STILL
WATERS

STILL WATERS

AN FBI K-9 NOVEL

SARA DRISCOLL

KENSINGTON
PUBLISHING CORP.

www.kensingtonbooks.com

KENSINGTON BOOKS are published by

Kensington Publishing Corp.
119 West 40th Street
New York, NY 10018

All Kensington titles, imprints and distributed lines are available at special quantity discounts for bulk purchases for sales promotion, premiums, fund-raising, educational or institutional use.

Special book excerpts or customized printings can also be created to fit specific needs. For details, write or phone the office of the Kensington Special Sales Manager: Kensington Publishing Corp., 119 West 40th Street, New York, NY, 10018. Attn. Special Sales Department. Phone: 1-800-221-2647.

Library of Congress Card Catalogue Number: 2022940970

The K with book logo Reg. U.S. Pat. & TM. Off.

ISBN: 978-1-4967-3506-5
First Kensington Hardcover Edition: December 2022

ISBN: 978-1-4967-3507-2 (ebook)

10 9 8 7 6 5 4 3 2 1

Printed in the United States of America

STILL
WATERS

CHAPTER 1

Napoo: A British slang term from World War I, a pronunciation of French *il n'y en a plus* or *il n'y a plus* ("there is no more"). It means something is finished, inoperative, or someone is dead.

Friday, October 18, 8:44 AM
Boundary Waters Canoe Area
Superior National Forest, Minnesota

The boat ghosted over water, slicing almost silently through a vivid reflection of blue sky and wispy clouds. At the edge of the narrow lake, stands of pine towered above ragged piles of granite, while mist danced atop the still surface near the shoreline. High overhead, a raptor glided, wings outstretched, riding the upper-level wind, its prey safe far below.

Not yet time to kill.

At the front of the boat, the black Labrador stood with his front paws braced on the curve of the inflatable bow, his head high, nose constantly scenting the air, the plume of his tail waving back and forth. A dog in his element, on the hunt, waiting for the first sign of the trail.

"Has he got it?"

Meg Jennings, search-and-rescue dog handler for the

FBI's Human Scent Evidence Team, took her eyes off her dog just long enough to glance over her shoulder at the man clad in a wet suit, buoyancy control vest, and air tank, sitting farther back in the boat. Like her, he was perched on the rounded side of the boat, but he also held a GPS unit in one hand, careful to ensure only he could see the screen.

Meg moved to keep her eye on her dog, but turned her head enough that her voice would carry and not get lost in the wind the boat generated as they traversed the lake. "I don't think so. I'm still learning Hawk's signs for a water-based search, but based on his physical stance, he hasn't picked up anything yet."

Meg turned her attention back to Hawk and tightened her hold on the leash, wrapping it around her hand one more time. An experienced search-and-rescue dog, Hawk had done water searches before—as he had after Hurricane Cole struck the Eastern Seaboard the previous year—but those had really been transports over water to get to land searches. And as a black Lab who loved his time in the water, Meg didn't want him to get overenthusiastic about catching a scent and leaping out of the boat to track it like he would on land.

Have faith. You know he's better trained than that.

She did know—a simple voice command would keep him in place. And, in case of a crisis, the use of his "don't mess with me" name—Talon—demanded instant compliance. Even if he did go overboard, not only was he an excellent swimmer, but he wore a life jacket, just like the humans in the boat.

Safety first. You couldn't help a victim if you were in trouble yourself.

Today they were training a different skill. On land, Hawk was an excellent tracking and trailing dog over a range of terrains and through varied conditions. But there were times when a search ended at a body of water where it would be more useful if he could continue. Granted, any search over water was bound to actually be more in the purview of the dogs of the FBI Victim Recovery Team—who were trained to search out human remains versus the living victims, who were the target of the Human Scent Evidence Team— but cross-training would only improve their overall search success. It was a sad but true fact that not all their searches ended in a live rescue.

Special-Agent-in-Charge Craig Beaumont, who led the Human Scent Evidence Team, had approved Meg and Brian Foster's request for this training weekend. Brian and his German shepherd, Lacey, were often paired with Meg and Hawk because of how well the dogs worked together and their resulting success rate. The handlers and their dogs were mandated by the FBI to refresh and upgrade their training as part of their positions on the Forensic Canine Unit, but when Craig heard that part of the weekend was also a trials competition against other law enforcement agencies, he gave his enthusiastic approval. Outside his office, Meg and Brian had shared a high five, pleased their strategy to sell the trip to Minnesota, based on Craig's competitive nature and his love of showing off his teams' skills, had been successful.

Brian and Lacey were somewhere out on the water as well, but considering the breadth of the Boundary Waters Canoe Area and the number of small lakes and rivers, they could be anywhere this morning. Part of the Superior Natural Forest, Boundary Waters was a widespread interconnected chain of waterways, distant from any towns and even most roads. Visitors to the area generally portaged their way into the interior. For these trials, the organizers, Search Dogs of America, had picked an area still accessible by land vehicles, allowing the competitors and their dogs to drive in, instead of being solely reliant on boating skills.

However, as this was a designated wilderness area, the SDA had sought, and received, approval to use outboard motors for the training sessions, since the distance to be covered was considerable. Nonpolluting equipment was required as part of the agreement, so the boats used electric outboard motors.

At first, the lack of noise as they left the shore had seemed jarring, but Meg quickly settled in, enjoying being able to talk without shouting and to hear birdcalls coming from the surrounding forests. There were four people accompanying Hawk: Meg, Charlie Allen, the pilot, Claire Hughes, the trainer, and Salvatore Gallo, the diver. It was a small group, but each of the eight dog-and-handler pairs involved in the training needed a full team each morning, so they were running with the bare minimum of personnel. Had it been an actual search, there would have been a separate team of divers in a second boat. But, in this case, they were looking for a "hide"—a perforated metal canister containing a small piece of decaying human tissue. Unlike other areas in the world, in the United States, training could be done using donated human samples, instead of pork or another substitute, so the dogs were able to learn on the precise blend of decomposition chemicals they'd need to react to in a real situation.

The water search mimicked their typical land search strategy with an important reversal. On land, they'd start downwind, working into the breeze, weaving back and forth, trying to catch a telltale particle of scent. When he found it, Hawk would weave out of the scent plume, then turn and come back into it, cutting across the scent cone until he came out the other side. Then he'd move back into it, each pass getting narrower and narrower as he worked his way to the origin of the scent cone and a single pinpoint location.

However, for water searches, the strategy was to start

upwind and work down, crisscrossing the body of water laterally in a similar pattern to Hawk's land route. They followed the wind, hoping Hawk would react the moment he entered the scent plume. Then, they could go back upwind, taking him out of the scent, and back in on shorter and shorter passes, until they found the exact position of the hide.

Meg knew this was going to be a challenge, even for a trained scent dog like Hawk. Land scents were one thing—scent particles were blown by the wind in predictable patterns, even if differences in altitude and urban or geographical obstacles got in the way. That was their bread and butter, and, as a team, they consistently nailed it. But Meg wasn't sure how Hawk would do today. His nose was sharp, but this search would require leveled-up skills. The hide was likely thirty or forty feet below the surface of the water, possibly dropped into silt or underwater plant life. Scent particles from the decomposing tissue had to filter out of the container, into the water, and then diffuse up to the surface, where they would catch the wind. The number of particles making it to open air would only be a minute fraction of what Hawk was used to working with. Not to mention, out here in the middle of the lake, the wind had picked up considerably; so, would the air current simply whisk away what small amount of scent remained? And even if Hawk caught the scent, once they took him out of it, would it be possible for him to catch it again and again as they narrowed down the location?

He was good, but was he *that* good?

The moment Hawk's stance changed, Meg knew they were about to find out. His body tense, his tail still, Hawk leaned out, his nose working frantically. His rear end wiggled, dipped, and then he had to catch his balance as the boat bobbed slightly. He let out a series of sharp barks.

"Good boy!" Meg stroked a hand over his hip. "His

alert is normally a sit, but I think he's figuring out that won't work on water."

"He tried to sit, but didn't like how it made him unsteady, so he adapted." Short and slight, with her wavy, blond-streaked hair whipped into a frenzy by the wind, Claire grinned in approval. "Smart boy. Bring us around and let's try another pass."

The moment they left the scent plume, Hawk relaxed, becoming more watchful than intent.

Meg studied him, cataloging how he was actively working this search. "Apparently, we're both learning as we go. How long does it take for the dogs to pick this up?"

"It depends on the dog. Experienced dogs, like Hawk, can sometimes nail it on the first try. In that case, we're doing more training of you as his handler, so you know how to help him, since he's utterly reliant on you getting him and his nose where he needs to be out here on the water. It's the handler's responsibility to direct the boat pilot. If you can't get him to the exact location, he can't help you. I'll show you how it's done this time. Tomorrow you're going to show me." Claire looked over her shoulder to where an older man with stooped shoulders and a belly that hinted at a love of beer sat at the tiller. "Charlie, bring us around one hundred eighty degrees. I want to narrow this down."

With a bob of his black ball cap, Charlie arced them in a curve.

"We're on the north side of the lake," Claire continued. "I want to circle to the south side and bring him into it from that direction to get an idea of how far across the breadth of the water we need to limit the search area."

"Have you ever had dogs so into the search they jump out and try to do it themselves?"

Claire's laugh answered the question before she spoke.

"Oh yeah, then it's fun to drag them into the boat by their life jacket. But they can't search that way. They'd have to expend too much effort swimming to be able to concentrate on picking up scent this scant."

An image filled Meg's mind—Hawk in the Potomac River about ten feet in front of her, his head above water as he swam as if his life depended on it around sunken World War I vessels. It hadn't been his life at stake, but her sister Cara's. Hawk had unerringly led her, her partner, firefighter/paramedic Todd Webb, and her sister's partner, *Washington Post* investigative reporter Clay McCord, to where a maniacal killer had tied Cara to one of the disintegrating ships, and left her to drown as the tide rose. Hawk had saved Cara's life that day, but it had been hard work and the scent had been 100 percent above water and essentially a glowing neon arrow for the dog. The scent he was looking for today would be *much* harder to find.

"No swimming for you today, buddy. At least not until we're back on shore."

Hawk turned around at the sound of her voice, his tongue lolling in a canine grin, and wagged his tail.

Sometimes she swore he understood every word she said, and not just her commands.

The boat circled to the north, then east, coming within about thirty feet of the shore, the mist eddying around them as the winds eased near the trees, and then headed north again.

"Find it, Hawk. Find the scent again." As part of the training, before they'd left shore, the dogs had been exposed to a small bit of decaying tissue to give them the mixture of scents they'd be looking for out on open water. Hawk could find human scent in the wilderness, or, if given a specific scent, could find it in the midst of a crowd, but this was an odor Meg wasn't sure he'd even identify as human. He might just think it was a game to find rotten eggs, for all she knew.

They were back to the center of the lake when Hawk's motion stilled, and he leaned forward over the bow. Another twenty feet and he barked twice.

"Good boy, Hawk."

"Back west again, Charlie, out of the scent. Then north and we'll come south into the plume." Claire's eyes were fixed on the dog. "He's doing great." Her gaze flicked up to Meg. "Do you see what we're doing here?"

"You're essentially gridding off the scent."

"Exactly. This isn't like a land search. You're unlikely to have any concentration of scent over a one-hundred-yard swath, especially on a lake this calm. There are currents because of all the interconnected waterways. But it was a dry summer, and not much rain so far this fall; as a result, the levels are down, and the water isn't running like it does in the spring. And keeping in mind the hide has been in place for about two hours, you need to get a feel for how far the molecules have diffused laterally in the water and then up to the surface. The highest concentration will, of course, be directly above the hide, but depending on how deep it is, how long it's been there, and the dog's sensitivity, he may alert farther out. Part of the process is training them with a second tell, or watching for them to develop their own, when they're over the most concentrated scent on top of the hide. So, more than on land, you have to work out the details of the search before you step into the boat—how long a victim has been missing, the currents in the body of water you're searching, wind and weather conditions. You're a team on land, but even more so on the water. He's the nose, but you have to be the strategic brains of the search."

"Does that team aspect sometimes doom the dog if the handler can't lead the search well?"

"Absolutely. The best nose in the world won't help if you can't get it to the site of the victim."

"No pressure," Meg muttered, her gaze fixed over Hawk's head to the expanse of water beyond.

"I'm not worried. I know about you two."

Meg's head jerked back to stare at the trainer.

"I'm helping out the SDA this weekend, but I'm not a Minnesotan. I'm from Maryland. And I know about some of your cases." Claire smiled down at Hawk. "I pay attention to news stories with dogs. And you guys keep making headlines."

"My sister's partner is with the *Washington Post*," Meg said dryly. "I can't do anything without him wanting to write about it."

Claire chuckled. "I bet. But as I said, I'm not worried. You're established, and I can see the bond between you. You'll nail this."

The boat circled around and then motored south again.

"Okay, Hawk, find it, buddy. Find the scent."

This time, there was almost no hesitation before Hawk alerted with a triple bark.

"Is the scent stronger here?" Meg asked. "Or is he figuring out what he's supposed to do?"

Claire waved both hands back and forth. "Could be one or the other. This early in his training, it may just be him recognizing the scent earlier. Later, when he's more established, it will indicate a greater concentration." She gave new orders to the pilot to circle around.

Their circles became smaller and smaller.

One circle netted them no scent, but Claire wasn't concerned. "Knowing where the scent *isn't* is just as important as knowing where it *is*. And he can't direct us, so we're reading between the lines of his response, especially while you're learning too."

On the following circle, as they came around to the east,

Hawk let out a sharp series of barks and threw himself down on the curved edge of the bow, his head dangling over the side as his nose stretched toward the water.

Meg shortened the leash, keeping a solid hold on it as she leaned forward to see into the water, but she couldn't distinguish anything in the murky depths. "Is this it?"

"Charlie, mark this spot, and let's circle back to it." Claire studied the dog almost hanging off the boat. "I know it's in this quadrant, but I don't know the exact location. They only give me a vague location to determine if the dog has missed the mark altogether, so we're not wasting training time. They don't want me to know specifics so I can't influence you or Hawk. This entire process has to be dog led. And I'd say he's done that."

The boat moved in a tight circle, slowed, and stopped when Hawk barked again. "Hawk, good boy. Come back into the boat. Sit." Meg's eyebrows curved upward in surprise when the dog didn't move. She gave the leash a tug, but met the resistance of solid muscle.

"He may not want to move, even at your command. He thinks his job's not done because he can't find the concentrated scent yet."

"Give me a few minutes, and I'll be able to confirm if we're in the right place," Sal said, his eyes still fixed on the GPS unit in his hand.

"You know where the hide should be?" Meg confirmed. "It's still transmitting?"

"Yup."

Meg waited for a few beats of silence, battling back her competitive nature and a sudden need to shake him. "And?"

"We're right above the signal."

Every muscle in Meg relaxed in relief. She knew it was silly—this wasn't a real search, there was no life on the line, and likely in a search like this, there never would be—but Hawk staying at the top of his game was important to both of them.

"I just need to check," Sal continued. "It's doubtful the transmitter has become dislodged at the exact spot of your dog's alert, but let's make sure." He pulled his goggles down into place, slipped his mouthpiece in, and bit down. He looked at Charlie, who held the coil of rope Sal would take down with him to indicate if he had any trouble. Charlie gave him a thumbs-up, which Sal returned. Then he glanced quickly over his shoulder to make sure the water was clear, raised his right hand to cover his regulator with his palm, holding his goggles in place with two fingers, covered the goggles strap with his other hand at the back of his head, and rolled backward over the edge into the lake with a shimmy of flippers. He surfaced, gave the occupants of the boat the okay signal, grabbed the rope, and disappeared under the water. Charlie let the rope play out, a black stripe every ten feet marking Sal's progress. Ten feet, then twenty. Then more, stopping just short of sixty feet.

Straightening, Meg looked over the edge as the water settled into its normal choppiness. "That's pretty deep."

"A little deeper than intended, for sure. We try not to make these first forays discouraging for the dogs. We thought it would be more like forty feet here, but sometimes the topography of these bodies of water isn't as consistent as we think."

"How hard will it be for him to find the hide?"

"Shouldn't be too bad. The tissue is in a container, attached to a floater on a four-foot cord, so he's looking for the floater, not the hide, which could be lost in the plant life or sediment at the bottom of the lake. It's going to be dark down there"—Claire squinted into the sun-bright sky—"even on a day like today, but he has his flashlight."

They waited for a few minutes in silence. Hawk wanted to stay perched on the bow, so Meg left him in peace, sitting beside him, one hand resting on his sun-warmed fur just behind his navy-blue-and-yellow FBI life jacket. The wind gently blew every loose strand of long black hair not tied back into her ponytail around her face. Even though they'd been enjoying an unusually warm fall, the breeze was cool, but here on the open water, the sun kept them from being cold. Motion at the edge of the lake caught Meg's attention, and for a moment, she wasn't sure what she was looking at as something moved across the water. But then it was joined by another, and another, and another, and she realized a family of otters was swimming near the shore. A smile curved her lips as they cavorted in the shallows; as a city dweller, albeit one who often did searches through outdoor environments—moments for work, not relaxation—she didn't get much of a chance to just enjoy the peace of nature.

Which was exactly what Todd had told her when he was convincing her to turn this trip into a mini-vacation.

Todd. That made her wonder how he and his brothers were managing at the campsite. Hopefully, they'd brought everything they'd need because there would be no dashing out to a store to pick up supplies, not way out in the wilderness like this.

"Two tugs," Charlie announced. "He's coming up. Keep in mind he's going to have to do a three-minute safety stop at fifteen feet to avoid the bends." He started coiling the rope, which lay lax between his hands as the diver rose in the water.

Finally the float broke the surface, bright white to catch the light of the flashlight below, followed by a stream of bubbles and then Sal's head as he surfaced.

He spit out his mouthpiece and grinned up at Meg and

Claire as his right hand broke the surface, holding a silver metal tin with circular perforations in the top of the magnetic lid, and a loop on the side where a woven cord was neatly tied, before disappearing into the water. Meg was instantly hit with a waft of putrid sulfur that turned her stomach.

With a bark, Hawk dropped back into the boat, his tail wagging furiously.

"Good boy, Hawk. You did it!" Meg followed her praise with a jerky treat, which he happily sank down on the floor of the boat to eat. "I don't normally reward him with food after a search, but I want to make connections in his head right now."

Claire nodded her approval. "Totally agree. This is new enough for him that you want him to understand he did it correctly."

Charlie dropped the rope, pulled the lid off a rectangular plastic bin at his feet, and extended it. "For the love of God, put that away."

Sal tossed the canister into the bin, and then Charlie set it on the floor, allowing him to reel in the cord and floater. He snapped the lid on tight and turned his face into the wind, trying to breathe only fresh air. "How can something that small stink so much?"

"Decomp chemicals are nasty, no doubt about it." Claire waited as Sal kicked his way out of the water, giving a twist as he did to sit on the side of the boat, his flippers still in the water. "Was Hawk precise? Was the hide right here?"

"Not only was it right here, when it dropped, it burrowed into the silt by a good six inches." Sal studied Hawk as he happily finished his treat. "He not only nailed the location, he did it sixty feet down and with less scent than usual because it had to percolate through the silt before it hit the water to filter up to the surface. I'm impressed."

Claire ran a hand over Hawk's head. "Me too. Good boy, Hawk." She looked up and met Meg's eyes. "Land and water capabilities. With this added skill set, you guys are going to be in great demand."

Meg beamed down at her dog, taking in his eyes, so bright and alert, as if to say, *What's next?* "Hawk says, 'Bring it on!' "

CHAPTER 2

Briefing: A meeting before a search during which search teams are given information in order to initiate and execute the search.

Friday, October 18, 11:28 AM
Boundary Waters Canoe Area
Superior National Forest, Minnesota

"Meg! Over here!"

The sound of her name drew Meg's attention up the hill, away from the water's edge, where they had disembarked fifteen minutes earlier, and along the path leading into the forest. She instantly recognized Brian Foster's tall, athletic form and dark hair. The arm he waved over his head and the German shepherd sitting at his knee only cemented the identification. She waved back and changed direction. "Hawk, come on, boy, let's go see Lacey." At Lacey's name, Hawk's ears perked and his pace quickened. Meg chuckled and grinned down at her dog. "You two are like an old married couple who can't bear to be separated for long."

As Meg climbed the hill toward Brian, she took in his cargo pants, unzipped navy FBI windbreaker, and Henley beneath, all of which were splattered with water. "Did you swim to shore?"

"Not me." Brian cast a flat stare down at his dog. "Her." Lacey grinned up at Meg, her long pink tongue lolling sideways out of her mouth, her tail thumping packed dirt scattered with a bright carpet of autumn's fallen color, her spiky fur telling the tale of a quick swim after her morning's work.

"Couldn't resist, could she?"

"Not even kind of. Good thing it's a warm day for this time of year. How did you keep Hawk out of the water?"

"I didn't." Meg pinched a fold of Brian's shirt between her thumb and index finger and rubbed the wet material. "I stepped away when he shook off. And then sat in the sun with him on the beach for ten minutes to dry off."

"Yeah, I didn't quite make it out of range." Brian rolled his eyes, but then belied his exasperation by dropping a hand onto Lacey's head and stroking fondly.

Like she would for Hawk, Meg knew Brian would do anything for Lacey. Always would have, but following Lacey's near-fatal brush with a cougar in the spring, their bond had only grown stronger as he'd nursed her away from the brink of death, and then coached her back into top form. "How did you guys do this morning?"

"Fantastic. Lacey got it on the first try. It took her a few rounds to pinpoint the exact position because the hide was located in an area of the lake where the wind funneled around a corner, making an eddy. But we've dealt with obstacles like that on land, haven't we, Lacey-girl? We just had to apply some of that strategy to this new situation and she narrowed it down once the trainer and I got her into the right location. How about Hawk?"

"Nailed it."

"Of course he did. Like we expected anything else from either of them."

"I admit I wasn't sure. It's not like either of them are Theo," Meg said, referring to Scott Park's bloodhound, the best nose in the Human Scent Evidence Team. "Knowing how sparse the scent is, I wasn't sure how either of them would do."

"Oh, ye of little faith. I knew they'd rock it." Brian peered uphill toward a clearing. "Now they need to rock the first trial. As far as I'm concerned, either of them can win, but it needs to be one of them, not one of the other teams. Craig is a little overly invested in our whipping some serious ass this weekend."

"I'll say. He's competitive at the best of times, but did you see when he realized the Connecticut State Police were going to be sending a team?"

"Oh, yeah. I mean, sure, it's one of the oldest K-9 teams in America, but him being buds with the department's lieutenant colonel really brought out his competitive side."

"Hey, it got us here. I can work with it. Or you can." Meg's gaze traveled from Hawk to Lacey. "I agree. As long as one of us takes it this weekend, I'm happy. We're two teams against six others. That's a one-in-four chance."

"With these guys, we have a better than one-in-four chance."

"Totally agree." She pushed back the cuff of her jacket to reveal the time on her fitness tracker. "We better get moving. We're supposed to start at noon, right?"

"Yes. And I want to take ten minutes to give Lacey a light meal. I don't want her weighed down and, while she had a good breakfast, I don't know how long this search will be. I want to give her a boost." Brian shrugged to resettle the backpack he carried, just as Meg did, that contained all their supplies.

"Me too. Let's move then."

Brian and Meg made their way into the woods, following the path up the hill to the clearing above. Once there they moved toward the edge of the forest, avoiding the other dogs and handlers rapidly filling the space, and gave their dogs a little high-energy kibble and some water. They downed a couple of energy bars themselves, because the dogs weren't alone in needing to keep their energy high during the upcoming search. Then they buckled their now-dry dogs into their FBI vests, signaling it was time to go to work. Leaving their backpacks together at the edge of the trees, they both put on fanny packs carrying a minimum of emergency supplies, including their satellite phones. By eleven fifty-five, they joined the group of handlers and dogs milling in a loose circle, mostly as single teams, but one other pair of handlers and dogs stood together, as Meg did with Brian.

Meg scanned their competition. During the drive out, while Todd was at the wheel, she'd taken the time to look up the groups entered in the trials, and while she didn't know the individual handlers' names, she knew their organizations. Everyone was out of official uniform, but wore the more casual call signs of their organizations—like the FBI windbreakers she and Brian wore—and the dogs wore the colors and insignia of their departments.

A chocolate Lab in a khaki vest with the Connecticut State Police crest sat patiently at the feet of his handler, a broad-shouldered man with an umber complexion and muscular build, his kinky black hair shaved close to his scalp. He looked as relaxed as his dog, his eyes scanning the circle, his smile a flash of white teeth. He stood in cargo pants with his hiking boots braced, his hands tucked inside the kangaroo pocket of his Connecticut State Police hoodie, the leash emerging to droop nearly to the ground beside his dog. His gaze landed on Meg and Brian and his smile broke wider. He gave them a nod, before moving on to study the other competitors.

Meg leaned into Brian. "CSP handler over there just

picked us out. Apparently, the competition is being echoed in their office as well."

"He looks pretty mellow about it." Brian frowned. "I'm not sure if that's because he's easygoing, or because he thinks he has us whooped before we even start."

"CSP only sent one team, so that helps. It's the New York State Police who sent two."

She nodded toward where two men stood with matching German shepherds, both wearing green camo police vests. They sat motionless, but they constantly watched the dogs around them. Meg noted that even here, the animals were working in tandem, just as Hawk and Lacey would, with each dog covering their own side of the circle. Unlike the CSP Lab, these dogs were at attention, the leashes between them and their handlers held with almost no slack. The two men were both in cargo pants and navy New York State Police jackets to ward off the breeze. Their high and tight haircuts paired with their unsmiling faces made them look unnaturally militaristic in the typically more relaxed search-and-rescue crowd. The matching outfits and haircuts almost made them look like twins, except one man had dark eyes, while the other's were ice blue.

"I don't like the look of those dogs," Brian murmured.

Meg studied the New York State dog teams. "While we all do tracking, they definitely look more like apprehension dogs than search-and-rescue. When I was on the Richmond PD with Deuce, we saw a lot of dogs like that. Always on, always vigilant. As a patrol dog in urban Richmond, Deuce was like that to a certain extent." Meg felt a pang as she thought about her days in the RPD, patrolling with her German shepherd, until he was cut down apprehending a suspect, and died in her arms while they waited for help to arrive.

"Why would they be here for a weekend training like this?"

"Probably because the New York State Police so heavily trains its dogs for apprehension, I bet they have a lot of dogs to fill that role. But it's a big state, with a lot of natural spaces, so having some dogs capable of water searches would be useful. They have somewhere around one hundred dogs in that department, so they can afford to diversify skills. And while I can see the need for training, those dogs look like machines." She looked down at Hawk, lying placidly at her feet, and Lacey, sitting quietly between herself and Brian. "Makes our two look like amateur hour."

"Until we get started. They're just resting until it's time to go to work. They know the drill."

"They sure do. And those dogs may be on alert because they're in work mode with their vests on. Now, *that's* a beautiful dog."

"Which one?"

"The black Belgian Malinois from Wyoming, to the left of the staties."

The long-haired Malinois wore a black vest that blended into its fur so well, the black-and-yellow crest with the silhouette of a rider on a bucking bronco popped bright. Laramie County Sheriff's Office. A tall, leggy redhead stood beside the dog, her hair tied back in a no-nonsense ponytail. Wearing yoga pants and a Laramie County sweatshirt, she bounced on her toes, like a runner jonesing in the starting blocks. Her eyes darted around the circle as if trying to take everything in at once. Like its handler, the dog also appeared unsettled, sitting tall and straight, almost as if the leash was just a little too tight.

"Gorgeous dog," said Brian, "but she could loosen up her hold on him a bit."

"I was thinking the same thing. She's either nervous

about the trial or the dog misbehaving, and is keeping it close. Too close."

"It's just a competition. If they don't win, their jobs aren't on the line."

Meg sent Brian a sideways glance. "So we're not worrying about winning now?"

"Hell no." He shot back a sly grin. "*They* shouldn't worry about it, though, because we've got it in the bag."

"That's better." Meg took in the next team. A petite woman, her blond hair heavily threaded with gray, wearing a blue-and-gold tracksuit with the Cook County Sheriff's Office shield embroidered over her left breast, stood beside a massive tan-and-black bloodhound. "Look at the size of that bloodhound. His ears are bigger than my spread hand."

"He's massive. At least he looks alert and ready to go. Makes Theo look like a slug."

Meg chuckled. "Never stand when you can sit. Never sit when you can lie down."

"If this one is energetic and has a typical bloodhound nose, he may be our toughest competition. Unless he moves like Theo, and then we have nothing to worry about because the trial is based on time. And if he's not like Theo, then he must be well trained; otherwise, that's a lot of dog for someone of her build to handle."

The look Meg sent him could have chilled water. "Her build or her age?"

"Her *build*," he repeated. "She may be the oldest competitor here, but if she's in shape—and it sure looks like it to me—then she can run circles around your average couch-surfing twenty-something. But she's petite for a dog of that size."

The last team was another German shepherd, this one in a navy vest with the symbol of a bear inside a sheriff's star. The man holding the leash looked like he'd just stepped off his surfboard and run up from the beach, from his sun-kissed tan, to the bleached-blond curls that flopped over his forehead, to the baggy, wrinkled khaki pants and the loose Henley under his navy jacket. His dog looked equally Zen.

"Is that beach boy from the Los Angeles County Sheriff's Office?" Brian asked.

"Looks like it."

"You think they need a dog who can find people in the concrete canyon of the Los Angeles River?"

"That's mostly the LAPD in the downtown urban center. Get out of the city and into the mountains where the sheriff's office has jurisdiction, and these dogs are tracking through nature and around bodies of water and rivers. They have the Pacific as well, but what they learn here will be less useful there simply because of currents. A body in the ocean isn't going to stay in place."

"I wonder if he takes his dog surfing?"

"You laugh, but there are lots of dogs who surf, and there are lots of owners who love sharing the activity with them. I mean, really, what's surfing but another type of parkour?" Meg referred to the exercise she and Brian did with the dogs, where they put the dogs through their paces of balance and agility using steps, blocks, railings, teeter-totters, jumps, and tubes.

"When you put it that way . . ."

Meg pointed in the direction of a man and woman dressed in SDA red-on-black windbreakers cresting the top of the hill. "Looks like we're about to start."

Brian interlaced his fingers, turned his hands palm out, and stretched, cracking his knuckles. "Excellent. Let's do this."

The man and woman stepped to the end of the circle, inserting themselves into the group, the CSP officer stepping sideways with his dog to give them a little more room. The woman was middle-aged, with gray sprinkled through her short brown curls, but her face revealed the slightly wrinkled weathering that spoke of an outdoor lifestyle. Like the man, she wore jeans and scuffed, muddy hiking boots, with a windbreaker over a wiry frame. Holding a clipboard, she stepped forward a pace into the circle, her eyes scanning the participants with a smile. "On behalf of Search Dogs of America, welcome to you all. I caught the last part of your training this morning and it looked like things were going well. And the trainers said they were encouraged about how smoothly the session had gone."

One of the two New York State handlers leaned toward his colleague and murmured something that made the other man crack a grin. Meg glanced sideways at Brian to see if he'd seen it, only to find his narrowed gaze fixed on the two men who were apparently making fun of either the SDA spokeswoman or the training they provided.

But the woman continued, seemingly having missed the exchange. "I'm Teresa Bowfin, regional director of North Central SDA, and the organizer of this weekend. And I'm happy to introduce you to Isaac Thatcher, our main trial judge. Isaac has been in search-and-rescue for about thirty years with a number of goldens, and is still active with the California Rescue Dog Association with his current golden, Petunia."

Easily twenty years older than Bowfin, Thatcher still had the build of a man who did regular exercise. Most judges in canine activities were previous competitors, and were often owners and trainers, so Meg wasn't surprised Thatcher would still be involved in search-and-rescue. It wasn't age that slowed a handler down; it was their health or that of their dog.

Thatcher raised his hand in greeting. "Welcome, all. And you're close, Teresa, but I've only been in search-and-rescue for about twenty-five years. I'm not *that* old." He gave Bowfin a mock-stern look, and then ruined it by chuckling and running a hand over his graying sandy hair. "I'm looking forward to seeing you all in action shortly."

"As am I," Bowfin continued. She raised the clipboard she'd been holding against her hip. "Now, because I was involved in the organization of the event and spoke to some of you personally, I asked one of the trial observers to assign each of you a randomly selected number for your starting position in this afternoon's trial. This is the order." She scanned down the list. "First up is Rita Pratt, Laramie County Sheriff's Office."

All eyes swiveled to the redhead and her Belgian Malinois. Pratt gave Bowfin a short nod.

"Next is Brian Foster, FBI Human Scent Evidence Team."

Brian raised his hand in acknowledgment.

"Next is Shay McGraw, LA County Sheriff's Office. Then Lamonte Dix, Connecticut State Police, Mandy Fief, Cook County Sheriff's Office, and Damon Glenn, New York State Police."

As the names were called, Meg found the handlers where they stood with their dog in the circle, mentally naming each one. They'd be together all weekend, and even though they were competitors now, the search-and-rescue world was small and every fresh contact could be a new person to rely on in a future search scenario.

"Finally we have Meg Jennings, FBI Human Scent Evidence Team, and Gerhard Elan, New York State Police," Bowfin continued, and then lowered her clipboard. "I'll be starting you off at your given time over there, in that break in the trees where the trail leads away from the water. Each dog will be given a scent sample of the hide you'll be looking for. You'll start on that trail, but don't expect to stay on it. Taking air currents into account, we've set the hide so at a certain point along the trail, your scent dog will pick up the odor and will redirect. If you stay on the trail to the end, you've missed the hide. The trial will be timed, with your synchronized time marked at the find by two independent trial observers when you call your dog's alert. A third trial observer will be stationed out of sight along the trail, and Mr. Thatcher will be observing the entire trial directly streamed from a number of remote satellite cameras, which will feed to his laptop here. Afterward, times will be calculated and we'll announce the leaderboard. We'll space the competitors out by ten minutes to ensure no one is being visually followed."

"What about trails being followed?" Pratt asked. "I'm first, which means every path I leave is an advantage to everyone who comes behind me. And by the time the last team goes through, they'll have a huge advantage."

"What the . . ." Brian muttered under his breath.

Meg was equally surprised. Any competitor who had done a trial like this before knew how the run would work. Random selection made it as fair as possible, and, yes, perhaps the first competitor could lay down a trail, but it all depended on airflow and eddies and the dog's working pattern. This wasn't going to be a straight trail to the hide. First the dogs had to find the specific scent and then narrow in on it. Chances of any dog following in a previous dog's exact footsteps for the entire run were practically zero.

Bowfin's frown said she had no time for this kind of protest. "If you're letting your dog lead, unless he or she is purposely following the previous team and not the specific scent of the hide they're tasked to find, they'll be making their own way. There will be no disadvantage. It's all up to the dogs. Any other questions?" She paused for a moment, scanning the group, but no one spoke. "No? Then we'll meet back here at four o'clock for the results of the first trial. Best of luck to you all."

"Good luck, partner." Brian held out his fist and Meg bumped hers against it. "Let's nail this."

CHAPTER 3

Rural SAR: A search conducted across farmland or woodland in a sparsely populated area.

Friday, October 18, 1:05 PM
Boundary Waters Canoe Area
Superior National Forest, Minnesota

The forest was quiet, with only the barest whistle of wind rustling the treetops far overhead. Below, there was only the rhythmic pounding of Meg's hiking boots and Hawk's paws on the dirt trail. They'd started five minutes earlier, having given Glenn ten minutes to get ahead of them. They were on the trail, moving at a steady jog, having used some of their lead time to do a quick warm-up by jogging around the clearing and doing a few stretches, so by the time they were able to start, both she and Hawk were raring to go.

The trail led them deep into the woods. Tall stands of autumn-bright trees surrounded them, and thick ground cover laid a carpet on both sides of the path. The forest was dense, a mixture of deciduous and evergreens, limiting their view of the surrounding area. Meg dropped her left hand onto the can of bear spray clipped to her yoga pants. She'd had to use it in the past, but hoped it wouldn't be a problem today, both from a safety and a time stand-point. If she got tied up avoiding a bear, it would eat into their trial time. But at this time of year, after a summer of nature's bounty, and as the bears looked toward hibernation, she hoped any bear she met would be fat and satisfied already, and the cubs would be old enough any mother bear wouldn't feel the need to instantly attack if she and Hawk crossed paths with them.

Been there, done that. Once was more than enough.

During the compound bow case in Georgia, she and Hawk had spent entirely too much time out in the middle of nowhere, including one terrifying night lost in the Cohutta Wilderness, where they'd fallen down a steep hill, losing all their supplies and communication equipment, then been tossed in a spring-swollen river, where they almost drowned in the rapids. After they dragged themselves out of the water, Meg was nearly bitten by a rattlesnake, and then they were set on by a pack of coyotes. All she wanted today was a nice quiet run through the forest. The trail could be as hard as necessary, but if she didn't see so much as a squirrel, Meg would be happy.

Hawk had yet to find the scent, but Meg wasn't worried. If she'd been the one setting up the hide, she'd have put the cross-breeze from it at least ten minutes into the run, and, more than likely, out of this thick forest where the scent would be somewhat strangled by the lack of airflow, risking competitors missing it altogether. She could tell from Hawk's stance that he was in the zone, his head high, nose working furiously, sampling the air, waiting for that first hint of scent. His tail was high and his pace was brisk. He was on the hunt.

He'd find the scent. He always did.

The path led up a steady incline, more and more of the forest floor broken by large spears of moss-covered granite erupting through the dirt. In front of them, the trees grew sparse, and then they broke out on top of a cliff face.

"Hawk, slow. We're not going to risk a misstep up here."

Hawk instantly obeyed, slowing from a trot into a walk, knowing instinctively to stay away from the edge. The path here was easily twenty feet across, a cleared area over flat-topped slabs of rock, and they both gave the edge a wide berth.

Meg's heart rate immediately spiked. For someone who was afraid of heights, even hugging the tree line was entirely too close to the edge.

Part of her brain could appreciate the stunning vista: The sun shone down onto the sinuous river that flowed along the bottom of the cliff, bound on either side by wide swaths of forest. The warm fall had extended the full colors of autumn a few extra weeks, and the valley below was a glorious spattering of brilliant crimson, fiery orange, and luminous amber. Water sparkled below, from the river at their feet, to the scattering of lakes in every direction. From this height, the varied landscape of the wilderness around them was laid bare.

The rest of her body reacted with an adrenaline spike that screamed *Run . . .*

If Todd had been here, he'd perch on the rock, dangling his legs over the edge as he soaked up the beauty below. She, on the other hand, would only ever be up here for work because she had to be.

Speaking of work, time to move this along. "Come on, Hawk. Find the scent. You can do it, buddy."

Safely over the top of the cliff face and back into the trees. They'd only gone about forty feet when Hawk's pace slowed, his head high, and his tail held tall and motionless.

He has it.

"Good boy, Hawk."

She ran the tips of her fingers down the warm fur near the base of his tail as he looked back at her, his eyes bright. If she ever thought she'd dragged him into search-and-rescue, and demanded too much of him on these searches, it was moments like this that reassured her that her dog was never happier than when they were out working together. Unless he had Lacey with him as well—that was pretty much a perfect day from Hawk's point of view.

"I knew you'd get it. Now follow the scent, Hawk." She dropped back a few steps, letting out the long leash between them a little bit, giving him more room to work.

Hawk ran along the path for another thirty feet or so, and then slowed only momentarily, before turning between a giant oak and a pine tree to enter the undergrowth, cutting back at an angle to the direction they'd already come.

Meg scanned the area around them. Bright with autumn's hue, the forest was still thick, shorter trees and bushes filling a lot of the open spaces, with ground cover spreading over the rest. Large boulders dotted the area, shaded pale green with lichen and moss. There was a slight trace of a breeze she hadn't been able to detect before, likely why Hawk had been able to pick up the scent. Recalling Pratt's complaint, she studied the greenery around them, but couldn't spot a sign of any of the competitors who had gone before them—not a broken branch, crushed stem, or a boot print left in soft soil. If they'd come this far, they'd gone a slightly different way.

Hawk immediately fell into his typical search pattern, working downstream of the scent, running nearly perpendicular to the scent cone until he lost it, then looping back into it, working his way toward it in ever-narrowing passes. He kept up as fast a trot as he could in the thick under-

growth, staying true to his direction with his only devia-
tions being for obstacles.

Meg checked the time on her fitness tracker. Just past
twenty minutes in, and from Hawk's behavior, they were
closing in.

The sound of running water met her ears, pulling her attention from her dog to the terrain to the southeast, where
the forest seemed to open up into the light beyond. She'd
given Brian a hard time about getting wet this morning
and now she was possibly going to get her own dunking.

They broke from the trees to a ravine probably sixty
feet wide. Water wound between the two forested bound-
aries to trip over jagged rocks in a parallel triplet of waterfalls. Below, the river spread wide and shallow over the
bottom of the ravine, pooling at the bottom of the waterfalls, then separating into multiple channels to slither
through a tumble of larger rocks. As Hawk came to stop
at the edge of the twenty-foot drop, a quick scan of both
sides of the riverbed cemented her strategy.

Twenty feet wasn't great, but she could handle it. She'd
certainly handled worse.

"Down, across, and then up again, Hawk. Then we'll
have to pick up the trail again on that side." She unclipped
his leash from his vest, coiled and stuffed it into her jacket
pocket. Not that she anticipated any issues, but Hawk's
freedom of movement was paramount in any situation
where he could fall. Or where she could, taking him with
her. Better for them to be separated. And, as usual, she was
the part of the team at a disadvantage. Hawk's four feet
and lower center of gravity would make this a much easier
exercise for him.

"Hawk, come." Quickly judging the easiest and safest
route down to the riverbed, Meg led the way, following a
series of ledges and rocky outcroppings to drop down

below. What she did in ninety seconds, Hawk did in thirty. "Show-off. You're going to beat me here too. With me, Hawk." She wound her way across the rocky riverbed, staying atop the larger rocks as the water rushed around them. Meg picked her way carefully, selecting each rock and testing her weight on it to make sure it wouldn't roll underfoot, whereas Hawk gleefully jumped from rock to rock, sure-footed in every movement. As always, it made Meg glad for the hours she and Brian spent taking the dogs to parks and playgrounds to run around climbing sets and over stone walls. The agility he showed in each outing made him confident in the real world. She wouldn't have him any other way.

Partway across, Hawk paused, his nose angled high, sampling the air, and elation punched through Meg. *Still has the scent.*

They made it to the far side, and then Hawk led the way up to the top in a series of leaps as Meg steadily climbed behind him. Straightening to stand, Meg clipped on his leash. "Okay, Hawk, find it."

They were off again. Back into the woods, pushing through branches and dancing around trees as they jogged up a steep rise.

Hawk faltered as they topped the rise, first darting in the expected direction, then abruptly doubling back. He stopped, his head swinging first in one direction, then the other.

"Hawk? What's wrong?"

It wasn't unheard of for him to lose the scent. It had happened before, but usually he signaled that loss with a whine. Now he was silent. Studying him, Meg could only identify his behavior as confusion.

An obstruction blocking the scent, so it's weaker in this location? A second scent cross-polluting the air?

Meg scanned the terrain upwind. Part of her job as the

handler was to logic out any challenges the search pre-
sented. Obstacles, like a building or a large hill, could direct scent up and over their heads, causing Hawk to miss
the scent altogether. Or, depending on wind speeds, if the
scent fell on the other side of the obstacle, swirling eddies
could form at ground level and the scent exiting the eddy
could go in any direction. It was a mild day, starting to
border on cool now, so convection—hot air rising and taking scent with it—wouldn't play a part. But the terrain itself, all hills and valleys to obstruct or channel the wind,
increased the difficulty of the search.

But this was what they did. They knew how to work
this.

She and Hawk were standing on top of the hill, so the
scent should have been blowing directly over them. And
while they'd just been in a hollow, the ground upwind was
relatively flat. Hawk had already brought them through
the worst of the terrain so far.

Meg crouched down beside Hawk, running a hand
down his back soothingly. "Hawk, you're doing great.
Just keep it up." She knew he didn't understand all her
words; he was smart, but no dog was fluent in English.
But he absolutely understood her tone and what her touch
conveyed. Love. Trust. Partnership. And, most important
in this moment, patience to get the job done right. "You
had the scent, buddy. Find it. Find the scent."

Hawk took three steps forward as Meg straightened,
then paused, changed direction, took two more steps.
Stopped again.

Then he seemed to settle, picked a direction, and settled
into a trot. Meg relaxed fractionally; he had the scent
again.

But forty-five seconds later, he didn't.

Meg was entirely baffled. She'd never seen him behave
like this before. He seemed . . . lost.

"Okay, Hawk, clock's ticking here. Let's go to where you lost the scent and start again. Come."

She hurried them back to where he'd first seemed conflicted. She crouched down next to him. "Let's start again. Let's find the scent. Do your best; no lives are on the line, it's just a competition. We can do it, buddy. Now find, Hawk. Find."

She pushed to her feet, gnawing on her bottom lip. Wins were important and a bad search could rattle a dog's confidence. It was why on sites like Ground Zero, after 9/11, when the dogs didn't find anyone alive, rescuers hid in the rubble so the search-and-rescue canines could have a "win," even if the humans knew it wasn't real. It would keep dogs from getting depressed and keep them on task. And the last thing Meg wanted on a weekend when she needed Hawk on point with new training was—

Hawk pivoted, picking his direction, his steps sure. Either a fresh wave of scent had reached him, or he'd resolved any conflicting scents, but he'd chosen his target and was back on the trail, his head up, his gaze laser focused on the terrain in front of him, and his tail waving proudly.

There's my boy.

After that, it was less than five minutes to the hide. Hawk pushed his way through a dense thicket of bushes, Meg right behind him. Thorny branches snagged her shirt and grasped the edges of her hair as she squeezed through after him and she had to raise her left forearm over her face to protect her eyes. Then she was on the other side, and dropped her arm to find Hawk sitting proudly at the base of a towering white pine, his tail thumping the dirt happily.

Meg circled the tree to find a perforated silver container tucked into the lee of two gnarled roots. "Alert!" she called to the trial observers. She couldn't see them, but they could see her, and her time would be marked on her call. She checked her stopwatch—thirty-seven minutes and twelve seconds. *Way too long.* But she lavished praise on her dog nonetheless. "Good boy, Hawk! Good job!"

After that loss of time, they certainly weren't going to come in first for this course, but there were still two more to go. They weren't out of the running yet. And Brian and Lacey may have already nailed this round. She'd be happy to see them take first place.

They'd pull back, and she'd get out her GPS and get them to the clearing, avoiding the path they'd just followed so they wouldn't run afoul of the remaining team.

Then they'd see who'd won the day.

CHAPTER 4

Chairborne Ranger: A term describing intelligence personnel who spend most of their time sitting at a computer.

Friday, October 18, 3:52 PM
Boundary Waters Canoe Area
Superior National Forest, Minnesota

Meg knew from the moment she stepped into the
clearing that Brian's run had gone well. He exuded
confidence and Lacey stood beside him, alert and proud.

"Hawk, come. Let's go see Lacey." They crossed the clearing to meet Brian halfway. "You look chipper. Nailed it?"

"Oh yeah." Brian's smile made him look like a doting
dad. "My Lacey-girl was on point. Right in the zone."

"Nice!"

"Hawk nailed it too?" When Meg paused, Brian studied her expression, his own falling. "No?"

"Definitely not." Meg kept her voice pitched high,
happy in tone for Hawk's ears, even though her words
were not. "I'm not sure what happened, but our search
went sideways."

Brian stared in surprise. "Like didn't find the hide, sideways?"

"No, he found it, but it took way too long and he got

majorly sidetracked. He was really off his game for a while there. I have no idea what happened."

"It must be going around then. Elan's shepherd was caught peeing on the course by one of the trail cameras."

"No way. Then he's—"

"Automatically disqualified, yeah. So on the bright side, someone did worse than you. You think Hawk got distracted by something the organizers couldn't control? Bear scat or some other kind of animal droppings? Or a dead animal?"

"Maybe. I certainly didn't smell anything like that, but we know his nose is way better than mine. One thing's for sure, if our whole weekend is going to be like this, the win is in your hands, though not for lack of . . ." Meg trailed off as raised voices carried from the far side of the clearing. "What's going on over there?"

Near the trail entrance, Pratt stood nose to nose with Fief, leaning in aggressively. Their dogs stood nearby, both shifting restlessly from foot to foot, picking up on the anger flowing between their handlers. The fur on the back of the Malinois' neck was ruffled. Her nervous handler of a few hours ago was gone; now she oozed arrogance.

Hands on his hips, Brian studied the two women. "Looks like a dustup. Think we should go break it up?"

"I don't like the look of the Malinois. The last thing anyone needs is a dog going protective because he thinks his handler is in jeopardy."

They jogged across the clearing as several other handlers turned to stare at the two women, and Elan and his shepherd broke from the trees to join the group.

Bloodhounds were often mild-tempered and mellow, but this one was definitely looking stressed. And the moment the Malinois dropped into a crouch, baring her teeth, Meg broke into a run with a command to her dog to sit and stay. Brian echoed the command for Lacey. The last thing they needed was two more dogs mixing into an already-tense situation.

"What's going on?" Meg yelled from fifteen feet out, hoping to distract both humans and dogs.

Pratt's gaze darted in Meg's direction for just a fraction of a second. "Nothing you need to get involved in."

"You're going to have everyone involved if you end up triggering a dog fight. And God forbid anyone gets injured. We're from different forces, but we're colleagues. Whatever it is, we can deal with it like adults."

"Some people aren't graceful losers." Pratt kept her eyes locked on the older woman.

All the handlers Meg knew would be more concerned about how their dogs were reacting than what another handler was doing. It didn't say anything good about Pratt that she didn't spare her Malinois a glance. "They haven't released the times yet. We don't know who won."

"You didn't mark your own time?" Now Pratt turned on Meg, but then her gaze dropped to Hawk sitting with Lacey twenty feet away, their eyes glued to their handlers. "I guess with that disadvantage, you might not want to."

Irritation flashed into the red haze of temper. "*Pardon me?*"

"Don't get me wrong, Labs make great therapy dogs." Her gaze slid sideways to Lacey. "But nothing compares with a shepherd type for drive. And that unbeatable nose."

Meg was about to snarl back a response, when Brian clamped a hand over her wrist, his firm hold telling her he had this.

"Shepherds are great." Brian's voice was full of calm, the mediator stepping in to break things up. "But every dog has his or her strengths and weaknesses. And as far as the nose goes, I'm sure none of these dogs can beat . . ." He trailed off as he took in the bloodhound.

"Nova," Fief supplied, correctly reading his pause.

"Thank you. Nova," Brian continued. "One of our colleagues works with a bloodhound. Theo's amazing."

"Be that as it may, it still all comes down to time. It doesn't matter how good a dog's nose is if you can't get them to move."

"You goddamn know he can move," Fief spat. "You ungrateful bi—"

"Look!" Brian interrupted. "Here comes the judge. Time to hear how we all did." He hooked a hand around Fief's upper arm, pulling her sideways a few steps with him. "Come stand with us. Come on, Nova. Lacey, here, girl." He turned to look over his shoulder. "Meg. Meg!"

Meg threw him a dark look, then turned her back on Pratt and marched after Brian, calling her dog as she strode across the clearing.

They stopped on the far side and Brian let go of Fief's arm. "My apologies. I didn't want the dogs to decide they needed to protect anyone. And it was pretty clear words weren't going to cool things down. Are you okay?"

"Yes." Fief's snappy tone clearly conveyed the opposite. "Thank you."

Brian turned to Meg. "Take a breath."

Meg had half a mind to march over to Pratt to continue the conversation. "She called Hawk a 'disadvantage,' " she hissed. "Like he was a doddering fourteen-year-old. *A disadvantage!*"

Brian grabbed her by both shoulders, whether to cement her to the spot or to get her attention, Meg wasn't sure.

"Breathe," he ordered. "You were already off balance because of how this course ran. Also, you wouldn't be half this angry if she'd just insulted *you*."

"She went after my dog."

He gave her shoulders a soft squeeze, then released her. "I get it. I'd have had the same reaction if she'd said that to Lacey, and then you'd have been the one holding me back." He elbowed her gently in the ribs. "Of course I didn't have to, because I have a glorious shepherd type . . ." He winked at her and then rolled his eyes at the stupidity of the whole idea. A sharp whistle attracted his attention. "Here we go. Okay, Lacey, let's find out how far out in front we are."

Beside Meg, Hawk shifted restlessly, reacting instinctively to Meg's temper. She ran a hand down his back. "Sorry, bud, I'm not mad at you. The rude lady across the clearing just said some nasty things about you." Thatcher stepped into the circle, accompanied by two young men and a young woman, and Meg straightened and focused her attention on the trial organizers.

"Can I have your attention," Thatcher called. "Thank you, all, for such a great first attempt. For those who didn't feel they did as well as they'd have liked, the winner will have the best cumulative time over the three consecutive trials, so there's still time to improve. All times were confirmed by at least two of our three trial observers. This is the Trial One list of competitors in order of their trial times." He raised a clipboard with a sheaf of papers, their edges fluttering in the breeze. "Rita Pratt and Ava, 29:41. Brian Foster and Lacey, 30:18—"

"What the hell?" As he stood partially behind Meg, Brian's low words were full of outrage. "That's not right. I had 29:07. That would have put us in first place, not second."

"Lamonte Dix and Chewie, 31:32." Thatcher continued. "Damon Glenn and Samson, 34:56. Shay McGraw and Yoshi, 35:49. Meg Jennings and Hawk, 37:11."

"Wow, sixth place," Meg murmured. "We sucked even more than I thought."

"Mandy Fief and Nova, 38:27. Gerhard Elan and Odin, disqualified from Trial One." Thatcher dropped the clipboard to hold it against his side. "Now, I realize some of these results may not be exactly what you wanted."

Meg thought Elan's stony stare should have turned the judge into an ice sculpture then and there.

"But tomorrow we'll do it all again," Thatcher continued. "Fresh slate. And before that, Teresa asked me to pass on to meet at the shore, like you did this morning, at eight o'clock. You'll form the same teams as today, but they intend to make the hides more challenging for the second round of water training."

Considering how their first water search had been inadvertently more difficult than intended, Meg wondered if it really would be more challenging.

"In the meantime, enjoy the natural beauty of the area. There are some fantastic hiking trails, if you'd like to get out a bit more. To ensure we had the entire site to ourselves, we had to wait until this late in the season, but it's just us and the training staff here, so you can have the run of the place. Have a great evening and we'll see you tomorrow morning."

"I'm going to go talk to that judge about my time," Brian said. "I know it's just a competition, but if they have my time wrong, who else is also incorrect? Lacey, come."

"I'm with you. Hawk, come."

They found Thatcher in a huddle with the three trial observers, their voices low, when Brian marched up to them, Meg on his heels.

Thatcher looked up and cut off his instructions to the team. "Yes? Can I help you?"

"I'd like to contest my time," Brian said. "Who are the trial observers noting the finishing times?"

"That was us." A man in his early twenties raised one hand. He wore track pants, hiking boots, and a backward ball cap over his dirty-blond hair. He motioned to the young woman beside him, dressed in an oversized hoodie and yoga pants, her brown hair in a choppy pixie cut. "We noted everyone's time when they called their dog's alerts."

"I was tracking the time too. You have my time wrong. It's off by more than a minute."

"We had synchronized clocks and noted the same time. I didn't add anything and neither did Shannon."

"You have the wrong time," Brian insisted.

"There's an easy way to settle this," Thatcher said. "Hand me your clipboards." As the two observers passed him their clipboards, he looked at Brian. "The numbers are added by hand, individually as the trial progresses. Their independent paperwork is then combined in my final copy, but in case of discrepancy, we go back to the originals."

Each clipboard held a chart. The left-most column contained the competitors' names and the names of their dogs, listed in order of departure. The first column beside the names was filled with a list of start times, handwritten in black ink; the next was the listed clock time the hide was found by each participant; and the last column was the final run time for each team, both handwritten in blue ink. A quick scan down the names found Brian's with the trial time 30:18.

Meg did a quick calculation to ensure the trial observer's math was correct. It was.

"I'm not sure what happened, but that time is wrong," Brian stated. "I always time my own trials so I know how we're doing throughout the run. Lacey found the hide at 29:07."

"That's not what I saw. And our clocks are synchronized to Ms. Bowfin's as she sent each team out at the beginning of the trial. Did you start late?"

"Everyone left on time," Thatcher said before Brian could answer. "As judge, I was watching to make sure the participants left exactly on time or else we would have needed to compensate."

"You had cameras," Brian argued, scanning their faces, finally landing on the last trial observer, a second young man, short and stocky, in jeans and a red plaid shirt. "Did you record the footage?"

"We intended to, but had technical difficulties," Thatcher answered before the third observer could. "Which is why we have multiple trial observers at the hide. Dean, is the resulting run-time correct?"

"Yes." Irritation stressed Dean's single word.

"Then the time set by the trial observer holds," Thatcher said. "Best of luck in your trial tomorrow." He walked away from Meg and Brian, the three observers following behind, Dean throwing Brian a narrowed glare before striding after the others.

Brian stood watching them go, his hands jammed in his pockets, his shoulders high. "That was useless."

"Unfortunately, as the judge, Thatcher has the final call on the matter."

Meg scanned the group of competitors as they drifted out of the clearing. Fief had been the first one to leave, her steps driven by temper, her bloodhound beating a rapid clip beside her. Glenn and Elan and their shepherds were next, Elan moving with a slight limp that made Meg wonder if he'd had a fall on the course. Dix and McGraw and their dogs followed. Standing near the trail leading toward the water, Pratt stood watching them, a satisfied smile curving her lips, the victor magnanimously letting everyone else go first. Meg suspected she was forcing every competitor to walk past her and her dog, parading past the winner. Pratt's earlier nerves were definitely gone now and her hold on her dog was greatly relaxed.

"You're definitely not the only one who's unhappy with how the trial went. Including me. I mean, the first part of the search went fine. It took Hawk a bit to find the scent cone, though considering the placement, I suspect it took everyone that long. But partway into it, he got totally confused. Started second guessing the trail. Then we lost several minutes going the wrong way and backtracking before he snapped out of it and homed in. It was so unlike him."

"Interesting you'd say he was confused. I've never seen that reaction from him. Or Lacey. They might lose the trail because of terrain or air currents, but they don't get confused."

"It's just so weird." Raising her head, Meg noted they were alone in the clearing. "No point in hanging out here. Let's go find Todd and Ryan. They'll have camp fully set up by now."

Back down the hill to the water, where the boats were tied up for the day. Several of the pilots had pulled out folding chairs and now sat near the water's edge, chatting and keeping an eye on the site. At this time of year, there were considerably fewer hikers and portagers in the Boundary Waters Canoe Area, and no other registered campers at this site, but they'd make camp nearby to make sure the boats remained secure. As they passed the pilots, Meg gave Charlie a nod; in response, he raised two fingers to his forehead in salute. Then they entered the forest again, starting the hike to the campsite, up the hill and farther along the lake.

As they walked, the dogs companionably between them, Meg kept turning the details of the trial over and over in her mind.

"Hey." Brian tapped her upper arm. "You in there?"

"Yeah. I'm just thinking about how that went."

"And?"

"Did you notice the first two of you who went at the beginning placed first and second? And from then on, it mostly fell apart, with the exception of Dix."

"What does that tell you?"

"I don't know, but something seems off to me somehow. Hawk's confusion, your time being off, the disqualification. This should have been straightforward. And yet . . ."

"It wasn't."

"Yeah. We'll have to see how tomorrow goes. No pressure, but Craig's desire to win is all on you now. Hawk and I are unlikely to catch up." At the sound of his name, Hawk tipped his face up to Meg and she gave him a quick stroke as they walked.

"I'm only a few minutes in front of Dix, with two trials still to go. You know how quickly a trial search of this length can turn. Do an extra pass in the scent cone, overshoot the cone and then have trouble finding it again, or miss it altogether because of air eddies, and that lead could evaporate."

"Or he could have the same difficulties. And you're less than a minute behind Pratt. She's the one to beat. And after that little display, I'd really love to see you do it. You just need to pick up some extra time, beat the pain-in-the-ass front runner, and stave off the competition."

Brian simply rolled his eyes at her.

No pressure at all.

CHAPTER 5

Black Swan: An extremely rare or unlikely event that may be impossible to predict.

Friday, October 18, 4:46 PM
Boundary Waters Canoe Area
Superior National Forest, Minnesota

"There they are. You can't miss our glow-in-the-dark tent." Meg pointed to where a large, blindingly orange tent was pitched next to two smaller tents in quieter shades of green and blue.

"That's . . . obnoxious." Brian's lip curled as they walked along, Lacey heeling at his knee. "Is Todd trying to avoid being shot at during hunting season?"

"Fair question. You ask him." Her gaze found the four men relaxing in folding nylon camping chairs in a loose group around a blazing campfire. Two chairs in the circle remained unoccupied. "I don't care about the color, as long as I'm comfortable. He knows I'm only going to go camping with him if there's a decent bed where Hawk and I will stay warm and dry, and if there's good food. I can deal with cleaning off in the lake for a weekend, and cooking over the fire, but there better be a generator to recharge my satellite phone—"

"Because God knows there's no cell signal this far out," Brian muttered.

"—or I'm not going to be there."

"Does he know you were willing to do this training weekend before he said he'd come and organize the camping aspect? For all of us?"

"No. And don't you dare tell him."

Brian snorted a laugh. "Are you kidding? He arranged our tent and the double air mattress and is catching the fish we'll be eating for dinner. I'm not telling him anything."

"Smart man. Not to mention his brothers contributed all the alcohol for the weekend, because Craig is picking up the camping fees."

"And while I'm not going to overindulge, I'm absolutely going to enjoy an adult beverage by the campfire."

"After that goofy trial we just did? Followed by that insane argument we had to break up? Absolutely. Besides, I hear there's some nice boxed wine, white *and* red, with your name on it."

"Really?" Brian's tone raised several notes in interest.

"And even wineglasses. Plastic, but still, wineglasses."

"I need to camp with you more often. This was not what I was expecting."

"I can rough it. I just don't see why I should. And that means you shouldn't either."

Brian slung an arm across her shoulders. "Babe, if my heart didn't belong to Ryan, it just might be yours."

"But for that smart, beautiful man, you and your amazing dog could have been all mine." She waved an arm over her head. "Hello!"

Todd lounged in his chair, his jean-clad legs crossed at the ankles, his hiking boots perilously close to the fire. A beer bottle dangled from his right hand over the edge of the chair arm as he angled, laughing, toward his brother

Josh. But at the sound of Meg's voice, he turned, a smile curving his lips at the handlers and dogs approaching. "Hey, Foster. You muscling in on my girl again?"

Brian released Meg to hold out both arms in surrender. "I keep trying, but she has this thing for tough, brawny firefighters. I just don't get it." He grinned and circled the group to where his husband, Ryan, sat on the far side. He dropped into the empty chair beside him as Lacey squeezed between them to greet Ryan.

"At least your dog likes me." Tall, slender, and blond, Ryan looked like the academic he was, even in casual camping clothes. His neatly styled, medium-length hair and precisely trimmed beard definitely set him apart from the men around him who were clean-shaven because of the masks they had to wear as part of the job, with their hair cut short to fit under their heavy helmets. "Hey, Lacey, how are you?" Leaning forward, he got a long lick from Lacey before looking up at Brian, a devilish glint in his eye. "See?"

"I dragged you, an archivist, away from your desk in the middle of DC and all its modern amenities, and out into the wilds of Minnesota. How can you doubt my love for you?"

"It's a question that basically answers itself." Meg sidled in front of the chair beside Todd and was about to sit down, when he grabbed her hand to stop her. "What?"

"That's my chair. I'm sitting in yours." Todd pushed out of the navy camp chair and stepped aside, his open palm offering her the chair.

She eyed the chair suspiciously—it had six legs instead of four . . . and were those hydraulics on the back legs? "What's the catch?"

"No catch. I bought this chair specifically for you. It

won't bite. I was just sitting in it to prove it." He took her by the shoulders, maneuvered her in front of the chair, and pushed her down into it.

Meg settled into the chair, but then jerked when it suddenly shifted backward as he released her. She leaned forward and the chair moved with her, so she cautiously leaned back again. "You bought me a rocking chair?"

"One specifically made for camping." He sat down in the chair next to her and watched her rock back and forth a few times. "Like it?"

Meg met Brian's eyes across the flames and could see his laughing approval. "I do. You're making camping worth my while."

Todd flipped open the cooler between them, pulled out a chilled cocktail in a tall, slender can, and held it out to her.

She slipped the can from his fingers, eyed it. "A mimosa?" Her gaze shot to him. "What did you do?"

"Do?"

"You got me a rocking chair"—she swayed back and then forward again—"which is nothing short of awesome, and one of my favorite cocktails. You're buttering me up." Her eyes narrowed with suspicion. "What did you do?"

His grin was accompanied by an overly exaggerated eyebrow waggle. "Nothing . . . yet." When she smacked his arm, he chuckled. "I'm just bribing you with a fun camping experience, so next time it won't be like pulling teeth. For an outdoorsy person, you're really picky about where you bed down."

"Blame my mother. My father would have camped, but Eda Jennings wouldn't hear of it. It was a nice hotel or a historic inn or nothing. As a result, Cara and I both feel the same way about it. We love a good hike, but when it's time to sleep, we want a comfortable mattress, hot and cold running water, a way to recharge our phones, and a connection to the outside world." She cracked open her can, took a long swallow, slid it into the cup holder in her chair, and leaned back, weaving her fingers over her stomach. "Our needs are few." Todd's crack of laughter had her imitating his eyebrow waggle.

"Todd, you're doomed."

Todd turned to face his youngest brother.

Seated beside Ryan, Luke looked so much like Todd, Meg had done a double take the first time she'd met him. Not that she should have been surprised—from their height, to their blue eyes, to their long black hair, she and her sister, Cara, looked so similar, many people thought they were twins. The resemblance was equally striking between Todd and Luke. Luke's eyes were green instead of Todd's gold-flecked brown, and his dark hair was slightly shorter, but the bone structure was strikingly similar. Put the brothers in similar plaid shirts over white T-shirts, as they were now, with vacation stubble because their respective fire departments weren't ordering them to shave, and they, too, nearly looked like twins. Once she'd met Stephen, their father, she realized they were cookie-cutter molds of the now slightly-weathered original. Josh, their middle brother, had the auburn hair and paler complexion of their mother, but his stature was all from his father. All three brothers were tall, broad, and muscular, just like Stephen. And, similarly, they had followed their father's footsteps into the firehouse. Stephen was now retired from the service, but his legacy was carried on by his boys, two of whom remained in his department in Baltimore. Only his oldest had stretched his wings a little farther, becoming a dual-trained firefighter/paramedic with DC Fire and Emergency Medical Services.

"How am I doomed?"

"No hot and cold running water." Luke looked sideways at Josh.

Josh simply toasted his brother with his beer bottle. "Doomed."

Meg leaned back a little farther in her chair, enjoying the smooth motion. *Pretty good for a folding camp chair.* "Nah, he'll be fine for a weekend. That's our list of wants. Todd knows he can make the rest of the experience so enjoyable, I won't notice the lack of warm water. I have to say, I'm loving this fire, so that's a good start. Also, I'm starving. Brian?"

"After that search? And the shenanigans that followed? Definitely starving."

"Shenanigans?" Josh asked.

"Food first," Meg said, "then explanations. Did you catch anything?"

Luke made a disgusted sound in the back of his throat. "Did we catch anything. So little faith."

"What Luke is trying to say is that dinner is cleaned and currently chilling on ice in the cooler under the table," said Todd. "You tell me when you're ready to eat and we'll make you a meal you won't believe."

Brian pointed at the fire. "Now. She's ready to eat now."

"She sure is," Meg agreed. "And I'll be even more ready by the time it's cooked."

"Dinner it is then."

The three Webb brothers insisted on doing everything, and Meg was impressed with how fast they pulled the meal together. Luke was the head chef, preparing the trout fillets with lemon, oil, and herbs, and then panfrying them over the open fire in a giant cast-iron pan.

"I told you this was why we made it a road trip instead of flying," Josh quipped. "I couldn't get him to leave that damned pan at home, and the baggage fees for it would have been unbelievable."

Luke didn't look up from his skillet. "It was an adventure. Admit it, you had a great time."

"Yeah, yeah. You tell yourself that." But Josh's grin belied his words.

It *had* been an adventure. They'd packed Todd's F-150 and Josh's F-250 with the camping gear needed for all six of them, and then Brian, Ryan, and Lacey had joined Meg, Todd, and Hawk, and they'd set out as a convoy to Minnesota. Two days of travel, two nights on the road, and a stop at a local grocery store and bakery for everything they'd need for the weekend to eat like kings. After an early start this morning, they'd dropped Meg and Brian off for training, while the brothers and Ryan set up camp.

By five thirty, they were sitting down to pan-fried fish with foil-wrapped baked potatoes cooked in the coals of the fire, a huge green salad, and fresh rolls from the bakery, with a box of mixed desserts and coffee waiting for them after the meal. Along with beer and white wine.

As they gathered around the picnic table, pulling up chairs to the ends to fit everyone, Josh brought the handlers back to their day. "So . . . shenanigans? Did your training go off the rails?"

Meg met Brian's eyes across the table. "No, actually that part went fine. It was the trial afterward that was . . ."

"Weird," Brian finished for her through a mouthful of salad.

"Definitely." She summed up the trial for the table, starting with her own run, then passing the baton to Brian to fill in his experience, and then, together, they described the argument in the clearing and the time disagreement.

"I don't get it," Luke said. "When you gotta go, you

gotta go. What's the big deal about the dog peeing during the trial?"

"Those are just the rules," Brian said. "No urination or defecation during the search."

"Ever? When you guys are out looking for a lost kid, you don't let them go?"

"No, no," Meg laughed. "For some of those searches, we can be out for hours and hours. And the last thing you need is a dog distracted because he needs to pee. If we need to take care of business, we do, and keep going. But in a trial, that's part of the discipline you're demonstrating. This trial was a little longer than most. Many are done on closed courses or at commercial facilities and time differences can come down to seconds; but because this is out in the middle of nowhere, they had the space to make it more challenging. But still, thirty to forty minutes isn't a long time for a dog to wait to go. And handlers know to give the dog time to go beforehand."

"Why did it happen then?" Ryan asked.

"You know, that's a fair question." Brian picked up his plastic wineglass, swirled the straw-colored liquid a few times, and then set it down, untasted. "Like seriously, that's a fair question." He poked the fork he held in his other hand at Meg. "Why *did* it happen?"

Meg pulled away slightly as he came a little too close for comfort. "Watch where you're waving that. It doesn't happen much, but it does happen. But . . ." Her voice trailed off as she stared off sightlessly past Brian's shoulder.

He shifted slightly, suddenly coming into her focus. "But what?"

"What would cause him to do that?"

"Needing to go?" Luke suggested.

"Well, sure," Brian said, "but the dogs are trained not

to do that without permission when they're in work mode."

"But what's going to induce a dog to do that without permission?" Meg asked.

She and Brian stared at each other for a moment before they spoke over each other.

"Instinct," said Meg.

"Another dog's urine," said Brian.

"Wait, so another dog peed there, so that dog did too?" asked Josh.

"Ever taken a dog for a walk and it stops at every fire hydrant to pee?" Brian asked.

"Sure."

"The dog is reacting to the scent of urine from another dog. It's instinctual to mark that spot with their own urine. Mark it as their territory."

"Okay. But what's the big deal with it happening on the trail you guys were on?"

"Because out in the middle of nowhere, close to a hide in a trial, what are the chances of another dog having gone there and it being fresh enough to distract a trained K-9?"

"You're implying that scent was planted there on purpose." Accustomed to how Meg's mind worked, as well as being well versed in the team's problem solving, Todd was already three steps ahead of his brothers. "You're talking about sabotage."

"That sounds overly dramatic." Meg shrugged. "But, yeah, I guess I am. Someone purposely trying to throw dogs off the scent."

"You said Hawk seemed confused and distracted while on the search."

"If it was fresh urine laid down just before the trial started, that would explain it. And maybe because of the angle Lacey came in at, it wasn't so bad and she managed to sort out the scents without you knowing there was a conflict. But then if Hawk came through the worst of it, that might explain why he was so off his game."

Todd finished chewing and set down his fork. "Any chance it could have been a natural occurrence? Not someone walking their dog, but something naturally occurring? A wolf or a coyote? A bear? Wouldn't that make more sense? Occam's razor and all that?"

"Meaning the simplest explanation may be the best explanation? That we're reading something sinister into a situation where coincidentally a few other things just happened to go wrong?"

"Maybe? You guys spend so much time working cases, it might be easy to read something nefarious into an innocent situation."

Meg gave a self-deprecating laugh and took a sip from the wine she'd moved on to for dinner. "There you go again, being the levelheaded first responder. You're probably right. And I probably need to drink more wine and relax." She tapped her wineglass against Brian's. "You too, apparently."

Brian picked up his glass and toasted her. "I'll drink to that. Now, that was truly amazing. But did someone say dessert?"

"Oh, don't worry, we have dessert," said Luke. "But don't eat so much dessert you won't have room for Josh's famous campfire nachos this evening. You won't want to miss that."

"Campfire nachos?" Ryan asked. "You need that giant skillet for those too?"

"You can do it in a skillet, but the key is to layer the chips deep, interspersing with multiple layers of cheese, then dump on a pile more toppings and cook it long enough over the fire to turn it into a hot, gooey, cheesy

mess. To pull that off, you need a cast-iron Dutch oven."
Josh's grin was a devilish flash of teeth. "I happen to have
brought one. You know, since we had to make the drive
because of Luke's massive skillet."

"You guys are serious campers."

"You come camping with us, you eat well. And campfire nachos are truly a thing of beauty." Todd rubbed his
belly. "Just give me time to digest dinner and I'm there."

"Sounds like they're not to be missed." Meg bumped
her shoulder against his. "I'll drink to that."

CHAPTER 6

Bodyguard of Lies: "In wartime, truth is so precious that she should always be protected by a bodyguard of lies." (Sir Winston Churchill)

Friday, October 18, 10:12 PM
Boundary Waters Canoe Area
Superior National Forest, Minnesota

"What time are you guys heading out tomorrow?" The sentence was muffled as Meg pulled a sweatshirt over her head, then worked her arms into it.

Todd toed off his unlaced hiking boots, lining them up neatly by the zipped tent entrance. "We're going to start at seven thirty. That gives us at least a good ninety minutes of prime fishing. Luke wanted to start at six thirty. Josh told him he's on vacation, and if Luke woke him up before six thirty, he was going to cheerfully murder him." He chuckled. "Have to say, I might do the same."

"You boys have an interesting way of showing you love each other."

"It's what guys do. Nothing says 'I love you' better than threats of mock violence."

"Actually, someone else's threats of real violence and

a sibling standing in the way is the best way to say 'I love you.' "

"Hell yes. As the oldest, let me tell you, I can absolutely pick on the two of them. Someone else tries it, they have to deal with me. And whichever other one of us isn't at risk." In thick socks, he sidled around the large inflated mattress in the middle of the tent. "Did I forget anything?"

Meg scanned the inside of the tent. It was a huge six-person tent, big enough to have a center divider to split it into two sections, though that divider was tied out of the way to make room for the large, double blow-up mattress, covered with two joined sleeping bags and full-size pillows. A large woven throw rug flowed out from under the bed to ward off the autumn cold coming through the ground. Todd had tucked Hawk's spare dog bed into the corner of the tent by Meg's head. A folding camp table with a Coleman LED lantern and a pair of two-way radio handsets sat on his side of the bed. Underneath, cords ran from the portable power station to her satellite phone, charging on the table. Their duffel bags, currently open on the bed as they changed for the night, would be neatly stacked against the tent wall.

"I don't think so. I think you covered all the bases."

"We aim to please."

"You're sure Josh and Luke don't need a hand out there? It's a lot of stuff to pack away."

"They said they didn't. I trust them to let me know." After several hours gathered around the fire—Todd was right, campfire nachos *were* a thing of beauty—they'd decided to call it a night, the guys wanting to get an early start fishing, and Meg and Brian having their next round of training at eight in the morning. Ryan, not the fishing type, was perfectly happy to relax with the weighty biography of Theodore Roosevelt he'd been saving for his uninterrupted reading time during vacation. Luke and Josh had insisted on packing away the food, coolers, and garbage themselves, safely locking it all into the covered bed of Josh's truck and away from curious wildlife.

"Okay. Then I'm going to hit the restroom one more time before bed, and make sure Hawk does the same. You need to come?"

"I'm good."

"Men. You can save yourself a ten-minute walk and just wander into the forest thirty feet that way." She tossed a thumb over her shoulder and into the thick underbrush behind the tent.

"You know it."

"Not quite so easy for us. Hawk, buddy, let's take a walk."

"Catch." Todd picked up the heavy-duty rechargeable flashlight and tossed it to Meg, who neatly caught it. "And this." He followed it up with one of the handsets.

Meg slid the handset into the side pocket of her yoga pants. "You think I'm going to run into trouble and need to call for help?"

"Nah, and if you do, you and Hawk know how to handle yourselves. But just in case."

"Yes, Dad. Hawk, come."

She unzipped the front panel of the tent, slipped through, and held it open for Hawk, then zipped it shut behind them.

For a moment, she simply stood and took in the quiet of the night. The campsite was now deserted. Their chairs ringed the banked fire, now only a faint glow of the last of the embers, and the picnic table was bare, with all signs of food, drink, and refuse whisked away. Looking up, she saw a panorama of stars flowing overhead. Now, without even the light of the fire to dim their brilliance, they hung thick in the night sky, a sparkle in the dark envelope opened through the break in the tall trees towering all around. Through the branches, flashes of a gibbous moon spread silvery threads of light over the path leading away from the camp. In the distance, the low hoot of an owl contrasted with the whistled *whip-poor-will* of the eponymous bird. Closer, she heard Ryan's voice, quiet, followed by the low rumble of Brian's laugh from inside their tent.

"Hawk, come."

Meg didn't need to leash him for a short walk, when voice commands would keep him by her side, so they left the camp and started down the lane—twin ruts, flanked by grass, a winding curve through the trees. When they'd booked their campsite, knowing they'd be a larger party than those strictly here on their own for the training and trials, Meg and Brian had reserved the most distant campsites, knowing they'd be able to combine them to create enough room for everyone and all three tents. However, the rest of the competitors were set up in the main campsite area, closer to the road and the restroom facilities near the entrance to the campsite, and both the beach and the boat ramp to the lake for those setting out by water.

They walked down about fifty feet of road before the trees opened out to the north to a larger camping area. Eight or ten tents were spread out around the space, some dark, some glowing from within with lantern light. The smell of woodsmoke still lingered in the air, but the fire pits were banked and dark.

Meg and Hawk quietly continued down the road, as the trees closed in again, until they reached the campground's main crossroads. Ahead lay the road that led to the small parking lot and the eastern campsites, where the SDA organizers and trials teams camped. To the north, a road angled down toward the water, and to the south, another led out of the campgrounds and toward civilization. On the southwest corner stood the small cabin that housed the men's and women's restrooms.

Business done, they reemerged from the cabin to stand on the gravel crossing. In the distance, moonlight shimmered on bobbing water.

"Let's go take a look at the lake, Hawk. We may not have a chance to see it this peaceful again." Side by side, they walked down the hill until they hit a fork in the road. Instead of taking the road to the right, which led down to the beach and all the boats pulled up on the sand waiting for tomorrow's training, they took the smaller road to the left. About forty feet out from the water, gravel gave way to dirt, and then, five feet out, to sand. The boat launch was nothing more than a section of shoreline cleared of grass and water plants to allow vehicles to back into place to slip their boats into the water before parking in the nearby lot. Ground cover and small, scraggly bushes lined one side of the launch just short of the sand, and two canoes lay upside down on a small section of grass on the other. Meg could see why the SDA organizers had the teams setting up one hundred feet down the shoreline where they could load multiple dinghies at once and could beach the boats together overnight.

They walked to the lake's edge, where the water rippled only slightly under the push of the breeze. The moon hung low overhead, a shifting trail of silver light sweeping across the lake toward them. Over the far side of the lake, a shimmer of green light rose above the trees, undulating and pulsing as it melted into purple, and then into the blackness of the sky overhead.

"Look, Hawk. We don't get to see northern lights like that at home."

Meg knelt down and slung her arm over her dog, the sand cool under her knees. He gave her cheek a lick in response, and then stood still under her arm. They stayed like that for several minutes, Meg's eyes fixed on the flowing ribbon of color, simply enjoying each other's company, as well as the peace and stillness after a long and occasionally unsettling day.

Finally Meg stood up and brushed the sand off her knees. "Going to be another busy day tomorrow, so we better hit the hay. Also, Todd's going to think we got lost in the woods. And the last thing we need is three first responders thinking they need to stage a rescue." Keeping that in mind, she pulled out her radio and signaled his.

"You lost?" She could hear the smile in his voice when he answered.

"Funny guy. No, we took a quick detour down to the lake because it's a pretty night. We're on our way back now. Didn't want you to worry."

"Appreciate that. See you in a few."

She tucked her radio into her pocket. "Hawk, come."

He fell into step, perfectly heeling at her knee, and they climbed the hill back up toward the crossroads. But Meg's steps faltered when a voice floated down to them. Female and full of rage.

"You'll do as I say, you stupid bitch. When I tell you to stay, you stay. You don't come find me."

Meg crested the rise to find Rita Pratt with her Belgian Malinois slinking at her side. Pratt wrapped the leash around her hand, shortening it severely, and then turned away from the dog, hooking the leash over her shoulder, dragging the dog onto its back legs. Then, joining her two hands together, and bending away from the dog, she hauled on the leash, pulling the Malinois right off its feet.

Hanging it by its neck.

Meg froze in disbelief for a fraction of a second as the dog let out a strangled cry of fear and pain, and then she was sprinting, Hawk keeping pace beside her. "What are you doing? Put that dog down!"

Pratt spun around, the dog still dangling in midair, before surprise loosened her hold, and the dog dropped to the ground to stand, head down, sides heaving like bellows, shaking like a leaf.

"Mind your own business, Jennings," Pratt snarled.

"I sure as hell won't. Not when an animal is being abused." Meg stopped ten feet from Pratt, not sure how out of control she was and wanting to give her some space. "Hawk, sit. Stay." He obediently did as commanded, keeping his eyes not on the injured dog, but her infuriated owner.

"That's not abuse, that's discipline."

"The hell it is."

"When you have an aggressive dog, you have to remind it occasionally who's alpha."

"That dog's not aggressive. She's terrified of you. Look at her!"

But Pratt didn't spare a glance for her dog. "She needs to be reminded who's in charge."

"That's not how you train a dog. Positive reinforcement builds a bond. Negative reinforcement only builds fear."

"Don't you dare lecture me. You with your docile little therapy dog."

An image of Hawk, his teeth buried in Giraldi's shoulder as he slowly strangled Meg while she lay on her own hallway floor, rose in her mind. *You have no idea, lady.* "There's no excuse for what you're doing. I'm going to report you to both the SDA and the Laramie Sheriff's Office. You'll lose your dog. Hopefully, she'll go to someone who'll treat her with kindness and respect."

"You wouldn't dare." Pratt took a step forward, and even in just the silvery light of the moon, her face flushed an angry red. "And even if you did, no one would believe you, so you'd be wasting your time. Get the fuck out of my business." She gave the leash a brutal yank, jerking her dog forward. "Ava, come." And then strode away, her dog hurrying to stay in step with her.

Meg watched them go, shaking with rage. While she

didn't condone adults abusing each other, the abuse of children and animals generated a special kind of fury in her. And to witness it herself? She was glad she'd been able to put a stop to it—this time—but it explained a lot about the animal's behavior earlier. Ava was terrified of Pratt.

She couldn't let that stand. When she got back into civilization, she was going to submit a formal complaint to Pratt's commander. She knew if she asked, Craig would throw all his influence and weight behind her to ensure the dog was removed to safety and no other K-9 ended up in Pratt's hands.

She lay a hand on Hawk's head, stroking, feeling a slight tremor run through him in reaction to both another animal's pain and her own rage. "It's okay, Hawk. You did well. Good boy." She let out a long sigh. "What on earth did we get ourselves into this weekend? Nothing's gone right. Come on, let's go to bed."

They walked back, keeping their footsteps quiet. When they passed through the larger campsite, all the lights were out and nothing and no one moved. Meg had no idea which tent was Pratt's, but the lack of movement made her wonder if Pratt had returned to the camp or had dragged her dog off somewhere else.

With nothing else she could do tonight, they moved on, down the path and into the quiet calmness of their own campsite.

She opened the zippered door, let Hawk go through, then bent to enter herself and zipped the door closed. She turned around to find Todd already inside the sleeping bag, wearing a warm, faded DCFEMS sweatshirt, his arms tucked behind his head.

His smile dissolved and he pushed up on both elbows. "What happened?"

She let out a rough laugh. "That obvious, huh?"

"It is to me. You're upset. I just talked to you and you were fine. What happened since then?"

When he started to roll out of the sleeping bag, she waved him down. "Don't move. I'm coming in. Hawk, bedtime, buddy."

Hawk stepped into his bed, turned around three times, and settled with a gusty sigh.

Todd stayed upright, his sharp gaze locked on her. He'd asked her twice, and was clearly going to wait her out at this point. Reaching into the sleeping bag, he pulled out a pair of her sweatpants he'd been warming with his own body heat.

"Thanks. You really are making this weekend as comfortable as possible for me."

"The way this weekend is going so far, it's the least I can do."

"You don't know the half of it."

He gave her a pointed look, but waited patiently when she held her silence.

Meg unlaced and removed her hiking boots, setting them opposite Todd's at the doorway, and shimmied out of her yoga pants. She stepped into the sweatpants, then without taking off her sweatshirt in the cool outdoor air, she wiggled out of her bra, extracting it through one sleeve.

"It always amazes men how women can do that."

That cracked a half smile from Meg. "It's one of those X-linked skills we have."

She double-checked that Hawk was comfortable, and drew a thick fleece blanket up over him, tucking him in, just leaving his eyes and nose exposed, so he'd be warm as the temperature dropped overnight. Then she unzipped her side of the sleeping bag and slipped in. Todd's body heat already made it deliciously warm inside their cocoon.

As his arm slipped under her, drawing her in, she rolled to lie with her head on his shoulder, one leg hooked over his thighs.

Then, as his fingers slipped under her sweatshirt to stroke up and down her side, she told him about her encounter with Pratt.

He waited until she talked herself out, talked out the rage, and the pity for an abused animal. Only then did he speak. "She needs to be reported."

"I know. I will. How could I not?"

"There are some who wouldn't. You're not one of those people. I can hear the helplessness in your tone. And the rage. You'll do the right thing."

"Yeah. I think I'll wait until we're out of here, but then I'll take it to Craig. If he doesn't want to submit an official department report, I'll do it solo, but I'd rather have the force of the FBI behind me. It will have more impact."

"It's still you who witnessed it."

"Yes, but when you lose a handler like that, there's a chance you lose the dog too. They're bonded to one handler and sometimes transfers don't work well. And some of these departments, they can't afford to buy a new dog. In reporting her, I'm hurting them and the good work that dog does. Don't get me wrong, I'll do it, but it's not as simple as pointing a finger." She was silent for a minute, and he waited her out. "This afternoon, before the trial began, she looked twitchy, and Ava . . . she seemed stressed. But then they came back afterward, and Pratt was all 'look at us.' And yeah, they'd taken first place."

"I've seen you and Hawk up close and personal. Most people would think the dog does all the work, but I know better. It's teamwork between you. He has the nose, but you have the logic to get that nose where it needs to be. You have a fantastic success rate together, but separately, it would be nothing impressive. But how you describe

Pratt and her dog, it isn't a partnership, it's a dictatorship. How did they work well enough together to take first?"

"That's a damned good question. And let me assure you, I'll be watching them *much* more closely tomorrow during the next phase of the trial. And if she mistreats Ava at any time, I'll call her on it, then and there."

"Hopefully, in front of additional witnesses to strengthen your testimony."

"That would be nice, but don't hold your breath. She was brutal to that poor dog tonight, but only because she thought no one was watching. I caught her off guard."

"I bet you did. But tomorrow is another day. And if you're going to be on your guard, and be watchful, you need to be at your best tomorrow." He stretched away from her, cool air flowing into the sleeping bag as he extinguished the lantern, the tent settling into quiet darkness. He snugged her in closer, warming her again, pressed a kiss to her forehead, and then rested his cheek against it. "I know it's easier said than done, but try to turn your brain off. There's nothing more you can do tonight. You can bring Brian up to speed tomorrow morning and you can work together to keep an eye on that dog. And then at the first opportunity, you can do what you can to bring her actions to light. In the meantime, try to rest."

"Sounds like good advice."

She curled into Todd, but the sound of Ava's cries kept ringing in her head.

Sleep was a long time coming.

CHAPTER 7

Tooth-to-Tail Ratio: Military jargon for describing the ratio of war fighters and the number of supply, medical, and transport troops needed to support them.

Saturday, October 19, 8:34 AM
Boundary Waters Canoe Area
Superior National Forest, Minnesota

Meg turned her face into the wind and stared out into the distance. She put out her hand to steady herself as the boat gave a small bounce over the choppy surface of the lake. Hawk shifted slightly where he stood in the bow, but stayed steady, holding still, his head high and his nose in the air.

He'd awakened that morning bouncing with energy and ready to take on whatever task she threw at him. Which was good, because Meg felt utterly drained. She knew her restlessness all night must have kept Todd from a deep sleep, because he disappeared before she was even out of bed, returning with a steaming cup of coffee ten minutes later.

She struggled onto one elbow, shivering slightly as cold air swept into the tent through the open tent flap. "What time is it?"

"Six fifty." Todd zipped the flap closed behind him, shutting out the cool draft.

"And everyone is up?"

"I haven't seen Brian or Ryan yet."

Meg accepted the plastic mug he handed her, wrapping her hands around its warmth and taking a careful sip of the steaming brew. "You're a miracle."

"Not me. Josh. You thought nachos were all he can do over a campfire? Coffee is a necessity. Especially after late evenings with beer and nachos around the fire. And Luke's making breakfast, so take two minutes with your coffee, then get up and get dressed, and come on out. We're going to eat and hit the lake and won't be back before you need to get to your training, so this way we can all eat together."

"He's doing a full breakfast on a campfire this early?"

"Bacon, eggs, toast. Nothing fancy, but enough to keep you going through the morning and possibly into your next trial."

"Bacon . . . Brian will be forced to get up. Lacey is a fiend for bacon. She's not allowed to have much—too salty—but the moment she smells it, she'll be all over Brian to let her out of the tent."

She wasn't wrong, and five minutes later, Brian staggered out of his tent, his hair standing up in every direction, following his dog as she made a beeline toward the campfire and the wafting scent of bacon. Ryan emerged two minutes later, looking like he not only owned a hairbrush, but knew how to use it.

They sat down to what Meg was surprised to find was a hearty breakfast while the stars started to fade overhead as the sky lightened. Then the Webb brothers made sure they had all the gear they'd need in the truck, which was parked behind the tents, still hooked to the boat trailer towing the three-seater drift boat they'd rented in Duluth. As they headed to the truck, there was a spirited negotiation around who would get the first shift at the oars to get them out into the middle of the lake. With a wave, they circled the truck around the campsite, back down the narrow lane, and toward the boat launch for a few lazy hours of fishing.

"Luke's going to lose that one," Ryan said.

Meg stared after them as they drove away slowly, watching for anyone else who might also be up and about. "Yeah, I suspect so. Baby of the family, and all that. This is what you get when you come to a lake that requires special permission for any kind of motorboat."

Brian poured himself another cup of coffee from the tin pot still sitting on the table. "I bet they're going to love doing it that way. More of a challenge, more teamwork. And who needs the gym when you can get your activity outdoors?"

"Not to mention, a much better story for the firehouse," Ryan said.

"You know, you may be right." Brian considered Meg thoughtfully. "So all that about a comfortable bed, and it still looks like you had a terrible night."

"Gee, thanks. You're such a gentleman." Meg refrained from sticking her tongue out at him.

"Just calling it like I see it. Was the mattress uncomfortable?"

"No, it was fine. It was what happened before bed." Meg caught Brian and Ryan up on what she'd seen the night before and her plan to report Pratt to her superiors as soon as the weekend was over.

"Holy hell." Brian was appalled, just as Meg knew he would be. "I'd have had trouble sleeping too. I'd have spent the whole night second guessing letting her go and whether I should be calling her boss at three in the morning. And worrying about that dog."

"That was exactly my night."

"You sure you shouldn't be reporting her now?"

"I want to wait to make it an official complaint. It will have more impact and I seriously want this to stick. I could reach Craig via the sat phone, but he's out of the office this weekend, and who's to say the Laramie County admin types aren't as well. It can wait two days. She's not going to pull a stunt like that in front of anyone here, so we just need to keep her in sight as much as we can."

"I'd be happy to help out there. Ava will be fine this morning, as they'll be in a boat with a trainer, pilot, and diver, and then we have the second trial this afternoon. That will keep her with other people for much of the day. Are you sure the dog isn't in imminent danger?"

"No guarantees, but I don't think so. As rough as she is with her, that dog is also her bread and butter. She does anything severe enough to hurt the dog, they're both benched. And it would certainly take her out of the running to win the competition this weekend, which she seems pretty focused on. It gives us a tiny window of opportunity."

Both Meg and Brian were watchful as they made their way down to the beach, but neither spotted Pratt and Ava. After that, they separated, meeting up with their own boat crews, and preparing for their next training sessions. Meg put it all aside and focused on the training. There'd be time to deal with Pratt later. Right now, she wanted to give Hawk's training every bit of her attention so they both learned everything they could from the trainer while they were with her.

They'd been on the water for about five minutes and Hawk was alert, but didn't show signs of having detected the scent.

Meg turned around to Claire. "This hide will be trickier than the last one?"

"It's supposed to be, but your first one was a lot more challenging than we initially intended. This one may be a piece of cake for him. Now, you're in charge this time. You direct Charlie. You saw how Hawk responded yesterday as we got him closer and closer. You can do it. Just let Hawk lead the way. He won't steer you wrong."

"*I* might steer him wrong." At Claire's pointed look, Meg held up both palms in surrender. "Kidding. Are we all on Lake Insula today?"

"Sort of. If you've looked at this lake on a map, you'll know it's actually six or seven interjoined bodies of water. The satellite view kind of looks like a sprawling, nightmarish Rorschach test. And Hawk was in the closest area to the campgrounds yesterday, so we're going farther afield today. If he smells anything in this section, we're just going to whisk him out of it. Charlie will let us know when we're starting. He doesn't know where the hide is exactly, but he knows the approximate location."

Meg glanced back at Charlie, who sat with one hand on the tiller, his eyes fixed straight ahead over Hawk's head to open water. She followed his gaze, but all she could see was trees, and none of the interconnected waterways Claire referred to. But that wasn't her job. Charlie would get them there, and then Hawk would do his thing.

She focused on Hawk now, standing in the bow, his ears flapping in the breeze. Today was cooler than yesterday, with low-lying clouds scudding toward the northeast, blocking the sun. The wind carried a bite, its gusts stirring the surface of the lake, and bumping them over the white-caps. But none of it bothered Hawk, who swayed and adjusted his balance as needed.

An icy wisp swept down the back of Meg's collar, a

shiver following it straight down her spine. She pulled her windbreaker in tighter around her throat, took a breath, and pushed everything but the current search away for later. She'd be more in the zone if she wasn't so exhausted, but this was the nature of searches—you worked with what you had. For today, Hawk had her.

Sorry, buddy.

They skimmed over the dark lake waters—it was probably too deep in this section of the lake to use for training—and after ten or twelve minutes, Meg could see the trees didn't actually enclose the far end of the lake, but opened into a wide channel. They shot down the channel flanked on either side by tall trees—so colorful it was akin to flying through the low-frequency end of a rainbow—pushed by wind that formed a natural tunnel through the gap.

Charlie eased back on the throttle, the front of the boat settling a little more level. "A little shallower in this area. Gonna slow down a bit." His gaze fell to the GPS in Sal's hand. "How we doin'?"

"Right on target. We'll be through in a couple of minutes."

"Roger that."

The quiet purr of the motor was amplified in the narrow channel, but after a few minutes, they burst into open water, the sound falling away into the lake basin.

"Here we are," Charlie confirmed. "You tell me where to go."

Claire sat back and gave Meg a nod of encouragement.

A study of the sky and cloud cover confirmed the wind direction for Meg. "Angle to the northeast, please, Charlie. Stick to the middle of the lake and we'll narrow it down from there."

"Aye, aye, Captain." He flashed her a grin and altered their course to suit her directions.

Satisfied with their course, Meg stayed focused on Hawk, who was alert and happy, but lacked the intensity that came with identifying a scent. The repetitive screech of a white-and-gray herring gull drew her gaze momentarily upward as it soared overhead on outstretched wings. She came back down to earth quickly as Hawk leaned forward over the bow, his nose working furiously, and then gave two sharp barks.

"Good boy!" Meg scanned the area around them, judging the distance to shore in both directions, as well as the airflow as it moved down the lake. She bet the hide was to the west of them. "Charlie, take us west, please, circling around to the shore, backtracking us by about a hundred feet, and then come northeast again, halfway between here and the shore. I'd like to bisect the area and narrow down the scent cone."

Claire's silent nod of approval eased a little of Meg's tension. Looking left, then right, she marked a tiny open area of beach to the east, and a distinctive double pine tree to the west, two tall trunks rising from a single root ball, to mark the maximum distance down the lake for subsequent passes.

It took them a few minutes to do the loop, and then come back up the lake in a parallel path to their first pass. Meg shifted a little closer to her dog, running her hand over his flank. "Good boy, Hawk. You found it the first time. Now find the scent again. Find, Hawk."

He didn't look back at her, but the tilt of his ears told her he was listening to her every word.

She spotted the double pine about fifty feet ahead. If they got that far, she'd miscalculated that the scent was on this side of the lake. In which case, they'd have to circle back the other way—

Hawk dropped down from standing to lean on his forelegs, stretching his neck and head out over the water, and barked.

"Good boy, Hawk." She whipped around to the stern of the boat. "Charlie, cut the engine, please."

The engine died, the boat going silent as they rocked on the choppy waters.

Meg studied Hawk. He'd moved to hang over the port side of the bow, his body still stretched out.

They were close.

She stuck an index finger in her mouth and extended it into the air, confirming wind direction. The intensity of Hawk's stillness told her they were close, but how close? She looked down the lake, back toward the channel. And realized she was looking at the key.

The channel was a wind tunnel. The wind exploding outward from its length would spread wide to run over the surface of the lake. Which meant the scent appeared to be from the west, which was how Hawk was searching for it on the west side, but the origin was actually to the east. Behind them and to the east.

"Charlie, I need you to circle around to the east, but back a bit closer to the channel, then come up slowly be-tween here and our previous midpoint." She caught Claire's eye. "I know he's leaning out to the west, and is indicating he smells the scent from that direction, but look at the way the wind channels into the open in this spot. It's not a straight line. That would necessitate going over the trees and we're too close to the shore with a breeze this stiff. The chimney effect would have the scent overshooting us. Which means he's scenting the air current we're feeling at water level, which has expanded out from the channel. And that places the hide behind us and to the *east*."

"That seems like a reasonable strategy to me," Claire said. "Let's test it out."

Charlie took them around and out of the scent cone. Hawk relaxed back to standing, alert and watchful, but not alerting. Yet.

"That's good, Charlie. Take us northeast. No, no, a little more to the east than this. That's it. Perfect." She knew they were getting close, could feel it in her gut, and shortened the leash in her grip, anticipating Hawk's enthusiasm. She was glad thirty seconds later she had, when Hawk practically launched himself off the bow, far enough that the leash on his vest stopped him as he dangled one paw in the water.

"Charlie, stop. Sal, mark it here." She turned to her dog to stroke and praise him for a job well done before swiveling to the diver. "How'd we do?"

Sal's grin said it all. "I'd work with you two any day. Nailed it a second time."

Relief swept through Meg, energizing her out of her exhaustion. "It's all him."

"That's not what I just saw." Claire ran a hand over Hawk's head, but her eyes were on Meg. "He was indicating on the wrong side of the boat, but you understood scent patterns enough to identify he was actually steering you a little wrong. He was reporting what he smelled. You got him where he needed to be. Your previous experience told you how to do that; you just translated it from land to water." She patted Meg on the shoulder. "Well done."

Sal was only in the water for a short time before he returned with the putrid-smelling hide and spit out his mouthpiece. "Practically right on top of it." He snickered at Charlie as he jammed the hide into the container and then snapped the lid on it, isolating the rancid odor. He kicked his way into the boat to sit on the edge. "Claire, I think we're making it too easy on them."

"You may be right. We'll have to come up with a way to make it really tricky for them tomorrow." She laughed at Meg's look of horror. "Don't you worry about that now. Just enjoy the win. You did great!"

Meg threw an arm over her dog and received a wet kiss in return. "We did great."

Teamwork for the win. Always.

CHAPTER 8

Pseudo™ Corpse: A training aid for training cadaver search K-9s. Sigma's Pseudo™ Corpse comes in several formulations like Distressed Body Scent (Trauma and Fear Formulation), Corpse Scent Formulation I, Corpse Scent Formulation II, and Drowned Victim Scent.

Saturday, October 19, 9:28 AM
Boundary Waters Canoe Area
Superior National Forest, Minnesota

"Let's get you back to shore," Claire said. "I bet we'll be the first team back. Charlie, that means you'll get the best spot for your chair by the fire."

"Hell yeah. We've even got time to do a little victory lap. We finished so quickly, we can afford a little sightseeing. It's a pretty lake. I haven't been up this way so far." The engine purred to life and Charlie took them up the lake, staying relatively close to the shore.

Trees whipped by, along with small bays and longer stretches of rocky granite rising into jagged cliff faces more than ten feet high. As they buzzed past a small island in the middle of the lake—a flat-topped slab of rock from which sprang a handful of tall pines—they spotted a bright red canoe pulled up on a shallow ledge. Behind it, a young couple sat in chairs in front of a navy-blue tent. They waved cheerfully and Meg returned the gesture.

Arrowing up the lake, Charlie cut across the far side and then banked around in a giant figure eight, bringing them around to head south.

"Look!" Meg pointed to the eastern shore where four deer paused just inside the tree line, remaining frozen until the boat shot past. But Hawk stayed at the front of the boat, his ears flapping and his head high, his eyes straight ahead. Shaking her head, Meg gave her dog an affectionate pat. "I don't think Hawk even saw them."

"I bet he thinks we're still training. But that was the only hide on this section of the lake."

But Meg continued to stare at her dog, now considering him through a professional lens. "Are you sure? I stopped watching him so closely because we were done, but if we were on land, I'd say he was in the scent cone. He's alert and focused like he has something."

"There could still be scent filtering up from our own hide. It takes a while for it to disperse. So that's still a ways in front of us, blowing in this approximate direction."

"That makes sense." Far ahead, Meg spotted the distinctive double pine tree. "Then it will never get strong enough for him to alert on, and we'll lose it up ahead. It's okay, bud, more tomorrow." She patted Hawk on the flank, smiling when he didn't even glance in her direction. "Man, he's *focused*."

"It's why he's so good at what he does. He's one hundred and ten percent in."

"That's my boy. Wait . . . Hawk?"

Hawk let out a whine, his head whipping from side to side.

Meg knew that whine. "He's lost the scent."

"Already?"

Meg looked up the eastern shoreline, her gaze stopping

at an open channel that led to another section of the sprawling lake. "I don't think what he was tracking came from in front of us," she said slowly. "It came from over there, that other arm of the lake." Hawk looked up at her and whined again, then bumped against her knee. "He's really unsettled." She looked back again. "Any harm in circling around and seeing what he was after?"

"I was thinking exactly the same thing. Charlie," Claire called, "bring us around again. We want to take that side cut we just passed."

"Can do." Charlie eased the tiller sideways, starting the turn. "Something interesting there?"

"We're not sure. Maybe."

Charlie took them in a tight loop and then motored them back north. "That inlet there?" he called as they approached it.

"Yes." Claire's eyes remained locked on Hawk as they drew closer. "We'll know in a second if it's something real."

"If it is, you'll see his posture change." The boat arced toward the channel and Hawk abruptly leaned into the wind, pressing his paws into the inflated curve of the bow, his nose furiously sampling the air.

"And there it is." Claire looked out over his head, down the short connecting waterway. It was, at most, about a half-mile straight shot through the surrounding forest, to open water on the far side. "Work it. We don't have a final confirmed destination, but he's sure something is out there. Let's see what he leads us to. Sal, you game to go into the water again if needed?"

"Absolutely. Let's see what he can show us."

"Great." Claire beamed down at Hawk.

"You're enjoying this." Meg couldn't keep the smile out of her voice.

"Sure am. I love watching these dogs at work. And

these training exercises are great, don't get me wrong. But there's something about the thrill of a real search, not an artificial situation where some of us know exactly where we should be going. And in this case, there's no missing child to stress us out. He's probably picking up a dead animal. Did you see those otters playing by the shore? Could be a water mammal like that. But decomp is decomp; they'll smell similar to Hawk. He's impressed me so far. I want to see him do it again."

They moved through the short waterway in only minutes, breaking out into an elongated, narrow section of the lake, dotted with small, rocky islands, each so low the trees springing from them looked like they erupted from the lake itself.

"Your call," Claire said. "Where do you want to go?"

"Any chance he could be scenting someone else's training hide?" Meg asked.

Claire shook her head. "We're too far north for that. The eight teams fanned out considerably closer to our launch site, going east and west mostly."

Meg looked overhead to check the direction of the cloud movement was unchanged. She studied the lake and its unbroken natural landscape—choppy water bouncing the shallow boat, rocks, trees, the forest coming nearly to the water's edge, leafy bushes crowding the waterline, and thick stands of bulrushes invading the shallows, their fluffy seed pods exploding atop yellowing stalks. "Let's play this straight. Charlie, take us southwest. Let's get Hawk out of the scent cone and work him back into it."

"You got it." Charlie adjusted their course and set a steady speed headlong into the wind.

"It's a straight shot across this area of the lake." Meg took her eyes off the landscape long enough to check Hawk's posture—no change—and went back to her perusal. "Those islands won't alter the scent path significantly, though there may be some minor dead space downwind of them. If we pass them and he's still in the cone, they won't affect the final search."

"That's my read as well," confirmed Claire. "Hawk, lead the way for us."

They bumped over the lake, spray rising up on either side of the boat to be swept away by the wind behind them. Hawk stayed focused ahead of them, his head up, ears flapping in the stiff breeze, tail waving. Charlie maneuvered them between two rocky islands, but Hawk's stance didn't change. Whatever he was after was still in front of them. They were almost all the way to the far side, when he deflated slightly, whined, and turned to look back at Meg.

Meg threw a quick glance over her shoulder, but the engine was already fading as they slowed. "Charlie, that's as far as we go. Now let's turn around and get back into the cone."

Charlie eased them around and then took them northeast. It took about ninety seconds for Hawk to indicate he had the scent again.

"Getting closer." Meg threw a glance at Charlie. "Circle around to the west and come back into this area about a quarter mile to the west."

It took a number of passes as Meg became more and more clear on Hawk's indications before she called it. "He's not reacting to this one in quite the same way. Not lunging like we've seen from the hides." She looked around, marking their spot in the middle of this section of the lake, likely in the deepest area. "And you think it's maybe an otter? Wouldn't they be more likely to die near the shore?"

"Not necessarily. And I'd assume, physiologically they'd be like humans. They might float initially, but would eventually sink simply because flesh is denser than water. The air in the lungs can help keep a body suspended, but it will sink after a short time, and then that air is replaced by water. Unless it's a chubby otter."

"Fat otters float?"

Claire matched her shrug with a chuckle. "Maybe? I can only speak to humans. The more fat tissue on a body, the longer it will float. Skinny people sink like a stone."

"Maybe it's a skinny, athletic otter. Or was." She turned around to Sal, with an apologetic smile. "You still willing to go searching down there?"

"Sure. We'll know either way within about ten minutes." He dug in the waterproof bag at his feet and pulled out a wristband with a compact camera attached.

"Is that . . ."

"A GoPro? Yeah. Waterproof model, good to two hundred feet, which is deeper than this lake. If it's a dead otter, I can give you photographic proof."

"For the love of God, don't bring it up," Charlie groaned. "That canister is bad enough. I don't need an entire rotting animal corpse up here."

Sal grinned, a near feral show of teeth, as he slipped his hand through the wrist strap and cinched it tight, adjusting the camera so it stood facing forward. The large button on the top would make it easy to operate, even with the dive gloves he pulled on next. "Make it worth my while?"

Charlie gave him a mock punch on the shoulder. "I'm not paying you to not gas us to death. You want on my boat, no rotting carcasses."

"Spoilsport." But Sal ruined the insult with a laugh.

He finished his preparations; then he gave them a wave and rolled backward into the water, the rope playing out behind him again. It ran over the edge of the boat, finally stopping just past the eighty-foot mark.

"How could this have gone wrong?" Meg asked.

Claire gave her a questioning head tilt. "What do you mean—wrong?"

"I assume we're wasting Sal's time."

"Not at all. Divers need practice too. You've set up a situation for him that isn't a cakewalk. The training exercises are made to be obvious to the dive team, in case we don't have someone as experienced as Sal. The placement in the body of water, the GPS tracker, the bright white float . . . it's all designed to make things underwater as easy as possible. But an old pro like Sal? He loves a challenge like this. There are plenty of things that give off decomp gases. We're just waiting to see what this thing is."

"You don't think Hawk was tracking a ghost?"

"Not at all."

"Even though he wasn't as definitive about the location?"

"That could partly be because of what he's trailing. We gave him the scent of a specific state of advanced decomp and then sent him out to find that exact scent. But decomp is a process and a sliding scale. Whatever's down there could be fresher than the hide sample." She ruffled Hawk's ears. "He's still learning, but he's doing spectacularly well."

They waited patiently, or least Meg tried to. The first two minutes Sal was gone, she took in the beauty of the land around them. But as the minutes ticked by, she started to fret. Then as more minutes ticked by, she started to sweat.

"This is taking a long time." Meg leaned over the side, as if she'd be able to see something—air bubbles, movement in the water, or Sal resurfacing. But there was nothing. "Are we sure he's not running into trouble?"

Charlie held up the rope. "He'd let us know if he was. Remember, he doesn't have a set location for this find, so it's going to take him longer."

"Or we didn't get close enough and it's a wild-goose chase."

At that moment, the rope in Charlie's hands jerked twice. "Here comes your answer."

"Anyone want to lay bets? Do I have any takers on an old rubber tire?" Sure that for all his good efforts and intentions, Hawk hadn't succeeded this time, Meg attempted to make light of it all so Hawk wouldn't sense any disappointment from her.

"Not from me. My money's on your dog," Claire said.

Meg knew Sal needed to do a safety stop before surfacing, but it felt like those three minutes ticked by slowly enough that fifteen had passed. A surreptitious glance at her watch confirmed she was simply being impatient to prove her dog's skills were solid. And that she hadn't wasted everyone's time this morning.

Sal's head finally broke the surface of the lake and he spit out his mouthpiece. The eyes that met Meg's were serious and shadowed with trepidation.

"What happened?" Meg leaned down and offered her hand. He slapped his around her wrist, and she gripped his forearm hard and hauled him aboard so he sat on the side of the boat. "What did you find?"

Sal pulled one knee up so he could turn to face into the boat, drew in a deep breath, then released it. "A body."

Charlie froze in the act of coiling the rope. "Like . . . an actual person?"

"Yes. And she hasn't been down there long. Hasn't been nibbled on yet."

"Have there been any missing persons reported?" Claire looked from Sal to Meg to Charlie, who shrugged.

"Not that I know of," Sal said. "And no one has called us to report one since we left camp, yet here we are. We need to call the authorities."

"Depending on how long it takes for them to get out here, they may need you to do the recovery."

"If they want that, I'm pulling in a couple more divers. And we'll need the equipment in my truck. And proper photography gear. And we'll need a real boat, not this dinghy." Sal threw a grimace at Charlie. "Sorry."

Charlie waved it away. "It *is* a dinghy. We don't need more than that for this kind of training. Also, this way we can use smaller electric motors on a lake that's not supposed to have outboard motors at all." He stared over the side to the dark waters below. "How accurate was Hawk?"

"Close. Close enough when you're talking about an unknown missing person in a body of water this size. We're not right above her, but my dive watch has GPS and I marked the location. I can get us back to her."

Meg zipped open her fanny pack. "I can call it in from here on my sat phone."

"Wait."

She froze at the urgency in his tone, her fingers just dipping inside. "Why?"

"You need to know a bit more before you call in the cavalry."

Meg stared at him for a moment, not liking the set of his mouth or the flatness of his eyes. She zipped the pack closed. "What do we need to know?"

"I took photos. They're not well lit, because I only had my flashlight to light the scene." He stripped off his dive gloves and then unstrapped the camera. He brought up photos on the color screen that covered the rear of the camera. "As I said, it's a woman." He paused on a picture, and then looked up to directly meet Meg's eyes. "I think I've seen her. I think you have too."

He turned the camera around so Meg could see the screen.

The photo had a murky blue cast to it, like all the other colors of the light spectrum had been filtered away. Only a narrow beam of light restored color to a nearby swath of the scene. A woman's head and torso were visible, her dark hair fanned out around her head in a suspended cloud. Her eyes were wide open and staring. But it was the symbol, light against black near her left collarbone, that Meg's brain struggled to resolve, upside down, and on an oblique angle.

Then she understood.

Shock sluiced like ice water over Meg, leaving her chilled and shaking.

The star contained the bucking bronco of the Laramie County Sheriff's Office.

Hawk had found Rita Pratt's body at the bottom of Lake Insula.

CHAPTER 9

Spin-up: Preparation and immediate execution of a short-term mission.

Saturday, October 19, 10:41 AM
Boundary Waters Canoe Area
Superior National Forest, Minnesota

"**D**o you know her?" Claire's voice trembled slightly with shock.

"I think so." Meg felt like her brain was rebooting and she was having trouble connecting her thoughts, so she didn't want to cement an identification. "Have you got a shot that's straight onto the face to confirm?"

"Yeah." Sal flipped forward a few photos and extended the camera again.

Meg took it, staring into the display, as Claire leaned in, pressing against Meg's shoulder, to see the image.

There was no doubt about it, especially as Sal had tried to light the photo better for identification. It was definitely Pratt. "It's one of the other competitors. Rita Pratt, out of the Laramie County Sheriff's Office." She turned her gaze away from the image of Pratt's lifeless face and up to Claire's. Only then could she drag in a breath and try to reorder her scrambled thoughts. "I don't understand. She should have been out on a boat. How is she here? Dead?"

Get it together, Meg. You've seen bodies before.

She forced herself to flip through the rest of the photos. A wider shot showed Pratt wearing what looked to be the same yoga pants and black Laramie County Sheriff's Office jacket that Meg had seen her in last night.

Was I the last person to see Pratt alive? Unless her death wasn't an accident . . .

Thoughts were madly tumbling over each other, so Meg closed her eyes, drew in a breath to settle herself, and took charge, as likely the one with the most law enforcement experience on the boat. "We need to call for assistance. The problem is our location. None of you are from around here, are you?"

All around, negative responses. It was what she expected, assuming SDA had brought in qualified instructors and teams from across the country. But it definitely made things harder now.

"Is that a problem?" Claire asked.

"Not so much a problem as a lack of information. We're in the Superior National Forest, so federal property makes it federal jurisdiction, but we're so remote, I suspect we'll need county backup."

"You think this is a crime?"

"I don't know. It may have been an accident. Though, if so, I'd love to know how she got all the way out here. Whether it was a crime or an accident, an investigation is required." Meg unzipped her fanny pack again and dug through the contents until her fingers closed over the squat black handset with a thick antenna. She pulled out the phone, then extended the antenna to its full six inches.

And dialed a number saved in memory.

"Beaumont."

The sound of Craig's voice settled some of the jagged edges in Meg's gut. "It's Meg."

"Meg! How's the competition going?" His voice took on a sly note. "Kicking some CSP ass?"

"Yes, but I don't think that's going to matter anymore. I need help."

"Anything." All jocularity dropped from Craig's voice. "What happened?"

She knew he'd make the immediate leap to whatever was needed to help his people. Craig was the definition of a team player, and his teams were everything to him. "Hawk and I are out on water training. He found the hide, but when we were on the way back, he alerted on another scent. So for fun—" She had to stop to let out a ragged laugh. "For fun, and because he'd been doing so well, we let him lead us to what we assumed was the dead animal he smelled. Except it wasn't a dead animal. It's a dead woman. Eighty feet underwater in Lake Insula."

Craig let out a low curse.

"Worse than that, it's one of the other competitors. Rita Pratt from the Laramie County Sheriff's Office."

Craig's second curse was considerably more colorful. "Any chance it was an accidental drowning?"

"I can't say. Hawk identified the location of the body and our diver went down to investigate. He found her below and took photos for primary identification."

"Good work on Hawk's part. When did you find her?"

"Sal just came up from below. I don't know who to call. It's federal land, but incredibly remote. If the Minneapolis field office dispatches an agent, they'll be at least four or five hours getting here and we might be losing the light by that time. We can't leave her down there as fish food in the meantime."

"I agree. Let me see if I can get you local support. In

such a remote spot, it still could be a while before they get to you."

"Then I'll need directions from them or the field office on how to hold the scene. I'll text you my coordinates so you have the exact location."

"Thanks." Craig's heavy exhalation carried down the line. "Never a dull moment, eh?"

"I'd like a dull moment."

"I'm sure you would. Just hang in there. I'm on board and will get you the assistance you need. I can do it all from here, so I won't waste time going into the Hoover Building."

"Thanks, Craig. Really."

"No thanks required. Now, hang tight. I'll call you back in ten or fifteen . . . as soon as I can update you as to who is coming and how to hold the scene. Talk soon." Then he was gone.

Meg texted Craig their coordinates and then dropped the phone into her lap. There were so many things she wanted to say to him—about Pratt, about their interactions—but there hadn't been enough privacy for that.

"That was your SAC?" Claire asked.

"Yes. He's an amazing coordinator and he'll make sure we get what we need." She stared into the blue waters of the lake, not actually seeing it. "Including local support. What are the chances of them having a dive team on staff?"

Sal waved away the suggestion. "Small, at best. As long as they tell us how they want it handled, I can bring in a couple of other experienced guys and we'll team up. We can fully document the scene before we bring her up, since no one from law enforcement may be able to get to her down there. Do you want to make contact with them now so they can be ready to go when we need them?"

"Let's give it ten and see what Craig says, but then, yes, we should contact them. They'll be coming back to camp around now, so they should be able to head straight out." Meg's gaze dropped down to her dog, who sat beside her, his eyes fixed on her. "Oh, Hawk, I haven't even told you how well you did." She bent over him, giving him a brisk rub and a kiss on the top of his head. "Good boy, buddy. You found her. We're going to bring her home now." She looked up at Claire. "Decomposition would have started at death, but it wouldn't have progressed far at this point. Do you think Hawk picked up on the combination of some low-level decomp scent mixed with a normal human scent and that was enough to alert him?"

"That would be my guess. He may also have smelled blood if she's injured in any way. Or he could have picked up on fear pheromones in her sweat if she was in danger before her death. These are both scents he knows well from live body recovery on land. Whatever the combination, it was enough to grab his attention, but only because we were lucky enough to be in the right place at the right time with the right wind conditions."

With a jolt, Meg suddenly realized what she'd missed. "Wait. Where's her dog?" She whirled back to Sal, who now sat with both flippered feet inside the boat. "Did you see a dog down there as well?"

"No, but I didn't keep looking, once I found her. Eighty feet down, it's murky. Only minimal light from above, especially on an overcast day like this. And I only had my flashlight, not the kind of lighting we'll use for the recovery if they want us to do that."

"Until we know what happened to Pratt, we may not know what happened to Ava. But she certainly wasn't wandering alone around the other competitors or the boat crews, or we'd have known Pratt was missing. Then again, there were four boats beached this morning when we left, so the other teams were still gathering. Back at the campsite, they'll know by now that Pratt didn't show and will have already raised the alarm. But they know all the boats are accounted for, so it's clear she didn't head out on the water on her own."

"Which would be why they haven't wasted time contacting the boats out for training, and why we didn't know she was missing. You know, her dog may be lost in the woods somewhere," Claire suggested.

"It's a possibility." Meg looked down at her phone, as if willing it to ring. *Come on, Craig.*

Craig didn't call for another five minutes. The boat fell into silence, each person so consumed with their own thoughts that they all jumped when her phone rang. The display showed Craig's number.

"How did you do?" She jumped into the call without preamble.

"I have help coming to you, but it's not going to be fast."

"An agent from the field office?"

"Yes, but that's not all. I brought Peters up to speed on what's going on." The head of Criminal, Cyber, Response, and Services Branch of the FBI, Executive Assistant Director Adam Peters ran the Forensic Canine Unit, the larger unit to which the Human Scent Evidence Team belonged. "Two of his people are involved—"

"Involved?"

"Not directly, but he felt that since two of his people are on-site and in competition with the victim, and as we currently have an unknown cause of death, he didn't want it to look like the FBI was going to walk in and run the case, sweeping our own involvement under the carpet."

"That's ridiculous. It *is* FBI jurisdiction."

"Agreed, but Peters wants transparency. He had me reach out to the Lake County Sheriff's Office, as well as the Minneapolis field office. An agent is incoming, but he'll be at least four hours. I gave the sheriff your coordinates and, as you said, you're in the middle of nowhere."

Meg's gaze skimmed the lake and the surrounding forest. "You can say that again," she muttered.

"But they have a problem."

"No dive team."

"Correct. They're a small unit responsible for a huge area of land, but only ten thousand people. They're out of Two Harbors, which is ninety minutes south of you. So he's coming, but it's going to take the sheriff some time to get to you. However, one of his deputies is in Ely. Twenty-five miles as the crow flies, but it will likely be an hour to get there. I told Sheriff Olsen you were there with professional divers. He wants your dive teams to work with his deputy, a . . ." There was a pause and Meg could imagine Craig searching through his notes for a name. "Deputy Sheriff Kline, to recover the body."

"We can meet Kline at the campground."

"Not you. He wants you and your team to stay there to ensure no one tampers with the scene."

"Tampers with a body eighty feet underwater? Does he know how unlikely that is?"

"Extremely. But it's their case now, even if in conjunction with the FBI, and I get the feeling Olsen is a stickler for rules. You're to stay and maintain the scene, so to speak."

"Brian has his sat phone on him. I can call him and he can meet the deputy and organize the dive team." Sal attracted her attention by waving four fingers. "My dive support is suggesting four guys to do it. They have cameras with them, so they can document everything below, since the sheriff won't be seeing the body in place."

"That's good. Call Brian and set it up. Kline is on his way and has your sat phone number. I want you to keep me in the loop on this."

"Will do. Thanks, Craig. I wasn't sure how to organize the recovery without assistance."

"I got you. Call me in a few and let me know what's going on."

"Will do. Thanks." Meg disconnected the call.

"Who are they sending?" Charlie asked.

"Local sheriff and his deputy out of Lake County. An FBI agent is on the way, but is delayed getting here simply because of how remote we are. I'm going to call Brian, my colleague at the Human Scent Evidence Team, who is also here this weekend. He'll organize everyone on land." She met Sal's gaze. "What do we need? Besides the real boat?"

"The deputy may have some instructions, but from the dive standpoint, we're going to need a real camera with video capabilities and proper lighting. You're not going to have law enforcement down there to document the scene, so you'll need us to do it."

"You've done this before."

Sal nodded, his eyes going flat and his jaw tightening in a way that sketched his role in the recovery of the dead as well as any words could. There was a reason he was dive support on a weekend of scent training—he'd done it in real life.

"Tell me what we need. And we'll try to make sure you have it. And give me the names of the divers you want."

Meg made notes in her phone as Sal outlined in detail what they'd need and what they had on hand.

She had just finished when her sat phone rang in her hand. Looking down, she saw Brian's number. "Hey."

"Where are you?" The worry in Brian's voice carried clearly. "You were supposed to be back here more than a half hour ago. And Pratt never showed up to do her training this morning and no one can find her."

We can . . .

"Sorry. I was literally just about to call you."

"You're okay?"

"Yes, Hawk and I are fine. So is the rest of my team. But I need you to meet with Deputy Sheriff Kline from the Lake County Sheriff's Office. And I need you to put together a dive team. And bring them out to where we are. I'll provide the GPS coordinates."

"Meg . . ." Brian drew the word out on a note of warning. "What's going on?"

Meg let out a long sigh. "On our way back from finding the hide, Hawk picked up on something and we let him lead us to it. What he scented was Rita Pratt at the bottom of the lake."

"*Dead?*"

"Yes."

"Oh my God."

"Tell me about it. I called Craig from here and he has both FBI and county sheriff's officers incoming."

"This is federal land, so that explains the agent, but why the sheriff?"

"Peters wants to be transparent because the body was found by one of his people."

"Damn. Craig brought Peters into it?"

"He felt he had to because of the nature of the competition, et cetera. Peters wants interagency cooperation, but otherwise seems to be hands off. Craig has been doing all the heavy lifting. Now, Sal, my diver, has sketched out what he needs, including three more divers. I'll text you the full list of equipment and personnel. Then I need you to bring them out here. Can you leave Lacey with Ryan?"

"Of course. Are you okay?"

"Yeah."

"Do they have any idea how long she's been there? I mean . . . were you the last person to see her alive?" The last came out as a partial whisper.

"Maybe. The thought has occurred to me."

"Does anyone else besides our group know about . . . you know?"

"I don't think so. Now, I need you to meet Deputy Sheriff Kline at the roadway entrance to the campgrounds. You need to bring the biggest boat we have; the one we're in isn't big enough for all of us and a body."

"It sounds like we'd better come out in a couple of boats."

"Probably a good idea. Once you're on the water, it'll take you about twenty to thirty minutes to reach us." She scanned the darkening clouds overhead. "Hopefully, it won't be pouring rain by then."

"It would be our luck. Okay, I'll see you as soon as I can. I'll text you and let you know when the deputy is here, and again when we're leaving."

"Thanks. And one more thing?"

"Name it."

"Can you quietly let Todd know what's going on? He's going to worry and he doesn't have a sat phone, so I can't contact him directly."

"I'll find him as soon as I go back to the camp to drop Lacey off with Ryan. They'll be long back from fishing. I'm going to go put this in motion now. I'll tell the SDA organizers as well. They're going to hear sooner or later anyway, and clearly we need to put a halt to the weekend's activities."

"Thanks. I didn't think of that, but, of course, you're right. See you when you can get out here."

"You will."

She ended the call, then texted Brian the lists they'd already compiled. After, she kept her phone in hand, knowing there would be additional communication. But the text that arrived fifteen minutes later still surprised her.

Brian told me. Are you okay? - T

Word had made it through to Todd, and Brian had given him his sat phone to make contact.

Yes. It's chilly out here but we're holding the scene.

Are you okay?

The repeated question made it more than clear he wasn't asking about her comfort. The question being asked by him wasn't just if she was in a good place mentally, as well as physically; it was quietly loaded with so much more. He knew about her argument with Pratt the night before, and he may have also deduced she might have been the last person to see Pratt alive. If Pratt hadn't died by misadventure or by her own hand, there were going to be fingers pointed in her direction if word of the argument got out without an actual eyewitness account substantiating Pratt's abuse.

Fear teased at the edges of her thoughts, but Meg locked it out, refusing to let it through. She'd done nothing wrong.

Todd would know where her thoughts would take her. But she was talking to him on a government device, so caution was warranted.

She texted back a reply she knew he'd read more into than the message itself conveyed. **This is unexpected. I'm hanging in.**

His return message came almost immediately. **I'll be waiting for you at the beach. No matter how long it takes.**

Todd's concern and his constant readiness to stand with her brought comfort. Always the first responder, the need to help was hardwired into him, but for those he loved, he'd go to the ends of the earth. And no matter how often her job put her into dangerous positions, he was always there to support her, even when her lack of care about her own risk made him uncomfortable. After her last case, when she'd been attacked and nearly killed in their home, she'd sat down with him. They'd talked through how the risk of each of their jobs affected the other, and how to handle the stress while knowing each of them had to tackle the inherent dangers of their profession alone. They now better understood each other, each acknowledging that while they might not be able to mediate those risks, they understood the stress the other felt because of it.

She sent one last message: **I'll be watching for you.**

She slid down to sit on the floor of the boat, smiling when Hawk lay down beside her, his length against her leg, his warmth slowly seeping through her yoga pants to comfort her. She pulled her windbreaker in a little more tightly to try to keep out the wind, which now carried a chill edge.

But the shiver that ran down her spine had nothing whatsoever to do with the weather.

CHAPTER 10

Poisoned Pawn: A tempting target whose capture would ultimately be self-destructive.

Saturday, October 19, 12:16 PM
Boundary Waters Canoe Area
Superior National Forest, Minnesota

"Here they come!"

Charlie's cry had Meg sitting up straight from where she slumped, her eyes on the far shoreline.

She turned around to find three boats speeding directly for them—from the spray rising around them, they were moving at a good clip. She checked the time; Brian had worked fast and the deputy must have sped all the way there for them to be arriving already.

Two of the boats were similar inflatable dinghies to the one in which she currently sat, but the third was a rigid inflatable boat—or RIB—the bow rising feet above the water, a vessel large enough that the pilot stood behind the center controls.

Enough room in front to transport a body.

There were three men in each boat, but they were too far away for her to identify the pilots and divers. However, as the gap closed, she picked out Brian in one of the smaller dinghies, seated on a bench seat in the middle of the craft, braced with both arms as the boat bounced over the waves. He waved one hand and she waved back.

Just seeing him eased some of her tension. Brian, who knew everything about Pratt, and who would be supportive no matter what happened. Who could make her laugh, distracting her with his dumb jokes.

It was exactly what she needed.

The boats slowed and then circled Meg and her crew, cutting their engines so they drifted together. One of the men in the RIB stood up from where he sat behind the pilot. He was of medium height, with a thick build, dressed in dark brown pants, a beige uniform shirt, and a brown jacket to match his pants. His dark hair was ruffled from the ride, but his blue eyes were sharp, examining and cataloging each occupant of their boat. Meg had met more cops like him than she could count—the cops who built a first impression before you opened your mouth. The kind of cop who, nine times out of ten, underestimated her, the nice lady with the dog, not seeing the ex–patrol cop until she made their mistake clear to them.

As expected, his gaze skimmed over her, dropped to Hawk, who still lay beside her, and moved on to Sal, someone he clearly considered useful in this situation. Meg and Hawk had been useful, but they'd done their job and now were just window dressing.

He had no idea.

"Ahoy there." He hooked his thumbs in his heavy utility belt, just in front of the sidearm on his right side, and focused his attention on the two men in the boat. "I'm Deputy Sheriff Kline, and I'm here to coordinate this recovery." His gaze fixed on Sal. "You are . . . ?"

"Sal Gallo. I work with the SDA on their dive recoveries in the northwestern states."

"You've done this before? Recovered remains. Or bodies."

"Yes, sir."

"And you've identified the location of the body?"

"Hawk led us right to it." Sal smiled down at the Labrador. "Second day doing water searches and he's already a complete pro."

Kline's gaze flicked to Hawk with only minimal interest, but then slid back to Sal. "I need the body brought up, but I need the scene documented first. I can't go down there with you, but we need a full record of the site."

"We should be all set there." Sal turned to the tall, slender blond man in a wet suit in the RIB. "Hank, you've got my gear?"

"Sure do. Found it in your truck, just where you said."

"Great." He swiveled in the direction of the diver with black hair and dark mocha skin in Brian's dinghy. "Sanjay, you've got your camera equipment?"

Sanjay nodded. "All ready."

"Thanks. And, Marv, thanks for pitching in."

The last diver, sitting on the edge of the third dinghy, a redhead with pale skin covered with a spray of freckles, raised a hand in acknowledgment.

Sal looked back at Kline. "We're all set. Ever done an underwater recovery before, or do you want a rundown of our process?"

A flicker of displeasure shadowed Kline's face, then was gone. "First time for me."

Doesn't like not being the one leading the charge.

"When I went down the first time, because I didn't know what I was looking for, or its exact location, I set up a standard grid-pattern search. I located the body and marked the exact GPS position."

"Is it obstructed in any way?" asked Hank.

"No. The bottom of the lake is rocky in this section,

and she's settled on top of some larger boulders, but not caught in them."

Kline stared down in the depths of the water. "Any idea how long she's been down there? Or why she's still down there?"

"Not that long from the body condition. This lake is well stocked with fish, but they haven't started to nibble yet, or at least not so much it's noticeable. And it's because she hasn't been down there long that she's still down there. Bodies are denser than freshwater, so they always sink eventually. It would be a different story in salt water, but here, in a lake like this, someone with her build would sink pretty fast."

"No need to weigh the body down?"

"No, sir. It's only after the dead body starts to really decompose and gases are produced that it becomes buoyant. She hasn't been dead that long."

"She was seen yesterday," Claire interjected. "Right, Meg?"

Meg tried not to jump when called out. Or jump to conclusions. *She doesn't know about last night.*

But before she could answer, Brian jumped in. "She took part in our trial yesterday afternoon. When we left the meeting place, around four thirty yesterday, she was still there with her dog."

"And you didn't see her after that?"

"No."

Meg noted the brevity of his answer. He told the truth—he hadn't seen Pratt, but the way the question was worded, Kline could have been asking both of them. "Sal, what's the recovery plan?"

"Because I drove into the site, I have all my standard emergency gear I keep stored, so I can light out as soon as a search is called. As part of that equipment, I have my full body recovery system."

"System?" Kline asked.

"Basically, it's a body bag made of fine nylon mesh so it drains as it's hauled out of the water, but contains everything else associated with the body. It's a long bag with a U-shaped zipper; inside are double straps to secure the body. There are external straps that go around the bag to secure over the top with matching loops. It has big carrying handles all around it and has a fifty-pound lift bag to give us a boost while bringing it to the surface." Kline's furrowed brow stated that more explanation was needed, so Sal continued before the question could be asked, "A lift bag is exactly what it sounds like. Hank?"

"Hang on." Hank bent down, rummaged for a minute, and then straightened, holding a bright yellow, flat, tear-shaped nylon bag with an open end.

"It works on the same concept as a hot-air balloon, which is why it has the same shape." Sal pointed at the flat, narrowed end. "The bottom is open. We take it down like that, but when we get the body loaded in, we'll fill the bag with air from our tanks, using the spare regulator, and then we'll carabiner it to the body bag strap loops. Just as the name implies, it will lift fifty pounds of weight, making it easier for us to work together to raise the body to the surface. There's four of us, so three of us will stay on the bag's handles, and one of us will occasionally have to release some air from the lift bag through the dump valve as we ascend. Air expands as you rise through the water, so you have to compensate or else you risk an uncontrolled ascent. But before we do all of that, we'll document the scene."

"Photos and video," stated Kline.

Sal's lips compressed briefly, as if he was biting back words. "As I said, I've done this before." He turned away from Kline. "You guys ready?"

The divers answered in the affirmative and for the next

few minutes they busily prepared for descent, putting on their wet-suit hoods, checking their scuba gear, and working out transportation of the equipment. Then they rolled into the water, were passed their equipment, and disappeared beneath the surface. Meg followed the bright yellow of the body bag for a few moments, until it was carried too far below in the dark water to be visible from the surface.

Brian leaned over to talk to his pilot, who fired up the motor to push them a little closer to Meg's boat.

As they came alongside, the engine died, and Brian grabbed the rope running across the gunwale of Meg's boat. Charlie, sitting in the stern, reached for Brian's boat. Brian gave him a two-fingered salute of thanks.

Meg shifted to Brian's side of the boat as Claire moved down to the far end to sit with Charlie, giving the handlers some privacy.

Brian peered over the edge to where Hawk lay beside Meg. "Good boy, Hawk! You're kicking ass and taking names this weekend."

Hawk raised his head at the sound of Brian's voice, the thump of his tail expressing his pleasure at seeing a trusted friend.

Brian flicked a glance toward Kline, who was talking to the pilot of his boat, then leaned in closer, and dropped his voice. "How are you?"

"Chilly." Brian's flat stare and raised eyebrows had Meg frowning at the second failure of that response with another man who knew her too well. "Okay, fine. Unsettled. I'm not sure what happened here."

"One of a couple of things happened here." Brian started counting with the fingers of his free hand. "One, she was seriously unhappy and took her own life."

"That's not the impression I got yesterday."

"Me either, though to be fair, sometimes those in crisis

mask their intentions even from those who know them well, which we did not."

"True, but why come all the way out here to do something like that?"

"Got me there." He raised another finger. "Two, she slipped and fell in and managed to drown. A total accident."

"And then got all the way out here? Or was here to begin with? How?"

"All questions worth asking." Another finger. "Or three—"

"She pissed someone off enough that they killed her. And they brought her out here to dump her body and hide the murder." Meg met Brian's green eyes. "That's the one I keep coming back to."

"We certainly saw the kind of bad behavior yesterday that could lead people to hate her."

"After my run-in with her last night, I certainly didn't have any love for her."

"Yeah. About that . . ." Brian trailed off, but the worry shadowing his eyes finished the thought for him.

"Only our group knows about it, as far as I know. But she and I weren't exactly quiet, and we weren't that far from their campsites or the bathrooms. Yes, it was late, but you'd just gone to bed, and I was still up. Others could have been, too. I'm going to have to cop to the sheriff or the incoming FBI agent about it."

"You're worried that if someone saw the two of you and they tell before you do, it's going to look bad."

"Absolutely. If I were the sheriff and thought one of the competitors was purposely hiding something, I'd want a close look to figure out why. They may think that argument was part of a greater disagreement and I killed her over it."

"I'm calling BS on that. You've never killed before, not even in the line of duty."

"What about Brett Stephenson?"

"You weren't responsible for his death. I was there and saw the whole thing. He slipped and fell while you were trying to save him. You weren't responsible then, and aren't now. If they give you a hard time about it, I can always say Lacey and I were out doing our business, witnessed the whole thing, and saw you leave her in one piece, alive and well, to go back to your tent."

Meg laid her hand over his, where it clenched the rope. His fingers felt as cold as hers in the brisk fall wind. "You're not doing that."

"Babe, you know I'd do whatever you need."

She gave his hand a squeeze. "I know. And I love you for it. But not this. You will not put yourself in legal jeopardy for me."

"But—"

"No." Her tone of voice firmly slammed the door on the possibility. "Not happening."

"Fine." Displeasure coated his tone. "But you know it's going to look bad if she met an unforeseen end."

Her stomach clutched with nerves, but Meg made sure it didn't show on her face. "I know. But I've done nothing wrong. Have faith."

"We'll see," Brian said darkly.

They sat in silence as the minutes stretched long; Meg occasionally stroking her dog, Brian fidgeting or worrying the rope between his fingers.

Brian finally broke the silence. "Todd wants updates, but I brought my sat phone with me, so he's out of luck."

Meg looked up to find Brian's gaze fixed on one of the islands in the middle of the lake. "He said he was waiting at the beach."

"He's going to be waiting for a while at this rate."

"He's going to know this isn't a fast process, even if he doesn't really know how time-consuming it will be. How long have they been gone?"

Brian checked his watch. "Thirty-five minutes."

"It could easily take that long to get down there, find the body, do full photography and shoot video, then pack the body into the bag, get it ready for transport, attach the lift bag and come up. And then they have to do a safety stop on the way back up. It all takes time."

"They probably are also doing a check of the immediate area, once the body is packed, to make sure they haven't missed anything. And that's going to take even longer." Brian blew out a gusty breath of impatience. "You going to text Craig and give him an update?"

"I will, but not yet. I'd like to know what we're looking at before I loop him in."

Silence fell again across all three boats, as if the occupants were in suspended animation, just waiting for the return from below for the world to keep spinning. In the RIB, on a bench behind the helm, where McDermott, the pilot, still stood, Kline sat still as a statue. Meg hadn't seen him twitch even once while they waited; he sat motionless, his eyes locked on the water where the divers had gone down. Waiting.

It was a full fifteen minutes later before Charlie called, "They're coming up. But they're bringing the body, so this is going to take a little time."

Seven minutes later, the bright yellow lift bag broke the surface, followed by four heads.

"Well?" Kline called.

Sal pulled out his mouthpiece. "We've got her."

"Full photos and videos?"

"That too. Bringing her aboard your boat?"

"Yes."

They towed the bag, struggling with the awkward weight that tended to sink now there was no buoyancy assistance. But they slowly circled around to the RIB.

"Hang on," the pilot of Brian's boat called. "We'll come around to your other side and can help pull her up from the water."

"Gotta go," Brian murmured, releasing his hold on Meg's boat as the engine fired up and they slowly pulled away.

The pilot was careful to give the divers a wide berth, but still ease himself in as close as possible. Craning his neck to look over the rounded side of the boat, he shot a fast glance at Brian. "Can you grab a handle and help lift? I need to stay on the tiller to get us out of the way, in case we start to crowd the divers."

"Sure."

Brian moved to the near side of the boat and looked over the edge. Meg could see the calculation in his eyes as he took in the orientation of the divers and his own position in the boat, before bracing his knee on the rigid middle seat, clamping his left hand over the edge of it, and then reaching down into the water with his right hand. Opposite him, McDermott and Kline reached down on the far side for the bag.

"Got it," Brian called. "You solid?"

"Yeah." Kline's voice floated up from where he was curled over the side of the boat. "Ready on three. One. Two. *Three.*"

With matching groans, the three men dragged the waterlogged bag out of the lake.

"Hold it there!" Sal's voice came from out of sight, down below. "Let it drain or you'll flood the deck."

Water sluiced out of the bag as it ran through the mesh. Brian glanced at Meg, grimacing from his awkward, frozen position.

"That's good." Sal's voice was now closer to Meg as he moved away, in case the bag was dropped. "Now Kline, McDermott, keep hold of the handle you have and also grab the one at your own end. Foster, you're going to have to extend out as far as you can until they can lift her over the side of the boat, then you can release. At that point, Kline and McDermott, you'll be able to lower her down just with the handles at both ends."

"Ready?" Kline asked. "Do it now."

The two men hoisted the bag over the side of the boat as Brian extended as far as both arms would go before being forced to let go. "Got it?"

"We got it." McDermott staggered sideways slightly on the wet deck and then caught himself. He and Kline lowered the bag to the deck and then straightened, breathing heavily. "That was heavier than I anticipated."

Sal had swum around to the rear of the RIB and now climbed up the curved metal ladder hooked over the side. "They always are."

Meg moved to where she could get a better view; Claire and Charlie joined her, each looking over the side of the larger vessel. The body bag was laid out in the open space in front of the helm, in plain view from their angle.

"Are you going to examine her here?" Meg asked. It wasn't as simple as morbid curiosity. Meg needed to know exactly what had happened to Pratt; maybe then the tightness constricting her chest would ease.

Then she'd know where she stood and could decide how to handle the situation.

"Yes." Kline stood, hands on hips, staring down at the bag. "Chain of custody has transferred to me; I need to confirm what I'm getting. How do I get into this thing?"

"Like this." Sal removed his flippers and squeezed in around the bag. He unzipped the bag down one side and halfway up the length, until he hit the end of his reach. "You do the same on your side."

Kline took over from there, running the zipper the rest of the length and then down the short side. He and Sal grabbed the top flap together and peeled it back.

Rita Pratt lay inside, secured into the bag with a strap across her upper chest and another across her hips. Her hair was a loose, ropey tangle around an unnaturally white face, and her open, staring eyes were covered with the blue-white haze of death. Her head was held at an odd angle, as if it had been jammed into place as rigor mortis set in, freezing the body in place.

Been dead for at least twelve hours.

"No obvious sign of injury," McDermott said. "So she drowned?"

"No obvious sign at first glance." Crouching down, Sal worked the straps he'd secured eighty feet below on the bottom of the lake. The buckles released and blue nylon fell away. "But this is what you need to see." With his gloved hand, Sal gripped Pratt's shoulder and rolled her toward him.

Claire gasped out loud, but the shock wave that struck Meg trapped the air in her lungs, leaving her silent.

The back of Pratt's head was a mass of tangled hair, blood-clotted bone fragments, and exposed brain tissue.

Perhaps she'd had a catastrophic fall.

Either that, or someone had hit her with enough force to shatter her skull.

CHAPTER 11

Kill Chain: A military concept of target identification, dispatching a force to the target, and the decision and order to attack the target, resulting in its destruction.

Saturday, October 19, 2:07 PM
Boundary Waters Canoe Area
Superior National Forest, Minnesota

The sight of land after so many hours out on the wind-tossed water was a relief to Meg. She wanted off this boat, and she wanted to warm up.

What she really wanted to do was roll back the clock to last night before things had gone so badly wrong. Back when Pratt was still alive. She hadn't liked the woman—she wasn't alone in that feeling—but she certainly hadn't wished her dead.

But was it at the hands of misadventure or by someone's actual hands? That was the real question.

Any doubts she had about being forthcoming with authorities concerning her argument with Pratt last night were wiped clean away at the sight of the catastrophic damage to Pratt's skull. She knew law enforcement and the way investigators ticked when it came to undeniably violent death. She needed to come clean about the incident, because withholding information would only make her look guilty when they found out. The FBI agent was hours away; she just needed a few minutes with the sheriff as soon as they got to shore.

Kline's boat led their small flotilla, the three dinghies following slightly behind.

As they closed in on land, it became evident a crowd had gathered. Word must have spread as Brian had put together the recovery team and as the deputy had arrived, and everyone in camp had come down to wait for their return.

To see the dead. Possibly to glory in it?

It was widely believed that some killers returned to the scene of the crime to revel in their lawlessness, as well as the chaos and hardship it caused. Or because they considered themselves smarter than law enforcement and wanted to watch them stumble around trying to solve the crime. Or even as a demonstration of their power, that they could stand there and watch both the investigation and the police, who were powerless to stop them. But returning to the crime scene wasn't possible here, so bringing the body back on shore might be the next closest thing.

Of course, considering their remote location, with everyone on-site and all activities abruptly stopped, their return would naturally attract attention. In which case, it would look suspicious if any one person *didn't* come down to the beach.

Meg scanned the lake's edge. While the largest crowd gathered at the water's edge, four men stood slightly up the hill, separate from the jammed mass on the beach. Even from this distance, Meg could pick Todd out from where he stood with his brothers, Ryan, and Lacey.

He'd said he'd be waiting. She'd never doubted for a

second he wouldn't. But, nonetheless, just the sight of him gave her the first easy breath in hours.

Her gaze dropped to the three uniformed men standing at the waterline—solid marble pillars of beige and brown, surrounded by an undulating sea of color. Meg pegged the tall man in the center as Sheriff Olsen. There was no overt marking, no sheriff's badge on his jacket she could see from this distance, but his manner, the way he held himself, the coolness of his gaze as it fixed on the officer in the lead boat, stated unequivocally this was a man used to being in charge.

Likely, this was also an officer who didn't see much in the way of violent crime. In a county with a small, mostly rural population, it was likely the sheriff's office saw more drug overdose deaths than violent killings. If this crime was intentional, this would be the kind of case that would occupy the sheriff's entire attention, as well as that of his deputies.

And that was before the FBI showed up. Not to mention the cops here as competitors. If Meg was already thinking about the case from an investigative angle, surely at least some of them would be too.

Especially if, like herself, they'd had a dustup with Pratt this weekend or had a history with her.

Meg needed to be transparent about last night, and to spin it as information the investigators might want because it spoke to Pratt's character. Hopefully, she wasn't the only person who'd seen Pratt be rough with her dog.

Which brought Meg around again to Ava. Where was the Malinois? It had totally slipped her mind to ask Brian, but hopefully those on shore would know the dog's whereabouts.

Kline's boat came into shore first, the others slowing to give it space to come into the shallows. McDermott tipped the outboard motor out of the water as they glided up on the beach. A crowd of pilots, search-and-rescue handlers, and trainers waded into the water to secure the boat, while the law enforcement officers stayed planted on the shore, watching with matching grim expressions. Kline hopped out of the boat and began issuing orders. A couple of men jogged up the beach and disappeared behind the crowd; in under two minutes, they returned, shook out a large tarp, and spread it over the sand. Then Hank and McDermott carefully lifted the zipped body bag and passed it down to Kline and several pairs of willing hands, who moved in to carry it onto the beach, carefully laying it on the tarp.

McDermott and several other men dragged the boat up onto the beach at the far end from the crowd, where there was a clear stretch of sand, then waved the other three boats into shore.

After the dinghies were also beached, Brian joined Meg, who stood with Hawk on his leash at the water's edge as they stared into the mass of people gathered around the body bag.

"I didn't think it would tell us anything, but I wanted to check who showed up to see the body." No one was near them, but Meg kept her voice low anyway. "At first glance of the people we know, I don't see anyone missing. The competitors are hanging back with their dogs, but they're all here."

"There are some faces I don't know, probably pilots and divers."

"Or SDA trial officials we didn't meet yesterday."

"That too. But everyone I can think of who we've met, I can see here."

Meg jammed her ice-cold hands in her pockets, her shoulders riding up near her ears, as she studied the on-lookers. Their faces showed a range of emotions—fear, horror, morbid curiosity, fascination. Some were crowding in, hoping for a glance at the victim, while some stood back, but couldn't look away, as if rubbernecking at a traffic wreck.

Brian nudged her arm. "Come on, we've seen more than we wanted already."

"Give me a minute. I want to talk to Sheriff Olsen."

Brian's gaze sharpened. "About what?"

"You know what. About last night. Think about that injury. We can't be under any illusions now that Pratt wasn't murdered. It was one thing to not answer Kline out on the water when it could have still been an accidental drowning, however unlikely. But now it's violent death and they're going to be looking for a killer. My hiding that argument at this point is a big mistake. When they find out, I'll look guilty as sin."

"*If* they find out."

"*When* they find out. Stuff like this always comes out eventually. And then it would be even more damning. Better to be straight up with them now."

Meg approached the crowd, trying to get close enough to the sheriff to catch his attention. "Sheriff Olsen!"

Olsen, conferring with Kline, didn't even look in her direction.

The noise of the gathered crowd rose as speculation abounded. Meg caught indistinct snatches of theories: Suicide. Drowning. Murder.

"*Sheriff Olsen!*" she tried again.

This time, Olsen glanced toward her, then leaned into Kline as he said something.

Probably telling Olsen I was part of the team that found Pratt.

"Sheriff Olsen, I'd like a moment of your time."

"Busy. Thanks for what you did out there." He turned his back to her.

"If you really want to do this, you'll have to do it later." Brian's voice came from behind her left shoulder. "He's not going to want to talk to any witnesses until he's got the beach cleared. He'll find us when he's ready."

"I guess you're right." Meg rubbed her hands up and down her chilly arms. "I could go for a cup of Josh's coffee." She looked up the hill to where their men still stood waiting for them. "Let's go meet Todd and Ryan, who are at least smart enough to stay clear of the crowd. Hawk, come."

They circled the group, already breaking apart slightly as Olsen bellowed at them to move away, and turned their backs on the chaos as they started up the dirt road.

As soon as they cleared the commotion near the shore, Todd, his brothers, and Ryan moved to meet them halfway.

As he neared, Todd held out both hands to Meg, and she automatically pulled her hands from her pockets and reached for him, nearly sighing when his warm fingers closed over hers.

"You're freezing." Todd pressed her palms together, then rubbed her hands, chafing warmth into her chilled skin.

"We were out there in the middle of the lake for hours. Temps are dropping and the wind gusted the whole time. I didn't realize how cold I was."

"That windbreaker could only do so much, and your hands were exposed. No danger of frostbite, but it would have made for an uncomfortable few hours." He met her gaze and held it, his steady and calm. "Now, before you say 'fine,' how are you really?"

That brought a twitch to the corner of her lips. The man knew her too well. She darted a quick glance around the circle. She could trust Brian with absolutely anything, Ryan was steadfast and trustworthy, and, while she didn't know Josh and Luke nearly as well, everything she'd learned about them said they were as solid as their brother. And already considered her family.

She could talk freely here.

"That . . . was not good. And it was a shock. Not only to find a body, but for it to be someone I knew. Someone I'd clashed with."

Josh stepped closer, Luke following his lead, and glanced down the hill at the people milling on the beach. They were too far away to be heard, but, clearly, he was taking no chances. "Can you tell what happened? Does it look like she drowned?" He paused, his gaze fixed on the sliver of yellow from the bag visible through the onlookers' legs where it lay on the beach. "Or *was* drowned?"

"We're going to need an autopsy, for sure, but from what we saw"—Meg's gaze flicked to Brian, where he stood between Lacey and Ryan—"it's unlikely she drowned."

"Meaning?" Ryan asked.

"Catastrophic head wound," Brian said. "The back of her head was bashed—and I mean *bashed*—in."

"You saw the injury?" There was knowledge in Todd's eyes. In his position at DCFEMS, he'd seen the worst of what could happen to a human body in so many ways.

"Yes." Meg released his hands to raise one of hers to the back of her head, down toward the base of her skull. Turning her back to them, she spread her fingers wide.

"The wound was that big?"

"Yes." She dropped her hand and spun around. "And not just big. Deep. She hit, or was hit, *hard*. You could see down to bone." A shiver ran down her spine, and Meg was sure it wasn't from the temperature, but from the memory of that heinous wound. "Hell, past bone, right down to gray matter."

Luke whistled. "That kind of blow would have to be fatal, right?"

"Absolutely." There wasn't an ounce of doubt in Todd's tone. "When they do the autopsy, it's unlikely they're going to find water in her lungs. This is in no way definitive, but was the wound bloody? Let me be more specific—coming out from the water, was there clotted blood in the wound?"

Meg and Brian exchanged glances before Brian answered. "Yes. Her hair was matted with it."

"And it was in the wound," Meg added. "What do you mean by 'definitive'?"

"Blood will clot underwater. It's a biochemical reaction, and water doesn't interfere with it, but if the body is in an area of high water flow, clotting factors can be washed away, inhibiting clot formation."

"The bottom of a lake isn't exactly high water flow," said Josh.

"Agreed, but a forty-foot drop to the bottom would be if she was killed and immediately dropped overboard while there was still blood pressure in the body."

"Eighty feet," Meg clarified.

"Even more so," Todd said. "The body will sink through that depth, the water flowing around it, washing away some of what isn't clotted. Assuming she was struck on land, there would be lots of time for the wound to clot while she was carried out to . . ." He trailed off. "Wait. That's quite a way out, isn't it?"

"Took about twenty-five minutes with the outboard-motor boats," Brian said.

Josh gave a cynical snort. "They don't actually think it was an accident and she slipped on shore, hit her head on a rocky piece of shoreline, fell into the lake, and drifted that far out, do they?"

"If they do, they're not thinking the situation through with any kind of level head," Luke stated.

"I'm with you there." Meg turned around to look down

the hill. Sheriff Olsen and his deputies were huddled together by the body bag, while the crowd still hung around, though with a gap of about ten feet around the bag. "Claire, our trainer, explained how a body behaves in salt water and freshwater. In freshwater, like a lake, a body would be expected to sink almost immediately. Especially, a lean, muscular body, like Pratt's. A person with a higher fat content might float longer, but I got the impression it would not be by much. Say Pratt met with some kind of misadventure on her own. Maybe her dog ran off in the dark and she went after her, slipped, hit her head, and fell into the lake. She would have been found *a lot* closer to shore, even if it was closer to the shore in that location. But it's unlikely she was on land in that area. It's twenty-five minutes away as the crow flies at outboard-motor speed. To hike to that shoreline? In the dark? That would take all night."

"And then some," Brian said. "And you'd never make it. In the dark, in unknown territory, with this amount of reported wildlife? It would be idiocy."

"There are other boats in this area," Todd said. "The small boat launch has a couple of canoes stored there temporarily. Since only people associated with the weekend's activities are on-site, I assume someone here this weekend brought them to do some canoeing during their downtime. She could have easily borrowed one during the night, as the boat launch is isolated from the rest of the campgrounds by forest. No, wait, that doesn't make sense. If she did that, one of the canoes would be missing, but they were both there when we took the boat out this morning."

Meg looked out across the lake, where small whitecaps rose in the wind over the dark blue-gray waters. "You may be onto something though. If someone else killed her, if they borrowed a canoe and took her out onto the lake, dumped her far from camp, and then brought the canoe back, they may have thought it was their best chance of not being detected."

"In a campground full of scent dogs?" Josh's tone was pure skepticism. "They'd be crazy to think that."

"Except they wouldn't," Brian said.

"No, they wouldn't," Meg agreed.

Josh looked from one to the other, clearly confused over something that seemed so obvious to him. "How?"

"These dogs are greased lightning on land. It's what they do. If Pratt was missing, and the alarm was raised this morning, with all of her stuff in her tent, you would have seven expert dog teams splitting up to search for her as soon as everyone returned from training. If the body had been on land, with scent samples available from her belongings, we would have found her, no question. But these dogs are just learning how to do water searches. They're not necessarily good at it yet. If a car or truck wasn't available to the killer to drive the body out of the area, then dropping the body in a deep part of the lake actually makes the most sense. Especially if it was anyone involved in the training, because after the first day, you got a feel for how deep they were placing the hides for dogs who were just learning. It would be unlikely a dog would be looking for scent in that area, and, even if they were on top of it, there would be no guarantee they'd detect the body. The dogs are being given a strong decomp scent to track in this training, to make sure they can find it. Assuming she was killed and dumped, the killer may have thought, reasonably, that no dog would pick up the body's scent because the strongest decomp gases were still a day or two in the future and we'd have left by then."

Todd nodded. "And it may have taken longer at that depth where the water is colder."

"Claire and I were talking about this out in the lake. There may have been just the beginning of decomp scents, but she thought Hawk might have also smelled the blood, had there been an injury—"

"There sure was," muttered Brian.

"—or fear pheromones in her sweat if that was what she experienced just before death."

"Which she would have, if someone murdered her. Let's assume that's the case," said Todd.

"Don't think anyone with a brain would think otherwise," Josh countered.

"How would the killer know where to take her?" Todd continued. "He or she had to move a body in the dark, get to a boat, and then get to a location on the lake where the water was deepest. How did they manage all that successfully without detection, and how did they know where to go?" Todd paused, his gaze dropping to Hawk, sitting quietly at Meg's knee. "And how did they do it without Pratt's dog raising holy hell? If someone laid a hand on you, Hawk would go crazy. And you know how sound carries in a quiet wilderness like this. Everyone would have heard and come running. Even if we hadn't heard, every dog in camp would have, and would have raised the alarm."

"That's another of my concerns." Meg turned to Brian. "Before you came out in the boat, had no one found Ava running around on her own?"

"No, but I don't know what happened while I was out there."

"If she hasn't been found already, she needs to be. She could be abandoned in the woods somewhere, or hurt, or has been attacked by local wildlife. The investigating agent will likely want to know all about Ava. As far as where to dump the body, we all received topological maps of the area before we arrived. And a nautical chart of Lake Insula, since it was the location of the training."

"Why would they do that?" Luke asked. "Wouldn't they want you in the dark about your competition search area?"

"It's meant to put everyone on a similar footing. Assuming some contestants would do the research, they made sure everyone had the info. And that included the topography of the lakes in this area. Everyone, from the SDA officials to the competitors, trainers, divers, and pilots, all had the same data."

"Not to mention," Brian interjected, "if we were on a real search, the first thing Craig would do is pull topo maps of the area. It increases the speed of the search, and it's a safety thing."

"So knowing where to go isn't in question. How they got there, though, is. I think the idea of borrowing someone's canoe is solid. It was clear last night, with a three-quarter moon to light the way on the water. And the wind didn't pick up until this morning, so a mostly smooth lake for canoeing. And paddling means silence. Even the electric outboard motors create noise, and then we're back to the quiet-wilderness problem. Any motor firing up in the middle of the night would have attracted attention."

"Depending on when the killing happened, it could have taken all night to paddle out and back," Ryan said. "Whoever did it should be exhausted."

"Or wired from the kill," Meg suggested. "Back in my days on the RPD, you'd see perps like that. High on the thrill of the kill. High on the feeling that they got away with something."

"Or they're mainlining caffeine," Todd said. "Either way, there may not be a physical tell." His gaze drifted past Meg's shoulder to the crowd on the beach. "They're not going to actually open and examine the body there, are they?"

Brian shook his head. "I wouldn't think so. Kline got a good look at it out on the boat. And they're not going to allow a public viewing, with everyone standing there. The only reason we saw it was because he knew he wouldn't have any privacy on shore and he wanted to know what they were dealing with."

"Multiple deputies," Meg pointed out. "My guess is they'll send the body off with one of them now. Maybe Kline to preserve the chain of custody. At least until the FBI gets here."

"You've already got the sheriff here. Why would you need the FBI?" Luke asked.

"It's a national forest, so it's federal land. That makes it federal law enforcement's jurisdiction."

"It won't be a conflict of interest for them to be involved?" When five pairs of eyes locked on him, Luke shrugged. "What? She's a federal employee and she found the body."

"Not just me."

"Okay, your dog found the body. Everyone else helped with the recovery?"

"Well . . . yes."

"But would your dog have found the body without you?"

"It's not like on land," Brian explained, "where the dog has full autonomy to lead us where they want to go. Unless they're going to swim, they need us to help them find the way."

"Brian . . ." Todd's tone carried a low warning.

"What? I'm answering his question."

Meg laid her hand on Todd's arm. "You don't have to protect me. Brian, Luke is trying to nicely point out that any investigator is going to question that we found the body. Because sometimes the person who finds the body is the one who put it there."

"What? That's utter garbage. Besides, if you'd dumped the body there, you would have avoided helping Hawk actually find it. See? Garbage theory."

"But a proven truth on many occasions." She turned back to Luke. "And that's why my SAC called not only the FBI but the county sheriff's office. To avoid even a hint of favoritism. The FBI has jurisdiction, but will work with the county to find the suspect. They'll get started right away and will catch the agent up when he or she arrives."

"They'll start right away so they can grill everyone on-site before they bugger off," Josh stated.

"Pretty much. I tried to speak to Sheriff Olsen, but he's tied up dealing with Pratt's body right now. If he doesn't come find me, I'll find him later. For now, what I really want is a cup of coffee and to warm up by a fire." Meg met Todd's eyes, finding understanding there. She not only needed the warmth and solace, but she needed fifteen minutes to try to disconnect from the whole situation and find her center again so she was ready to meet any questioning coming from law enforcement.

"I can put on coffee," Josh offered.

"And I got the fire," Luke countered.

Reaching around Meg, Todd slipped the leash from around her wrist. "Here, Hawk." He waited as Hawk came to stand at his knee before he took Meg's hand. "Let's head back. They'll find you when they want to talk. By then, you'll be warm, and will have had a chance to catch your breath. On top of that, when was the last time you ate?"

"Breakfast. But I'm not hungry."

"I'm sure we can find something that appeals to you, even if it's just a snack. Or one of those god-awful energy bars you two eat. But you need to keep your energy up. Hawk, come."

They headed up the hill and then took the road toward their campsite.

As they rounded the corner, Meg looked back down the hill where the four Lake County officers were clustered around the body bag.

And knew without a doubt, it was only a matter of time before they came gunning for her.

CHAPTER 12

Calling in the Pickets: Concentrating available forces into a single group.

Saturday, October 19, 2:31 PM
Boundary Waters Canoe Area
Superior National Forest, Minnesota

They entered their campsite, which looked exactly like how they'd left it that morning, but now felt almost foreign to Meg after the day she'd had.

Todd led her to her rocking camp chair, gently settled her into it, and gave her a push to get it rocking. "Stay down, we'll do the rest. Hawk, down." He waited until the dog lay down beside Meg's chair. "Good boy." He unhooked the Lab's leash and ruffled his ears. "Stay with Meg."

Behind him, Luke was already building the fire, and Josh was getting coffee on to perk.

Brian fell into the chair to her right and unleashed Lacey, who flopped down on the grass beside Hawk between their chairs.

Meg let her head roll sideways to look at Brian. "I didn't ask how this morning went."

Brian grinned down at Lacey. "Good. Great, actually.

Better than yesterday; she's getting the hang of it. And I didn't mess her up by taking us in the wrong direction."

Meg laughed. "That's how I felt too. Hawk was totally on point—possibly more on point than I ever suspected, given how the rest of the morning went—but I was terrified I'd steer him wrong. Literally. It's so much easier on land and they can just tell us where they want to go."

"Amen to that." He held both hands out to the growing flames in the fire pit. "You going to update Craig now?"

"Good thought." Meg pulled out her phone and speed-dialed Craig, putting the call on speaker and holding it between them so Brian could hear.

It barely rang twice before being picked up. "Meg, hi. What's the update?"

"Hi, Craig. I'm here with Brian and we have you on speaker. We got her up from the bottom of the lake in a body bag, and the Lake County Sheriff's Office has custody."

"Your ID was correct? It's Deputy Pratt?"

"No doubt about it. Brian and I got a look at the body after they brought it up. Craig, the back of her head was caved in. Either she fell and hit her head hard, or someone did the job for her. And unless Todd is wrong, she was dead awhile before she hit the water."

"And, from what you described, she was way too far out to have drifted there herself."

"In a lake? I mean, there are rivers feeding into it and flowing out from it, but it's not like an ocean current. I don't see any way she falls into the lake where the campsites are located and ends up where she did without help."

A loud sigh came through the phone's speaker.

Meg stared at Brian, seeing the same look on his face she expected was on her own. *Something is off.* "Craig, what's going on?"

"She lodged a complaint against you. It went right up to Peters."

"*WHAT?*"

All motion around the campfire ceased and every face swiveled in her direction. Todd, who had been at the table preparing food, dropped his knife and strode toward her.

"She sent a message to her commander after eleven o'clock last night reporting you for animal abuse."

"What the f—"

Meg threw up a shaking hand to cut Brian off. "Who did he contact?"

"Peters and myself both received the same e-mail around midday. I didn't see it because I was busy helping you, but because I'd looped Peters into the situation, he was at his desk at home and he saw it. Then *I* got a call from *him*."

"What's she accusing me of?" Meg wasn't sure if the tremor in her voice was from fear or fury, but when Todd's hands dropped to her shoulders from behind her chair, she knew others could hear it too.

"She said she ran into you last night, Hawk was misbehaving, and you were mistreating him. She said you were hanging him over your shoulder and she had to step in before your dog lost consciousness. Or his life."

Ripping away from Todd's loose hold, Meg came out of her chair. She jabbed the button to take the call off speaker and then stalked past Brian to pace the grass at the outskirts of the campsite. In her peripheral vision, she noted Brian now stood beside Todd, watching her, but the red haze clouding her vision blocked everything else out. "Jesus Christ, Craig. That's what I caught *her* doing. We had a blowup about it last night just before bedtime. I was going to report her to her superiors on Monday."

"It looks like she beat you to the punch."

"No one is going to believe me now when I say the same about her."

"Likely that was her strategy."

Regret burned hot. Regret she'd waited to make an official complaint, and that, in her fury, she'd threatened Pratt with the complaint in the first place, allowing Pratt to turn the tables on her.

The grass only afforded her about twelve rage-filled strides before Meg was forced to turn around to retrace her steps. "Craig, you know I'd never do that."

"I know."

The straight-up honesty, said in such a simple and calm tone, defused some of her fury and her steps slowed. "Thank you."

"No thanks required. Meg, in all the years we've worked together, I've never seen you treat Hawk with anything other than love and respect. You don't need to stoop to mistreating him, because he wouldn't act out like that. He'll do what you ask of him without hesitation because of that love and respect. This is utter bullshit."

Meg stopped pacing and simply stood, head bowed. "You have no idea what a relief it is to hear you say that. What about Peters?"

"He'll say the same. We're not about to throw you under the bus. We're standing with you. But you realize you have a big problem now."

"Yeah, I can see that."

"She's dead, and you may have been the last person to have seen her alive, besides her killer. Did anyone see you two arguing? Did anyone else see her mistreating the dog?"

Meg's gaze shot over to Brian. "Not that I know of. Brian told me he'd say he was with me, but I won't let him do that. He wasn't there."

"Yeah, he's not doing that."

"Thanks. It's the thought that counts, but . . . no. And,

yes, it's a problem because I'm going to get flagged with it. There will be questions about last night."

"Have you told anyone about last night?"

"I tried to tell Sheriff Olsen when we got to shore, but he was tied up dealing with Pratt's body and the crowd gathered on shore. I wanted to tell him before there was any chance of him finding out about it, but that ship has apparently already sailed. It was clear he was going to be a while, so we left them on the beach and came back to our campground. I just wanted to warm up." She turned to the group to find a frozen tableau—Todd and Brian still by her chair; Luke crouched by the fire pit, his fire poker in one hand, the tip buried in the grass beside his boot; Josh by the coffeepot, clutching a pot holder; and Ryan hanging back by the picnic table, as if unwilling to intrude. Her gaze settled on Todd. "I wanted family."

"I get it. You've seen death before, but this is different. You're smart. The moment she was found, you had to be worried. And only more so, once violent death was confirmed."

"That was when I knew, for sure, I needed to talk to the sheriff."

"Do you need me to come out there?"

Meg was genuinely touched by the offer. "No. I'm not ruining your weekend for this. Any more than I already have, I mean."

"You're not ruining my weekend. And if you need my support, if Brian needs my support, I can be there in five or six hours, depending on flights." There was a pause, and then he said, "I'm going to look into them."

"Craig, really, you don't have to. Though I appreciate the offer more than you know."

"I'm still thinking about it. I think it would only be to the good if I was there, especially once the investigating agent arrives. You know they're going to look into everyone involved, and when they look into you, they're going to find this accusation."

"If she was alive, I think she'd be pleased with this."

"She sounds like she was a real sweetheart. Let me see what I can work out. How rough is the camping out there?"

"Pretty rough." Meg let a little disapproval color her tone, hoping it would back Craig off.

"Nice. I love getting away from city life. The rougher, the better."

Meg slumped in defeat.

"I'll let you know what I decide. In the meantime, play nice with the county cops. Be square and transparent with them. You have nothing to hide. But it might not hurt to talk to the other competitors and the SDA reps to see what the scuttlebutt is. They may be freer with their intel with you than with the sheriff and his men."

"They might not, once it becomes clear I'm the prime suspect," Meg muttered.

"Then work fast. And try to dig up as much info on Pratt as you can. Someone killed her. Someone knows something."

"The tricky part will be getting them to tell me. Thanks. I'll update you again when I have more. Hopefully, later today."

"Sounds good. Hang in there."

Meg ended the call and spent a long moment staring at the phone in her hand. Then she walked back to the group, who still stood silently watching. She took a deep breath and addressed everyone. "Pratt reported me to her superior officer last night, accusing me of the abuse I caught her doing." Brian started to draw breath, but she pinned him with a look and a raised index finger, and he swallowed whatever he'd been about to say. "It's gone up the chain to both my special-agent-in-charge and my executive assistant director."

"There is no way in hell either Craig or Peters believes that charge." Unable to hold back anymore, Brian's fury was palpable.

"No, they don't. In fact, Craig is possibly going to fly out. Which tells you how bad this looks."

"Because it now looks like you killed her before she could report you." Todd's voice was flat, but Meg could hear the worry behind his tone, and it ripped at her. Once again, her job was piling stress on him. On them.

"Yes."

"And what about the charge? What could come of it?"

The answer was on the tip of Meg's tongue, but she simply couldn't force the words out.

Brian seemed to sense her inability to put the horror into words, and stepped into the breach for her. "The FBI doesn't own our dogs, so they can't take them away and give them to another handler, but that's not the big problem. The big problem is that both DC and Minnesota have enacted legislation that provides protection to pets in domestic violence situations. This might qualify and could include anything from directions on the animal's care to an order to remove the animal permanently from the owner's possession. In both jurisdictions, pets are considered property, and the powers that be will deal with them as if they're any common household object, like, say, a blender."

Josh's head snapped toward Brian, his mouth open in surprise. "That's ridiculous. Pets aren't property."

"They are according to the state. And can be removed as such."

"After only one supposed incident?"

Meg found her tongue again, all her fear pouring out in

a rush. "It's not like she's accusing me of tapping his rump with a rolled-up newspaper. She's accusing me of attempting to *kill* him. That's more than enough to support the immediate removal of an animal."

Todd grasped Meg's hand and squeezed hard. "That is *not* going to happen. We won't allow them to take Hawk away from you."

"You may not have much choice, especially if they also suspect me of murder." To her amazement, Meg's voice was steady, which was a miracle considering the terror that shook her to her core at the thought of losing her dog.

When she'd lost Deuce, cut down far too young, Meg never intended to put her heart on the line like that again. But in retreating to her parents' animal rescue, and finding the desperately ill, abandoned black Lab puppy, who needed her to even have a slim chance at survival, she'd found that deep connection again, and found a second heart dog. She'd gone into search and rescue with that recovered puppy, then a hale and hearty one-year-old, because it was a way to stay in the law enforcement world with a dramatically lower risk to her dog. Not zero risk, as her work had proven on many occasions, but less.

She'd expected Hawk to live his full life span at her side. Had orchestrated so many aspects of their lives to ensure that. And now to have the risk of losing him at only four, still in his prime working years, when he might have up to eight, or, if she was lucky, nine more years ahead of him, was terrifying.

The only way to counter this was going to be to prove her innocence by proving Pratt's guilt, by figuring out how she died, and at whose hands. More than that, it had to be done this weekend while everyone was still on-site. She figured she had maybe an extra day or two at most, because she anticipated both branches of law enforcement would temporarily hold everyone on-site, instead of allowing them to scatter out of their jurisdiction to the four corners of the country. But it was still going to be a significant challenge. And in times of crisis, when knowledge was power, she needed every advantage she could get.

She gave Todd's hand a squeeze and then released it to pull out her phone.

"Are you calling Craig back?" Todd asked.

"No, Craig's already doing everything he can. It's time for the big guns." She entered another number she knew by heart, and then waited until the line was picked up, the knot in her stomach loosening slightly at the familiar voice. "McCord, it's Meg. I need you."

CHAPTER 13

Prepper: A synonym for "survivalist" which came into everyday usage in the early 2000s. The prepper actively prepares for both natural disasters and societal disorder.

Saturday, October 19, 2:49 PM
Boundary Waters Canoe Area
Superior National Forest, Minnesota

Meg ended the call and sat back in her chair, dropping her satellite phone in her lap.

"Here. Fuel up."

She looked up to find Todd standing in front of her, a steaming cup of coffee in one hand, and a fat sandwich on a paper plate in the other.

"You need food. No arguments. I know you're not hungry, but you can get one sandwich down. Turkey, with lots of mayo and a touch of Dijon, just how you like it." He laid the plate in her lap. "I'd suggest eating it sooner rather than later, or you'll lose it. Someone seems interested. Or someones."

Meg followed Todd's gaze down to where Hawk and Lacey sat at attention, ears perked, and gazes locked on her sandwich.

Todd extended the mug. "And coffee. Tank up."

"Yes, Dad." She accepted the cup, wrapping both hands around the mug to draw its heat into her still-chilled fingers.

He crouched down so they were eye to eye. "I don't know what to do to help you." He kept his voice low, a tiny bit of privacy as the others bustled around the camp. "You're covering, but I know this has you scared. I'm sure no one else can see it—"

"Brian can. I can see it in his eyes too, because the thought of anyone taking our dogs from us is terrifying." She took a deep breath, and blew it out slowly. "I'm not ashamed to say this terrifies me. But I'm not going to just sit by and allow it to happen either."

"Tell me what I can do. Whatever you need, whatever Hawk needs, we'll do it. Can you officially give him to me, so the worst that would happen is you can't work with him? Or what about giving him to Brian or Cara, if he can't officially be under the same roof as you?"

As an experienced first responder, Todd was always calm in a crisis. To any outside eye, he radiated control. But to her ear, his concern carried in the speed of his words, in their emphasis. He wouldn't be scared for himself, but he was for her. She lifted one hand from her cup and laid it against his cheek, his skin cool under her now-warm fingers. "Thank you." She leaned forward and pressed her mouth to his, holding for a long moment.

When she pulled back, his eyes locked on hers. "For a sandwich and coffee?"

"Well, yes, for that too. But for taking care of me." Her gaze dropped to Hawk. "For taking care of *us*. For always being open to whatever crazy adventure I throw you into, headfirst."

"You know I'm up for whatever you need. We all are.

You need anything, Josh and Luke are there. You're family. There isn't any question."

"I know. And I appreciate it. I know Brian is there as well. Although as a fellow competitor, Brian will also be under the magnifying glass, just not as much as me, once word of Pratt's complaint gets out."

"What's going on with McCord? He's looking into Pratt's history?"

"It's going to be a working trip for McCord."

"Trip?"

"Did you think he wouldn't be on his way as soon as I said I needed him?"

"Yeah, I guess he wouldn't look at it any other way."

"We'll see him sometime tomorrow depending on flights. He was researching options while we were on the phone. And making notes on what happened and who Pratt is. He's going to show up with as much background as possible. Employment history, past deployments, previous partnerships."

"McCord can be a gold mine."

"It's amazing what he can dig up and what he can sweet-talk out of people. But I'll take it."

As Todd straightened, Brian wandered over and sat down beside her with a pointed look at her sandwich. "Eat."

"The two of you are a pair of mother hens." She took a long, slow sip of her coffee, then picked up her sandwich, glared at both men, and took a bite.

"Thank you," Todd and Brian said in unison as Meg rolled her eyes.

"So, what's next?" Brian asked. "Are you planning on waiting for the sheriff and his boys to show up to question you, or do you have something else in mind?"

"Something else. Something from our earlier discussion is sticking with me and I was turning the idea over in my head while I was talking to McCord."

"What's that?"

"When we were talking about why the body was in the water, and that we would have found her if she'd been on land because specific scent samples are available." She glanced up at Todd, who looked down pointedly at her plate, so she picked up her sandwich and dutifully ate another bite. As she chewed, and then washed it down with some coffee, Josh and Luke drifted over, both with their own coffee cups and one for Todd. "The seed of the idea is there. We've recovered her body, but we can still track her movements."

Brian looked away long enough to accept a cup of coffee from Ryan, but when he turned back to her, she could see he was following and was 100 percent on board. "That's a great idea." Brian took a quick sip of his coffee, flinching slightly at the heat. "You want to offer our services. But I see what you're doing—you want to offer our services *right now*. Before they get wind of Pratt's accusation. So you're not going to talk to the sheriff about last night now?"

"I intended to tell him. I want to be transparent, but the abuse charge changes everything, because they'll read motive to kill her into it. As soon as he hears about the argument and the charge, he's going to cut me off from the case entirely. And you with me, as we're colleagues, and he'll assume—rightly—that you're on my side. If I don't tell him, I can offer for us to help them along, and try to leverage as much info as possible about Pratt. Actually get into her tent and look for the best items to use for tracking."

"You think they'd let you do that?" Ryan asked, settling into the chair beside Brian.

"Not on our own, but I'll suggest one of the deputies accompanies us."

"We'd get an inside look at her belongings," said Brian.

"Exactly. For starters, I'd like to see if her cell phone is there. She wouldn't have had it out there with her. No signal, so what would be the point? That's when she'd carry her satellite phone. But she'll likely have one with her things, because it would have worked until she got into the wilderness, and it could hold a gold mine of information. Not that I'll be able to see it, because the sheriff will take it, but I'd like to know what they're learning."

"How do you think that's going to look when word of your argument comes to light?" asked Josh.

"Like I'm guilty as hell, and I'd be lying if I said that didn't worry me. But I've got to find a way out of this. Pratt is the key. Finding out what happened to her, finding out more about her, that's crucial to figuring out what happened last night. I think it's worth the risk of not telling Olsen right away."

"Well, I like it," said Brian. "It's better than sitting around waiting for the boom to fall."

"We're going to need to move fast."

Brian tapped her plate. "Eat up. Then we'll head to the beach."

"How will that work?" Josh asked. "I understand the dogs will follow her known scent, but won't you need every search team on-site? She'd been here more than a day and had to run in and out of the tent, going different directions a bunch of times."

"Good point, but our dogs are pretty incredible." Meg rested a hand on Hawk's head, where he sat, his nose an inch from her knee, his gaze still fixed on her sandwich.

"I think he wants your turkey," Luke commented.

"Oh, he does, but we have a strict no-feeding-at-the-table policy, even when the table is my lap. If we're about to start a search, I'll give him some high-energy food to keep him rolling. Trust me, he's not starving to death."

She turned back to Josh. "Search canines can essentially tell time."

Josh's face wrinkled in confusion. "Like a watch kind of 'tell time'?"

"Sort of. It has to do with how strong the scent particles that make up the trail are. Let me give you an example. Brian and I had a run-in with a mama bear and her cubs in the spring."

Beside her, Brian groaned and rolled his eyes.

"We were on a ridge at the peak of a mountain," Meg continued. "We actually crossed paths with the bears, but if they'd gone by fifteen minutes earlier, we'd have missed them and Brian and I would have had no idea they were there. However, the dogs would not only know we'd crossed their path, but would be able to tell you which direction they'd gone. They'd be able to tell the older section of trail from the newer."

"So you'll be looking for the newest trail. Her last trail."

"Exactly. Theoretically, one team would do, but we'll offer both teams, in case we have any conflicting paths. Better to split up."

"And you think they'll allow you to do this?"

"I think I can sell it to Sheriff Olsen that it's in his best interest to know what her final steps were. She left camp somehow. The question is how? And, again, where's her dog?"

"I should come with you," Todd said. "If the dog's hurt, while I'm not a vet, at least I know biology and could help out there. And if you need the dog carried back, I could help there too."

Brian's expression clouded with grim memory. "Take it from me, it's a struggle to carry a full-size dog out of the woods. She's a little smaller than Lacey, but an extra set of hands will speed up the process considerably."

Meg knew exactly what he was thinking of—when Lacey had nearly died following a cougar attack in the spring, Brian had saved her life by carrying her out of the wilderness in his arms. She squeezed his forearm in solidarity and memory. "Might actually be a good idea for each of us to take one of you strong firefighter types." She looked up at Josh and Luke. "Either of you two good with the medical stuff?"

Josh shrugged noncommittally, but Luke perked with interest. "I'm not officially trained as a paramedic, but I've helped out on a few medical calls when we've been short-handed and I've taken basic medical training. I'd be happy to tag along."

"Let's get the dogs fed and go talk to Sheriff Olsen if we can grab his attention for a few minutes. There's a possibility he won't go for it, but I'm going to push for it needing to happen right now. We're going to lose the light in a few hours, and it's important to hit the trail while it's still fresh."

"And while we may be able to save Ava," Brian added.

"That too." Meg pointed at first Todd, then Josh. "Get your hiking boots on and bring whatever you need for what could be a few hours out there. We'll bring our go bags, and throw in some extra water for you guys. But we need to be prepared to move as soon as we get the green light."

She quickly finished her sandwich and coffee and then stood, calling her dog. Going into their tent, she found Todd lacing on his hiking boots. He straightened, looked her up and down, and smiled. "You look better already."

"I feel better. Part of it is the food and coffee, so thank you again for that."

"More of it is having a proactive plan."

"You know me so well. I don't do well just sitting, waiting for the other shoe to drop. I'd rather go out and find it." She glanced at the time. "Let me feed Hawk. But time's a-wasting, and I want to be off-site by the time the FBI agent shows up. Olsen's not going to be happy about the abuse accusation. Up to the time it becomes official, I can play dumb, but once he knows, he'll rightfully block me from the investigation because I'll be suspect number one. Let's move now, while we still can."

CHAPTER 14

Survivalism: A movement that predates "preppers." Survivalists often go beyond preppers by training themselves in self-defense, urban and wilderness survival, and a variety of other survival skills.

Saturday, October 19, 3:32 PM
Boundary Waters Canoe Area
Superior National Forest, Minnesota

"**S**heriff Olsen!"

Only Olsen's eyes moved as he tracked toward the voice calling his name. He towered over the two deputies flanking him as they stood at the SUV's open driver's window. Kline sat inside at the wheel. With a last word to his officer, Olsen tapped his fist twice on the roof of the SUV and then stepped away as Kline eased the vehicle away from the beach and up the dirt track, away from the lake where someone had tried and failed to hide Pratt's death.

Probably on the way to the nearest proper morgue facilities, which could be a distance from all the way out here.

Meg and Brian ordered their dogs into the grass at the side of the rough roadway as the SUV slowly pulled past them. Through the darkened windows, Meg caught a dull flash of yellow taking up the entire rear compartment, confirming her assumption of Kline's current assignment. She looked away from the vehicle. What happened to Pratt now couldn't be her concern; what happened to Pratt last night needed her entire attention.

Meg raised one hand in greeting and she made her way down to the beach.

Olsen watched her approach. His gray hair was receding, and his gray goatee and pale hazel eyes, paired with a naturally light complexion and no sign of summer color, combined to give him a nearly albino wash.

Meg fixed a professional smile on her face and gave Hawk a wordless hand signal to heel as she approached the officers. She held out her hand. "Sheriff Olsen, Meg Jennings, FBI Human Scent Evidence Team. I believe you spoke with SAC Craig Beaumont earlier this afternoon."

Olsen looked to her hand and then back up to her eyes, but didn't extend his own hand in greeting. "Talked to him, yeah."

She dropped her hand to indicate the dog at her side, as if his refusal to shake was no slight at all. "This is Hawk, my search-and-rescue K-9. Hawk led us to Deputy Pratt this morning."

That softened Olsen's expression slightly as he glanced down at the Labrador. "Good work."

Meg seized on the mild praise and ran with it. "Thank you, sir. He's a smart boy. I actually wanted to offer our services"—she stepped sideways to ensure Brian and Lacey were visible—"and that of my colleague, Brian Foster, and his K-9, Lacey. I think we may be able to assist in your investigation."

Olsen hooked both thumbs in his utility belt and looked from one dog to the other, then back up to Meg, his brows raised in question, but stayed silent.

Meg kept the smile pasted on firmly and continued. "I'd like to offer the dogs to you. Something happened last night, and we can use the dogs' skills to possibly shed some light on Deputy Pratt's movements."

"How?"

Definitely a man of few words. Remember, this is the type who would allow a suspect to babble to fill the silence, increasing the chances of them screwing up. Keep it to "need-to-know" only.

"I don't know how many saw the deputy after we were all together following the first stage of the competition, but at some point, she and her dog, Ava, left the campground. No one has seen Ava, her Belgian Malinois, since yesterday. So there are actually two trails to follow— Deputy Pratt and her dog. They may move together or, at some point, might have been separated, but what happened to her dog may have impacted her own activities last night. We can use items from her tent, use some of her own possessions and that of her Malinois, to track them. The fact the dog is missing, and was not found with her, is noteworthy."

She forced herself to stop talking, using the sheriff's own technique against him to coerce him to talk.

"Why?"

"Are you familiar with the breed?"

"Not particularly."

"Belgian Malinois are very much like shepherds"—she glanced sideways at Lacey, who stood at attention at Brian's knee—"but with potentially a greater connection with their handler. All the Malinois I've known are beyond dedicated to their handlers. It's especially disturbing that Ava would have abandoned Deputy Pratt. In fact, to me, that suggests foul play. Something happened to that dog. Either she was forced to be separated from Deputy Pratt, and then couldn't follow, perhaps if the deputy was in a boat, or Ava was hurt or killed. I suspect the latter is a stronger possibility. Out here, in the wilderness, Ava would have had to be a very long way away for us not to hear a dog in distress. Something bad happened last night, likely to both of them."

Meg forced herself to meet and hold Olsen's icy gaze. And waited.

"And?" Olsen prompted.

"Right now, it's under twenty-four hours since they disappeared. There's a trail to follow, and light to follow it by, but not for much longer. We'd like to offer our services to provide you with information about the deputy's movements last night. With you, or your deputies, of course, to monitor."

Olsen looked over Meg's shoulder. "And they are?"

Meg turned to look back to where Todd and Luke stood.

At her small nod, Todd stepped forward. "Lieutenant Todd Webb, firefighter/paramedic, DC Fire and Emergency Medical Services."

Luke stepped up beside him. "Firefighter Luke Webb, Baltimore Fire Department."

"You gentlemen are far afield," Olsen said, but with more respect in his tone for men he likely considered on-the-job colleagues than he'd used for Meg.

She suppressed the desire to roll her eyes. Old boys' club, indeed.

"We came for a weekend vacation of fishing in your beautiful wilderness," Todd said. "But I'm also Meg's partner. Luke and I offered to come along, in case we find the dog and medical assistance is required. If you approve the search, we need to start right away before sundown."

Olsen shifted his weight and turned his attention first to the dogs, and then to Meg and Brian. For long seconds, the only sound was the whistle of the breeze in the trees and the cry of a loon, far out in the water. Then, "What will you need?"

"Access to her tent and belongings to find some items that will give us both her scent and Ava's. Four evidence bags, preferably plastic, to keep those items untouched by any other hands. Then we need to head wherever the trail takes us. With two teams, if we need to split up, we can do that. With some luck, we'll have some answers for you within a few hours."

"Becker, you go with Jennings. Murphy, with Foster. Grab some evidence bags from a cruiser first. I'll start interviews here, but if you haven't found anything by eighteen hundred hours, come on back."

"Yes, sir."

"Thank you, Sheriff. I'll be sure to tell SAC Beaumont about how helpful you've been."

"You do that."

Meg turned away from him, Hawk circling her to stay on her left side as they walked away from the sheriff and up the hill. She glanced sideways at Deputy Becker, who fell into step with her. "It's nice to meet you, Deputy."

"You too, Agent Jennings."

"Just Meg is fine. I was an officer on the Richmond, Virginia, Police Department, but now I'm officially a civilian handler working in conjunction with the FBI." As she had calculated, learning she was an ex-cop changed the way he looked at her. More than that, she knew it would get back to Sheriff Olsen. In only a few short hours, she was going to need him to not consider her his primary suspect.

After making a stop at one of the SUVs parked up the hill blocking the main entrance, they made their way to the main campsite to find Pratt's tent unattended. It was a lime-green two-person pop-up, with an oval base, located toward the back of the larger camp area, only a few feet from the forest behind it. Even though she'd walked through this area the previous night, Meg took the time to study the campground. Most of the tents were equally spaced about fifteen or twenty feet apart, but Pratt's tent was easily forty feet from the next closest, almost out of the designated camping area, and away from the shared fire pits and picnic tables.

She pitched her tent back here. She could have been closer to the others in the group, but chose this kind of separation. And the flap doesn't face toward the group, but instead faces toward the forest. Because she didn't want to mix with the other competitors or trainers? Because she was antisocial or thought she was better than the other handlers? Or so she could come and go unnoticed? To do what?

The other competitors and trainers were drifting into the campsite from the beach, now the excitement was over. Every other tent was pitched in expected spots, close to fire pits and picnic tables. A few tents in the cluster were a larger four- or six-person style—likely for the New York State Police contingent to hold two officers and two familiar and friendly dogs, or for trainers who knew each other and were doubling, tripling, or quadrupling up— while the rest were of the small two-person size, perfect for a handler and dog.

"Have any county officers been in the tent?" Meg asked. "We need to know if any trace scent was left by you." *More important, so we know if you've searched it already.*

"No one's been here yet." Becker looked around the tents and immediately unhooked his radio. "Becker to Olsen. Come in."

"Olsen, 10-4."

"Sir, you may want to come up to the campsite, up the road and to the west. The vic's tent is here and unprotected. Until additional officers arrive to search the tent, you may want to conduct your interviews in sight of it."

"10-4, Deputy. Incoming."

It was a case of closing the barn door after the horse had already escaped, because if the killer wanted to remove something from the tent, they'd had all of last night or any point during the day when everyone was down at the beach to do so, but Meg recognized the attempt to contain the scene. "Can we go on in?"

Becker studied the tent. "Do you both need to go in? I'd like as few people in there as possible. And I have to at least go as far as the doorway to observe whoever goes in."

"I can go in for both of us," Meg offered. "Something from Ava will likely be the easiest—a chew toy, some bedding. And if Deputy Pratt came in from Wyoming the day before, that will play in our favor."

"Why?"

"Normally, we like to use a piece of dirty laundry. Something worn that holds sweat and skin cells. She disappeared after the first day and was wearing the clothes she wore for the day yesterday, but we started so early, she would have arrived in Minnesota the day before and either set up camp then, or stayed somewhere nearby and drove the rest of the way in. Either way, because she wasn't coming from close by, there should be something we can use. A pair of used socks will do us." She handed Hawk's leash to Todd. "I'll be quick. Hawk, sit. Stay." She turned away, avoiding Brian's eyes because the silent communication she knew would pass between them might be obvious to the deputy standing only five feet away. She knew what he was thinking anyway—scope out the place, learn anything you can about her. She was going to, but knew that under the deputy's sharp gaze, she wasn't going to be able to gain much more than an impression.

Plastic evidence bags in hand, she unzipped the tent flap and pulled it wide. And froze.

If the sheriff and his deputies hadn't tossed the tent, then surely someone had beaten them to it.

The inside of the tent looked like a whirlwind had spun through. The deflated air mattress was kicked into the middle of the space, the sleeping bag lying over it a crumpled twist of torn fabric and wispy stuffing. The small camp table was tipped against the back wall of the tent, a battery-powered lantern lying wedged on its side. The dog bed, lying in the corner by the door, was ripped to shreds, and clothing was flung haphazardly in every direction.

"What the—" Becker reached for his radio. "Becker to Olsen."

"I'm on my way, Deputy."

"Sheriff, the victim's tent has been searched. I need you to see this before we remove anything from it."

A muttered expletive came through the radio; then, "Hold the scene. I'm coming."

Brian had inched forward with Lacey and peered over Meg's shoulder. "Damn. Who was looking for what?"

Meg looked sideways to find Brian only inches away. "That's the question, isn't it?" She looked back into the tent and then glanced at the deputy. "I can see some items we can use. A couple of rope chew toys, some socks and underwear, hopefully used. Once Sheriff Olsen has seen it, we can pull out only those items with his approval, and get out there." She did another quick scan of the tent contents, knowing there was nothing significant she'd find now, and let the flap drop.

Meg, Brian, Todd, Luke, and the dogs stepped toward the middle of the campground as Olsen strode down the road and into the campsite. He headed straight for the tent; then Murphy lifted the flap for him as he leaned in.

"How bad is it?" Todd asked.

"Pretty bad. Someone was clearly looking for something, likely something incriminating. From the mess in there, it's hard to tell if they found it, gave up the search, or were interrupted in the middle of it. It wasn't just that they tossed the place; they cut up the dog bed and sleeping bag, apparently looking for something. What was she hiding? Something that pointed at someone she had a history with?"

"No one has indicated a history with her," Brian said. "And I didn't see anything yesterday that led me to think any of them knew her. I mean, all the handlers were new to us. We're familiar with some others from those forces, but all of them were new to me."

"Me too. But there's something we're missing, that's pretty clear at this point."

"Did you see her cell phone in the mess?" Luke asked.

"No. It could be under a pile of clothes, or it could be gone."

"If it's someone with a long history with her, there may be evidence on that phone," said Brian. "It may be in a different spot at the bottom of the lake. There's a small chance a dog *might* find it, but we'd need an experienced electronics-detection dog for that."

They waited for ten minutes while Olsen and his men took photos of the tent and made notes.

Then Olsen beckoned her over. "What do you need?"

"There are two rope chew toys in there. One just knotted rope, one with a ball attached. I need the item picked up with gloves on or by turning the bag inside out, and then the bag sealed shut. And I need socks or underwear or a shirt that's obviously been worn. Two articles, bagged separately."

It took another five minutes with all three men in the tent before Becker and Murphy emerged, each holding a pair of clear, plastic zippered bags, which they passed off to Brian and Meg. Meg handed the bagged rope toy to Todd, and then studied the sock. "That looks used. Good."

"We found two socks balled up and stuffed into a pair of damp hiking boots."

"Probably got wet coming in from the morning's search on the water and changed to dry socks and boots for the afternoon competition. Was in a rush, so she just jammed them in a corner, intending to come back to them."

"Then never did. Do you need anything else?"

"No." Meg looked to where Olsen still stood inside the tent, the flap flipped open over the top of the dome. "Are you both free to leave?"

"Yes. More officers are nearly here."

Meg met Brian's eyes and he nodded. "Then we're ready. Let's see if we can figure out what happened last night."

CHAPTER 15

High-angle Rappel: A descent by rope at an angle greater than 45°.

Saturday, October 19, 4:41 PM
Boundary Waters Canoe Area
Superior National Forest, Minnesota

Hawk and Lacey trotted ahead of Meg and Brian, their leashes stretched long. Both dogs were head down, following the scent trail. Meg and Brian power walked behind them, letting the dogs set the pace down the dirt path, dotted with small rocks and veined with tree roots. Around them, the forest rose straight and tall, the wind no more than a whisper in the treetops far overhead. Todd and Luke followed behind; then the two deputies brought up the rear.

Meg and Brian both wore their go bags, the search-and-rescue backpacks that went everywhere with them so they were always ready for a search if needed. The packs were loaded with water, food and treats for the dogs, high-energy snacks for the humans, rudimentary first-aid supplies, tools, climbing cord, flares, and their satellite phones. Todd wore a modified version of his working med pack, but it still contained an extensive medical kit, as he knew how far out in the wilderness they were camping, and how far away medical assistance would be in case of an emergency. If anyone was hurt, he was prepared to stabilize the injured until they could get back to civilization.

In this case, at best, the injured would be a dog.

Meg suspected that if they were able to find Ava, she'd be beyond their help. Meg knew if she herself had been murdered, Hawk would lose his mind, and only his own death would stop him from raising the alarm or taking down the killer.

Hope for the dog was low on her list. What she was more hopeful of was finding some trace of where or how Pratt was killed. Although with their current run of luck, she might have been transported somewhere by water and then killed. It was a large lake with a long, rambling shoreline. If the trail led the dogs to the shore, then they'd have to cover every inch of shoreline.

They had a campground full of tracking dogs, but if one of the handlers was the killer, they couldn't trust any of them. The only one she trusted was Brian.

It made her wonder how fast Craig could mobilize Lauren and Rocco, and Scott and Theo, if she needed them. Probably quickly, as long as they hadn't been deployed somewhere else since she and Brian had left town. She'd been too distracted to ask Craig when she talked to him.

Back at the campground, the dogs had cast about for scent and had a few false starts separately, beginning a trail, then falling back.

When the two deputies looked skeptical, Meg had stopped long enough to reassure them that this was what she expected. Pratt had been in and out of her tent several times, so they were looking for the freshest scent. But when the dogs had separately chosen an unmarked path into the forest that met with an established, cleared hiking path, they knew they were on the right track. Fifteen minutes later, the dogs were still confidently on the same trail. Neither used the zigzag usually employed in the scent cone; they were following what was, to them, a clear scent trail. No need to use scent cone strategy.

"You're sure they know where they're going?" Murphy called.

"Absolutely," Brian called back. "You see how they're keeping their noses to the ground and nearly have us at a jog? We're not driving them; they're practically pulling us. They have the trail." Facing forward again, he glanced sideways at Meg. "It makes sense this is where she'd go."

"Keeping to a trail, you mean? Instead of cutting through the forest?"

"Yeah."

"Well, if it was after eleven when she headed out"— Meg threw him a pointed look, not wanting to spell out her eyewitness testimony—"it would have been dangerous to pick her way through a rocky forest with only a flashlight. But an actual hiking trail wouldn't be so bad. As long as she didn't run into a bear or a wolf."

"You'd like to hope Ava would have given some warning about that if the wind was blowing in the right direction." Brian studied the two dogs. "They've definitely picked up on her."

"Or on both of them. That could be why they're so sure. Doubled scent." Meg eyed the hill the dogs were leading them up. "It looks like this goes up a fair way."

"Maybe she fell off a cliff?"

"And then swam out several miles, including through several channels, to die in the middle of the lake? Not buying that one."

"No, you're right. She had help."

An insistent tug on the leash had Brian breaking into a jog, and Meg joined him. The dogs, feeling the back pressure on the leash loosen as their handlers sped up, broke into a run.

"They have something," Meg threw over her shoulder. "Stay with us."

For the next few minutes, Meg was conscious of the huffing and puffing from behind them as they ran up and down a series of hills, the forest thinning to their right and the lake water visible through the trees. Brian rolled his eyes skyward, then tossed her a sly grin and laid on the speed. A chuckle behind her heavy but steady breathing, Meg stayed with him, knowing very well the out-of-shape county deputies behind them were likely getting their workout of the month, maybe of the season. Glancing back behind her quickly, Meg met Todd's eyes, confirming her suspicions that for two firefighters used to running up stairs in sixty pounds of gear with one hundred pounds of hose over their shoulder, this was practically a walk in the park. She just hoped neither of the deputies collapsed, because she'd have to leave them with Todd to deal with as she stayed with Hawk.

Down into a shallow valley, then up another, steeper rise as the trees thinned. Then they broke out into a rocky clearing at the top of a hill. In the east, the sun was sinking toward the horizon, painting the thin layer of clouds in vibrant tones of amber and fuchsia. Thirty feet below, the lake stretched out toward the distant treed shoreline.

Meg and Brian immediately pulled back on their dogs as she tossed him a look that clearly implied, *Not again*. "Hawk, slow." Meg shortened the leash, wrapping it around her hand a number of times. Hawk was well controlled, but this close to an edge, she wanted a tighter hold on him. "Find, Hawk, but slow."

The dogs started forward together, their noses still down, but angling closer and closer to the edge as Meg's heart pounded faster.

"Hawk, stop. Sit. Brian." Meg stopped and waited as her dog did the same.

"Lacey, stop. Sit." He moved to stand beside his dog. "What are we looking at?"

"Look at the dirt. No!" She threw out a hand as if to stop him from moving forward. He was too far away for her to touch, but he froze. "Sorry, I don't want to disturb that area. You see those tracks? It must have rained sometime before we arrived and it hadn't totally dried out by last night."

"I don't . . . wait. Yes, I do. Boot prints. Closer to the edge. They're kind of indistinct. But I see them. There's a lot of them, like they were dancing. Or, more likely, fighting."

"Yeah, I don't like this at all. And the dogs were headed for the edge. We need to look over."

"Let us do that," Todd offered, with a quick glance sideways at the two deputies, who stood, red-faced, their chests heaving. "You don't want to get that close to the edge with the dogs, in case something spooks them."

Meg's gratitude was clear in her eyes as Todd gave her an excuse to stay away from the edge. "Make sure you avoid that section over there, because there are a bunch of boot prints. Deputies, do you have cell phones with you?" At their nods, she pointed to the dirt by the edge. "You might want to shoot some photos of that area while the light is still good."

"We'll stay clear of it." Todd stripped off his jacket and handed it to Meg, and then pushed up the sleeve of his sweatshirt and held out his left arm to his brother. "Counterbalance me in case I need to lean out."

Luke pushed up the sleeves of his jacket and shirt, and clamped his left hand over Todd's forearm. "Go for it."

Todd stepped nearly to the edge and looked over, holding still as he scanned the area below. "Need to get closer." And took another step, right to the edge.

Meg was gripping the leash so tightly the woven cord dug into her palm. She wasn't near the edge, but Todd being so close kicked up her heart rate. "See anything?"

There was a long pause, then, "I can see Ava. She's not moving." He and Luke stepped back from the edge and returned to where Meg and Brian stood with their dogs.

"We need to get down there," Meg said, "but there's no direct way from here. Possibly the only way to recover her body would be by boat."

"If Pratt went over with her," Brian reasoned, "that might have been how she was retrieved as well. And if she was already in a boat, why take her back to camp when you could dump her somewhere she'd hopefully never be found?"

"That doesn't make any sense. The easiest way to have handled it if she went over the edge was to leave her there to be found. It would look like an accident."

"Unless there were marks on her body from a struggle?" Todd countered. "Or something on her the killer couldn't risk having found. Because you're right, it would have been more straightforward and much less risky to leave her there. Assuming she went over, of course." Todd looked back at the edge and the sheer drop beyond. "How much climbing cord are you packing?"

"One hundred feet is about as much as we can fit in with everything else we carry. Brian has the same. And we each have three or four carabiners."

"Which I'd need a harness for, so, unfortunately, they're not useful to us today. But what you have will do and then some." He took his jacket from Meg and shrugged into it. "How's your rope work?" he asked Luke.

"Stellar. How's yours?"

"I teach it to the probies. There's no easy way down the cliff. No defined trail, no straightforward climb, and the bottom is a killer spread of uneven boulders that will break into pieces anything that falls on it from a height. And that could be a killer drop even onto a softer surface. Now, we have two coils of rope to get us down the cliff and then some, but no harness."

"You're thinking of an old-fashioned body rappel," Luke stated.

"Yeah. Specifically, a South African rappel. Ever done it?"

"As part of emergency training. I may be a little rusty on it."

"I teach that emergency training. I'll make sure you're set up right." Todd looked from Meg to the two deputies, who joined them again. "I wouldn't try this without the proper equipment if it was a bigger drop, but we can make it safely down a cliff of that size with the minimal equipment we have. If that dog is alive, it will need immediate assistance. But not having harnesses means we can't take any of you with us."

"We can access this location from the water," said Becker. "We'll radio Sheriff Olsen and he can get one of the pilots to bring him out. They'll probably get here faster than we did."

"Good plan." As the deputy pulled out his radio, Todd turned to the handlers. "Meg, Brian, we need your cord."

Meg pulled her sat phone out of her jacket pocket. "Can you tuck my phone into one of your pockets? That way, you can talk to us on Brian's and let us know what you need."

"Good idea." He slid it into the inside pocket of his jacket.

Meg slid off her bag, opened it, and pulled out blue-and-black climbing cord, tightly coiled and wrapped almost from end to end, making a surprisingly compact bundle for the length it contained. "I appreciate you check-ing, but what are the chances Ava is still alive, now we know where she is?" She kept her voice low so the dep-uties wouldn't hear her.

"Extremely low, though not impossible. Keep in mind, if she didn't die on impact, it's been about eighteen hours and she's most likely passed." The grim look in Todd's eyes told Meg he was sure the dog was already gone. "If she's alive, I'll need one of you to pull up a rope, tie a hitch knot, and lower my pack to me."

"We can do that."

"If she didn't make it, at least one of us will get a look at Pratt's potential death scene before the sheriff comes in and blocks it off." He patted the back pocket of his jeans. "And I just happen to have my cell phone on me. Useless as a phone in this area, but great as a camera."

"You wily man. And you wonder why I love you."

Todd flashed her a grin and then turned to stand, hands on hips, studying the trees that stood about fifteen feet from the cliff edge. "Those will do."

"To anchor you?"

"Yes." He took the cord from Meg and strode to the tree line.

Luke joined him, holding Brian's green-and-black coil. He pointed to two sturdy trees, a red pine and an oak standing about six feet apart, both tall enough that their lowest branches were over six feet up, leaving the thick trunk exposed below. "Those two?"

"Yeah, they'll do nicely. Loop the cord at midpoint."

"Check."

The men uncoiled and shook out their cord, looped it around the trunk of their tree, and then adjusted the cord so the midpoint of the length was around the tree. Holding the rope in both hands, they ran the cord back and forth a few times, ensuring it moved easily and didn't snag. Walking to the cliff, Todd studied the edge, and then kicked a loose stone or two off to the side before tossing his rope over to tumble to the rocks below. Luke did the same.

Todd peered down to where the cord pooled on the rocks below. "Perfect length for this. You ready?"

"Yup."

"Watch your hands. We're doing this without gloves or carabiners, which makes us the friction to slow the descent, so do what you can to avoid rope burn." He looked over to where Meg and Brian stood with their dogs and the deputies. "We're going out. It should only take a couple of minutes to get down there, so we'll know where we are soon enough. Luke, strap up. I'll talk you through it, to make sure you're solid." He picked up the two strands of blue cord and stepped between them. "Cross the cord over behind your back and bring it out again to the front. Then bring the cords together and step over them on both sides so it loops between your legs." As he instructed, Todd carried out each step, slowly winding himself into the rope, keeping an eye on his brother as he did the same. "Bring both strands over to your right hand, wrapping it once over your forearm to let your jacket sleeve take some of the friction. Now grip the ropes coming from the tree in your left hand, and the spare length in your right. Test out how the rope is lying and adjust if needed." He leaned back into the ropes, holding them tight in his clenched fists.

Now Meg could see it. "That's why you're not using the carabiners. You've wound the cord so it's your harness."

"Yes. The trick here is to lean back and out as far as possible to keep the ropes tight and supportive. We'll essentially be walking down the cliff perpendicular to its face. Carabiners would be more efficient if we had a harness, but my gear's in DC. Didn't see this little excursion happening." He adjusted his weight in the ropes slightly. "This works for me. Let me see yours." Luke angled toward his brother. "That's good."

Meg met his eyes and silently mouthed, *Be careful*. He nodded in acknowledgment.

"We're going down. We'll let you know how it goes." He looked at his brother. "Ready?"

"You bet."

"Keep your eyes open for any kind of falling debris. We're working without helmets, but we both have one hand we can safely free up quickly if anything comes loose. And over we go. Remember, maneuvering over the edge and getting horizontal is the hard part. Take it slow. We're in no rush."

They both backed to the precipice, and then, making sure they had a solid grip on the climbing cord, stepped to the edge.

"Heels over the edge and let yourself out slowly, tipping back as you go."

Meg suspected Luke didn't need directions, but Todd had instinctively reverted to instructor mode. She kept her eyes locked on his hands, all that was keeping him from a fatal drop. With his left arm nearly fully extended, he gripped the two ropes that fed from the tree in that hand. His right hand held the doubled extra cord and also the right-most cord coming from the tree closer to his torso. Every few seconds, he'd release the right rope, loosen his hold on the feeder ropes, and sink a few inches, before gripping tight again and clamping back on the rope supporting his body. As he went over the edge, his hiking boots secure against the granite face of the cliff, he tipped from vertical to nearly horizontal by loosening the rope, but keeping his feet planted. Then he eased himself down the cliff face.

"Look at them go." There was wonder in Brian's voice. "I'd kill myself if I attempted that stunt."

"Firefighters. They're handy folks to have around."

"As Todd has proven on several occasions."

Meg extended Hawk's leash. "Hold him for a minute?" She dropped her voice so the deputies couldn't hear from where they'd stepped up to the edge to watch the Webb brothers' progress. "They're good, but I'd still like to keep an eye on their progress. I think I can do it without freaking out if I go back a bit so I can see them on an angle."

"You bet. Take my phone with you so you can call him once he's down."

Meg found a good spot about twenty-five feet away where she could see along the cliff face as it curved, without getting too close to the edge herself. The bottom fell out of her stomach as the base of the cliff finally came into sight down below, a rocky expanse of jagged boulders, splashed by the wind-driven waves.

Her heart squeezed as her gaze settled on the still body of a dog in a crevice between a cluster of boulders. Casting her gaze upward, she found Todd and Luke. They worked slowly but steadily, the ropes supporting them in midair as they walked down the cliff face. Meg noted that Todd's attention was split, checking on Luke often, making sure his technique was solid and he wasn't taking any risks.

A few minutes later, they were both safely finding their footing on the rocks at the base of the cliff, unwinding the cord and shaking themselves free.

Meg dialed her own number and waited while Todd pulled out the phone and answered. "I can see you from where I'm standing a little eastward. All good?"

Todd's head turned as he tracked along the line of the cliff until he found her. "Yeah, that was textbook. We're going to check on the dog now."

"Put the phone back in your pocket and leave the line open because you'll need both hands to climb over those rocks."

They'd landed about fifteen feet away from the dog, and it didn't take them long to clamber over rocks to her. Meg knew the dog's status from the grim expression on Todd's face as he turned to look up at her before he pulled out the phone.

Poor Ava, living such a terrified life, ended far too early. May peace guide your way over the Rainbow Bridge.

"Gone, likely last night. The body is cold. And broken." Todd paused, his head bent as he looked down to where Luke knelt by the dog's head. "This was a terrible landing. I'm not moving her, so the sheriff can see her in her original position, but it's clear from how she's lying that at least two legs are broken in multiple places."

"It might be a blessing she didn't survive. If it was catastrophic damage like that, she would have been in agony and may never have truly recovered. Hang on, we need to get Becker and Murphy in on this discussion." She returned to Brian, relieved him of Hawk's leash, and called the deputies over as she put the call on speaker. "Todd's on the phone," she told them. "Ava's dead."

"Lieutenant Webb, do you think she survived the fall?" asked Murphy.

"I doubt it," Todd replied. "If she did, I don't think she lasted long after. She certainly didn't move from this position. Too many broken bones. But that makes me think . . . Meg, just how badly was Pratt injured?"

Meg was silent a moment as she thought of the brief view she'd had of Pratt's body. She'd been captured by her face, by her open staring eyes, but, closing her own eyes, tried to rebuild the memory. And realized one of the reasons why she hadn't noted anything much was because there was nothing to note. "I think the head was it. It was all Sal specified, and if they'd lifted her and her limbs were unduly floppy, I think they'd have noticed and said something. Thinking back, I didn't really concentrate on much besides her face, but if her arms and legs had been positioned oddly, I'm pretty sure it would have caught my attention. Brian?"

"I agree. The head injury was terrible." Lacey, on her feet, pulled against her taut leash, trying to step away, and Brian glanced at her in confusion. "Lacey, stay."

"It was. What about her other injuries?"

"I didn't see any either."

Meg nodded her agreement. "If that's true, and the head wound was all there was . . ."

"Then she didn't go over the edge with her dog," Becker finished.

"That's what I'm thinking. Thanks, Todd. Let me call you back in a bit. We need to look around up here."

"Message received."

Meg knew Todd's use of the common firefighter radio sign-off wasn't just a habitual way of ending the call. He was acknowledging the deputies would be busy, so now was the time to look around and snap pictures.

She looked down when Lacey pulled against the leash again.

Brian shook his head at his dog. "Lacey, stay." He looked back to Meg. "It sounds like it's a mess down there."

"Skeletally, that dog is in pieces." Meg looked toward the soft dirt at the edge. "And we have that. You have pictures of it?"

"Yes." Murphy took a step toward the edge, then stopped. "That looks like a scuffle took place." He turned to the handlers. "But if you don't think Deputy Pratt went over the edge . . ." His gaze skipped to the lip of the cliff and then over toward the woods.

"She might have died up here," Becker suggested.

Lacey barked.

Everyone stopped and stared at the shepherd.

"She might have died up here," Meg repeated. "Brian, I think Lacey's trying to tell us she's picked up on something."

Brian loosened up on the leash. "Sorry, Lacey-girl. Show me what you smell."

She went unerringly to a spot in the tree line about fifteen feet from where footprints dented the soft earth. But when she would have pushed into the bushes and undergrowth, Brian pulled her back. "Lacey, sit. Guys, take a look at that spot. There's damage to the greenery."

The low scrubby bush at the border of the rocky ledge had a broken branch. Below it, a clump of leafy stems was crushed and bent.

"We don't want to get the dogs too close if that's evidence," Meg said. "Deputy Becker, can you take a look? Hawk, back up a bit."

"Sure." Becker slipped around the dogs and pushed aside the greenery with a spread hand, freezing in place when the movement revealed a jagged rock half buried in the dirt.

Meg's phone rang, and she sightlessly thrust a hand into her pocket to pull it out. She glanced down distractedly to see her own phone number. "Hey."

"Hey," Todd said. "It didn't take long because it's not a big area, but there's nothing here minus the dog. You could get a forensic team down here to go over these rocks with their fancy chemicals, but there's nothing visible Luke or I can find."

"That's okay, I don't think we're going to need it."

"No?"

"No." She stared down at the jagged chunk of granite, at the dark stain that flowed over the top, pooled in a small dip in its uneven surface, and finally puddled around the base.

So much blood.

"No," she repeated. "I think Lacey just found where Deputy Pratt died."

CHAPTER 16

Enhanced Interrogation: A euphemism for the systematic torture of detainees conducted by one's own side.

Saturday, October 19, 5:33 PM
Boundary Waters Canoe Area
Superior National Forest, Minnesota

The officers arrived with lights and equipment, by land and by water, as dusk sank toward night. Olsen came in by boat, directed from his deputies' original call to examine the dog and to have it photographed and removed as evidence. Another boat arrived to take Todd and Luke out of their crime scene. Yet more officers would hike in, accompanied by the county forensic specialist.

As soon as they'd been given the go-ahead to collect their climbing equipment, coil it, and stow it away, Meg and Brian had been summarily dismissed, and shooed away with their dogs like recalcitrant children. They'd gone without protest, wanting to return to camp to regroup and compare notes with Todd and Luke. They'd walked back to their campsite by the light of their flashlights, both lost in thought, comfortable with each other and the silence.

Coming down the road, they found their campsite busy with dinner prep. Josh and Ryan hovered over the fire, talking and laughing, while Luke dug through one of the coolers, pulling out tightly wrapped packages, and shaking off small pieces of ice. Todd bent over the picnic table, a row of corncobs and a heavy pot on the table before him.

Meg bent and unleashed Hawk. "Okay, boy, go ahead." She smiled as Hawk bolted for Todd, dancing around him once he reached the table.

Todd greeted the dog with a smile and praise, but when his eyes rose to Meg's, they were grim.

As Brian and Lacey angled off toward the fire, Meg followed her dog to the picnic table. She laid a hand on Todd's back, leaning in over his shoulder as he opened a cob of corn, stripped out the silk, pulled the husks around the cob again, and dropped it into the pot of water. "Are you grilling Mexican street corn?"

"I am. You think it's good on the barbecue, wait until you get it over an open wood fire." He pulled silk out of the next cob, dropped it onto a growing pile on the table. "It'll blow your mind."

"My mind could use some blowing after the last couple of days." She ran a hand up and down his back. "Yours might too. Thanks for doing the dirty work this afternoon. That can't have been pleasant."

"The trip down or the dog?"

"Both. There's no way that's a comfortable rappel with no harness. And the dog . . ."

"The rappel isn't that bad. When you use yourself as friction, there's always some pain, but if you're slow and careful, you can minimize it. But yeah, the dog wasn't pretty." He met her eyes. "I'm glad you didn't see it up close." His gaze dropped to Hawk, who sat vibrating be-

side them, his tail swishing back and forth in the grass.
"Too personal." He dropped the cob in the pot and
reached down to stroke Hawk's head. "Buddy, you know
this is a vegetable, right? Doesn't your nose tell you the
meat's over there?"

"Meat? You guys didn't catch anything this morning?"

"We did, but we planned steak for tonight's meal."

"Steak? We're living like kings." She smiled down at her
dog, whose ears perked at the word "steak." "Hawk's in."

"Does he actually know that word?"

"I wouldn't put it past him. He's a smart boy."

"No doubt about that. Can you do me a favor and tell
Josh I need room for the corn, in a few?"

"Sure. Anything else I can do to help? So far, you boys
have done everything from cooking to coffee to cleanup.
Brian and I could help with some of it."

"You could, but that was the deal. Uncle Sam is paying
for the campground and you're on a working weekend.
We can pull our weight. If we'd just gone off, the three of
us, we'd be doing the same thing. It's just more food. And
Ryan's right in there with us. You and Brian get to relax.
It's the only time all weekend that's going to happen."

"Tell me about it," Meg muttered. "Okay, see you at
the fire."

Three minutes later, she was comfortably rocking in her
camp chair beside Brian, a fresh cup of coffee in hand. The
two dogs were curled up between their chairs as Todd
pulled corn from the water and laid it out on the grill over
an area of the fire that Josh had let burn down to hot
glowing coals.

"That isn't the famous Mexican street corn, is it?" Brian
asked.

"It is." Water dripped from the corn, sizzling to steam
on the coals. "You're going to love it. Todd does this

amazing chili-lime mayo you slather on instead of butter, and then you sprinkle with Cotija cheese. It's amazing."

Brian rubbed his belly. "I can't complain about the food here. I would have thought the way this weekend has been going, my appetite would have vanished, but just the opposite."

"Fresh air and exercise."

"Don't forget stress."

Josh looked up from the fire, where he was about to lay the steaks on the grill. "You guys have had more than enough of that. Todd told us what happened with the dog. And he overheard the radio conversations about what you found up top."

"Where we think she died, yeah."

"There was a fight on top of the cliff?"

"Looks like there might have been." She looked sideways to Brian. "You were quiet on the way back."

"You too. I think we're both trying to process."

"What's your take on it?"

He took a sip of coffee, then cradled the cup in both hands and stared into the fire. "It looks like there was a physical struggle up there. They were near the edge; maybe the dog tried to intervene, lost her footing, and fell."

"Or maybe there was a fight and the dog moved to protect its owner." From where he tended the corn, Todd looked over his shoulder toward the dogs. "You know how your dogs will go to the ends of the earth to protect you. Meg, you were protected by Hawk from Daniel Mannew and Lou Giraldi. Brian, Lacey protected you from that cougar. One was shot and the other attacked by a wild animal while doing everything they could to stand between you and a threat. What if Ava did the same?"

"Meaning it wasn't an accident," Meg posited, "but Pratt was fighting with someone on top of that cliff and the dog got into the mix. Then the someone kicked or threw the dog over the edge." A shudder ran through her, hard enough for a ripple to run across the surface of her coffee as a terrifying image filled her mind.

She stood opposite Daniel Mannew on Miller's Knob at the peak of the Great North Mountain. Mannew, his back to a fathomless drop, was rigid as she leveled her Glock at him, his hands held at his sides, his handgun pointed at the ground.

The handgun that had shot Hawk only moments before.

Terror streaked through her at the thought of her dog being injured, or worse. She didn't know how badly he was hurt or where he was, but his whine of pain still echoed in her head.

"Mr. Mannew, it's not too late. Put down the weapon and we can work this out."

"You know who it's too late for?" The gun clutched in his hand started to vibrate. "It's too late for you—"

Hawk burst from the bushes with a snarl, launching himself at Mannew's gun hand, his teeth bared. He latched on, grinding bone and sinew, Mannew screaming in agony. The gun went off as they struggled, the bullet striking the earth halfway between Mannew and herself. Mannew grabbed a fistful of Hawk's fur as the dog jerked his wrist right, then left, until the gun went flying. But then, in trying to fight off the snarling dog, Mannew lost his balance and staggered backward toward the edge of the abyss. One step . . . two . . . three . . .

And they were gone.

"HAWK!"

She occasionally woke in the middle of the night, sweaty and panting, with the sound of her terrified scream still in her ears. Hawk had been caught by a ledge twenty feet down and in the end had saved the life of the man who'd nearly killed him.

She met Todd's eyes, and knew he followed her thoughts. "If that was me, and someone kicked Hawk over a cliff to his death, I'd have taken him apart limb from limb."

"Justifiable homicide," Brian said matter-of-factly. "I'd have done the same. The only thing I'd question there is how Ava would behave. Considering the abuse, would she protect the way Lacey and Hawk have? And how would Pratt react to the loss of a dog she mistreated so badly? There are a lot of unknowns we may never have answers to."

"What I wonder is if the scuffle at the ridge happened before, during, or after the dog died," Luke commented. "Either way, whatever happened up there, it ended with Pratt falling backward, likely fast and hard, striking her head on that rock hidden in the bushes."

"Fast and hard enough to have been helped?" Ryan asked.

Meg and Brian stared at each other before Meg answered. "Meaning, was she pushed or thrown, or did she lose her footing? That's a good question."

"Another good question is how she got from the top of that cliff to the bottom of the lake," Josh said.

"The killer must have carried her down," Meg said. "It might have been easier to toss her over the edge, but for whatever reason, the killer didn't or we'd have seen that in her body condition."

"You'd think if the killer carried her down, they'd have been splattered with her blood. Head wounds bleed like a bitch, and, even if Pratt's heart wasn't pumping, that's an awfully large wound. Unless the killer wrapped a shirt or jacket around her head, but then you'd still be left with bloody clothes as evidence."

"Unless it, too, is at the bottom of the lake somewhere. Tie it around a big rock and heave it over the side." Luke dusted his hands off on each other. "Problem solved."

"Time to let it go for now." Todd handed Meg a plastic wineglass, nearly full to the brim with deep ruby liquid, then passed a second to Brian. "I want you both to turn off your brains for an hour."

Brian tapped his glass to Meg's. "We can do that."

Dinner was a light affair, and Meg had the feeling everyone was trying extraordinarily hard to keep the conversation away from anything having to do with search-and-rescue, training, or the murder investigation. Afterward, they lounged around the fire, sipping coffee and complimenting the cooks on yet another excellent meal.

Brian leaned closer to Ryan. "We need the recipe for that corn." Sitting forward, he looked around Meg. "Todd! I need the recipe for that corn."

Todd tipped his beer in Brian's direction. "I can send it to you."

A flash of light dancing along the road attracted Luke's attention. "Incoming."

As one, the group turned to stare down the road.

Meg took her eyes off the disembodied light just long enough to glance at her fitness tracker for the time. *Getting late.* She looked up, knowing the hammer was about to fall. She'd rolled the dice, not talking to Olsen when she had the chance, hoping that finding out more information about Pratt would outweigh the consequences now coming her way. Hopefully, what they'd found that afternoon would justify that risk in the end.

She gripped Todd's arm. "Whatever happens, keep Hawk with you. We haven't had time to consider transferring ownership, but they won't take him away that fast."

His gaze followed hers to the bobbing flashlight. "Who do you think that is?"

"The FBI agent. And he's going to know about the abuse accusation, and that I've been in contact with law enforcement and haven't mentioned my run-in with Pratt last night. Keep Hawk with you."

"Meg, he's not going to cart you off to—"

She squeezed tighter. "We have no idea what he's about to do. Todd, please. I need to know he's safe."

At her feet, Hawk whined quietly and pushed his snout against her shin. Her sensitive dog, she should have known he'd sense her worry.

Todd pulled her hand off his arm, wove his fingers through hers, and gripped tight. "He's safe. I won't let anything happen to him no matter what."

She relaxed her grip somewhat and let out a shaky breath. "I'm sorry, I know I'm being stupid. I just can't help—"

"You're not being stupid. This is Hawk we're talking about. He's mine too, and I'm not going to let anything happen to him. Have faith. I do."

Her laugh was jagged, her gaze locked on the dark shape of a man dimly illuminated in the light of his own flashlight. "I hope you have enough for both of us." She turned to her right. "Brian?"

"Yeah. I got him." His tone was flinty. "He's wearing a suit and tie at a campground. That's a fed, for sure."

On the other side of the fire, Josh pushed to his feet, a welcoming smile on his face. He stepped forward a few paces, putting himself bodily between the stranger and the two FBI handlers.

Between the agent and me, Meg thought, knowing full well Brian was at the bottom of any list of suspects being drawn.

"You don't have to talk to him," Brian said. "You don't have a lawyer here. You can ask for one, and he has to stop everything now."

"If I jump to a refusal to talk without my lawyer present, when I haven't been accused of her death yet, I'll look even more guilty. They'll have to put a stop to the investigation and drag me to Minneapolis for questioning at the field office. If we have a hope of figuring out what happened, I need to be here. So I'll talk to him. *Carefully.*"

"Hello," Josh called.

The man stepped into the circle of light thrown by the fire, dropping his flashlight to his side to illuminate a small circle of dirt beside his shiny black dress shoe. His other hand slipped into the breast pocket of the suit jacket under his trench coat to retrieve a thin black flip case, opening and extending it. Firelight glowed off the gold of his badge. "Special Agent Jonathan Brogan, out of the Minneapolis field office. I'm here investigating the death of Deputy Sheriff Rita Pratt." His eyes scanned the circle, then stepped sideways to see around Josh, locking on the only woman in the group. "Ms. Jennings."

She paused for a second as she studied him, taking his measure. He looked young, likely an agent for a year or two at most. Lean and decidedly shorter than her own nearly six-foot height, he wore the typical Bureau uniform of dark suit and tie, white shirt. His light brown hair was cut short, with only a small amount of extra length on top. His face was set in neutral lines, with no hint of expression on his lips or in his eyes behind his utilitarian, rectangular-framed glasses. *Furthest thing from a social call.* "Agent Brogan." She gave herself a virtual pat on the back for her calm tone. "Nice to meet you."

"Which one is Foster?"

"That's me."

As Brian spoke, Josh returned to his chair, either his point made, or in the knowledge he couldn't stand in front of her anymore.

"I'd like to speak to you both about Deputy Pratt."

With a hand gesture to Lacey to stay down, Brian stood. "Sure. Can we do it here, or would you like to go somewhere else?"

"I want to start with Jennings." He turned to look around, spotting an unused picnic table closest to the tree line. "Does anyone have a lantern?"

"On that table there, closest to the orange tent." Luke pointed toward the table where the lantern stood in the dark to save battery power while not needed.

"Thank you." The eyes that met hers across the fire were dark. "Let's talk over there."

"Of course. Hawk, stay." She gave Todd's hand a squeeze and pulled her fingers free. She slipped out of the circle, the shiver that skittered down her skin not just the heat of the fire falling away as she stepped into the dark. She strode across the grass in the direction of their picnic table, dialed up the light on the lantern to halfway, and then led the way to the table on the far side. She sat down on the far bench so she could still see the group, but Brogan couldn't.

It made her feel better knowing they were all there, even if they couldn't help her. It reminded her she wasn't alone.

Brogan pulled out a spiral notepad and pen from his pocket. "Ms. Jennings, were you familiar with Deputy Sheriff Rita Pratt before this weekend?"

"No."

"You'd never worked any searches with her?"

"Not to my knowledge. She may have been involved in some of the mass-casualty events I've taken part in, like Hurricane Cole last year. Many different search-and-rescue organizations responded to the call for help. But if she was there, I never knew it. What I can say is she was unfamiliar to me when we met for the first competition. She and every other contestant. Which isn't surprising, because while the world of search and rescue is relatively small, within law enforcement, there are a good number of us. And we come from all over the country."

"Did you have any personal interactions with her this weekend? Interactions not part of the larger group?"

Time to look transparent.

"Two conversations with her."

"And what was the nature of these conversations?"

"You didn't mark your own time? I guess with that disadvantage, you might not want to."

Just the memory of Pratt's words lit the flame of Meg's temper, but she swallowed it down. "The first interaction was to break up an argument between Deputy Pratt and Deputy Fief. Deputy Pratt's dog was looking riled, and I didn't want to start the weekend off with any of the animals getting hurt. Brian and I walked over to calm things down."

"Deputy Fief described the interaction to me. She said Deputy Pratt insulted your dog."

Meg forced a careless shrug. "She made a generalization about Hawk's breed. She doesn't know him, so she really can't insult him."

"Deputy Fief said it made you angry."

Deputy Fief is trying to stay clear of this mess herself. "Irritated, sure. But not angry. Sometimes you just have to look at where a comment is coming from and brush it off because of that. It was a few comments back and forth, and then we broke up to find out the results of the competition."

"Where did you place compared to Deputy Pratt?"

Meg knew without a doubt he knew the answer to that question. "Sixth to her first."

"And did that bother you?"

"I want Hawk to give the best showing he can, but it was an off day for him. However, we were supposed to have two more opportunities to compete."

"Did you resent the fact she did so well when you did so poorly?"

Meg won the struggle to keep her spike of temper off her face. "Not at all."

"But now she's dead, and your friend Brian, your teammate, has essentially won the competition. Your team has won."

"He hasn't won. We haven't won. There won't be a winner. You don't end a competition that's only barely started and declare a winner."

"You could say your team won."

"But we wouldn't," Meg insisted. "If we did, it would be easy to prove it was a false claim. Not to mention, word of one of us dying during a competition weekend would keep the competition fresh in everyone's mind. Everyone will know Brian and Lacey, or the FBI team, if you want to put it that way, didn't win."

"But there is an advantage to winning?"

"For some. Not for me."

"Why not for you?"

Meg's gaze tracked over his shoulder to the group. Hawk sat up beside Todd, his hand resting on the dog's back, both of them staring directly at her, not letting her out of their sight. "Because the reasons you could make money out of a trial win don't apply to me."

"Why not?"

"Because I'm not breeding Hawk, so I don't care about his monetary value."

"Winning a competition could increase his value?"

"Sure, if he could be bred. But he's already valuable to me. To my team." Her eyes narrowed on him. "And to the FBI."

"Your connection to the FBI is immaterial. We brought in the Lake County sheriff to make sure we had an impartial investigator."

Meg wondered how far this agent was prepared to go to make sure it was clear he was impartial himself. She was willing to bet a long way. Also, if he was as wet behind the ears as she thought, he might be using this case to make a name for himself in FBI circles.

"A dog's breeding worth is the only advantage to come out of a trial win?"

"No, that's part of it, but not all. It's also a boon for the training facility. They can sell more training sessions, or charge more for their dogs when they sell them, because their dogs are medaled, that kind of thing. Again, irrelevant to me."

"His training facility doesn't need the boost?"

"It doesn't because it's me. I trained him."

"What about his breeder?"

"There isn't one. He was abandoned as a sick puppy on the doorstep of my parents' animal rescue. I helped nurse him back to health and we bonded. I trained him in search-and-rescue once he was better, and we joined the Human Scent Evidence Team." Irritation was crawling into Meg's tone, and she took a breath and beat it down. "As I said, winning the trial wasn't why I was here this weekend."

"What was?"

"The training. Underwater search-and-recovery was a skill Hawk and I didn't have."

"We'll circle back to that. But let's come around again to the conversations you had with Deputy Pratt. You said there was a second."

"Yes. Last night—"

"What time?"

"I didn't look at the time, but it was after the group had

broken up to go to bed. I went to the washrooms by the front entrance, and then Hawk and I wandered down to the lake and stood there for a few minutes. It was a pretty evening, bright moon, still lake, not too cold yet. A nice show of northern lights. Very peaceful. By the time we'd turned around and headed back to camp, it must have been ten forty-five or eleven o'clock." Meg put all her chips on telling a believable story. In the end, the abuse accusation was Pratt's word against her own. If she could convince this man she told the truth, she might be able to talk her way out of this. "And that's when we crested the rise and ran into Deputy Pratt, struggling with her dog."

Brogan's eyebrows rose, but he remained silent.

"Ava was misbehaving in some way, and Deputy Pratt had the dog in a stranglehold. Had the leash over her shoulder and was dragging her dog off the ground by the neck so she couldn't breathe. When I saw what was happening, I sprinted toward her, yelling at her to put her dog down. I must have surprised her, because she dropped the leash and Ava fell back to the ground. Luckily, she was okay." She met his eyes and put every bit of truth into her words. "I was going to report her to her supervisor first thing on Monday morning for her abusive behavior toward her dog."

"That's very interesting. Because she reported you to your supervisors for the exact same abuse that night."

"Absolutely untrue. I'd never treat my dog that way. I'd never need to."

"That's not her story."

"Of course, but you can't ask her, to be able to judge for yourself." The moment the words left Meg's mouth, she kicked herself for letting the edge of her temper slip free. She wasn't wrong, but that statement could be taken in entirely the wrong way.

"That's true. Someone has ensured I can't talk to her, to be able to judge if she's telling the truth."

"Or if she was lying."

"Whoever killed her guaranteed her story died with her."

"Whoever killed her ensured every story she had to tell died with her. She was not a favorite around the camp."

"That's for me to decide. Tell me more about finding her body. You said you wanted your dog . . ." He trailed off, and looked down at his notes. "You said his name was Faulk?"

Anger clawed down her spine. He knew her dog's name. He was trying to put her off balance. *Definitely going way out of his way to make sure he isn't showing any favoritism to someone who is essentially a teammate.* "Hawk. Like the raptor."

He made a note in his pad and underlined it twice for emphasis. "Right. Hawk. You wanted Hawk to pick up this new skill."

"Yes."

"And he was so good right out of the gate, he managed to find a body at the bottom of the lake after two sessions."

"You've talked to my team?"

He flipped back one page, skimmed, then back one more. "Yes. Charlie Allen. Then Sal Gallo and Claire Hughes. Their stories all match."

"Because they aren't hiding anything. Hawk picked up on the scent of something we thought would be a dead animal, we had some time to spare, so we let him lead us. It turned out to be Deputy Pratt."

"From what I understand from Hughes, you're in charge of establishing the final search site. You 'read' "— he made air quotes around the word, communicating he thought the reading was an act—"what the dog tells you, decide when he's found the target, and then you call the search. You essentially pick the location."

"No, the dog picks the location."

"But the dog isn't capable of walking on water. You have to get him to the site."

"Yes. And everyone else in the boat could also see and read Hawk's alert signs. Ask Claire. As the trainer, she watched Hawk on the search. She can back me up."

"I asked about that. She did. And then I asked if the dog was so well trained you could order it through hand signals no one else saw to act the way he did."

"You have to be kidding me." The words burst out before Meg could stop them. "Are you trying to craft a conspiracy theory to fit the established facts?"

"You were once a Richmond PD officer, as I understand it. Is that correct?"

"Yes," Meg ground out.

"Then I'm sure you're familiar with how far a guilty individual could go to cover his or her own tracks. I'm just being thorough."

"Your theory is that I killed her, somehow managed to get her body out into the middle of the lake, without my personal or search-and-rescue partners noticing my absence, and then led my dog back to the site the next day to discover the body." She threw both hands out, palms up. "Why on earth would I do that? It's exactly the wrong thing to do if I was trying to hide her death. It makes no sense."

"It does from a certain perspective. The trial would be stopped, and with the current leader dead, your team would be declared the winner. And the only person who saw you mistreat your dog wouldn't be able to tell her story, putting you at risk of losing your dog."

"Except she did tell. A story, that is. Not anything resembling the truth. I'd have had to kill her right away to stop her from telling her superior officer. It doesn't make sense. Any investigator would see that."

"I don't." His voice was flat and stone cold. "And you could have left your tent after everyone was asleep and done what needed doing."

"I don't sleep by myself. My partner, Todd, was in bed with me. There's no way I'd be able to get out of bed without him noticing. He's a firefighter. He's used to waking at all hours of the night for a call. He goes from deep sleep to on his feet in under two seconds. I couldn't leave without him noticing. Ask him."

"I will. I think that's all I have for you for now."

Meg swung out from the bench seat and stood. She'd only taken one step when Brogan's voice sounded behind her.

"I need you to stay in camp. No returning home yet."

She spun around slowly to face him. "Just me?"

"No, everyone. I'll be ensuring all your supervisors know you need to remain here a while longer. They're law enforcement. I know I'll have their full compliance." He twisted on the bench, looked back toward the fire, and stood. "What's this firefighter's name?"

This firefighter. Everything he said seemed designed to get under her skin. "Lieutenant Todd Webb. DC Fire and Emergency Medical Services."

"Thank you." He strode past her, quickly crossing the grass to return to the fire as she followed. "Mr. Webb."

"Yes." Three voices spoke in unison.

It was almost enough to make Meg smile, though she noted Brogan purposely dropped Todd's official rank to gain the upper hand.

"Mr. Todd Webb."

Todd didn't move from his chair, his face set and his eyes hard. "Lieutenant Webb."

Brogan looked like he might be grinding his teeth, and

several seconds ticked by, filled only by the crackle of the fire. "Fine, Lieutenant Webb. I'd like to speak to you for a moment."

"Sure." As he moved past Meg, Todd had enough time to brush her fingers with his and give them a quick squeeze.

She turned to follow them as they walked to the picnic table and sat down. Todd's stiff posture and rock-hard expression told her Brogan was about to hit a brick wall.

Good. Give him hell, Todd.

CHAPTER 17

Collectors: Ordinary soldiers who gather information or capture prisoners while on patrol.

Saturday, October 19, 7:24 PM
Boundary Waters Canoe Area
Superior National Forest, Minnesota

Still seated in front of the fire, Meg's attention was constantly drawn back to where Todd sat, facing Brogan, her partner's expression chiseled from granite. She couldn't hear his answers, but could see them growing more and more clipped.

"Why is this taking so long?" There was unease in Brian's voice. "Todd didn't know Pratt, had no contact with her."

"But might have had motive to kill her for my sake." Meg pulled her collar up a little closer around her throat and burrowed farther into her jacket. The evening had turned cold, and even the fire wasn't enough to warm her. Though she could admit to herself it was more likely stress leaving her chilled, rather than the air temperature. "Wait, Brogan is standing up." She looked sideways at Brian. "You're probably next."

"Terrific." Brian's deadpan told her how much he wasn't looking forward to the conversation.

"You'll be fine. Just tell the truth."

"Uh-huh."

"The truth. If I find out you lied for me, I'm going to call you on it in front of Brogan." When he simply glared at her, she softened her tone. "I'm beyond grateful you'd consider it. But this isn't your fight."

"Yeah, yeah, I got it. Here he comes."

Brogan joined the group, his gaze finding Brian. "Mr. Foster, I'd like to speak with you, please."

Brian stood. "Sure."

As he stepped out of the circle of light, Todd strode across the grass toward them. He didn't spare Brian a glance as he passed, but kept his eyes locked on the group around the fire. Stepping into the glow from the flames, Todd circled around to drop into his chair beside Meg, giving her a dark look.

"What happened?" she asked, her gaze flicking toward Brian to see how he was doing. Brian, always the pro, had a pleasantly neutral look on his face. *Perfect. That kind of cheerful nonchalance will piss off Brogan.* "Was he questioning you because he thought you might be responsible for Pratt's death?"

"No, nothing like that. He thinks I'm a sloppy drunk."

"*Pardon me?*"

"You heard me. He thinks I was so intoxicated last night, I was sleeping off a bender, which allowed you to slip out of the tent to go kill Pratt unnoticed. Well, not in so many words, but that was clearly what he was aiming at. Blowing up your alibi."

"Because you had a couple of beers on vacation? You, a firefighter, who has a job where people's lives depend on you being dead sober most of the time?" Luke sneered. "That's BS."

"That's putting it lightly," Josh chimed in. "You set him straight?"

"Oh yeah." When he turned to Meg, a lot of the anger had drained away, to be replaced by concern. "He's gunning for you."

"Yeah, that was the impression I got as well."

"If he starts the investigation with the suspect already picked out, he may just concentrate on information that strengthens that idea."

"Confirmation bias, as McCord would say."

"Why would he do that?" Ryan, quiet and watchful through much of the evening, now spoke up. Lines of worry for Brian were etched around his eyes and mouth, and his gaze kept darting to where Brian sat on the other side of the campsite.

"I got the impression he's fighting to look like an impartial investigator. Two FBI handlers are involved and he wants to appear squeaky clean. Also, I think he's relatively new. He may be trying to make a big impression on his unit head. But don't worry about Brian. Brogan may be looking for more information from him and confirmation of what I've told him, but I don't think he has Brian in his sights. There's no reason for him to be there."

"No, there isn't. So then . . . who should be?"

"That's really the question, isn't it?" Staring deep into the flames, Meg reviewed the people on-site for the weekend in her head. "I know McCord is incoming, and he's going to be doing as much research as he can on the way, but I want to talk to the other handlers."

"To see who else knew her?" Luke asked. "You think they're going to admit to that?"

"There's a lot of crossover work in search-and-rescue, especially when it comes to mass disasters." She turned to Todd. "You remember Virginia after Hurricane Cole?"

"Yeah, the place was lousy with search teams, most with dogs. They came from all over."

"Right. It's not unlikely at least one of them had come into contact with Pratt on a big search."

"Still not sure you're going to get anyone to 'fess up to that," Luke insisted.

"You may be right. But I'd like to get the lay of the land. And I'd like Brian to help me." She checked on him again, to find the same patient expression still plastered on his face. "He must be driving Brogan to distraction. I've seen that look on his face many times. It's his I'm-just-humoring-you expression."

Josh chuckled. "That should annoy your agent."

"Let me assure you, he's not *my* agent. But when Brian's done, I think he and I should take the dogs and go do a little investigatory work. Find out how everyone else is doing, and who's talked to who. And sometimes the best way to do that isn't to talk to the handlers about themselves, but about what they've seen."

"Oh, I get you." Luke's smile was broad. "No one is going to incriminate themselves, but they might be willing to incriminate the guy in the next tent over."

"That's my thought. It's a small campground, and it's hard for anything to happen no one else sees."

"Do you have any indication anyone heard you arguing with Pratt last night?" Josh asked.

"You've got me there. To the best of my knowledge, no. But I can't be certain what someone else might have said to Brogan."

"You told him about your argument with Pratt?" Todd asked.

"I told him from my perspective how the interaction went down, but he could easily think I've just turned the incident around. Any investigator worth his salt would."

"What about having Craig talk to him? Craig knows how you handle Hawk."

"I've been thinking about that. I want to touch base with Craig tomorrow . . . if he doesn't end up here himself. He said he was looking into flights. I'm not sure what his plans are." Movement on the other side of the clearing caught her attention. "Looks like they're wrapping up. That was relatively quick."

"Brian didn't have as much contact with her, dead or alive," Ryan said.

Not wanting to worry Ryan, Meg stifled the comment that Brogan knew very well that Brian would have come in first if it wasn't for Pratt. Should have come first no matter what, since he'd actually had the best time.

Brian and Brogan stood from the table. Brogan scanned the group before turning back to Brian one last time, and then striding off down the road away from camp. Brian picked up the lantern, returned it to their picnic table, turned it off, and then headed toward the group.

Meg waited until he approached before calling out to him. "Feeling a little burned from having your feet held too close to the fire?"

Brian rolled his eyes. "He's like a dog with a bone. And he had an odd focus on my drinking habits." Todd's cynical bark of laughter drew Brian's gaze. "Did I miss something?"

"Did he want to know how much you drank last night?"

"Actually . . . yes."

"I'm pretty sure he wanted to know if you could have slept through any activity in the camp. Like Meg sneaking out in the middle of the night?"

Now it was Ryan's turn to laugh. "He probably would have slept through *me* getting up to sneak out in the middle of the night. Unless Meg banged the coffeepot like a gong outside our tent on her way out, he'd never wake up. He's a deep sleeper. A couple of glasses of wine wouldn't have made a difference."

"Sad, but true," Brian agreed. "He didn't dwell on that, though. His real push was about the trial, since that was my main exposure to her. I told him about interrupting her and Fief arguing. He made notes about that, and I assume he'll follow up, but he really wanted to know how you and Pratt interacted."

"He seems to think I did it. But rather than sitting by the fire, waiting for the boom to fall, what about you and I and the dogs go do a little reconnaissance?"

Brian rubbed his hands together. "I like the way you think. You have some sneaking around in mind?"

"I'm thinking right out in the open. We're just a couple of outraged handlers pissed at the heavy-handed FBI and worried about the other handlers."

"Who we know work day in and day out to save lives, so who else would have a motive?"

"Exactly. Get them to talk about each other, talk about their training and dive teams. Maybe they haven't worked with Pratt before, but one of their team members has."

"And they may be more likely to talk to us, just one of the guys, so to speak, rather than someone waving a badge in their face. You want to go now?"

"Yeah, I thought that might be the way to do it. People may still be out and about around their fires. We can divide and conquer so it doesn't look like we're together."

"Works for me." Brian stood and gave a low whistle to Lacey, who immediately stood and trotted over. "Come on, Lacey. We're going behind enemy lines."

CHAPTER 18

Ex Turpi Causa Non Oritur Actio: Latin, "from a dishonorable cause an action does not arise." *Ex turpi causa*, also known as the "illegality defense," is a legal doctrine that states that a plaintiff is unable to seek relief or damages for injury incurred during the commission of their own illegal act. As an example, "If two burglars, A and B, agree to open a safe by means of explosives, and A so negligently handles the explosive charge as to injure B, B might find some difficulty in maintaining an action for negligence against A." The reasoning for the illegality defense was proposed by Lord Mansfield CJ in July 1775 when deciding Holman v Johnson, a case involving tea smuggling. The seller sold tea to the defendant in Scotland knowing the tea was to be smuggled from Scotland into England. The seller sued when the defendant did not pay for the tea. Lord Mansfield CJ held that the agreement could be enforced because the seller had himself done nothing unlawful.

Saturday, October 19, 9:08 PM
Boundary Waters Canoe Area
Superior National Forest, Minnesota

Their plan was for Meg to go first, walking through the campgrounds to pass by to the bathrooms on the far side. Brian and Lacey would then follow a few minutes later, putting them into the campgrounds first.

Meg and Hawk started down the road and into the darkness, lit only by the splash of light from her flashlight on the dirt road. The sound of their own campfire—Luke and Josh poking at each other in what, Meg suspected, was an effort to raise everyone's spirits—quickly died away, only to be replaced with the sound of voices in front of her. She broke from the trees into the larger campground.

A quick glance showed two large fires burning, surrounded by multiple chairs, the sound of voices coming from each. But she kept walking, Hawk heeling at her knee, through the campgrounds and then into the trees and toward the front entrance.

She used the bathroom and had just stepped out into the cool night air with Hawk when Mandy Fief came around the corner of the building, her bloodhound at her side. "Deputy Fief!" Meg pressed a hand to her breastbone and laughed. "You startled me." She looked down at her dog, who stood at ease at her side. "Clearly, not Hawk, though."

"If Hawk is like Nova, he knew a full minute ago we were coming." Fief laid a hand on the top of the bloodhound's droopy head. "Though right now, there are enough strangers around here, and enough stress, she's constantly on high alert. And it's Mandy. No need to be so formal."

"One of my colleagues has a bloodhound. Theo is the mellowest dog I've ever met. Sometimes he's a little too mellow, but Scott has a way of gently prodding him along that he responds to." Meg studied Nova, noting her bright, watchful eyes. "Nova seems a lot . . . sharper. Theo often seems like he's teetering on the edge of a coma." She smiled to soften her words, knowing the best way to build a bridge with another handler was through their dog. "And we know what dogs are like—they're so sensitive and they pick up on our stress. At least Hawk does." She let her tone drop, allowing the dark to creep in. "Especially right now."

"Because of Rita."

Familiar use of the first name. "Yes. Have you seen Special Agent Brogan? That man's on the hunt."

Fief rolled her eyes. "Like a terrier after a rat."

"Did he talk to you?"

"I'm not sure 'talk' quite covers it. I'm thinking 'interrogate' describes it better."

Meg circled her with Hawk at her side, pulling them slightly off the path and into the shadows under the pine trees, in case anyone else came through to use the washrooms. She dropped her voice to lend an air of confidence. "I don't know who he talked to before me, but he already knew she and I'd had words after the trial. And then, of course, he wanted to know about how I led the recovery teams to the body."

"But you didn't. Hawk did."

"He's not so sure about that. He thinks that since Hawk wasn't literally in the water, leading the way, I steered the boat to that exact location. And how would I know where the body was . . ." She trailed off.

"If you hadn't put it there yourself," Fief finished. "The man knows nothing about how we work."

"He doesn't, and that's getting in the way of his investigation. He doesn't understand search-and-rescue. We're all about life. This kind of violence, it's not who we are.

He's looking in the wrong place." Meg thought her own justification was pretty simplistic, but the words coming from her own mouth rang true out loud. She needed Fief to trust her, to confide in her, which meant she had to believe Meg didn't think she herself was involved.

Fief stepped in a little closer, her gaze darting around them as if to ensure they were alone. "Where should he be looking?"

"Not at us. But we're not the only ones here. What about the dive teams? Or the pilots? Or the trial organizers? Sure, some of them also have SAR backgrounds, but some likely don't. I just don't know who to point him at. All I know is I wasn't responsible for her death and I have my partner to vouch for my presence last night. So he can keep looking at me all he wants, trying to make his point about favoritism, or he can actually do his job and find the person responsible."

"Favoritism?"

"He's FBI, and a real eager beaver. I think he's trying to prove he can run an impartial investigation when two in his pool of suspects work for the FBI. It's one of the reasons why the Lake County Sheriff's Office is involved. It's FBI jurisdiction, but the sheriff and his deputies could arrive and run point faster, and they can help run the investigation, since they don't have anyone involved. But even with them assisting, he seems . . . fixated."

"On you."

"So far, but it won't stick. Before everyone scatters, I'm trying to see who else might be involved. I mean, if it's not us handlers, and I don't believe it is, then who could it be? My problem is, I don't know the others. Have you worked with any of them before?"

"A couple of the trainers on other SAR deployments, but not any with Rita, so I can't say anything about their working relationship with her. The divers are all totally new to me. And I don't know anything about the SDA organizers, but . . ." She stopped, her brow furrowed as she worried the bottom edge of her jacket between thumb and index finger.

"But what?"

"I overheard an argument last night."

Shock jolted through Meg momentarily before she remembered Brogan already knew about her argument with Pratt. If anyone had actually heard them, it would only be to her advantage.

"Between?"

"Rita and Shay McGraw. They were arguing about a past SDA trial and he accused her of rigging this weekend's trial."

"Really?" That was not the direction she'd thought the conversation was going. "Rigged so she'd win?"

"That was the accusation. From the bits I could piece together, it sounded like they had an agreement to fix each other's trial runs in a competition last year. A you-scratch-my-back-I'll-scratch-yours setup, but it doesn't sound like it worked out for McGraw and his dog."

"But did for Pratt?"

"I think so."

"How did they cheat on it together? Weren't they both in the competition?"

"They were, but at different levels. McGraw was an up-and-comer and was NW2. Pratt and her dog were NW3 Elite."

The National Association of Canine Scent Work ran national trials throughout the year, which were beneficial to competitors trying to nail a win for the various reasons Meg had explained to Brogan. But the trials ran in levels of nose work skills from NW1 to NW3, with truly skilled dogs competing at the NW3 Elite level. That was the level of the professional SAR dogs here this weekend, but all of them had worked their way up the skills ladder.

"That would do it." Meg looked down to take in the two dogs sitting patiently by their handlers. "McGraw wanted to win because he had his eye on a professional SAR career and needed the accreditation of a competition win to catapult to NW3 and beyond as quickly as possible. And Pratt wanted . . . ?"

"Possibly just the glory." Fief's tone was sour. "As you saw, she wasn't a great winner, now imagine how she'd be as a loser."

"Not good, I bet. They were helping out on each other's levels?"

"Sounded like it. You know how those competitions go. They're perennially short staffed, so they're happy to take any volunteers as trial observers or judges. I'm not sure who took what role, but it was clear McGraw thought she'd screwed him, taking the glory for herself and not allowing him a win too."

"That actually says a lot about her personality if they weren't even competing at the same level. I mean, I can see if they were at the same level, she might not want to allow him a win, but what harm to her was there in letting him take the win at NW2? He helped her win, and then she double-crossed him."

"I think that's how it went down. And he accused her of cheating again this weekend."

Brian's words rang in Meg's head: *"What the hell? That's not right. I had 29:07. That would have put us in first place, not second."*

The first trial had too many inconsistencies, from timing to a dog urinating on the course. But if Pratt was set up to win, all the other chaos could be explained through trial observers or a judge—or both—who had a hand in giving Pratt an unfair advantage.

"What was her response?" Meg asked.

"She totally blew him off. Called him paranoid and left him standing there, shouting obscenities at her."

"Threats?"

"No overt threats, but it was clear he thought she was a real bitch."

"Does Brogan know this?"

"I mentioned it to him. He was going after me for the argument we had in front of everyone else, and I wanted him off my ass."

"Good for you. He should know about it. He needs the whole picture. And why would he be on your ass? You had one argument with her because she was in your face. That's hardly a motive for murder."

The hesitation was microscopic, but Meg caught it before Fief smiled her agreement.

"Not even close to a motive." Fief's gaze flicked past her to the washrooms. "We're going to go do our thing. Best of luck to you in dealing with Agent Brogan."

"Thank you. Have a good night."

"You too. Nova, come." They disappeared into the washrooms.

Meg stood for a moment as the door shut behind them. *Something going on there. That is* not *the whole story.*

She had information now on Shay McGraw, and, though Fief had downplayed it, that kind of rage could spur a man to murder. But apparently McGraw wasn't the only one hiding something.

Now to see if the other handlers knew some gossip about Fief, just as she had known about McGraw.

CHAPTER 19

Closed Circle of Suspects: A common element of detective fiction where the list of suspects is limited because of restricted access by outsiders.

Saturday, October 19, 9:39 PM
Boundary Waters Canoe Area
Superior National Forest, Minnesota

Meg scanned the tents and twin fires as she and Hawk stepped into the main campsite. It was difficult to see who was sitting around each fire, but it looked to Meg like almost all the handlers and trainers were there. The only person she could definitively pick out was Brian, who stood at the near fire talking to . . . was that Lamonte Dix? There was an empty chair by that fire, which Meg assumed was Fief's.

Definitely needed to head for the other fire. She didn't want Fief to raise the alarm that Meg was pumping competitors for information. Besides, Brian had it covered.

Meg strolled by the first fire, noting in her peripheral vision that Brian didn't glance her way, though Lacey watched Hawk as he walked past.

She was about twenty-five feet from the fire when someone on the far side waved her hand over her head, and, squinting, Meg realized it was Claire. She waved back and made her way around the fire in Claire's direction, noting the two New York State Police handlers sitting side by side, both with a beer in hand.

Claire stood up and gave Meg a hug. "How are you doing?"

"I'm okay. It's been quite a day."

"It sure has. You out for a walk or can you take a load off for a few minutes?"

"Hawk and I were just down at the washrooms, but I saw the fires on my way past and thought I'd wander by and say good evening to everyone. Make sure everyone was doing okay." She looked out across the fire to Elan and Glenn. "You guys hanging in?"

Elan merely raised his beer, but Glenn nodded and said, "Yeah."

She considered Elan, slouched loosely in his chair. "You're okay? I thought you might have gotten hurt yesterday." At his confused look, she clarified. "I thought you were limping when you left at the end of the trial."

"Ah, that." His smile was sheepish. "I wasn't watching where I was going and tripped over a damned root. Wrenched my back a bit. Nothing serious, just a careless moment."

"I've done that myself. You have your eyes on your dog and the next thing you know you're stumbling over something on the path you didn't see. Glad that's all it was." She scanned the group, seeing the now-familiar faces of trainers she'd seen during the past two mornings. But this was only the dog personnel campsite. The pilots and divers were in the campsite near the beach; she made a mental note to stop there tomorrow.

"Here." Claire dragged over a folding chair, pushed hers a foot to the left, and pulled the new chair in between herself and a middle-aged man with light hair and eyes.

Meg was 90 percent sure he was Brian's trainer. She smiled and extended a hand. "Meg Jennings, FBI Human Scent Evidence Team."

The man shook her hand. "Carl Evans, National Search Dog Alliance."

"Nice to meet you. You guys do great work."

"Thank you. My golden, Baxter, is the brains behind the operation. He's at home, hanging with the family this weekend, while I'm working like a . . ." He chuckled. "Dog."

"You must miss him like crazy. I hate being separated from Hawk."

"Yeah, I do. But we've had a busy summer, and spent two straight weeks at the end of August at the Quincy Fire in northwestern California. He's due for a break. And my wife will spoil him rotten while I'm away. He may not even notice I'm gone. I, on the other hand, feel like my left arm is missing." Evans grinned down at Hawk, who lay between her chair and Claire's. "So that's the famous Hawk, huh? The one who found the body?"

"That's him." She ran a hand along Hawk's back, his fur soft and silky under the glide of her fingertips. Hawk heaved a contented sigh. "He did all right this weekend. Learned a new skill and put it into action successfully. I'm really proud of him."

"As you should be." Claire leaned around Meg to look at Evans. "Carl, this dog is born to do water searches. I hardly had to teach either of them anything. They're totally in sync."

"Yeah, the team I have this weekend is solid too."

"I think you had my partner, Brian Foster. And Lacey."

"Yes, that's them. Great team. Overall, I'd say we have a very good roster this year."

"Possibly too good," Meg muttered.

"Too good? How's that?" Claire asked.

"Special Agent Brogan from the FBI seems to be gunning for me. Thinks it suspicious Hawk found Pratt's body. Thinks I steered us to that location."

"That's BS if I ever heard it," Claire said. "I explained that to him, but I guess I wasn't clear enough. I was there. You were following Hawk's signals. You didn't give him surreptitious hand signals for him to react like that; he did it all on his own. Then you read his alert signs and narrowed the search field. You didn't take him somewhere he didn't want to go." Claire sat back in her chair and pulled a covered travel mug from the drink holder in the arm. "If Brogan doubts my word that was an entirely dog-led search, I'll be happy to go over it with him again and set him straight. Send him here tomorrow if he's pestering you."

Meg laid a hand on Claire's forearm, and squeezed. "Thank you, really. You don't have to do that, so I appreciate that you want to."

"I'm happy to, honest."

Meg looked across the open flames to the troopers on the far side. "Brogan seems to have a head of steam for the handlers and doesn't understand how we tick. That saving lives is in our blood. Did he give you guys a hard time?"

"He tried, but we didn't have much to give him," said Elan.

"You didn't know Pratt? Weren't on any deployments with her?"

Elan shook his head. "I never met her."

"Even if we had, we were together in the tent that night," Glenn said. "Brogan was pushing for alibis. A couple of people are on their own, like Pratt, but most of us are paired up."

"Or more," Claire said, "if we don't have our dogs with us."

Glenn pointed at Claire with the mouth of his beer bottle. "That too. We weren't looking at the time, but we figure we were up until two or two fifteen, just shooting the shit."

Elan nodded in agreement with a sheepish smile. "Kinda lost track of time. Damon and I, we work in the same force, but not in the same troop. So we like to catch up when we get together and that was the first time in . . . what was it . . . six months?"

"More like eight," Glenn corrected.

"Eight months. So we talked for a while, then hit the hay for this morning's training."

"If you were up that late, did you hear any movement in the campsite?"

Elan looked over to where Pratt's tent stood—just a shadow in the dim play of firelight. "No. But if she was in and out of her tent, it would be too far away to hear from here. Same for a lot of the other handlers. We're that tent there." He indicated a four-person red tent situated on the far side from Pratt's tent, right at the border of the trees.

"You could ask Deputy Fief," Glenn suggested. "Her tent is closer. And considering their relationship, she'd be more likely to keep tabs on Pratt."

The hair on the back of Meg's neck prickled upright, but she carefully kept her face blank and her voice light. "Relationship?"

Glenn snorted a laugh. "Sorry, not what I was implying. Fief was Pratt's mentor."

"Really?" Caught off guard, Meg couldn't keep the surprise out of her tone.

Even though she used her first name, Fief made it sound like Pratt wasn't that familiar to her, that she was just someone she clashed with at a competition. But is this actually a matter of the student having outshone the master?

"Yeah. Fief taught Pratt the search-and-rescue ropes, nose work skills, and helped her get her job in Wyoming."

"How do you know this?"

"Talking to her last night. She was *pissed* about Pratt's attitude after the first trial. Fief thought she deserved a lot more respect than she got."

"And maybe didn't like the fact that Pratt was lording her first-place finish over her when she came in last."

Evans winced. "Ouch."

"I didn't know they knew each other," Meg said. "Puts a different spin on the argument we interrupted. I thought it was two competitors sniping at each other, but keeping their history in mind, it was a lot nastier than I thought."

"It must be hard to feel like you're past your prime and the one you trained is now the hotshot."

"And you and your dog may be on the way out." Glenn shook his head sadly. "That has to suck. No one wants to feel irrelevant."

"As working handlers, we all know we'll hit that moment," Claire pointed out. "Our dogs will get older, or will get injured. Or the physical stresses of the job will become too much for us as handlers. It's a physical job, and the end of active SAR comes for all of us. We know it's coming, but that doesn't mean it'll be easy when it's time."

"No, it doesn't." Meg noticed Brian and Lacey were walking away from the group and back toward camp, and turned the conversation to the water-search training, asking the New York State Police handlers how their searches had gone.

Finally she made a show of checking her fitness tracker. "Look at the time. I'd better get back to my own fire or my group is going to wonder what happened to me." Meg stood and called her dog. "I hope you all have a good night. See you in the morning."

There was a chorus of "good night," and with a last wave, she and Hawk headed along the edge of the forest and back to the road.

By the time they got to their own fire, Brian was seated

beside Ryan, a glass of wine in hand. Seeing her approach, he threw her a wave. "Come, sit. I have dirt."

"Good. Me too." She reclaimed her rocking chair as Hawk lay down beside Lacey.

"Here." Todd pulled a can from the cooler and passed it to Meg. "You could probably use something to relax after the day you've had."

"And then some. Thanks. Brian, what did you learn?"

"Some good stuff. Dix and McGraw were both at the fire at first, and Fief joined us later. Dix didn't have much to offer. He says he didn't know Pratt, had never seen her before yesterday. But McGraw had a couple of interesting points. He'd been in a competition with Pratt last year, where there were rumors of cheating. He says it was Pratt, but she was never caught."

"Did he say how he knew this?"

"Rumor mill. He didn't have any definitive proof about it, but when things were screwy yesterday, he says he started nosing around."

"That's very interesting, because Fief says she heard Pratt and McGraw arguing last night. McGraw accused Pratt of cheating this weekend, but that was based on his previous experience where they had agreed to cheat to help each other in a competition, except she double-crossed him. She got her win, and he didn't."

"Funny. He left out that part of the story."

"I bet he did."

"And Fief wasn't there yet to contradict him. He did suggest Pratt was cheating again to make sure she won this competition."

A memory tickled Meg's brain. "Brian, remember the weird point Pratt made before the competition about being first?"

Brian laughed. "Sure I do. It *was* weird."

"What did she say?" Todd asked.

"Basically, that in going first, other competitors could simply follow the scents of her and her dog, rather than the hide, straight to the win."

"Did she have a point?"

"No. For starters, arrogance alert, she was implying she was going to find the hide and everyone else was riding her coattails. But the dogs are following a specific scent, not the random scents of every dog and handler who've gone before, so it made no sense."

"But do you see what she did there?" Meg asked. "She was setting the ground work to make her win look harder than it was. Because she already knew she was going to win."

"Doesn't this lend credence to what you suggested last night about someone tampering with the course?" Ryan asked.

"That was my thought," Brian said. "But then who's she cheating with? The judge? The trial observers?"

"All of the above?" Josh suggested.

"Could be." Meg took a sip of her drink and stared thoughtfully into the dancing flames. "Brian's time was off, and then there's our theory about the urine contamination of the course. It couldn't have been any of the other competitors, but given the time gap between competitors, there was time for someone else to quickly pass through, especially if it was between Dix and Glenn."

"And since they only would have had so much urine, they could only cover so much area," Brian said. "You said Hawk seemed confused, whereas Elan's dog peed on the course. You may have skimmed the area, while he went right through it."

"That would make sense. And then for the trial time, all that's needed is to have the two trial observers who are noting the time either being in contact or changing the time by an agreed-upon amount. Then add in a judge who upholds the observers' results no matter what they are. Note that they only tinkered with your time because you were getting too close to the lead time."

"If they'd messed with too many people, it would look like a setup," Todd pointed out.

"Good point." Brian toasted him with his wineglass. "My time would have put me in first, so they bumped me back to second. You were far enough back they didn't touch you. And they used the urine after Pratt to slow everyone else down."

"It sounds like you and Lacey missed it altogether. No distraction, better time. Sounds like you gave her a run for her money. So much so, you needed to be bumped back."

Brian rubbed a hand through Lacey's thick fur, and her head rose to gaze up at him. "That's my Lacey-girl. She's got skills."

"Yes, she does. So that theory gives us a line to tug. Did someone think they were going to be exposed, or did she threaten to expose them over the cheating?"

"Would that really be motive for murder?" Luke asked. "It seems a little over-the-top."

"Being exposed as a cheater would drum you out of the search-and-rescue and dog trials community, and make your work with law enforcement suspect. For many people, this is their life. More than that, it's their identity. Losing that identity would be devastating. It might seem like nothing to you, but to someone that hard-core in the community, it could be motive." Meg looked at Brian for agreement.

"Yeah, absolutely. We need to look into it more. What did you learn?"

Meg took them through her conversations so the group was up to speed.

"Let me get this straight," Brian said. "We have an aging mentor who's being shown up by her student, a past trial cheat who was frozen out from his win, potentially a cheating trial judge and multiple cheating trial observers, a handler who's been accused of animal abuse, and six other handlers who've been cheated out of a competition win." He ticked each possibility off on his fingers. "It could be practically anyone."

"Except you and me. But I feel like we're stuck in an English manor mystery with a dozen suspects who could all be murderers," Meg said.

"With possibly more that you haven't identified yet," said Todd. "And that's before McCord arrives. Then we'll see what he turns up."

"On that note, I've had it for the day. I'm going to turn in. You too?"

"Yeah. Who knows when he'll show up tomorrow, so we should get up early to be ready for him."

Meg pushed out of her chair to stand. "Then we'll see if we can finally figure out what happened here this weekend."

CHAPTER 20

Swimmer: A Coast Guard member who enters the water to save a potential drowning victim.

Sunday, October 20, 5:43 AM
Boundary Waters Canoe Area
Superior National Forest, Minnesota

Meg's satellite phone exploded into sound and light only inches from her head. She'd left it on top of her duffel bag beside the inflatable mattress. She groped for it and hit the talk button with her eyes only open to slits. "'Lo."

"Good morning, sunshine."

"McCord." She cracked one eye open to take in the darkness of the tent. "What time is it?"

"Coming up on a quarter to six."

"Feels like it too." She flopped down on her pillow. Beside their mattress, Hawk stirred in his bed.

Todd's arm came around her, pulling her closer and tipping his head against hers so his mouth was only inches from the phone. "Why so early? We didn't expect you until daylight."

"Good morning to you too. If you're us, it's still yesterday."

That jolted Meg a little more awake. "Us?"

"Morning, Meg." A different voice this time.

"Craig?"

"Yes, ma'am."

Now she was awake. "Where are you two?"

"That's why I'm calling," McCord said. "We're coming up on your campground, but I have no idea where you are."

"You're here?"

"Didn't I just say so?"

"It's too early to be cute, McCord."

"Too late."

"McCord . . ." It came out as a growl.

McCord chuckled. "You really are a bear in the morning, aren't you? Just like Cara."

"This can't surprise you. How did you link up with Craig?"

"When you called me, you told me he was thinking of coming out. So I called him, told him I was going to fly out to help, and he said he'd arrange flights for both of us. We were in the air by shortly after seven forty-five and landed in Minneapolis at a quarter to one this morning. He'd arranged for a car rental from the twenty-four-hour place at the airport and we drove north."

"You must be exhausted."

"We've taken turns catnapping while the other drives. But I wouldn't say no to coffee if you have it."

Todd snagged the phone from her grasp, but kept it angled so she could hear both sides of the conversation. "We have coffee. How far out are you?"

"According to the map app, about ten minutes."

"At the front entrance, there's a huge wooden sign announcing the campsite and outlining the rules. I'll meet you there on foot in ten and I'll bring you into our campsite. We're at the far end of one of the campgrounds, so getting in your car will be easier than explaining it to you when you'd be searching in the dark."

"Thanks. Appreciate that."

"You came all this way to help us. It's the least I can do. I'll have Meg's sat phone. Call me if you get lost."

"Done. See you in ten." And McCord was gone.

The phone went black, leaving them in the stillness of just before dawn.

Meg struggled up to sitting and laid a hand on Todd's chest. "Thank you."

"For going to meet them? We aren't going to be able to hide new faces, but we don't want to make a big deal of them being here, attracting attention. The quieter they come in, the better."

"No, that's not it. I mean, yes, it is, but that's not what I meant. You thanked him for coming out to help us. Not just me. *Us.*"

The Coleman lantern on the camp table flared into brilliance, and then he rolled back to her. "Because it *is* us. Anything that affects you or Hawk affects me, and vice versa." Todd sat up, his gaze falling on the dog on the far side of the tent. "It would kill me if they took Hawk away. Not the way it would you, but, in a way, he's my dog now too." His slight smile fell away as he looked back at her. "Someone is messing with our family. We'll do what's needed to protect it." He ran a hand down her arm. "And now, if I don't get moving, we'll have McCord honking at the front entrance, waking everyone for miles."

"Good thing for us, it sounds like Craig is driving." She threw back her side of the sleeping bag, shivering as cold air washed over her. "I'll get dressed and go wake up Brian. Will we be able to find the stuff for coffee?"

"Maybe, but just get Josh up. He'll do it. Tell him guests are incoming and I told him to get his ass out of bed." He flashed a smile rife with the joy of one sibling picking on another. "He can take it up with me later."

They left the tent three minutes later, Hawk trailing behind Meg as she made a beeline for Brian's tent, while Todd started down the road toward the main entrance, their largest flashlight lighting his way. Meg had one of their smaller flashlights, its light bobbing in front of her as she walked toward Brian's tent.

If she'd been groggy only minutes before, the cold snapped her awake quickly.

She stopped outside Brian's tent flap. "Brian. Brian, it's Meg. I need you to wake up."

There was rustling inside, then Ryan's voice. "Meg?"

"I'm sorry, Ryan, I need Brian."

"Hang on."

There was about ten seconds of rustling and low murmurs inside the tent before Brian's husky voice called her name.

"Brian, sorry to wake you so early."

"What's wrong? And before you answer, come in here. This is an idiotic way to have a conversation. Especially when I'm not awake."

She unzipped the flap, Hawk darting through the gap as soon as he could slip through. She followed him, once the separation was big enough, keeping the light on the ground and out of Brian's and Ryan's eyes. "You need to get up. Craig and McCord are on their way."

"Getting here when? What time is it?"

"It's not yet six, but they're only about ten minutes out. They've been driving all night."

That got Brian vertical and flailing for the lantern. He eased the light up gradually until the tent was dimly illuminated. "Hey, Hawk, make yourself at home."

Even as tired as she was, the sight of Hawk squeezing

onto the dog bed beside Lacey gave her a chuckle. "He just loves Lacey."

"She doesn't seem to mind sharing with him. You said they're ten minutes out?"

"Yes. Todd is walking down to the main entrance to meet them and bring them in. McCord has requested coffee."

"At this hour of the morning, I want it too."

"That's next on my list. Todd told me to go get Josh up."

"Might as well. Camp is about to get animated. Good thing we're separated from everyone else. Okay, we're up. We'll get dressed and meet you outside in a few minutes." He looked over at the dogs. "Just leave Hawk here. I'll bring them out together in a few."

Five minutes later, Meg sat in front of the growing fire Luke was feeding. She held her cold hands out to the flames and sighed. "Again, I'm sorry to drag you guys out of bed at this hour."

Josh waved it away with a casual flick of his hand. "We're firefighters. We're used to bouncing out of bed fully awake at a moment's notice at any time of night."

"Todd's the same. Professional hazard, I guess. But this is supposed to be your vacation."

"We can take a nap later if we need one. We've also got the rest of the week off, so we can catch up then." Josh slid the coffeepot onto the grate over the flames. "But we may not need to nap today, because I made the coffee extra perky."

"That's music to my ears." Preceded by the dogs, Brian and Ryan came into the circle of light thrown by the campfire. "Coffee and heat. The two things I want most right now." The crunch of tires drew his attention toward the roadway, where lights flashed through the trees. "Here they come."

A dark sedan pulled into the campsite, then pulled off

the road to park near Meg and Todd's tent. The back door opened and Todd climbed out, then leaned in, said something to the occupants of the vehicles, reached in farther, pulled out a duffel bag, and headed over to their tent. He dropped the duffel at the tent flap and then returned to the car.

Brian leaned in close, laughter in his eyes. "There goes your romantic weekend. Looks like you're rooming with McCord."

"You think that's funny, but consider this. If I get McCord, that means you get Craig." She smiled at the stark shock on his face and patted his arm. "There goes *your* romantic weekend."

"We never should have come."

"I think that's more than clear by this point." She stood, stepping away from the warmth of the fire to greet the approaching men.

They both looked exhausted. McCord, tall and blond, his usually sharp blue eyes dull with fatigue behind his wire-rimmed glasses, threw her a smile with a raised hand. "Fancy meeting you here."

"Smart-ass." But she pulled him into a hug. "Thank you. This weekend just keeps getting worse, and if anything else goes wrong—"

"It won't." McCord pulled back, holding her by her upper arms. "The cavalry's here now. And Cara sends her love. And says to call her the moment you have a chance."

"I will."

"And for the love of God, can someone pour me a coffee?"

"Coming up!" Josh called from the other side of the fire. "I'm good, but not that good. Give it ten to perk." He rounded the fire, holding out his hand. "Josh Webb."

"Clay McCord." The men shook hands. "I've heard about you and your brother." His eyes skimmed the group, falling on Luke. "Which, by process of elimination, has to be you. Granted, I'd be able to pick you out of a lineup just from your face."

"The genes are strong in this family," Luke said with a grin and a handshake.

Meg looked to where Craig stood just outside of the circle of chairs, looking strangely reluctant to come any farther. Shorter than McCord, with a stocky frame and salt-and-pepper hair, exhaustion carved deeper lines into his already-craggy face. "Craig. I don't know what to say. I mean, thank you, but you came all this way. You helped McCord get here too. A thank-you doesn't seem like nearly enough. But, come, sit down. You look like you could sleep on your feet."

With a tired smile, Craig stepped into the circle of light, giving her arm a squeeze. "Close to it, and I won't say no to coffee, once it's ready."

"Hey, who has the nice rocking chair?"

Meg looked over to where McCord was comfortably ensconced in her chair, his booted feet extended toward the fire, rocking gently back and forth. "That's mine."

"I like it."

"Me too. But you've come so far, the least a girl can offer is her rocker."

"Make it a rocker and a cup of coffee, and my research notes are yours."

"Done. But seriously, you have notes already?"

"Of course I do. Did you think I was going to spend time sitting in the airport and then on the plane doing nothing?"

"Actually, when you put it that way, it would be really unlike you."

"It would." He leaned back in the chair, linking his fingers over his belly, and tipped his face up to the sky. "Now that's worth the travel time. You never see stars like this at home."

Luke added another log to the fire. "They're there, just hidden behind the light pollution."

"Wait until tonight when the fire is out and the sun isn't just below the horizon," Todd added. "You think there are a lot of stars now, that will blow your mind."

"I wish Cara was here to see it."

"I wish this was a leisure trip so she could be with us to see it," Meg said.

"Next time. We should plan a trip out to a place like this. The dogs would love it. Cody especially. He could burn off some of that boundless energy in the lake."

"While you sit on the shore in a chair with your beer, lobbing tennis balls into the water."

"Perfect all around."

Craig, who had yet to sit down despite Meg's invitation, shuffled his feet. "Meg, before we get started, can I grab you for a minute?"

A chill of foreboding ran down Meg's spine. There was more in Craig's expression than just exhaustion, and that realization made her stomach pitch. "Craig? What's going on?"

"I want a quick word with you."

Meg and Brian exchanged uneasy glances, and Brian stepped partly in front of Meg as if to shield her. "Craig, what are you doing?"

Exhaustion disappeared behind the temper rising in Craig's eyes. "Brian, you're not helping. Meg, a word?"

All movement around the campfire ceased as all three Webb brothers picked up on the tension. Todd dropped the armload of firewood he was carrying and came to stand beside Meg. "What's going on?"

"My question precisely." Meg pushed Brian one step to

the right, but gave his arm a squeeze of thanks before she let go. "Whatever it is, you can say it here. I don't need privacy. Everyone is going to know within minutes anyway. Unless this is confidential, need-to-know FBI intel."

"It's not."

"Then just say it."

Craig looked like he was grinding his teeth, but then he threw up his hands, sent Brian a dark glare, and turned back to Meg. "You've been suspended from the team pending this investigation. I need your FBI identification. And your sidearm, once you're back in DC."

Craig's words hit Meg like a slap, the blow exploding out of nowhere, the aftermath leaving her ice-cold, her head spinning.

Off the team. No more working with Brian. Or Lauren. Or Scott. And Hawk not able to work with Lacey anymore.

Off the team. No more purpose, or camaraderie, or the thrill of the save. No more common goal with my dog.

Off the team . . .

She couldn't do any more than stare at Craig, but Brian still had his voice.

"What the hell, Craig? What are you thinking?" When Ryan grabbed his arm in an effort to calm him, Brian yanked it from his husband's grasp and held up a hand to stop him. "How could you do this?"

"It's not my decision. Peters made the call."

"Goddamn Peters—"

"He made the call he had to make." Craig's voice was rising, anger building in his tone. "He had a handler who was the last person to see the murder victim alive—"

"Not remotely true," Brian snarled. "The person who killed Pratt was the last person to see her alive."

"And then led authorities straight to the body," Craig continued, speaking over Brian. "You know how that looks."

"Only to someone who has no idea how the dogs work. There were knowledgeable witnesses inside that boat who watched Hawk lead them to the body, not Meg."

"Do you think I don't know that?" Craig was almost at a roar.

"Right now, I'm not so sure." Brian was close to matching his volume, their voices echoing in the quiet.

"Stop it, both of you." Meg's shaky words were soft, but cut through the rage like a knife.

Both men turned to stare at her.

"Meg."

She turned her head to find Todd beside her, and only then felt the arm he already had around her waist, supporting her. She had to blink a few times to bring his face into focus. "I'm okay."

"You're not even close to okay. But you will be. We're all here with you, and this isn't going to stick. Take a breath."

She did as he suggested, and took another as she gripped his hand, where it curled over her hip. Then she straightened her spine and looked past Brian to Craig. "This comes from Peters. But you agree with it?"

"God, no. I argued it was overkill. But you work for the FBI, and the FBI means structure and Peters is our director. And you know what? I don't think he's particularly happy about it either, but what's he going to do? You're the main suspect."

"That's bullshit," spat Luke.

Craig momentarily glanced in surprise at the stranger, kneeling by the fire, who inserted himself into their argument, but then turned his attention to Meg. "For now, you're the main suspect. I came here with McCord to get you out of this. You belong on the team, with us. But we have to do this right, so there's no hint of favoritism, no gray areas, no questions. And we have to do this making sure that charge of abuse gets expunged too." He rubbed the heel of his hand over his forehead like something was inside his skull, pounding to get out. "It needs to be clean. That's the best way to protect both you and Hawk. And then we can go home and forget this godforsaken weekend ever happened."

"I can help."

For the first time, Meg realized McCord was out of his chair and had closed ranks on her other side.

"That's why I'm here," McCord continued, laying his hand on her shoulder, giving it a squeeze. "Meg, it's why Craig brought me. I would have gotten here, but Craig got me here faster, and arranged for everything so I could spend my time digging through Rita Pratt's past. We can work together, and we can do this. For now, give up your connection to the FBI. It's only temporary. Play by the rules and don't rock the boat. It will allow us to work faster and quieter. We don't want any FBI agents looking at us right now. Once we have more information, we'll go to them."

"Brogan's a piece of work," Brian spat. "He's absolutely gunning for Meg. Going overboard in trying to look impartial."

"Brogan is the agent from the field office?"

"Yeah."

"Good to know. For now, if he asks, tell him I'm your brother-in-law." When Meg stared, McCord simply shrugged. "Close enough, and if he finds out I'm with the *Post*, he'll try to get in my way. Better he thinks I'm family and here for moral support. Or that I just came to fish."

Meg nodded, not trusting her voice. Letting go of Todd's hand, she unzipped the hidden pocket in the waist-band of her yoga pants at the small of her back and slipped out the flip case she carried, not daring to leave it in the tent, where it could be stolen in her absence. It was warm from lying next to her skin, like it was a part of her. Pulling away from Todd, she crossed to Craig and extended her identification.

Behind her, she heard Brian mutter something under his breath; she couldn't hear his words, but the tone conveyed his fury.

Craig took her flip case and slipped it into his pocket. "Meg, I'm truly sorry. If I didn't have to do this . . ."

The pain in his eyes answered any other questions she might have had. "Just hold on to that for me, for now. I want it back."

"I want you to have it back."

"Good."

She turned to the group. "Now what?"

"Coffee," said McCord. "Then let's get to work."

CHAPTER 21

Coming in Hot: Army jargon referring to aircraft coming in with guns blazing, or "locked and loaded."

Sunday, October 20, 6:03 AM
Boundary Waters Canoe Area
Superior National Forest, Minnesota

McCord looked around the campsite. "Where's my laptop bag?"

"Hang on, it's with your duffel by our tent. I'll get it." Todd jogged off into the darkness.

"Come sit with me." McCord waved Meg over and pointed to the chair beside him.

"One second." Meg stepped into the gap between Craig and Brian, who stood stiff, their faces averted. "If we're going to do this, figure out what happened and reinstate me, I need my guys on board. Brian, that means you not sniping at Craig for doing his job when he got jammed into a corner."

Brian made a noncommittal noise in the back of his throat.

"And, Craig, that means you not being angry with Brian for standing up for me. We're used to being 'one for

all, and all for one,' so our gut reaction is to always protect each other. But 'all for one' should include you too."
She looked from one to the other. "I need you both. You're
angry with the situation, not each other. We're all on the
same side. The side of the team." She pasted on a bright
smile and raised the pitch of her voice by several tones.
"And there's no 'I' in team, am I right?"

Brian gave her a flat look. "You're just being annoying
now, is that the idea?"

"Will it make you put away your inner guard dog?
Though I appreciate that he came out to play for a few
minutes."

Brian stared at her for a moment and then blew out a
long breath before sticking out a hand to Craig. "I'm
sorry for losing my temper. This whole weekend has been
a clusterfuck from the moment it started. We're a bit
stressed."

Craig grasped his hand. "I'm sorry too. Yeah, this isn't
the weekend we hoped for, in so many ways. Let's fix it."

"Agreed."

"Come on, then," Meg invited. "Let's find out what
magic McCord has managed."

"No pressure at all," McCord said, where he sat with
his laptop open on his thighs as it booted up. "Now come
back here."

"Coming." Meg returned Todd's smile as she sat down
beside McCord, where he repeatedly stretched his hands
out, fingers spread wide, before curling them into tight
fists, then stretching them out again. She studied him for a
couple of repetitions. "Hands stiff?"

McCord looked up to meet her gaze with a smile. "Nope,
probably because I do this so often. A dozen reps every
hour I'm awake. Keeps them loose and limber, so they
never stiffen up on me."

A vision of McCord at the end of August's blood diamond case flashed through Meg's mind. McCord, beaten to within an inch of his life, lying in the hospital bed, his face nearly unrecognizable from the bruising and broken nose, with both hands splinted after a mobster had tried to extract information by breaking them, one bone at a time. Also, with the visual memory, a shadow of the terror she'd felt seeing him unmoving—*dead?*—echoed through her. Once his survival was assured, they'd feared he might never regain full use of his hands, but McCord had worked hard, and Todd had worked alongside him and his physiotherapist once the bones had knit, guiding McCord through those early workouts, helping him recover first partial motion, and then full range.

Meg studied McCord's profile. "You know, if it wasn't for that slight bend in your nose, no one would ever know they tried to beat the stuffing out of you."

"War wound." He waggled his eyebrows at her. "Cara says it's sexy. And, as Cara likes to tell me, she's rarely wrong."

"It's a cross we women have to bear. Now, can someone get this man a cup of coffee, if it's ready?"

Luke held up an index finger. "Just ready now. How do you take it, McCord?"

"I'm a newspaper man. We all drink it black, like ink." McCord grinned slyly.

Meg rolled her eyes. "Don't quit your day job."

"What? It's funny. Get it, like newspaper ink?"

Meg patted his arm. "I got it. Someone get this man his coffee before he keeps cracking wise."

"Right here." Luke poured a steaming cup from the pot and passed it to McCord before looking at Craig. "Uh . . . sorry to have jumped into your argument. I'm Luke Webb, Todd's brother." He offered his hand.

Craig shook. "I guess I'd want my brother to defend my partner if her honor was in question."

"Coffee?"

"God, yes. Black. I hope it's strong."

"Oh yeah, extra strong this morning. Knew you guys would need it."

Luke made sure everyone had a coffee and then settled into his own seat.

"Okay, McCord." Meg studied him over her cup as he opened files on his laptop. "What do we know?"

"Is there anything you need to update me on?" He cocked an eyebrow as he looked over at her. "I know you." He pointed at Brian. "And you. The two of you don't sit still and let a case develop on its own. Am *I* out of the loop on anything?"

"As a matter of fact, yes."

"Knew it. Update me and I'll see if any of what you know clicks with what I have."

As McCord made notes, Meg and Brian took McCord and Craig through what they'd learned in their conversations. "And that leaves us with two groups of people to talk to today," Meg finished. "The pilots and the divers, though I doubt they'd have much of a stake in this."

"Agreed," said Brian. "There was contact between Pratt and the support workers, but not much; only her own team, as far as we know. Unless she knew someone from before and made quite an impression, I just don't see that as being particularly relevant."

"I suspect you're right. Which leaves us with a group that could be extremely relevant—the trial judge and the observers."

McCord paged through one of his documents. "You said Isaac Thatcher is the judge. And Dean and Shannon are the trial observers, with one unnamed male observer as well?"

"Yes. We don't know last names, but we can find out."

"Someone will find out. I'm not sure it's a good idea if it's you or Brian. Or any other competitor. And I also have a Teresa Bowfin. That's correct?"

"Yes. She's from SDA and is organizing the weekend."

"SDA is Search Dogs of America."

"Yes."

"I have the e-mail you forwarded me with all the participants' names and affiliations, as well as the team makeup. That's really helpful."

"Good. Have you been able to connect any of them?"

"Patience. Let me work through what I have so far, so we're on the same page. I'm only starting to dive into potential connections. It's a lot of names." He tipped back his coffee cup, draining it. "Can someone hit me again?"

"You bet." Josh grabbed McCord's mug and headed for the coffeepot.

"So, using as many different areas of public information as I could find, I tracked Pratt as far back as I could. Born and raised in Horse Creek, Wyoming, she attended Grand Canyon University in Phoenix, Arizona, where she got a degree in public safety administration."

"A degree like that says she had her eye on law enforcement from the beginning," said Craig.

Meg nodded. "That's how I see it too."

"And it looks like she always had the dog connection, because she supplemented her way through college working as a groomer. Then when she graduated, she went home to Wyoming and joined the Wyoming K-9 Search and Rescue. At the time, she had a German shepherd named Doogie. That group was where she got her real SAR training."

"Was that where she met Mandy Fief?" Brian asked.

"Just looking into that now. Give me . . . one . . . second."

"Where are you looking?" Meg leaned over to look at his screen. "More than that, how are you looking?"

"Satellite Internet. You can thank the *Washington Post* for that little helper. And I'm looking at LinkedIn."

"Seriously?"

He gave her a pointed look that clearly said, *You doubt me?* "Seriously. It's a platform frequented by professionals who want to look good by listing their every accomplishment, complete with time frames. It's a good place to start and then you narrow in on specific information."

Meg caught a quick flash of Fief's face at the top of the screen before McCord scrolled down her profile page.

"Bingo. She lists her volunteer work with the Wyoming K-9 Search and Rescue. And Pratt overlapped during the same time period. So the information they worked together, trained together, isn't disproven by this. Give me a little time and I'll get more than overlapping calendar dates. Now, Pratt joined the Laramie County Sheriff's Office four years ago, originally just as a regular officer. Two years ago, I have her moving to the K-9 unit. Media reports from the time list a dog as being purchased by the sheriff's office and put into her care. Considering when that was, if Doogie was still around at that point, he may have been too old for professional SAR activities."

"But she'd have the experience, so pairing her with a fully trained animal makes sense," Brian said. "However, if an abuse complaint was lodged against her, the department should have taken the dog out of her care while it investigated, because the dog was their property. And she'd likely have lost her job and the dog, if the claims were substantiated."

"Considering how she was treating Ava," Meg said, "I highly doubt it was her first time abusing her."

"Not a chance," Brian agreed. "Think of how twitchy Ava was when we first saw her before Friday's trial. I thought at the time she was uneasy because of the sheer number of dogs around her, but now I don't think that was it at all. She was scared of Pratt."

"Totally agree."

"She was one of three dogs," McCord continued. "All of them were cross-trained for apprehension—"

"Small unit, that's not a surprise," Brian interjected.

"One dog for narcotics, one for explosives, and Ava was tracking and search-and-rescue," McCord continued. "At least in the public sphere, I couldn't find any mention of disciplinary complaints, but I imagine departments keep that kind of thing close to the vest." He looked at Craig for confirmation.

"Correct."

"As far as media stories, there was the usual highlighting Deputy Pratt. School appearances, some apprehensions, lost children. She and Ava were sent out as support often inside the state, mostly to counties in the west for lost hikers, and often in the winter for avalanches. Snowmobilers and backcountry skiers seem to get into the wrong place at the wrong time, but Pratt and Ava were known to have a good success rate."

"No known crossovers with any of the handlers or trainers in those events?" Todd asked.

"Not as far as I know at this point, but I'm still working on it. From what you've said, only McGraw and Fief had known contact with her, but I want to confirm everyone else. While with the sheriff's office, she was deployed out of state for significant events. The sheriff's office's social media channels were a gold mine there. Tulsa, Oklahoma, in March 2016 after the tornado ripped through. Texas in 2017 following Hurricane Harvey, and then to Florida in 2018 after Hurricane Michael."

"It's possible any of the dog teams here could have been at those sites," Todd said. "Considering what we saw after Hurricane Cole."

"No one is admitting to it, if they were there," Meg said. "But, of course, being there doesn't mean contact with any specific team. Many of us have had firsthand experience with the chaos of a natural disaster like that. With the teams spread out geographically, a bunch of them could be in the city at the same time and never run into each other."

"Possibly, but I'm not going to take anyone's word for it." McCord scrolled farther down his document. "The one thing about those events is that groups document them pictorially to publicize fund-raising efforts, et cetera. I'm only starting to look there. But the be-all and end-all is Deputy Pratt doesn't seem to have done anything that stands out officially." He looked up at Craig. "As part of the investigation, will the FBI be looking for copies of her HR records with the sheriff's office?"

"If Brogan hasn't already made contact about it, I'll make sure both he and Sheriff Olsen are reminded to. That will speak to her personality in a more official manner. We know contestants found her abrasive and that led to some clashes, but what was she like on the job?"

" 'Abrasive' is one way of putting it," Meg said. "But take it from a woman who came up through male-dominated police ranks. Chances are good that kind of competitive personality was alive and well throughout her training. In many ways, it might have been the only way she made it through training, depending on what her cohort was like."

"Meaning it was self-defense?" Ryan asked.

"To an extent. Just like men, some women are naturally aggressive. And some dial it up because they think it's how the men will respect them. Or, just as important, leave them alone because they'll think they're a pain in the ass and not sexual-conquest material. A lot of women drop that act once they find their footing with their colleagues, but not everyone. You're right, McCord, the HR records could be enlightening."

"Yup. From a personal perspective, with research done late at night and no one to call at that hour, all I can tell you from her social media feeds is she's single. Both parents are deceased and she's survived by a brother. But I'd be surprised if the person responsible for her death is part of her life in Wyoming."

"I agree," said Craig. "Someone didn't follow her this distance and risk being seen as out of place to then kill her and toss her in the lake, when it could have been done with far better cover closer to home. This site is entirely too isolated for that."

"Not to mention crawling with law enforcement, or law enforcement adjacent types," Brian pointed out. "And we're a suspicious lot. Right now, we're expecting strangers with badges, but if someone had wandered in on Friday looking like Joe Camper, they'd have been questioned. These are valuable animals, and no one would risk some-one just strolling in to possibly mess with the dogs."

"Not to mention the boats and dive equipment," Meg said.

"That too."

"That line of thinking emphasizes one point to me. This simply isn't the best place to kill someone. Smallish group, everyone accounted for and traceable. No one in their right mind would plan this location for a murder. The kill site suggests it was an unplanned death, likely a crime of passion, but this cements it."

"And, for all the reasons you've outlined, we have a killer trapped in our ranks who may be increasingly desperate to not get caught," said McCord. "So let's leave Pratt and look at who may be responsible, knowing we have an incomplete picture, and nothing that stands out as an instant driver to kill. Let's look at the other handlers and trainers, because those are the people who are most likely to have come up against Pratt previously." He flipped to a new document, bringing up a chart. "There're a lot of people here, so I started with the handlers and am branching out to the trainers. Four people per boat with eight teams means thirty-two people in the training exercise alone, let alone the competition. On a first look at the ones I've covered so far, they look squeaky clean, with a couple of exceptions. The first one is one of the trainers. A Ron Stanley. Do either of you know him?"

"I met him last night around the fire," said Brian. "Just an introduction, though. Meg, did you meet him?"

"No."

"Then we aren't going to add anything." Brian turned back to McCord. "What do you have?"

"Stanley is with Snake River Search in Idaho. Specializes in cadaver and water recovery with his retriever, Jinx. There have been some complaints lodged against Mr. Stanley by male members of the search group that he's a sexual harasser. Nothing has stuck, though."

"Only into men?" Brian clarified. "I mean, any kind of sexual harassment is bad, but if he only goes for men, it seems unlikely Pratt was his target."

"Seems like it, from what I can find so far. But that opens a door for other interactions. Like, say, if Pratt had some dirt on him and was blackmailing him. I do have him also assisting with victim recovery following Hurricane Michael, but I don't know if they ever came into contact. I need to do more research there. And we have Gerhard

Elan. He appears to be a bit of a bad boy. He's gotten into trouble a few times in his department. Some investigations into excessive force when he was still a patrol officer, where he was eventually cleared of all charges. Accusations of having a gambling addiction, including sports betting while he was on LTD healing up after a crash that occurred during a police pursuit. His own force broke a big gambling ring, but they couldn't, or didn't, hang any charges on him."

"Wonder if there was some inside help with that?" Todd mused.

"Could've been. Bet it wouldn't be the first time. But, again, we might have had someone with a shadowy history, which might have been a blackmail pressure point. Now, you said Mandy Fief was her old mentor. I couldn't find anything nefarious about Deputy Fief, but she may not have liked being shown up by her up-and-coming student."

"Twice," said Brian. "Once in the trial, and a second time after the trial, in public, in front of a bunch of strangers and the SDA organizing team."

McCord winced. "Ouch."

"You know, most mentors expect if they've done a good job, they could be surpassed by one of their students." Craig took a sip of his coffee and stared thoughtfully into the fire. "That's your job, as a mentor, or as a unit director—training those who come after you. But there's a world of difference between losing to the student and being humiliated by them. That kind of shame and rage could be a real motive."

"It sure could be, especially if you have suspicions your ex-student may be cheating to get the win she's rubbing in your face. She may not have known that at the time Pratt was haranguing her, but she told you herself, Meg, that she overheard McGraw later that night accusing Pratt of cheating based on his past experience with her. That would be an extra kick to her humiliation, not being beaten fair and square. And then we have McGraw himself, who'd been burned by Pratt in the past and was carrying some baggage from it. So, already, we have a possible panel of potential suspects, and that doesn't even touch on half of the people here."

"And the strong possibility the judging team is in it, up to their ears," said Brian.

"Especially that," McCord agreed. "Assuming that's correct, I'd like to get a feel for why they'd do it. At first glance, it appears the only person who would be served by this cheating was Pratt. But there's no way they'd be involved out of the goodness of their hearts."

"Money?" Meg suggested. "Pratt paid them off?"

"Always a solid go-to as a potential motive. I can't get into their banking records, but the investigators will."

"What about blackmail?" Brian theorized. "Maybe Pratt had something on Thatcher he didn't want to get out. Something that bought her a first-place finish and his silence."

McCord considered him thoughtfully. "More complicated, but definitely worth considering." He turned to Meg. "I have more research to do, clearly, and I intend to get back to that later today, but I want to go talk to the judging team."

"You want me to come with you? Or Brian?"

"Absolutely not. If they were in cahoots with Pratt for her to win, the last thing they'd do is open up to a competitor who thought they'd been ripped off. But they might talk to a reporter."

"You'd go in as a *Post* reporter? And you think they'd talk to you?"

"Hell no. But what if I'm from *American Field Trials* magazine?"

"Who dropped by to investigate the murder?"

"Murder? Never. Totally uninterested in that. I came in for the last day of the trials to cover the winner, and only found out about the tragedy once I arrived. Murder isn't my thing, and isn't something the magazine would be interested in, but I could turn the article around to more of a day in the life of a trials organizing and judging team, since I don't have a trial to cover now."

Meg glanced at Brian, echoing the emotion she spotted behind the squint-eyed uncertainty on his face. "*Maybe . . .*" She drew the word out. "You'd have to be totally convincing."

"Like I just spent an hour with two real-life competitors who will teach me everything I need to know about trials, and then some, so I can ask actual questions? Including showing me your actual paths on a map and where you think things went sideways? And from that, find out how all this was set up and see if I can suss out any hint of cheating? That kind of totally convincing?"

"Exactly that kind. Craig, what do you think?"

Craig cocked an eyebrow at them as he sat with his hands wrapped around his coffee cup, as if trying to suck every bit of warmth into his cold fingers. "I think I'm off taking a walk right now, because I'm pretty sure I didn't hear any of that."

McCord grinned. "Enjoy your exercise." His grin broadened when Craig lifted his coffee cup, drank deeply . . . and then didn't move so he could hear the rest of the conversation. "You two set me up so I can carry this off. We have about two hours because it's way too early to show up right now. And then when I go talk to the judging team, you and Brian go talk to the pilots and divers. Start with your own teams and maybe that can be your entrance to the whole group. You think your teams would talk to you?"

Meg nodded. "Mine would, for sure. These are the people who helped find Pratt, after all."

"Great. Brian?"

"I'm sure mine will talk to me. They seemed like good people. We'll go down and give it a shot."

"Excellent. Afterward, we'll compare notes and we'll see where we go from there."

CHAPTER 22

Support Apparatus: Personnel or vehicles dedicated to special operations like dive teams, rescue boats, hazardous materials, or high-angle rescues.

Sunday, October 20, 8:47 AM
Boundary Waters Canoe Area
Superior National Forest, Minnesota

"Who's that?" Brian pointed ahead to the men sitting in chairs around a fire at the water's edge near a line of beached dinghies and several anchored RIBs.

Meg squinted into the brilliant morning sun to see a smiling man with curling dark hair. He was broad across the shoulders, wearing a bright red jacket, and waving one arm over his head. It took a moment for her brain to make connections. "Oh! That's Sal, my diver. I didn't recognize him at first. He was always wearing a wet-suit hood when we were on the boat. I honestly didn't know what color his hair was. Or if he had hair. Hawk, let's go see Sal. Come." She waved back and diverted with her dog toward his side of the circle. "Do you see your team here?" she asked Brian.

Brian was already scanning the circle. "Actually, no. But their tents are up there." He indicated the row of tents up the hill, half hidden behind a row of trees. "They may not be down yet."

"Or they've eaten and gone back up. We'll find out. Sal!"

"Good morning. How are you doing? You don't look any worse for wear for our adventure yesterday."

"I'm okay, thanks. You?"

"Just fine. Hawk, my man, come on over here. You're looking good." Hawk, who recognized Sal by scent, happily greeted him, tail waving madly, and Sal ran his hand down the Lab's back. "And who is this handsome boy?"

"Girl, actually," Brian corrected. "This is Lacey. I had to leave her on shore when I came out to help you yesterday. Lacey, say hello to Sal."

Sal roared with laughter, drawing several gazes, as Lacey sat and politely offered a paw. Sal gently grasped it. "Lacey, I'm already a fan. You two are making me miss my boys."

"You have dogs?"

"Three rescued Heinz 57 mutts. Not purebreds, but I love them as much as my kids."

"Absolutely nothing wrong with mixed breeds," Meg said. "Not to mention their hybrid vigor. Thank you for rescuing."

"I never buy from a breeder. Too many dogs out there already needing a home and some love." He poked the man sitting beside him in the shoulder. "Hey, Dirk, shift over and make room for the lady."

Meg put out a hand to stop him, but the young man was already out of his chair with a grin. "You don't have to move on my account," she protested.

"No worries. I'm going to head out on the water with the boys." Another grin, this one full of slightly crooked teeth. "They told us not to leave the camp, but they didn't say we couldn't go out on the water." With a wave, he was off at a jog toward the tents.

Meg released the breath she'd just drawn in to ask him to stop, her shoulders slumping.

"Did you need Dirk?" Sal's face was lined with concern.

"Not specifically." Meg dropped into Dirk's chair and Brian stepped in to stand behind her. "Sal, you didn't formally meet Brian yesterday. Brian Foster, my partner in the Human Scent Evidence Team. Brian, this is Sal Gallo."

Brian stuck out his hand. "Mr. Gallo."

The men shook. "Just Sal, really. Especially after you helped out so much yesterday."

"I didn't do much, not compared to you."

Sal turned to Meg. "What's going on?"

Meg leaned in closer and dropped her voice as the men around the circle continued to talk and laugh. "We're trying to nail down what happened. The FBI agent they sent . . ." She paused, trying to find the right words.

"He's a bit pushy, isn't he?"

Brian laughed. " 'Pushy' might be considered kind. But we thought that was just for us. We have a theory that it's because he's new, paired with him trying to make it look like the FBI isn't showing any favoritism to its own people."

"He may be worse for you, but he hasn't been great with everyone else. Honestly, he's barking up the wrong tree with us."

"That's why I wanted to talk to you guys." Meg met Sal's eyes. "I was there yesterday when you found her. I saw the look in your eyes, witnessed your reaction. Either I'm a terrible judge of character—and in six years as a patrol officer with the Richmond PD, I learned how to read people quickly, usually in a crisis situation—or finding her body was a total surprise to you."

"It was."

Meg sat back in her chair, loose with relief. "I didn't think I was wrong, but that solidifies it for me. I need your help."

"You have it." Sal stood. "Come on, let's take a walk down the beach. Brian?"

"I'm with you. Lacey, come."

They strolled down the beach with the dogs as if they didn't have a care in the world, finally stopping just before the sand gave way to a thick patch of yellowing rushes in the water bordering the path that led up to the clearing where the trial had started on Friday.

Sal turned to face them. "What do you need?"

"Hawk, sit. Good boy. Honestly, I'm ninety percent sure Brogan considers me the main suspect in this killing."

Confusion clouded Sal's expression, and then understanding lit his eyes. "Because you 'found' the body?"

"That's part of it."

"That's ridiculous. You have three witnesses in the boat who can testify you didn't find Pratt." Sal smiled down at Hawk. "He did. In fact, you were clearly trying to keep up with him." At Meg's shrug, he patted her arm. "You're learning, that's why we're here this weekend. No one expected him to pick it up this fast. And there were way too many facts beyond your control. Charlie, for one."

"Why Charlie?" asked Brian. "He's your pilot, right?"

"Yes. After Hawk made the first find, we had time to kill, so we were tootling around the lake just going wherever Charlie steered us. He didn't have a plan. It's a gorgeous area, so he was showing us the sights, so to speak. No one had any idea Hawk would catch a scent. Really, it was purely coincidental he did. Right place, right time, and with people primed to recognize his reaction."

"Did you tell Brogan that?"

"You bet I did." Sal jammed his hands into the pockets of his blue jeans. "But you want to talk to the boys to see if anyone knows anything."

"Yes. I don't know who's responsible, but it's someone

who's here. Maybe someone panicked after an accident, but there's an explanation as to how she got out there."

"Not on her own, that's for sure." Sal looked back up the beach. "Let me talk to the guys."

Meg grasped his forearm. "I can't ask you to do that."

"You're not asking. I'm offering. Now, I don't think any of the boys are responsible. That first night, after the trial, we were all around the fire. And word had filtered down about Pratt going after a couple of you. The boys were laughing about how preposterous that was, but no one gave a clue they knew her. No one said they'd heard of her, or had worked with her. Now, if they were planning to kill her, they likely wouldn't have."

"But we don't think it was planned." Brian kept his voice low, even though no one was near them. "We found where we think she was killed, and it looks like it was either an accident or a spur-of-the-moment killing. If that's true, then the evening before it happened, there'd be no reason to hide the fact they knew her."

"So that makes me lean more toward none of them knowing her or having a motive to kill her."

"Unless it was something like a random attack," Meg said. "A sexual assault gone bad? That kind of thing." The slack-jawed shock on Brian's face caught her eye. "What?"

"Jesus. I've been thinking of this all along as Pratt being targeted by someone who knew her, someone who had a grudge or a disagreement with her. But you think it could be anyone with a Y chromosome?" He sounded appalled.

"I don't have anything to substantiate that, but we have to consider it might be a random killing. I admit the chances are small, but we have to at least keep the option open while we pursue all other leads."

"Yeah, I guess."

"Give me a few hours to talk to these guys," Sal offered. "If you don't want them to get suspicious and clam up immediately, it would be better if it just, you know, came up in conversation. If you walk in and start talking to them, they'll wonder why you're asking questions. If anything seems off to me, I'll let you know. I mean, I'll let you know either way, but if I have concerns, I'll bump it up. Come back around . . ." He pushed his sleeve up to check an ancient, scuffed dial watch. "Two. I'll be able to hit everyone in that time. Some guys are already out on the water, some are heading out now. They'll be back for lunch. I'll do the rounds, and let you know."

"Sounds good. Thanks, Sal." Meg looked down at Hawk. "Okay, boy, looks like we need to go sit and wait while other people carry the ball for us. Sal, we'll see you this afternoon."

Sal followed them to the fire, then waved them off as he settled into his chair again.

Frustrated, Meg continued on. The logical part of her brain knew other people asking questions was smart investigating, but she didn't like being useless.

Suck it up, Buttercup. For now, you're doing yourself a favor by getting out of the way.

But she knew the next few hours, waiting for McCord and Sal to get back to her, were going to feel like days.

CHAPTER 23

Code One: Traveling to an emergency location with no lights or sirens.

Sunday, October 20, 2:26 PM
Boundary Waters Canoe Area
Superior National Forest, Minnesota

"Well, that was a bust."

Brian gave Meg an elbow bump as they stepped off the road and headed across the grass toward the nearly deserted circle of chairs around the fire. "No information is still good information. Sal's convinced no one knows anything. I believe him. He seems like a straightforward kind of guy."

"He is, and I believe him too. I guess I'm hoping we could take this list of names we have and either add to it or clarify it. And, so far, that's not happening."

"How did it go?" Ryan, in his chair beside the fire, tucked his bookmark into his book and closed the thick volume.

"Struck out." Brian flopped down in the chair beside him and scanned the empty campsite. "Where is everyone?"

"Todd, Josh, and Luke are out in the boat, but said they'd be back by three thirty at the latest, in case you need them." Ryan looked over his shoulder toward their tent. "Craig's asleep. He kept trying to stay upright, and I finally talked him into getting three or four hours of sleep. Not a full night, by any stretch of the imagination, but that will keep him going until tonight."

"Is McCord napping too?"

"No, he isn't back yet."

Meg froze partway into sitting down on Ryan's other side. "We thought, for sure, he'd be back by now. He's been gone for hours."

"He may have had to wait around to talk to people. Or maybe they gave him some leads?"

Meg dropped into the chair. "That would be a lot of leads."

"It would. So your diver didn't find out anything?"

"Sal? No. He didn't think any of them knew Pratt before this started, and came out of talking to them all thinking the same thing. Unless it's a random attack—"

"And this would be one of the dumbest places for a random attack," Brian interjected.

"Unless it was an unplanned, spur-of-the-moment, random attack," Meg clarified, "the person responsible isn't in that crowd." She slumped down in her chair. "Which cuts out almost half of our potential suspects."

"You don't think we have enough already?"

"I don't think we have enough promising suspects. Knowing someone didn't get along with her isn't enough to bump them to number one. If it is, then I'm number one."

Brian gave her hand a squeeze. "You'll always be number one to me, babe. Well, after Ryan. And Lacey."

"I'm honored to be your number three. But you know what I mean."

"Of course, I . . . Hey, there's McCord!"

Meg whipped around to see McCord walking toward

them. She surged to her feet at the sight of him—his face was haggard and his complexion was creeping toward gray. His shoulders slumped and he nearly shuffled. "McCord . . .you okay?"

"Yeah." He stepped into the circle and nearly fell into the chair next to Meg and tipped his head back, his eyes closed.

"You're lying to me."

McCord's eyes opened to slits. "What are you, my keeper?"

"Your keeper's sister. And said sister will have my hide if something happens to you."

"I'm fine." With a groan, McCord sat up straighter. "You know, this used to be easier."

"What was?" Brian asked.

"Staying up for over twenty-four hours. When I was in Iraq, I did it several times when we were under attack."

Meg rolled her eyes. "A—you're not under attack, so no adrenaline to pump you up. B—that was a decade ago. You're not the spring chicken you used to be."

"Oh, I get that message from my body every time I overdo it at the gym. Ah, to be eighteen again." He stopped, considered. "Ah, to have the body of an eighteen-year-old, but my current brain."

"There it is," Brian said. "That's the sweet spot. Everyone wants their younger selves, but not the unwired brain that went with it. So, what's the scoop on today's snooping?"

"You call it snooping, I call it investigating."

"Po-tay-to, po-tah-to. Give us the dirt."

"Fair enough. Let's start with the players, beginning with the organizers."

"Teresa Bowfin," said Meg.

"Yes, but also her assistant, Rob Monroe."

"I never met Rob." Meg turned to Brian. "Did you?"

"Rob's new to me."

McCord pulled a familiar spiral-bound notepad from his pocket and flipped it open. "Rob was apparently the organization behind the training teams. I bet you probably saw Rob down by the water on the mornings you went out for training, but didn't know who he was."

"Did he have anything to do with the trials?"

"No, he was strictly training. He said he'd never met Pratt, and I believed him. He did a lot of the heavy lifting for the weekend ahead of time, arranging for all the technical staff, the pilots, divers, and trainers, and made sure everyone had the equipment they'd need for this location."

"It sounds like Rob had a lot to organize. He didn't have to find the teams—we all signed up on our own—but must have had to find everyone and everything else."

"He had lists of people from past training sessions, but a lot of them weren't specific enough to train for these particular skills, so he had to scour SAR groups to find trainers for water searches. Pilots and divers weren't a problem, because any search group that deals with lakes or larger rivers has lists of both of those positions on hand."

"Did Teresa organize the trial itself?"

"Yes. She brought Isaac Thatcher on as the judge and they set up the three trials, only one of which ended up being used."

"Did she bring on the trial observers, or was that Thatcher?" Brian asked.

"That was Thatcher. He'd worked with all of them before in previous trials."

"They told you all this?" Meg couldn't keep the surprise out of her voice. "They bought your *American Field Trials* reporter act?"

McCord buffed the knuckles of his right hand on his collarbone. "Hook, line, and sinker. I came across as a gee-shucks eager-beaver reporter and you guys gave me enough details about how trials are run, as well as info about some past trials, that I was convincing."

"I wasn't sure it was going to work. Glad I was wrong."

"Lots of people are flattered when you show interest in what they do, so I buttered them up with my enthusiasm for pulling off a weekend like this with so many moving parts and such an extended competition. Really laid it on thick about how most competitions were short form, with the finds taking only a couple of minutes, and how this one took advantage of the natural environs, yada yada yada. They lapped it up. You could tell they'd had a stressful weekend, and my showing up was unexpected, but welcome."

"Did you learn anything useful? Keeping in mind the discrepancy in time we suspected?"

"Maybe. I had them run me through their specific setup here. Normally, on those shorter courses, as you laid out, they have the trial observers in specific spots, tracking everything. And when trial times are under three minutes, and fully observed, the most you can shave or add is in the fraction-of-a-second range. But this was too big an area, so they had a half-dozen remote trail cameras set up at designated points. The judge watched the cameras on a laptop in the clearing; one observer monitored a section of the course, and the other two were positioned close to the hide. That's Dean Whittaker and Shannon Litzer."

Brian threw Meg a disgruntled look. "Dean wasn't too happy with me when I questioned his times. Any cameras near the hide?"

"Yes, but Thatcher wasn't writing down the times. He was watching the competitors at all stages of the trial, so he could see the hide being found as part of that, but wasn't noting the time. Now, about the final time—both observers were working with timepieces standardized against the National Institute of Standards and Technology clock. They noted the time the moment the dog alerts—sits, barks, whatever—and the handler calls it. Both had a clear view to the hide, and it's expected their times will be within a second of each other. Each time is then noted on a chart on a clipboard they have with them. I made a big deal about that and asked to see them. What I saw is exactly what you previously described. Two sheets, hand-written, with numbers that fell neatly inside the one-second range per competitor."

"I still think it's possible those two trial observers may have been on the take," said Brian. "What about Thatcher?"

"I have nothing to substantiate this, but, in my opinion, he was involved. He wasn't twirling his mustache, but it was plain from the way he took over all conversations that he ran the show. Once he agreed to be the trial judge, all decisions were his, or his in conjunction with the SDA brass. The location for the weekend was picked before he came on board based on the training requirements, but he and Bowfin laid out the trial courses together, trying to mix up each day's particular challenges as much as they could based on the terrain. Once that was done, he brought in the trial observers and made sure the technology they needed for such a long course was in place."

"But they didn't actually record the trial," Ryan stated.

"I played dumb and asked them about that, and got the same 'technical difficulties' response you got, which I didn't believe for a second. I would bet money the cameras themselves are capable of it, but they couldn't afford any actual evidence of their collusion. They never set them up to record."

"So Pratt makes a deal with Thatcher," said Meg. "Thatcher then brings on two trial observers so he gets the results he wants. Makes you wonder if the third trial observer knew anything about it. Or . . . wait. The third observer. That has to be who contaminated the course."

Brian sat up abruptly, like he'd been poked with a cattle prod. "Of course. The other two had to be close to the hide, and Thatcher was watching the cameras up in the clearing. They said the third observer—"

"Leo Baeza," McCord supplied.

"He was watching a section of the trail, but all they had to do was pick a section out of the view of any camera, just in case anyone looked over Thatcher's shoulder, and contaminate that unobservable spot."

"Baeza was the quiet one. Didn't offer any information on his own, as opposed to the other two, who wanted to make a splash in *American Field Trials*."

"The other observers weren't tasked with running through after the first person found the hide to sabotage the course. Maybe Urine Boy wasn't so happy with his role in the whole thing."

"It did make me wonder if we might be able to flip Mr. Baeza, get him to talk." McCord had to stop to stifle a huge yawn behind his palm. "But that's only going to give us the details on what we think we already know, not on the murder."

"Still useful information," Brian muttered. "We don't want this happening again."

"True. Would there be any evidence of the urine? A container of some kind?"

"It would have been brought with them, since none of those players are here with their own dogs."

"I've been thinking about that." Meg leveled an index

finger at Brian. "Any dog urine could have done that, but what if they got urine from a female in heat?"

Brian whistled. "I didn't think about that. That wouldn't have affected a female, like my Lacey, so badly, but for males, like Hawk here, it could have really thrown them off. And did."

"Wouldn't take that much volume to do it either, but that would have worked for them. They might have come with a small bottle of it; it's not like they'd need a four-gallon bucket. My guess is, any container has been scrubbed with soap and water so no evidence remains."

"Except the guilt in Leo's heart, apparently."

"Any idea why they carried out this elaborate scheme?" Brian asked.

"Needless to say, they didn't admit anything to me and sketch out their motives," said McCord, "so I still think we need a warrant for their bank accounts. The more interesting question is, why was the win so important to Pratt? So much so that she was willing to put enough of her own money behind an entire team to help her win?"

"She had to contact them somehow. I'm sure seizing Pratt's electronics is high on the investigators' lists. They may find their answers there. But that doesn't help us with her murder. We're left with the entire judging team, all four of them, involved in the scheme for Pratt to win. Thatcher—planning, organizing, recruiting, and possibly pressuring those recruits. Baeza—contaminating the course with urine to try to distract every dog but Ava. Then the other two, Whittaker and Litzer—colluding to mess up the time of anyone"—Meg patted Brian's arm—"who might be close to Pratt. That's four more people to add to the list. Four more who had a connection to Pratt, and who couldn't afford to be found out."

His shoulders hunched and riding near his ears, Brian shook his head. "This list is getting pretty long. And it's still being added to. We're not narrowing down anything at all."

"Not so far, but we have to start with a list of people for McCord to do more research on. He may be able to find connections. Right?" When McCord didn't answer, Meg poked his shoulder. "McCord?"

McCord blinked owlishly a few times, squinting at Meg as if he was having trouble focusing.

"You okay?"

"I think my body has decided it's had enough and my brain is short-circuiting. I'm half asleep with my eyes open." He glanced at his watch. "Which is reasonable, considering I've been basically awake now for about thirty-two hours." His smile was sheepish. "Sorry, apparently the coffee has worn off."

"Don't apologize. You've gone above and beyond. You also lasted longer than Craig."

"Either that, or Craig is the smart one who knew when to call it quits." McCord awkwardly stood, then swayed.

Meg bolted to her feet, grabbing his arm to steady him. "Hey, careful. You end up in the fire and scar your pretty face, Cara will hold me responsible."

McCord tossed her a smirk and pulled his arm from her grasp, but carefully stepped between the chairs and away from the flames. "I'm bedding down in your tent?"

"Yes. We haven't set anything up for you yet, so just roll into our sleeping bag. Do you want me to get you up in a few hours?"

"Yes. Three hours, no more. Then I want to get back to research. There's a lot of dot connecting still to do."

"You okay to get there?"

McCord didn't answer, just gave them a wave and stumbled his way to the tent, disappearing inside.

"He'll be asleep inside of thirty seconds," Brian said.

"I think that's generous. I bet he's already out. Didn't even take off his boots, just went horizontal on top of the sleeping bag, and is already asleep. Deservedly so. But let's give him a few hours to recharge. You know McCord; he's the Energizer Bunny. Give him minimal time and he'll be back on his feet. And, hopefully, making the connections we can't see yet, to make that list smaller."

CHAPTER 24

Size Up: Rapid mental and verbal assessment of factors that influence an incident.

Monday, October 21, 6:32 AM
Boundary Waters Canoe Area
Superior National Forest, Minnesota

The barking invaded Meg's dreams.

She was in the dinghy with her crew, perched on the front of the bow, staring out into the thick gray fog as it surrounded the boat. Somewhere, lost in the mist, a dog barked. Hawk? And if so, where was he? Swimming ahead of them? Marooned on one of the islands?

She turned around to speak to Claire, but McCord sat in her place. Behind him, Todd manned the tiller as he squinted into the fog. Craig sat opposite her, wearing Sal's wet suit.

The dog continued to bark, and as she followed the sound, she realized it wasn't Hawk. She knew every vocalization he made, and that wasn't him.

But who was it?

With a jolt, Meg awoke, sitting upright. Beside her, Hawk whined.

In the distance, a dog barked, again and again.

Beside her, Todd stirred. "What's going on?"

"You hear that dog? Something's wrong. Hawk can sense it too." She unzipped her side of the sleeping bag and threw it back. "I'm going to go check it out."

"Not on your own, you're not. McCord, wake up."

"I'm awake." McCord's voice came from the bottom of the bed, near the tent flap where they'd cobbled together a bed for him. "I hear it too. Turn on the lantern so you don't step on me, and I'm coming with you."

Within minutes, they'd laced on hiking boots and tugged jackets over the sweats they'd worn to bed to ward off the chill. With Hawk on lead beside them, they stepped out into the cold dark of early morning, holding flashlights. Meg wore her go bag, which held any essentials they might need for a rescue, and Todd wore his med pack in case of injury; hopefully, they'd be prepared for whatever was out there waiting for them.

"Sounds like it's coming from over there." Meg pointed past their campground to the west, in the direction of the water, away from the other campsites.

"There's nothing over there, right?"

"From what I've seen, yeah. No paths. Just forest down to the water's edge."

The moon had sunk below a horizon lightening to a dusky purple as the sun edged toward dawn, but stars still shone overhead. They hurried across the campground and into the forest. Hawk, reacting to the sound of a dog in crisis, forged ahead, and Meg let him lead the way. She could follow the sound without him, but if he could get them there faster, all the better.

Keeping her flashlight focused ahead of Hawk, while Todd and McCord flanked her, keeping theirs on the ground in front of them to avoid pitfalls, they covered ground in the forest quickly as the sound of the dog got closer.

A big dog, but all the dogs here were big. Though she didn't think it was the bloodhound. One of the shepherds?

Meg jammed the toe of her boot against an embedded rock she'd missed in the dim light and stumbled, but Todd's hand shot out, lightning fast, and grabbed her, steadying her. "Thanks."

"Hawk's in a rush. Do we need to go this fast, before one of us really takes a tumble?"

"He seems to think so. That dog sounds panicked to me. It must sound terrified to him, so his natural response is to get there as fast as possible. Let's try to keep up, and I'll try not to face-plant."

Another few minutes and her flashlight showed the trees thinning, giving way to lower, thicker bushes and scrub. Then, with a final push through the greenery, they were out and at the water's edge just as the sky eased toward pink in the east. Meg had a quick flashback to the last time she'd stood at the water's edge with her dog and these two men as they'd desperately searched for Cara in time to save her life.

Who was in trouble this time?

To their left, the barking came closer and they shone their flashlights toward it.

A soaking wet German shepherd sprinted toward them on the narrow strip of grass and scrub that bordered the lake.

"Hawk, stop." Meg immediately closed the distance between herself and her dog. She could control Hawk with voice commands, but if this dog was aggressive, she wanted him on a much shorter leash and closer in case of attack. But the shepherd stopped about twenty feet from them, barked three times in quick succession, and turned and ran back from where he'd come.

"That dog wants us to follow him," McCord said.

"That's my take too. Hawk, come."

The lightening sky allowed them to jog after the dog without their flashlights. About fifty feet down the shoreline, the dog darted into the bulrushes at the water's edge. Arriving behind him, they focused their flashlights into the thick green stems, finding the dog in seconds.

A man was facedown in the water. From his cargo pants to his windbreaker, he was dressed all in black. He lay spread-eagled, his head wedged at an awkward angle against the thick, reedy stems. The shepherd had the man's jacket sleeve in his mouth, and was trying to drag him to shore, but the arm threaded through the rushes only jammed the body into the yellowing tangle.

Without hesitation, Todd thrust his flashlight into Meg's hands, slid his backpack off to drop it on the grass, and stepped into the water. "Keep the light on him so I can see. McCord, with me."

McCord didn't question the instructions and stepped into the cold water behind Todd. They waded into the shallows, shoving bulrushes out of their path as they fought their way to the far side, where the dog, nearly up to his chin in the water, braced his feet harder, straining to rescue the downed man.

"Meg, any way you can call him off?" Todd asked.

"Let me try. Hawk, sit. Stay." Meg ran through all the dogs she knew were on-site and hoped one of the names would catch the dog's attention. "Yoshi!" She waited a few seconds when there was no response. "Samson!" Nothing. "Odin!"

The dog's ears perked and she knew she'd hit pay dirt. And had a bad feeling the man in the water was Gerhard Elan.

"Odin, let go. Let go, Odin."

The dog kept pulling.

You never knew the commands for another handler's dog, but there were common ones that were more likely

than others. Her bigger issue was that dogs were trained to
listen to only their own handlers. And she had a bad feeling Elan would never speak to the dog again.

"Odin, release!"

The dog froze, clearly conflicted.

That's the one. "Odin, release! Release, Odin." She unhooked Hawk's leash from his collar. "Talon, *stay*." She
needed to get in there, to get the dog off what was likely
his handler, but didn't need her own dog in the mix.
"Stay." Her eyes locked on the shepherd, Meg stepped
into the lake. The chill immediately soaked through her
sweatpants, but she walked carefully toward the dog.
"Odin, release." Her tone was calm, yet forceful, an experienced dog handler expecting—demanding—obedience.

Odin let go of the sleeve.

While she'd been focused on the dog, Todd and McCord
had circled through the rushes to the far side, open to the
lake, and the moment the dog released the jacket and was
distracted by Meg, they moved in, pulling the body free of
the rushes.

Todd quickly flipped him. "I can't work on him here.
Let's get him back to shore." They both grabbed an arm
and towed the man toward shore. "Keep the dog off us."

"Got it." Only five feet from the dog, Meg gentled her
voice. "Odin. Odin, come here, boy. We have him. We'll
help him. Come with me. Come." Making a judgment call
as she studied the dog watching the men pull the body
from the water and onto land, she held out a hand, held
just over the surface of the water so it was low from the
dog's perspective. "I'm Meg. That's me, I'm Meg." The
dog hesitantly stretched out, sniffing her hand. Meg was
cautious; even a highly trained dog, who was fully compli-
ant for his handler, could be a wild card with a stranger,
especially if the dog thought the stranger was any kind of
threat, either to himself or his handler. Did Odin realize

they were helping? Or would he attack in defense of his handler? Knowing what was likely already taking place on land behind her—Todd attempting to revive the man using CPR, which could well resemble an attack through the eyes of a dog—she wanted to make sure the dog was restrained so Todd could work unimpeded.

If he even had a chance to save a life in the first place.

To her surprise, Odin turned his face up to hers and stepped toward her. Moving in, she snapped Hawk's leash onto his collar. "Odin, come." Not wanting to pull the dog into deeper waters, she led the way through the rushes and onto land, purposely stepping onto dry ground about twelve feet away from Hawk so the dogs stayed well separated. Hawk's eyes stayed locked on her and the strange dog, so, for emphasis, she gave him the hand signal to stay.

Turning her back on Hawk, Meg tightened up on the leash. "Odin, sit." But the shepherd stayed frozen, his eyes locked on the man, now lying flat out on the grass. She gave the leash a gentle tug to catch his attention. "Sit."

Odin finally sat, but almost came off the ground again as McCord sloshed past in the water. He grabbed Todd's pack and then slogged back, giving Meg as much space as he could with the unpredictable shepherd.

Todd bent over the supine man who lay with his jacket unzipped and flipped open across his limp arms. Todd was centered over the man's torso, his arms locked and hands layered over the middle of his chest as he counted off compressions. When he hit thirty, he gave the man two breaths and then went back to compressions. On dry land again, McCord dropped to his knees beside Todd. "What am I looking for?"

"My portable defibrillator, but I'll do it. I need you to take over. Hands-only CPR for you."

"I can do it."

"Get ready to switch off."

McCord moved in, his hands already stacked, and the moment Todd moved out of the way, McCord planted his hands in the same spot and pumped with an identical rhythm.

Todd unzipped his pack and started digging. "Keep doing that. One hundred twenty beats per minute. Do it to the tune of 'Staying Alive' in your head. That's the right pace."

"Good to know."

Todd pulled out a black-and-orange box and a pair of scissors.

"Only you would come to the wilderness with a defibrillator."

"I'm like a Boy Scout—always prepared. Break a limb, I'm prepared for that too."

Working quickly around McCord's hands, Todd cut the wet shirt open in a single line up the center just to the right of McCord's hands and up and over Elan's left shoulder. He flipped back one side to reveal pale skin. "On three, lift your hands off after the compression so I can pull this off," he told McCord. "One, two—" He counted off in time to McCord's compressions. "*Three.*" McCord lifted his hands about an inch off Elan's chest and Todd whisked the wet material away and jammed it in around Elan's sides.

"What is that?" McCord's voice sounded strained, like coming through gritted teeth as he continued compressions.

"What is . . ." Todd trailed off as he spotted where McCord's gaze was fixed.

Meg squinted, not wanting to get any closer. The flashlight Todd had tossed in the grass to light the scene reflected off three small, clear, rectangular plastic patches running in an uneven line down Elan's right side. "Are those . . . nicotine patches?"

"No." Todd shrugged out of his jacket and tossed it behind him.

His dark tone told Meg there was something significant at play here. "What are they?"

"Fentanyl patches. Strong ones too." His words were momentarily muffled as he whipped his sweatshirt off over his head, leaving him bare-chested.

"Look, you're a firefighter. We already know you're built. Do you need to flaunt it?" McCord complained.

"You want me to dry him off with your shirt instead?" Todd dried off Elan's chest, right shoulder and left side with his shirt. "This won't work well on wet skin."

"Oh, well, in that case."

"Given those patches, this may not work at all." He opened the plastic box and pulled out two rectangular pads with wires that led to the defibrillator. "But we're going to try." After turning on the unit, he pulled paper off the back of the first pad. "Stop compressions." The moment McCord was off, Todd attached the first pad high up on Elan's chest on the right side. He stripped the paper off the second pad and laid it on Elan's left side, curving from the front around his rib cage, and pressing it firmly for full attachment. "If he OD'd, this isn't going to work. Those patches are one-hundred-microgram-per-hour dosing, the highest you can buy, meant to be used one patch at a time. He's using three. And I'm not as prepared as I thought I was, because I didn't bring naloxone. I'm ready to deal with a range of injuries to one of our party, not an overdose of someone else in this crowd. But naloxone won't help if his heart's stopped." He sat back on his heels, studying the readout on the small screen.

"What's it doing?" Meg asked.

"Evaluating the heart rhythm." Shivering, he grabbed his damp sweatshirt and pulled it on again, following it with his jacket.

"He has one?" McCord's tone rose in question. Or disbelief.

"No. No surprise, since I couldn't find a pulse. And we have no idea how long he's been out there. It's shocking him now. Starting at two hundred."

"Is that a lot?"

"Standard shock. Works for most people." He was silent for a moment, his eyes locked on the screen. Then he shook his head. "But not this time. Charging to three hundred."

Meg exchanged an uneasy glance with McCord, and then looked down at Odin. The dog's eyes were fixed on his handler and he quivered, as if ready to leap to his aid. But Meg thought he sensed they were there to help Elan and wouldn't do him harm. Her gaze slid to Todd. She knew the expression on his face, heard his thoughts in her own head. But needed confirmation. "Todd?"

"Charging to three-sixty."

"How high does it go?"

"Three-sixty."

This was it then. If this didn't shock his heart into rhythm, they had another dead handler on their hands.

Todd was motionless for a long moment, his eyes locked on the small screen. Then he looked up. "I'm calling it."

Meg inched a little closer, keeping Odin close to her side. "He's gone?"

"He's possibly been gone for hours. The body is cold, but that could have been from the water temp versus a body cooling after death. I couldn't take the chance. I had to attempt resuscitation."

"Of course you did. Thank you both for trying."

"Thanks for keeping the dog out of our way," McCord said. "Do you know who this is?"

"Gerhard Elan, a trooper with the New York State Police. One of two New York state troopers here this weekend. I suspected it was him even before you turned him over, once the dog reacted to his own name."

Todd pushed to his feet to stare down at Elan. "Two deaths in two days. There's zero chance that's a coincidence."

"Is that a high-enough fentanyl dose to cause an accidental overdose?" Meg asked.

"Three hundred micrograms of slow-release fentanyl on a man his size? Not a chance. Normally, you'd be looking at two milligrams, just under ten times that amount, for an overdose. Three hundred micrograms could give a nice buzz. Enough of one that it would be easy to push his head underwater and keep it there."

McCord stood, shaking out his wet pant legs. "Meg, you're going to have to call in law enforcement."

"Great." She met Todd's eyes. "I've found a second body. Brogan's going to want to know where I was every second last night."

"The three of us found the body. And last night, you were with me."

"Then he's going to want to know if you were drinking last night."

Temper heated Todd's gaze. "Bring it on."

"You were also with me," McCord pointed out. "And you would have had to trip over me to get out, so there's no way you got past both of us to carry out your heinous deeds." He grinned at Meg when she nailed him with a dark glare. "Just trying to keep your spirits up."

"Don't try to keep them up in front of Brogan." But Meg appreciated his attempt at humor. She offered Odin's leash to McCord. "Hold Odin, please."

"Uh . . . he seems a little skittish and upset with everything that's happened here. Not that I blame him for that, but he's not going to bite me, is he?" McCord, who was used to Cara's well-behaved mini blue pit bull, Saki, and

greyhound, Blink, as well as his own hyperactive golden
retriever, eyed the shepherd with suspicion.

"Considering everything that's happened around him,
he's been really good. Don't be nervous; it'll be fine. If
anything goes sideways, we're right here." She extended
the leash again. "Take him down to the far side of Elan so
I can bring Hawk closer."

"Fine." He took the leash and led the dog past the body
and to the far side of the beach. "Sit, Odin." The dog sat,
but McCord left a little space between himself and the
dog. "What are you doing?"

"Getting Brian out of bed. Or attempting to." She
pulled out her phone and speed-dialed Brian. The phone
rang six times and she was getting ready to hang up and
call again, before it went to voice mail, when a sleepy
voice said, "Hello?"

"Ryan, it's Meg. I'm so sorry. I need Brian."

"His phone going off didn't wake him up. Hang on."

The sound became muffled, like Ryan was holding the
phone to his chest, but she heard voices, Ryan's repeatedly,
then Craig's, and then Brian's, slurred and indistinct.

Then his voice, clear, though husky. "Meg?"

"Sorry, buddy, I need you out of bed. You and Craig.
He's up?"

"Yeah."

"Put me on speaker."

"Sure." There was a brief pause. "You're on speaker."

"Craig, good morning, sorry to get you all up."

"What happened?" Although distant, Craig sounded
brisk and businesslike, already knowing Meg wouldn't be
calling in the darkness before dawn when they had agreed
to meet for breakfast at seven thirty—unless there was a
problem.

"We just found another dead competitor."

Brian's yelp of surprise was quickly replaced by Craig's

voice, in close proximity as if he'd snatched the phone away from Brian. "Who?"

"Trooper Gerhard Elan, one of the New York State Police handlers. I woke up to the sound of a dog barking, clearly in distress. Todd, McCord, and I went searching for it with Hawk and found him only a few minutes from our campsite. The shepherd's handler was lying facedown in the water and the dog was trying to drag him to shore, but the body was tangled in the rushes. I caught the dog, and Todd and McCord dragged him to shore. Todd had his med pack with him, did CPR, and then used a defibrillator, but there was nothing he could do. Elan may have been dead for hours. But now we need law enforcement."

"I'll take care of it. Give me your GPS coordinates and I'll sound the alarm and then we'll come down there and give you a hand." He paused for a moment, hesitation hanging heavy in the silence. "You know this looks bad. Finding a second dead handler."

She'd known from the moment they pulled Elan from the lake, known even before Todd had called his death. Recognized it in the knot in her gut, and the chill that skittered along her skin leaving goose bumps in its wake. "Yes. But there's no way I could have killed this one. You were with me last evening. Then, after that, I was in bed with Todd, with McCord stretched out in front of the tent flap. I'd have had to stomp over him to sneak out to kill anyone. It didn't happen."

"I know it didn't; I'm just telling you what it looks like."

Meg studied the body of the fallen officer, trying to catalog anything that looked out of place. The problem was, besides the fentanyl patches, nothing did. "There are no obvious signs of trauma. There is something that might have put him at a disadvantage, but there's no clear indications of how he died."

"That's going to be up to law enforcement and the medical examiner to decide. And that means we need to get them there. Give me your coordinates and then hold the scene. We'll be there in a few minutes."

Meg gave him her location, hung up, and dropped her phone into her pack. Then, pulling her spare leash out of her bag and calling her dog, she pushed down the fear that bubbled to the surface, and prepared to meet the onslaught of accusations she knew was about to come her way.

CHAPTER 25

Cascading Failure: A failure in one area resulting in failure in a different area that should not have failed.

Monday, October 21, 7:13 AM
Boundary Waters Canoe Area
Superior National Forest, Minnesota

It was less than five minutes before lights flashed through the forest, growing continually stronger and brighter. Brian and Craig broke through the trees, about ten feet down the shore, both stopping dead at the sight of McCord holding a strange dog.

"You're okay," Meg said. "His name is Odin and he's responding well to voice commands. No aggression so far. But, McCord, keep him separate. He may change his mind at any time and decide we're not helping his handler, but hurting him."

"Okay, Odin, come with me. Come." McCord led the dog a few more feet down the shore, close enough he was still loosely part of the group, but far enough the leash would keep the dog away from everyone else.

Craig and Brian came to stand beside Elan's body, with Todd, Meg, and Hawk.

Craig looked down at Elan, shaking his head, his lips a tight line. "I made contact with Brogan."

"Going to take him hours to get here?" Meg asked.

"I'm guessing ten minutes max." Craig met her surprised gaze. "He arranged with the locals to borrow camping equipment. He's in a tent on the grounds."

"Great news." Todd's flat tone expressed how he really felt about it. "Now you're here, and are of superior rank to Brogan, can you run interference?" He looked from Craig to Meg and back again. "Because we all know how this is going to go with him."

"I'm going to make sure he keeps his questioning fair and impartial, yes. But keep in mind that beyond his own style, Special Agent Brogan may have arrived here with his own set of Bureau instructions."

"Meaning his supervisor told him to be aggressive and insulting so it didn't look like he was giving Bureau personnel a pass?"

"He should never be that, but while he's leaning on all of you, someone may be leaning on him. Just keep that in mind." Craig crouched down beside Elan, his hands braced on his knees, as if forcing himself to not touch the body. Elan's shirt lay spread open over his jacket, the defibrillator pads still attached, the leads lying limp and disconnected in the flattened grass beside his body. Elan's head lolled to the side toward them, his skin sickly pale, his eyes closed, and mouth slack. Craig looked up at Todd. "Meg told me you tried to resuscitate him. No chance?"

"He may have been dead for hours. I couldn't find a pulse, but I moved on to CPR, as there was no time to waste. Defibrillation resets the existing electrical activity in the heart muscle when it's out of normal sinus rhythm; if he was flatlined, something I couldn't see without leads and a monitor, it wouldn't make a difference. I didn't think resuscitation would work, but I had to try."

"I'll make sure Brogan understands that."

"There's something else." Todd played his flashlight over the patches on Elan's side. He ran an index finger through the air an inch above Elan's skin. "See these?"

"Yeah. What is . . ." Craig bent to read the small type on the patches, froze, and then looked up. "Fentanyl. He OD'd?"

"Not at that dose. Not unless he took pills, smoked, or injected more of it. Or mixed it with something else altogether. But at three hundred micrograms, he'd have been high."

"High enough to have been helped into the lake."

"I'd say yes."

Craig swore under his breath. "Or maybe it was an accident. He was high and got in over his head. Literally."

"Also could have happened."

"That's not what Brogan is going to think, and you know it." Brian looked at Meg. "Right?"

"Yeah, that's not what he's going to think."

"Maybe he committed suicide," McCord called. "What if he killed Pratt, and there's a connection we haven't found, yet he knows would come out eventually. So he got high to make the ordeal less painful and then he killed himself."

"Then why drown?" Todd countered. "Just slap on another pack of patches and fade away painlessly."

"Maybe he did? Could he be wearing more patches?" Craig asked.

"He could. I didn't want to touch him more than needed. I had hands on him for CPR, which McCord took over while I got the defibrillator set up. But once I knew he was gone, everyone stayed hands off. Figured you'd prefer it that way."

"Good thinking. I'm going to wait for Brogan to arrive before having a better look." He studied the body. "As you said, nothing obvious beside those patches, though. No overt signs of trauma. No injuries or bruising."

"Unless it's on his back, because that's how someone held him underwater," Brian suggested. He froze, then slowly turned. "Do you hear that?"

"Hear what?" Feet away, Meg started toward him, but then caught a flash of light bobbing along the edge of the lake. "Here comes Brogan. No, wait. Is that . . . two people? Craig? Did Sheriff Olsen leave one of his men here?"

"I honestly don't know. Possibly?"

Meg directed her flashlight down the shoreline, but the two shadows were partially blocked by the edge of the forest and the encroaching greenery.

"Elan! Odin!" The bellow came with a wave of a flashlight. "Elan, is that you? Man, we've been worried."

There was a moment of silence as Meg exchanged uneasy glances with the men.

Getting closer, the shadow took on the distinct form of a tall man. "Elan?"

"That's not Brogan," said Brian.

"No, it's Glenn. And he's about to trip over the body of his dead tent mate. Can we switch dogs? Brian, you take Odin, since you're the more experienced handler, and I don't know if the incoming personnel will spook him." Meg held out Hawk's leash. "McCord, you take Hawk. I know them, sort of. Let me try to head them off before they get here."

Brian took Odin, and McCord jogged over to grab Hawk's leash. "Try to block them from the scene."

"I'll slow Glenn down, but I doubt he'll stay there. Hawk, stay. Stay with McCord."

"You slow him down," said Craig from behind her. "We'll do the rest."

Meg kept her flashlight low to keep from sliding in the

water, but as two men pushed through the branches of a pine at the shoreline, she snapped the light up. Dix came through first, Chewie at his side, with Glenn and Samson behind him.

"Lamonte. Damon." Hoping first names would keep things more relaxed for a few moments, Meg stepped up to the men, purposely blocking the direct path along the shore. "You're out early."

"One could say the same of you," Dix said, his gaze fixed over her shoulder to the men standing behind her. "We're looking for Gerhard Elan. Have you seen him?"

"He's missing?"

"He wanted some air last night." Glenn went up on his toes, trying to see around Dix.

"What time was that?" Meg wanted to get as much information from the men as possible before they knew what had happened, and might change their stories accordingly. She also was stalling for Brogan's arrival.

"Just after midnight. He said he was restless and wanted to go for a walk, but I was tired and had had enough. Just wanted to go to bed. He asked if I'd keep Odin while he went out for a few minutes of peace, and I said sure. I turned out the light and hit the sack, and fell asleep before he came back."

"*While he went out for a few minutes of peace.*" The line replayed in Meg's head, the disconnect jarring. It was the kind of thing you'd expect from someone who didn't understand the bond between handler and dog. The kind of person who didn't understand a quiet walk with your heart dog in the woods in the moonlight *was* peace.

"But then I woke up and something seemed off. I turned on the light and Elan wasn't there, and Odin was gone too."

"You think he came back for Odin and went out again?"

"Not sure. Either that, or Odin nudged the zipper up

with his nose and his leaving the tent on his own was what woke me up. All I know is Elan wasn't there, and that worried me." He craned his neck, trying to see better. "What's going on over there?" He gave Dix a nudge. "Let's go look."

"I would if I could get through." Eyes narrowed, Dix studied Meg. "Ms. Jennings, is there a problem?"

"Just Meg is fine. How are you involved here, Lamonte?"

"I woke up when I heard Glenn calling for Elan and Odin. I offered my assistance and here we are."

A light flashing through the trees from the direction of her own campsite attracted Meg's attention. *Brogan.*

"Okay, then, Meg, what's going on?"

"I woke up earlier to the sound of a dog barking. My partner and brother-in-law came down with me to investigate." She met Glenn's eyes. "The barking dog was Odin. He was trying to drag a body out of the lake. Damon, I'm sorry. It was Gerhard. He's gone."

For a moment, Glenn gaped at her. " 'Gone'? What do you mean *gone*?"

"He's dead. I'm very sorry."

"If that's a joke, it's in terrible taste."

"Meg, if you'd get out of our—"

Glenn didn't wait for Dix's request, but stepped into the water, wading around Meg, then jumped back onto the grass. Samson didn't hesitate, but jumped into the lake after his handler and up onto the path behind him.

"Damon, wait!" Meg hurried after him, Dix and Chewie hot on her heels.

Glenn broke into a run, but only managed about four steps before Brogan broke through the forest in front of him, causing him to jerk to a stop. Brogan took one look to his left—the body on the ground surrounded by four men and two dogs—and to the right—another man and dog pelting toward him—and threw up a hand toward Glenn. "Slow down!"

"I need to get through." Glenn was breathing hard, not from the run, but apparently from stress. "That's my buddy over there. Gerhard!"

"You're attempting to disturb my crime scene. There are entirely too many people here. And dogs." Distaste curled his lip. "Too many dogs."

"We're K-9 handlers," Meg said, struggling to keep her disgust at his attitude out of her voice. "Where we go, they go."

Brogan looked past Glenn to Meg and Dix. "Then let's get rid of the ones who don't need to be here. Mr. Dix, I need you and Mr. Glenn to vacate the premises immediately. And take your dogs with you."

"We wouldn't leave them behind." Irritation came through clearly in Dix's clipped cadence. "They're our partners. Glenn, come on."

Instead of answering, Glenn tried to shoulder past Brogan.

Brogan simply shoved him. "Back off. I get dragged out of bed before dawn, I'm not going to fight with you. You do as I say. Get gone."

Glenn's gaze was fixed on the limp form on the grass. "I just want to see him. Maybe you've got the wrong guy."

Meg laid her hand on Glenn's shoulder; it was rock hard under her touch, tight with tension. "Damon, it's not. I've seen him myself. You don't want to see him like this. Just . . . go back to your tent."

"And stay there. I'll have questions." Brogan turned his back on them and started along the shore toward the downed man.

"Great people skills," Dix muttered.

"Not even remotely," Meg agreed. "Damon, you need to go." She gave him a slight shake. "Damon."

"Yeah, I got it. Samson, come." Glenn spun on his heel and, pushing branches out of his way, shoved his way into the forest, creating his own path in his rush to escape.

"Chewie, come." Shaking his head, Dix followed Glenn more carefully, he and his chocolate Lab almost instantly swallowed up by the dark forest.

Meg strode back to where Todd, Craig, McCord, and Brogan clustered around the body, while Brian still stood out of the way with Odin, but where he could still hear everything. She took Hawk's leash from McCord with a nod of thanks.

"What the hell happened here?" Brogan demanded, looking straight at Craig. "You're Beaumont?"

"Yes," said Craig. "I'll let those directly involved explain; I arrived after the resuscitation attempt."

Brogan looked from Todd to McCord to Meg, with Hawk at her knee. His gaze dropped to the Lab. "Can you move your dog? He's going to contaminate my crime scene."

Meg was just drawing breath to snap at Brogan, when Craig beat her to it. "I'll have you know, that's one of my best handlers and her trained law enforcement canine. This isn't a dog park. These are my unit team members, and you will treat them with respect. This isn't their first death investigation. They know what they're doing."

Brogan looked startled, like it had never occurred to him his attitude was unsuitable to a superior rank, let alone one who commanded those he denigrated. "Yes, sir."

"Meg, please bring Special Agent Brogan up to speed."

Meg didn't let her lips even twitch at Craig's subtle reminder to Brogan that he may be the lead investigator, but he was standing beside a special-agent-in-charge. "Yes, sir." She turned to Brogan. "I woke around six thirty this morning to both the sound of a dog barking and Hawk reacting to it. It was clear the dog was in trouble in some way. My partner, Todd, my brother-in-law, Clay McCord, who is staying in the tent with us"—she held out a hand to indicate McCord, whom Brogan hadn't met yet—"and I came out to see what was going on. When we got to the shore, we found a German shepherd in the rushes over there." She pointed to where bent and broken bulrushes marked the spot where Odin had tried so hard to save his handler. "He was trying to drag a man to shore. The man was facedown in the water and unmoving."

Meg looked over to where Odin sat beside Brian. "Knowing we had three different shepherds here this weekend, but not knowing them well enough to identify by sight in the dark, I started running through the names. When I hit the name Odin, he responded."

At the sound of his name again, the dog sat up straighter, ears perked.

"Once we knew which dog it was, I suspected I knew the man's identity. I left Hawk on the shore and waded in to get Odin to release Elan. Once he did, Todd and McCord went in from the other side, flipped him faceup, and pulled him to shore. Todd?"

"He wasn't breathing and had no pulse when we brought him to shore so I could work on him," Todd continued without missing a beat. "I started CPR and then McCord continued while I got out the defibrillator I'd brought in my medical pack."

"You brought a defibrillator to a campsite." Disbelief hung heavy in Brogan's tone.

"I'm a paramedic. I knew we'd be in the wilds of Minnesota, hours away from a real trauma center, so I brought what we might need on-site. It wasn't my full pack, but had what I thought was essential."

"Good thinking," Craig said, with a hand wave that telegraphed *Move on . . .*

"Did three shocks—two hundred, three hundred, and

three hundred sixty joules. None of them restarted his heart. It will be the call for the medical examiner if he drowned, or if *those* had any effect." Todd pointed his flashlight at the patches on Elan's side. "Those are transdermal fentanyl patches, with the dose stamped on them. One-hundred-micrograms-per-hour slow release."

Brogan squatted down to get a better look. "Are those supposed to be used three at a time?"

"No. One hundred is the top dose in the patch. To be used singly."

"Three hundred would be fatal?"

"No, but it would be dangerous. The patches release a certain amount of drug per hour. With three of them applied at the same time, it's three hundred micrograms per hour, which is extremely risky. It would give him a high, could make him dopey or possibly unconscious, but it would take about two thousand micrograms to kill him. Now all we're seeing are these three patches. If he supplemented his dosing in any way, by pills or injection, or more patches we haven't seen yet, anything above one thousand micrograms would be likely to kill him. Anything above two thousand, would." Todd looked down to meet Brogan's eyes. "I have supplies for broken bones, to stitch wounds, antibiotics for infection, the defibrillator, allergy meds, bandages. But I didn't bring any naloxone because I know the people I'm with, and knew I wouldn't need it. So I couldn't have administered it, even if I'd wanted to."

"Would it have saved him?"

"Honestly, no. I think he was long dead by then, but the water temp will play with time of death."

Brogan stood. "I'll call Sheriff Olsen, and have him send officers in to take this body to Ramsey as well." He pulled his pad of paper and pen from his jacket pocket. "I'd like a full accounting from all of you on your whereabouts yesterday. Let's say from seven in the evening on, and we'll go back further, if needed."

"According to Glenn, Elan left their tent to go for a walk around midnight. That was the last time he saw him," said Meg.

"Then seven o'clock more than covers it."

"This will be easy for you then," Craig said. "All five of us here were together from that time until we split up around eleven o'clock to go to bed."

"Did any of you go off to the washroom on your own?"

"Todd went with me at eleven," Meg said, "but we were only separated for a few minutes."

"At most," Todd added. "Then we went back to the tent."

"Where I was bedded down at the doorway," McCord said. "No one left until we all did this morning, or they'd have to have literally walked on me to get to the tent entrance."

That caught Brogan's attention. "But you could have gotten out."

McCord shrugged. "I guess. Not sure why I would, though. I'd never met the man."

"You're not part of the competition."

"No."

"Neither are my brothers and I," Todd said. "We came for the fishing."

Brogan made notes. "The fishing, right."

Brogan's head was down, so he didn't see the glare Todd tossed his way before he turned away and started packing his gear into his bag.

"So, Ms. Jennings, this is the second body you've found." Brogan raised his eyebrows expectantly.

What are you waiting for? A confession? Not wanting to give him an inch, Meg simply stared back at him, a pleasantly interested expression firmly fixed in place.

Brogan frowned and flipped the page in his notebook with considerably more force than needed, the page partially tearing, the ripping sound overloud in the predawn quiet. "Do you have any comments on that?"

"I didn't find the first one, Hawk did. And I found this one with Hawk and two other people. So I'd agree I *assisted* in finding two bodies."

"Is there a point to this, Brogan?" Craig asked.

"You're not inserting yourself into this investigation, are you, sir?"

Craig's brows nearly disappeared into his hairline. His gaze flicked to Meg, whose expression said, *I told you so.* "Not at all," he said. "But I'd expect our officers to ask relevant questions, not make pointed statements. If you don't have any more questions for my people, or for Lieutenant Webb or Mr. McCord, I think they'd like to go get a cup of coffee, since their day started so early and so jarringly. They'll be available to you if you have any more questions later today. I, on the other hand, will stay here to help you hold the scene until Sheriff Olsen or one of his men arrives."

"Thank you, sir. Quite generous of you." Brogan's tone of voice directly contradicted his words.

"Meg, Brian, what do you recommend we do with Odin?"

"I'd recommend we return the dog to Trooper Glenn," Brian said. "If he agrees, it would make the most sense for him to keep Odin. He's familiar and so is his dog. The force will have to decide what to do with their asset in the long term, but our only immediate concern is for the dog's well-being. Meg?"

"I agree. Familiarity will be best for him and that keeps him with an officer in the New York State Police. Agent Brogan, do you have any objections?"

Brogan shook his head. "As long as Glenn remains in camp with both dogs, that's fine with me. Now, if you'll excuse me, I need to get Sheriff Olsen out of bed." Brogan walked away a few feet, pulled out his phone, and turned his back to them as he placed his call.

Craig stepped to Brian and motioned the others to join him. "Thanks, guys. Head on back to camp and we'll get this straightened out. I'll be back as soon as I can."

"We'll run over a coffee for you," Meg said.

"That would be amazing. Thanks."

They made their way back through the forest, retracing their steps. McCord went first with Todd, then Brian and Odin, and finally Meg and Hawk.

Meg considered the dog as they walked. Maybe they'd hold on to him for an hour or so, have coffee, eat breakfast, then return him. By that point, camp would be fully up and moving and they could ask a few questions.

And maybe find a few answers Brogan and his brusque manner would never uncover.

CHAPTER 26

Shaping the Battle Space: Preemptive actions before a major battle to give one side a decided advantage.

Monday, October 21, 8:16 AM
Boundary Waters Canoe Area
Superior National Forest, Minnesota

Meg and Brian stood just off the road, studying the bustling campsite. Meg had Odin on a tight, short leash, while Brian had both Lacey's and Hawk's leashes in one hand, both dogs standing quietly together on his left. The two campfires were ablaze, with handlers and trainers seated around both. "Let's go see a man about a dog," Brian said.

"Funny man."

"Hey, someone needs to try to keep this trip light. It's not doing so well on its own."

"You can say that again." As Brian drew breath, Meg threw up a hand. "But really, don't."

He grinned at her.

They crossed the damp grass to the farthest fire, where more people gathered. Glenn sat in a chair, near the flames, bent forward, his head in his hands. Dix sat on one side of him, McGraw on the other. As they approached,

Samson, who lay between Glenn's chair and Dix's, put his head up, scenting the air. Then, seeing Odin, gave a woof of greeting.

Glenn's head came up at the sound, looking confused until he spotted Odin. His hair was mussed, his jaw dark with an overnight growth of beard, and his ice-blue eyes bloodshot and splotchy with shadows.

"He looks like crap," Brian murmured.

"I'd like to think you'd look like crap if I was killed."

That stopped Brian dead in his tracks, but it took two steps for Meg to realize he wasn't with her. She stopped and let him catch up.

"Don't joke. We've come a little too close to that a few times recently and I don't want to go there."

"Sorry. That was stupid."

He squeezed her arm. "Stupid's allowed. You dying is not. Not even in jest. Come on." He raised one hand to the group as a whole. "Good morning."

"Not much that's good about it," Glenn said. "Except that big boy. Let him loose. Odin, come here, boy."

Meg dropped the leash and the dog immediately trotted around the circle to Glenn, who pulled him in and dropped his face into the fur at the dog's neck.

"He's really torn up about this," Brian said. He passed Hawk's leash to Meg and they moved forward together.

Dix looked up at them from where he sat on Glenn's right. "What are they doing with Elan?"

"We left the shoreline about an hour ago. They called Sheriff Olsen and were waiting for him or one of his people to arrive." Meg left out her second trip to the lake with coffee for both men; they'd still been there alone, standing in a stiff silence, and Meg had wanted to clear out of there as quickly as possible. If there was something she needed to know, Craig would make sure it got back to her. He had his own sat phone and knew how to reach her. "They'll transport him to Ramsey, to the medical examiner's office that serves Lake County. But we actually wanted to talk with you, Damon."

Dix pointed to a couple of folding chairs that lay collapsed beside one of the tents. "Grab those and join us."

"Hold Lacey." Brian handed off Lacey's leash to Meg, and brought the chairs over, one at a time, and opened them out, squeezing them in beside Glenn, while Dix and McGraw shifted sideways to make space. "Thanks." He took Lacey's leash and they sat down, the dogs settling beside their chairs.

Glenn stared down at Odin, sitting between his knees. "What can you tell us about Elan?"

"We don't know much," said Meg. "We got sent away from the scene pretty quickly."

"But you two found him."

"I wasn't with Meg at the beginning," Brian clarified. "She called me after they pulled him out of the water."

"You were alone when you found him?" Glenn's hands tightened on Odin's fur, but the dog didn't react.

"I was with my partner and my brother-in-law. My partner, Todd, is a paramedic; he did everything he could. But Gerhard was already gone."

"Goddamn it." Glenn's head sank low, his face hidden.

"You may be able to help us figure this out. You knew him best."

Glenn's head came up. His eyes were haunted and going bloodshot. "How?"

"I don't mean to be indelicate . . ." Meg dropped her voice. "But did Gerhard have a drug problem?"

"Like weed? Cocaine?"

"Fentanyl."

Glenn's eyes flared wide for only a fraction of a second before he recovered, but Meg caught it.

"You knew about it."

"It wasn't his fault."

"No one's assigning blame; we're trying to discover what happened. Was it the car accident?"

Glenn stared at her, shock etched into his features. "How do you know about that?"

"Word gets around." Meg left it at that, not wanting to reveal the asset that was McCord. "I understand he was critically injured during a high-speed chase."

"About two and a half years ago. Messed him up bad. Broke his left femur and jacked up his back."

"Back injuries are the worst. That's when he got hooked?"

Glenn looked away, out into the forest, worrying his lower lip.

"Damon, he was an officer injured in the line of duty. No one is going to think less of him." Meg ran a hand over Odin's head. The dog looked up at her and held her gaze, his eyes unfathomably sad. *You know he's gone, don't you?* "Those of us on the job know the risks. Know what an incident like that cost him, and the honest-to-God guts and drive he must have had to get back to work. The fact that he did, while in pain, really shows those guts."

"We didn't work in the same unit, but we stayed in touch, especially while he was recovering. I told him he needed more time, but he was determined to return to duty. They'd reassigned his dog when he was hurt, but he'd heard a new dog was going to be available, and he was sure as hell going to make sure he was in the running for it."

"That was Odin?" Brian asked.

"Yeah. And he was so happy when they assigned Odin to him. Elan did a lot of his training himself and they were a great pair."

"He seemed upset after the trial when he got disqualified."

"That was bullshit."

Meg glanced at Brian, recognized calculation in his gaze. "Why do you say that?"

"Because Odin's a pro. He'd never do that. Something hinky happened." Glenn froze, his eyes locked on Meg's face. "Wait a second. You think that too."

"We both do. The trial was rigged."

"Goddamn it!" Glenn's fist came down on his knee, and Odin jerked. "Sorry, buddy. Sorry." Bending low, he murmured to the dog and ran his hands over his thick fur. When he straightened, he was careful to keep his voice temperate. "Elan thought they'd failed that first trial. But if it was rigged . . ." His face suffused with color. "If it was rigged, then everything he felt about the trial, and about Odin's performance, his own performance, was false. What if he . . ." Glenn trailed off, his lips pressed together so hard they went white.

"You think he was so upset he took his own life?" Dix asked.

"That seems insane. It's a trial, for God's sake. And after Deputy Pratt's death, one that was never going to finish, so there'd be no winner declared. But . . ." Glenn paused, torn.

"But what?" Meg prodded gently.

"Elan wasn't having a great weekend. He tripped on the first course and hurt himself."

"I saw him limping on Friday afternoon, but when we talked about it on Saturday, he blew it off as nothing."

"He'd never admit he was hurting. And it would've been nothing to an average person, but Elan had a preexisting injury. He wrenched his back and was in severe pain." Glenn deflated. "Which he tried to control with fentanyl."

"There were patches on his abdomen," Meg said.

"That was the easiest way, he always said. Lasted all day and . . . wait. Did you say patches? Plural?"

"Yes. Three of them."

His gaze cast skyward, Glenn released a breath that collapsed him into himself. "It was only supposed to be one a day. It was some kind of slow-release deal. He must have really been hurting." He looked down at Odin, frowning.

"What if more than just the trial was on his mind?" asked McGraw.

Meg turned to look at him. "More than the trial?"

"Yeah. I mean, what if he . . ." McGraw stopped, as if unwilling to continue. "What if he did Pratt? I heard she's been involved in cheating in previous competitions. If Elan knew they'd been disqualified from that course, sure, they could do the other two, but there was zero chance of winning overall. I saw him on Friday. He was humiliated. What if that was enough to push him over the edge?"

"He would have had to know Pratt was behind the rigged trial," Brian pointed out.

McGraw rounded on Brian. "I suspected. Why wouldn't he?"

Brian drew back slightly at McGraw's sharp tone. "Slow your roll. I'm not saying he couldn't have known, just he needed to know for your theory to hold."

"Well . . . yeah."

The look Brian threw Meg made it clear he was struggling not to roll his eyes.

"But what if he did know," McGraw continued. "Killed her in a rage, then panicked and dumped her body in the lake, but it was found anyway. Now we're all under the microscope and the chance of the guilty party getting away with it is pretty small. Maybe he couldn't live with that."

Meg's and Brian's gazes met briefly before breaking

apart to study the others in the group. Dix looked contemplative, like he was mulling over the possibilities, whereas Glenn simply looked despondent.

"Damon?" Meg touched his knee. "You okay?"

Glenn shook his head. "I don't know what to make of all this. We came here for training and to run in a competition, and now Elan is dead and we're discussing if he took his own life because he was distraught after he killed Pratt?" He surged to his feet. "I need some air. Samson, Odin, come." He stepped out of the circle and strode past the tents and toward the main road, the dogs flanking him.

"I'm sorry, guys," Meg said. "It wasn't our intention to twist the knife. We're just trying to figure out what happened."

Dix held up a hand as if to stay her words. "Don't feel bad. You're not trying to poke at him. He's upset and I think pretty much anything would rile him up right now. I don't know either of them very well, but Glenn and Elan seemed close. Always hanging together when we weren't working. The whole thing is a shock to him."

"Is there anything else you guys can add?"

Dix rubbed one hand over his jaw as he stared at Glenn's empty chair. "Not really. I didn't know any of you before this, so I don't have a lot to add. I didn't know the personalities, and if there was cheating during the trial, I didn't see it. I'm sorry. McGraw?"

"I've already made suggestions." He stood. "I'm going to go see if Glenn needs anything. Yoshi, come." McGraw strode off in the direction they'd last seen Glenn, his German shepherd trotting to keep up with him.

Meg watched him go. "That went well."

"Everyone is on edge." Dix stood as well. "I'm going to get a coffee. Want one?"

"No, thanks, I think we'll head back to camp," said Meg, getting a nod from Brian. "Thanks for your time, Lamonte."

"No problem. See you around."

Meg was silent as they made their way to their own campsite.

Brian gave her a few minutes before he gave her a gentle push. "What are you thinking?"

Meg glanced sideways at him. "What makes you think I'm thinking anything?"

"Babe, you're always thinking something. But right now, you have that furrow"—he poked his index finger between her eyebrows—"that says you're mulling something over. What is it?" They walked for another ten feet. "Come on, spit it out."

"Does it seem a little too neat and tidy to you?"

"We've had two deaths. That's not neat and tidy at all."

"You know what I mean. One death is explained by the other. Elan kills Pratt because of the cheating, and then is so torn up about it, he ODs on fentanyl, and then throws himself into the lake when he knows he won't be able to save himself, and no one will come to his rescue because it's the middle of the night."

"I'm sure you noticed this solution was suggested by a man with a known history of cheating with Pratt."

"Because McGraw seeding a theory that takes one hundred percent of the attention away from him isn't suspicious at all." Meg rolled her eyes.

"From where we're sitting, it's clearly a ploy to divert attention. Still, it could have happened that way."

"Sure, but did it?" They walked on for twenty seconds as Meg organized her thoughts. "We've seen death, you and me."

"Too many times."

"The bombing in Cumberland, when all we found were charred body parts. The burial at Arlington Cemetery. All those bodies after Hurricane Cole. Not figuring out the puzzle in time to get to Bethlehem Steel to save Warren Roth."

"Brett Stephenson."

"Exactly. Death is messy. It's terrifying, and uncertain, and it tears the heart out of you. And this . . . this feels too tied up in a big red bow for me. We needed an explanation and there's one right there, just waiting for us. But for me, that explanation doesn't fit the mess of violent death, as we know it. It's just too pat."

"So what does fit?"

"I don't know. Maybe I'm wasting our time. Maybe we should shut up and let Elan take the heat off me."

"But since you know you're not responsible, and you don't think he is, someone else is walking free."

"That's part of it. Elan wasn't on our radar initially. We have this long list and he wasn't on it, and now he's the key."

"There are some who don't want to be looked at. They'd be happy to shine the spotlight elsewhere."

"That's what I'm worried about. Will Boy Wonder take the time to look into the shadows around the spotlight, or does he just want an uncontested win?"

"What if he still thinks you're in the shadows?"

"Then he continues to be short-sighted. And it's not just me on the line. It's Hawk. Just the thought of someone taking Hawk away terrifies me. But if I'm arrested for murder, or, worse, if I'm convicted, I'll lose Hawk anyway. And Todd, and my family, and you, and the team. My life, as I know it, will be over." She had to stop, had to concentrate on her breathing—in, out, in, out—as she tried to steady a heart that hammered like she'd just finished a half marathon. "Between the abuse charges and Pratt's death, too much of this could go sideways." She met his green eyes. "I'm scared."

He ran a hand comfortingly up and down her back. "I know. I would be too, in your place. But you have the whole lot of us. We're not going to let them take Hawk away, and we're not going to let them lock you away on a murder charge. We'll get it sorted out and we'll find who's responsible for it all. Let's go badger McCord and find out what he knows. And if he's still busy, let's devise our next plan of attack. Remember what McCord said. We don't sit around and let a case develop on its own; let's be proactive."

Meg threaded her arm through his as they walked down the road. "Thanks, pal."

"You bet. Now, let's figure this out."

CHAPTER 27

Church Raise: A training exercise where one firefighter sits atop a fifty-foot ladder, balanced vertically by only four ropes affixed to the top of the ladder. Each rope is controlled by an individual firefighter. The exercise is intended to develop teamwork and trust.

Monday, October 21, 10:41 AM
Boundary Waters Canoe Area
Superior National Forest, Minnesota

Meg stretched out on top of their sleeping bags, Hawk curled at her side, her hand spread over his back as his head rested on her thigh. She lay, unmoving, her eyes closed, but didn't sleep.

She'd retreated into her tent with Hawk for twenty minutes of peace. McCord was sitting by the fire, deep into research, flanked by Brian and Ryan. Todd and his brothers had headed out on the lake after breakfast, and Craig was off somewhere with Brogan and Sheriff Olsen. She'd wanted some time to gather her thoughts—to not talk murder, or competitions, or legal options if they tried to remove Hawk from her care.

She wanted to roll back the clock to Thursday, to change her mind about the weekend. New skills were always useful, but Hawk could have lived without this one. In the end, he hadn't needed that much training. They might have figured it out themselves based on their own knowledge of scent patterns and search strategy if they'd used imitation cadaver scents.

If only they'd stayed home. Spent the weekend curled up bingeing a new show on Netflix or going for a long hike through Rock Creek Park. Then she wouldn't be a murder suspect, in danger of losing her freedom and her family. She wouldn't have been accused of abusing her beloved dog and risking his removal.

If only . . .

Her fingers twitched on his back and she felt his head lift to gaze at her. "Sorry, buddy. Just ignore your neurotic owner." She smoothed his fur, and his head settled again on her thigh.

She tried to clear her mind, using one of Cara's deep-breathing techniques, but that only made her think of scuba diving . . . and what can be found while scuba diving. Scolding herself, she tried visualization, picturing herself sitting on a tropical beach. She sat on a towel, Hawk stretched out beside her, his black fur warm under the sun's rays. A few feet past her sand-covered toes, the waves rolled in rhythmically. She concentrated on those waves. In . . . out . . . in . . . out—

"Meg? You in there?"

She released a deep breath on a sigh. She seriously loved the man, but couldn't he have fished for another half hour? "I'm here."

The sound of the zipper came from the front flap, followed by a rustle. Then silence.

She opened her eyes to find Todd standing at the bottom of the air mattress, dressed in jeans, hiking boots, a hoodie, and windbreaker, staring down at her.

"Yes?"

"You okay?"

She laughed. "Is that a serious question?"

Shaking his head, he circled around to his side of the bed. He sat down on the mattress next to Hawk, stroking the head the dog raised in greeting as his tail thumped the sleeping bag. "Actually, it is. You're putting on a good front, but I can see this trip is taking its toll on you. That's why I offered to stay back this morning. To do whatever I could to help."

"I appreciated the offer, but Brian and I had to head out to return Odin and I couldn't bring you for that. Not to mention I already have Brian hanging over me. And you came along this weekend to get some guy time with your brothers. I'm not going to get in the way of that."

"First of all, you're not 'getting in the way' of anything. I love those two lunkheads, but we could go fishing any other weekend. They know you come first."

She linked her fingers with his, where they lay on Hawk's back. "Thanks. But we're in a holding pattern for now. All this morning got us was yet more confirmation we have too many potential suspects. And now the possibility being raised that Elan killed Pratt and then killed himself in his grief over that act." As Todd considered that theory, the calculation in his eyes told her he found it wanting. "Not seeing it?"

"Oh, I can see it. I'm just not buying it. Is the theory that he did it because he was so upset about an incomplete competition that doesn't mean anything significant to a career officer in the long run?"

"That's the idea."

"Elan knew, for sure, that Pratt was the brains behind the setup?"

"No."

The pointed look he gave her clearly said, *So?*

"Yeah, it's weak."

"It sure is."

She rolled her eyes up to look at the ceiling of the tent. "Which puts me firmly back at the top of the list."

He folded her hand into both of his. "You're not going to stay there. And a weak suspect isn't what we need to get you off the list for good. We're going to figure this out. I saw McCord out there. He's gnawing away on this like Hawk does on an elk antler. He's determined to work this through. Give him some time. He was happy with what he got accomplished yesterday."

"How do we know what he accomplished? He wouldn't share it with us last night because he didn't have the full picture yet." She could hear the frustration in her tone, but couldn't seem to filter it out. "God, listen to me. I sound like a whiny fourteen-year-old who's not getting her own way."

Todd chuckled. "You're frustrated and scared. It's okay to let that out. Better than bottling it up the way you're hiding how worried you are. About Hawk. About yourself. About what's at risk you haven't put into words, but I know is weighing on you."

His words brought all she'd been trying to keep at bay crashing down on her, fear blossoming, its razor-sharp petals unfurling to slice deep.

"Don't say you're not concerned," he continued. "I know you better than that."

"I'm trying not to worry." At his raised eyebrows, she sighed. "Okay, it's not working. The whole thing terrifies me. The thought of losing Hawk. Of what I'm doing to you."

"Doing to me?"

"We have plans, and all of this threatens them. It's not just my future at risk, it's ours. Our home. Our future. Our children." She pushed past the obstruction that seemed to swell in her throat. "Our *life*." She slapped her free hand over her eyes. "Why did we come here this weekend?"

"Because you saw it as an opportunity to expand Hawk's horizons. Not yours, *his*. And he loved it. You did too. You should have seen yourself that first day, talking about the training. You were so proud of him, just over-flowing, wanting to tell us about how he did so well."

Meg dropped her hand to look down at Hawk, an affectionate smile curving her lips. "He really did do well."

"And his accomplishments on Saturday were remarkable. That got lost in what he found, or, rather, who he found, but this was supposed to be a training weekend and he was working as well as any experienced cadaver dog. He's amazing."

Meg's smile melted, knowing she didn't have to hide her fear from Todd. "What will I do if they take him away? I can't do it. I can't lose him like that. Not after . . ." She dug under her sweatshirt for the chain that lay there, out of sight, whenever she wasn't on a search where she might risk losing it. She pulled the chain and its pendant out. Made of handblown glass, it was a swirling cloud of color—black, electric blue, and a soft smoky gray . . . all she had left of Deuce—his ashes. She wrapped her fist around the remembrance necklace. "I know Hawk would still be alive and breathing somewhere, but it wouldn't be here, with me. With us. I can't do it, Todd. I can't—"

He stopped her frantic flow of words with an index finger over her lips. "You won't. Look, I may have done something you may not be happy about."

Her eyes went to slits. If he thought she'd be unhappy about something he did before he'd even told her, he was probably right. "What did you do?"

"Craig and I . . . had a conversation yesterday."

"What kind of conversation?"

"The kind of conversation I probably should have had a couple of beers before, because I was likely wound too tight before we started. But it was right after breakfast, so it seemed a bit early. Still . . . might not have been a bad idea."

"Where was I during this conversation?"

"You and Brian had gone to talk to Sal. Anyway, I caught Craig on his own for a few minutes and let him know my opinion about Hawk and about your suspension."

Temper flared, driving away fear. "I don't need you to fight my battles. I'm not helpless."

Todd's crack of laughter startled Hawk upright again. "Sorry, buddy. Didn't mean to scare you. Mom said something hilarious." When he met Meg's eyes, there was no humor in his. "You're anything but helpless. You may be the strongest person I know, and that's saying something when you keep in mind the family I come from and that I work with a group of people who routinely run straight into burning buildings. But just because you aren't helpless doesn't mean sometimes someone else can't stand up for you. The suspension, the abuse charge, the potential murder charges—it's all garbage."

"It may be garbage, but it's real. I need Craig in my corner. If you piss him off—"

"I didn't. In fact, that was part of my calculation. I thought he'd be on your side, but I had to confirm. I admit I went in there, guns blazing, but Craig's attitude took that down pretty quick." He picked up her other hand so he could hold both in his. "He's going to make sure this gets fixed. He knows you didn't kill anyone. He's leaving McCord to work the connections and research for that, because if we try to help there, we'll only get in his way. But Craig's already working on the abuse allegation." He let go of her hands to mime balancing two objects, one in each cupped hand. "On one side, you have one complaint from someone who doesn't know you; on the other, years of working side by side with professional dog people who have seen you in the most stressful of situations, have seen how you treat Hawk during those situations, and how he responds to you." One hand dropped nearly to his thigh, while the other popped up to his shoulder. "It's no contest. He's building a list of people who will speak for you. If Brogan tries to take a run at you around that, he's not going to know what hit him. That charge is going to go away. And the suspension is a technicality. Craig needed to do it—hell, Peters needed to do it—to play along for now because of Pratt's death. Neither of them has any intention it's going to last more than a week or two. Hopefully, considerably less, if McCord works his magic." He cupped one hand to her cheek. "I know you're feeling unmoored and rudderless. But you're not."

A lump was forming in her throat and she swallowed hard to get past it. "It's hard not to feel that way. So much of this is out of my control. Everyone intends to put things back the way they should be, but I've lost my job, my purpose, and there's no guarantee I'll get it back. And I could lose my dog. And my freedom. And you."

He studied her face for a moment, indecision reflected in his brown eyes, and then he rolled off the air mattress to kneel beside the small adjacent table, sorting through items.

Meg stared at him. This was his response to her lamenting the loss of her dog and her career? "What are you looking for?"

"Dental floss."

"Dental . . . what?" She had to be losing her hearing. Or her mind. Or he was losing *his* mind.

"Found it." He shifted to sit on the air mattress, a small box of dental floss in hand.

Meg pushed up onto one elbow. "Dental floss."

"Well, sort of." He flipped open the top. But instead of a closed compartment with a spool of floss, the inside was hollow. He tipped the box and a brilliant flash fell into his hand. He picked it up and extended it to her, holding it between thumb and index finger. "I know we've talked about this, and it was always just sometime in the future. But Giraldi's attack on you two months ago, and nearly losing you in that attack, made me realize time is precious, and what was I waiting for? I had this crazy idea of giving it to you this weekend. Somewhere quiet, just us and Hawk. Maybe out on the lake in the boat under the moon. I was going to run with it, once we got here and I saw the setup. But then things went sideways, and I decided to put it off. But now . . ."

Meg couldn't take her eyes off the ring clasped in his fingers, couldn't even blink. The single, round-cut center stone was held into a silver band on both sides by a bezel that ran nearly half the length of the stone, leaving a small gap at the top and bottom. On each side, two smaller diamonds were bezel set into a filigree of leaves and swirls. She tried to draw in a breath, but shock left her lungs frozen.

"This is you, taking control," Todd continued, as if sensing she needed a minute for her brain to start firing properly. "This is you, not being unmoored and rudderless. We're committed to each other, to living together, but this is the next step I'd like to take with you. I know things are unsettled, but this is something you can count on, even if everything else goes to hell. You can count on me. On us. No matter what happens, or where you are, we'd be connected. Marry me; let's make it official."

Meg's lungs finally remembered how to work and she sucked in a breath. "Yes. Oh God, yes." She threw her arms around his neck and just held on for a moment before pulling back, cupping his face in both hands, and kissing him, long and slow. She shifted away in surprise moments later when Hawk, sensing something important was happening without him, ran his cool nose over both their cheeks, trying to get in on the action. She broke away, laughing. "Hawk, give us a minute, buddy. Good boy." She kissed the top of his head. "Down." He settled on the bed again and she turned back to Todd.

"Let's put this where it belongs." Picking up her left hand, he slid the ring onto her finger, smiling down at it. "Perfect."

"It really is." She angled her hand so she could see the ring better, the light that filtered through the tent sparkling in the depths of the stone as she tipped her hand back and forth. "It's beautiful."

"I was hoping you'd like it. Now, if you don't, I want you to tell me. McCord and I put a lot of thought into it, but it's your ring, and you need to love it."

"I do love it. McCord?"

"After the last case you worked with him, who better to help me pick out a ring than the guy who now knows everything about diamonds and where to get them. Also, in the early days of his recovery, it gave him something to work on. Deciding which shops and so on."

She gaped at him. "You and McCord went ring shopping on Jewelers' Row in Philly?"

He grinned at her. "Sure did. He knew everything about color and clarity and made sure we got a nice stone, and then we worked with a jeweler there to build an indestructible ring."

"Indestructible?"

"Well, as close as we could manage. You have a job where sometimes you end up in some challenging spots. If you want this to be a piece you can wear all the time, you can't have a ring with a tall stone, or only four claws, or pavé diamonds. So we went with a modern bezel setting for the center and side stones, in an Art Nouveau–style band. All in platinum, because it's a more durable metal, and can be polished if it gets scratched. But if you would prefer a different style—"

"No, I love it just the way it is." She met his eyes so he wouldn't question her sincerity. "Truly love it. And I love you for putting all that thought into creating a ring that works with my occasionally hazardous lifestyle." She studied the ring again. "Has Cara seen it?"

"Yes. She knew McCord and I were working on it because we did so much of it there."

"All those times you went over to help him with his physiotherapy."

"I always did. We tacked this onto the end of it. Anyway, Cara's seen it because she's been keeping it for me for the last week so you couldn't accidentally stumble over it at home."

"And she knows you planned to propose this weekend?"

"Your whole family knows."

"The whole family?" Hawk's ears perked high as Meg's tone rose. She stroked his head. "Sorry, buddy. I'll try not to go supersonic on you. You told all of them?"

"I admit I haven't talked to Emma," Todd said, referring to Eda and Jake Jennings's newly adopted daughter, a teenage girl caught in a sex-trafficking ring until she was rescued by Meg and Hawk, and then cared for by Meg's parents at their rescue as she found her balance again. Their bond had grown so strong, Emma was now legally part of the family, to everyone's great joy. "But I asked your dad for his blessing—"

"You didn't."

"I did. I respect your dad. I know it's not necessary,

but it's old-school, and a lot of older men like old-school. So then, of course, once I talked to Jake, Eda needed a word too."

"A word." Meg couldn't hold back a laugh. "She kept you on the phone for at least a half hour, didn't she?"

"You know your mom. She can talk the hind leg off a mule, as they say." He chuckled. "They're both over the moon. And sent along the message they want you to call ASAP."

"Of course they do. I have to ask—dental floss?"

"I wanted to bring the ring with me, but didn't want to carry it out on the boat, in case anything happened out there. I didn't think anyone would steal our stuff, but if they did, no one's going to steal dental floss. So I hid it in there and then left it on the table tucked behind a bunch of stuff so you wouldn't see it and decide you needed some. But that way, if someone came in and swiped my duffel, they'd leave the dental floss behind."

She tapped his temple. "Pretty ingenious. Now—"

"*Meg!*" The shout came from McCord, from outside. From the sound of it, he was still sitting by the fire.

Meg deflated at the sound of his voice as reality intruded once again. She looked toward the tent flap as if she could see through it. "What does McCord want?"

"I have no idea, but we can always ask him. There's a one hundred percent chance he'll tell us."

"Maybe he'll just go away."

"*Meg! I need you now!*" Another call from across the campsite.

Todd shrugged. "On the other hand, maybe he won't. Whatever it is, it sounds important."

"It does." She pushed up into a sitting position and dropped her hands over Hawk's ears. "Brace yourself," she said to Todd. "*Coming!*" she bellowed. She sucked in a big breath, let it out noisily. "I can do this." She looked down at the ring, at Todd's physical symbol of their connection. "*We* can do this."

"Yes, we can."

Meg rolled to her feet, called her dog, and moved to the tent flap. She held out her newly ringed hand, and Todd clasped it in his.

Together, with their dog, they stepped out into the afternoon sun to meet the next challenge.

CHAPTER 28

Flashover: The situation that occurs during a fire when the contents of a room give off flammable gases heated to their ignition point, so fire suddenly engulfs the room.

Monday, October 21, 11:02 AM
Boundary Waters Canoe Area
Superior National Forest, Minnesota

"You can stop yelling, we're coming."

Meg and Todd crossed over to the fire, Hawk trotting beside them, and then breaking away to head for Lacey, who sat with Brian and Ryan. McCord sat in what had become his spot, the chair next to Meg's rocker, a flat chunk of wood in front of him to use as a footrest as he sat with his legs stretched out, ankles crossed, his laptop open on his lap. Todd's portable power station sat behind his chair, powering his laptop and phone, its small solar panel propped against it, spread wide to recharge the battery. Brian sat on McCord's far side, leaning in to look at the screen McCord angled toward him. Ryan and Craig were next in the circle, and Josh and Luke, both with coffee mugs in hand, completed the group.

Meg dropped into her rocking chair. "What's going on?"

McCord looked up from his laptop. "First, let me make

sure I have this straight. Of all the people we've talked to, we had a limited list of those who said they knew Pratt before or who were linked to her. Fief, who mentored her, only to be humiliated by her later. McGraw, who cheated with her in a past competition and got burned for his trouble. Once she got here, Thatcher, Whittaker, Litzer, and Baeza helped her cheat in this competition. But beyond that, there were no direct connections."

"That's my understanding."

"None of the divers or pilots."

"No."

"Not Dix, Elan, or Glenn."

"No, not unless Elan got wind of her cheating this weekend."

"And none of them said they'd worked with her before?"

"No. I told you I asked them flat out. Where are you going with this?"

"I'm going here." McCord turned his laptop around. A Facebook page was displayed.

Meg leaned in to look at the page itself. "FEMA?"

"FEMA. They often document all the good stuff they do during mass disasters. Your tax dollars at work. But I want you to see this." He opened a photo in a post. In it, a group of five K-9 handlers stood with their dogs against a backdrop of devastation, a row of town houses in the background no more than a pile of matchsticks. The entire group, humans and canines alike, radiated exhaustion and none of them smiled. "It's dated October 11, 2018."

"Hurricane Michael. That's Florida?"

"Mexico Beach."

Meg winced. "Landfall."

"Yeah." He plunked the laptop on her thighs. "Take a good look." A thread of anger wove through his tone.

Meg scanned the image, feeling Todd press in from her left. The middle pair caught her eye immediately. "There's Pratt and Ava. Dead center. But we knew they were there."

"Keep looking. Anyone else you know?"

Meg scanned to the right and was surprised to see a face she hadn't seen in years. "Actually, yes. Pam Dennihoff, with her retriever, Goldie." She pointed at the woman on the extreme right of the photo. She wore a navy one-piece jumpsuit and carried a yellow hard hat under her arm. Her retriever sat at her feet, slightly angled so her FEMA work vest displayed the familiar logo. "She works with the Search Dog Foundation, but when disaster strikes, FEMA contracts her to bring in the dogs they need. I've worked with her a few times in the past." She looked up to meet McCord's flinty gaze. "And that's not what you're looking for." She studied the photo again, scanning over dogs—so many German shepherds—and then up to faces. She actually panned past the face to the left of Pratt, moving on to the final figure, before alarm bells clanged and her gaze snapped back. Using two fingers, she blew up the photo until only the middle three people in the photo showed.

She nearly hadn't seen it. Between the mud-smeared black jumpsuit, and the blue hard hat sitting low on his forehead, he'd looked almost anonymous. But it was the eerily pale eyes that finally jumped out at her. Ice-blue. Cold.

Damon Glenn.

Gasping, she sat back, and slowly turned to McCord.

He was nodding in satisfaction. "I thought so. You asked him. Did he deny knowing her?"

"You didn't know Pratt? Hadn't been on any deployments with her?"

Elan shook his head. "I'd never met her."

"Even if we had, we were together in the tent that

night," Glenn said. "Brogan was pushing for alibis. A couple of people are on their own, like Pratt, but most of us
are paired up."

"He dodged the question, now that I think of it. De-
flected." Fury filled Meg. He'd been stringing them along
the whole time. "Son of a bitch!"

"I'm missing something," Todd said, angling the laptop
more toward him. "What don't I see?"

"Him." Meg poked a finger at the screen. "That's
Damon Glenn. And he's standing right beside Pratt."

"Son of a bitch," Todd echoed.

McCord picked up his laptop and set it on his knees.
"He ducked that question for a reason. Maybe he thought
it would possibly put him on the list."

"Not telling us puts him at the top of the list," said
Craig. He met Meg's gaze. "You're sure that's him?"

"One hundred percent. McCord, did they name the
handlers in the photo?"

"No, that's why I wanted you and Brian to confirm
what I thought I was seeing. I haven't met him, but after
all this time trying to track these people, I know their faces
pretty well. We need to confirm that's him, but it really
needs to be from an outside source. This Pam. Could you
contact her?"

"I can, with an assist." She started to push out of her
chair.

Todd stopped her with a hand over hers on the chair
arm. "What do you need?"

"My sat phone. It's beside the bed."

"Got it." He got up and jogged to the tent.

"Meg," Craig called, attracting her attention. "Before
we go further with this, I have a couple of new pieces of
intel. I spent some time this morning with Sheriff Olsen
and Brogan. First off, agents from the Cheyenne field of-

fice searched Pratt's home, also in Cheyenne. And they found some interesting things there, including her laptop. Didn't take their computer forensic team long to get into it. Seems her e-mail program was set up for automatic access. And all her communication with Thatcher was right there. Seems she paid him thirteen thousand to help her win the competition, ten for him, and a thousand for each of the three observers he said he needed to recruit."

Meg tossed McCord a look that conveyed how unsurprised she was by this news. "You were right once again."

"You had to know they weren't doing it just for kicks," McCord said.

"And you remember how Pratt's tent was tossed?" Craig continued.

Meg nodded. "Hard to forget that."

"Looks like whoever tossed it may have missed what they were looking for. Olsen found a handwritten note hidden at the bottom of a box of tampons."

"That's a place most men wouldn't look," Brian muttered.

"Probably exactly what she had in mind," Craig continued. "But considering the note, she likely wanted to keep it as proof. The directions in the note were to meet that night at midnight, along that trail, with a GPS location for the top of that cliff."

"So now we know how the perp got her there," Meg said, anticipation rising. "Who was it from?"

"Isaac Thatcher." But as Meg drew breath, Craig held up a hand to stop her. "Hold that thought. Olsen took it to Thatcher, who denied it."

"Of course he did."

"And then followed it up with reams of handwritten trial plans and comments in a handwriting totally dissimilar to the note. Olsen even had him rewrite it verbatim. It looked nothing like the handwriting in the note and matched everything else he claimed was his."

"I assume he's going to get samples of everyone else's handwriting for comparison?"

"Yes. He got sidetracked by another dead body, but he'll be taking care of that. Of course, McCord may have just shortened the suspect list considerably. Which you're potentially about to confirm."

Meg leaned forward to look past McCord, who was head down again over his laptop, to Brian. "Did you ever work with Pam?"

Brian waved his hand in a *maybe* gesture. "I don't think I ever worked with her in person, but I've talked to her on the phone when she was trying to pull people in. Whatever it was, I wasn't available. Or we were already deploying as official FBI personnel."

"She's good people. Practical and straight-shooting. And has an amazing mind for details, which is what I'm hoping to put to work for us."

Todd returned and handed Meg her phone.

She smiled up at him. "Thanks. Go catch up on what you missed with Josh. He'll fill you in on what Craig just told us."

Todd gave her a questioning look, but sat down beside his brother and leaned in for the details.

"Who's the assist?" asked Craig.

"Lauren. I know she's worked with her. And if she doesn't have her number, she's in a better place to track it down for us. Have you deployed her and Rocco? Or are they in DC?"

"She's in DC, ready for deployment, but no current cases."

"Let's give it a try." She had every team member's number stored on the phone, and speed-dialed Lauren's number.

The phone rang only twice before being picked up. "Lauren Wycliffe."

"Hey, it's Meg."

"Meg, hi. Did you get back last night? How did the training go?"

Meg's gaze flicked up to Craig, whose eyes were fixed on her. Craig, who could practically have the slogan "Loose lips sink ships" tattooed on his shoulder, who would go to the grave with many of the secrets of the FBI never whispered from his lips. He'd guarded the secret of the accusation of abuse against her, as well as Pratt's death. Keeping her safe.

She really wasn't alone in all this.

"Actually, I'm still in Minnesota. So's Brian. Craig's here too."

"Craig? I talked to him earlier this morning. I assumed he was in the office."

"Nope. He's currently sitting on the other side of a campfire from me. I'll keep it short. We had a suspicious death here over the weekend, one of the handlers, and he came out to give us a hand."

"Crap, that is not what you thought the weekend would be."

"Not at all."

"I'm not surprised Craig came out, though. You know what he's like. Everything for the team."

"One hundred percent."

"Can I do anything to help?"

"Actually, yes. Do you remember Pam Dennihoff?"

"Remember her? The woman is a tornado sweeping aside anything in her path, but in a good way. How could I forget her?"

"Great. Do you have contact information for her? Specifically, phone?"

"I think so. Hang on." Ten seconds ticked by as Lauren stayed silent, then twenty. "Yeah, I have it. Got something to jot this down?"

Meg tapped McCord's knee and, wedging her phone between her ear and her shoulder, mimed writing something down. McCord hit enter a few times to get to a new line in his current document and nodded. "Yes, give it to me."

As Lauren read out the numbers, Meg repeated them, and McCord typed them in. Then Meg read them back in their entirety, one more time.

"That's it," Lauren confirmed. "Anything else I can do?"

"This is more than enough. Thanks, Lauren. I hope to be back in a day or two and I'll explain the whole mess to you then."

"I'll see you then. Stay safe, and if you need anything, call anytime, day or night."

"Appreciate that, thanks." Meg ended the call, then called up her contact list and entered the number into her phone. "I'm going to call Pam. I'm just going to move over there, where it's a little quieter." She stood, threaded her way out of the circle, and walked over to the deserted picnic table. She sat, her back to the group so there was nothing to distract her, and dialed Pam.

The phone rang four times and Meg was worried all she'd get was voice mail, when the call was picked up and a harried voice said, "Hello?"

"Pam, it's Meg Jennings from the FBI Human Scent Evidence Team. We worked together on—"

"I remember. It's nice to hear from you. Are you still working with that handsome boy? Hawk, right?"

"Yes, Hawk. And I am. He's doing great. We just learned water cadaver searches this past weekend, and he has a real knack for it."

"Does he?" The professional interest was evident in her tone. "Can I make a note of that?"

"You're still organizing for FEMA?"

"I am. And that's a valuable skill to have."

"Definitely make a note. Same note for Brian Foster and

Lacey. As always, all deployments have to go through SAC Craig Beaumont, but he's always willing to send us where we're needed, especially following a mass disaster."

"I like Craig. Unlike some unit chiefs, he doesn't grouse when I ask for help. That's good to know. I'll add it to my files on you two."

Of course she has a file on us. Über organized.

"But I'm sure you didn't call to update your skill set," Pam continued. "What can I do for you?"

"I'm involved in a case here in Minnesota." Meg thought it best not to outline her own involvement in the case. Pam was fair, but she didn't have time to get into the minutiae. "And I need some information about one of your deployments. Mexico Beach in October 2018. Do you remember it?"

"I remember it, all right. Landfall occurred while Michael was a Category Five storm. The storm surge was nineteen feet high at maximum. Total devastation."

"The kind of storm where you really need the teams afterward."

"Oh yeah."

"Do you remember the teams you had for that deployment?"

"I can look through my notes for specifics. Did you need something particular?"

No way around it. "Pam, we're investigating the suspicious death of Deputy Sheriff Rita Pratt from the Laramie County Sheriff's Office."

"Pratt? I remember her. She's dead?"

"Yes. It happened sometime Friday evening into Saturday morning."

"That's such a shame. She . . ." Pam's voice trailed off.

"What?"

"My brain is kicking in. You know I run a lot of deployments. Sometimes they begin to blend into one another. One tornado looks like another. One hurricane looks like another. Unless something different happens to make it stand out. Pratt stood out during that deployment."

"Did she do something wrong? Or make a significant discovery?"

"She didn't do anything wrong. But I had to handle an accusation of sexual assault during that deployment. With one of the other handlers. Needless to say, it makes the whole deployment stand out."

The hair on the back of Meg's neck prickled upright. "Can I ask who the handler was?"

"I don't think I can say. To the best of my knowledge, the case never went anywhere and no disciplinary action was handed out. She accused, he denied, the old boys' club blew it off, charges dropped. You know, the same old story."

"Too often, yes. Though things are getting better lately. How about this? If I give you one name, can you confirm or deny that's who was involved? I hate to ask this of you, Pam, but we're talking about murder."

There were several seconds of silence, then, "Yes."

"Damon Glenn."

The catch of breath on the other end of the line answered her question. *Son of a bitch, indeed.*

"That's who it was. You think he killed her?"

"I think he's hidden a past with her. According to him, they'd never met."

Pam's laugh was harsh. "Not even close."

"What happened between them, to the best of your knowledge?"

"I can send you my notes on it, but I'll give you what I remember first, so you have something to start with. You know what these deployments are like. You put people up wherever there's a place for them. Schools, community centers, hotels. Whatever is open, and has electricity and running water, if possible. For that trip, we got one of the American Legion posts in Panama City. It was a ways inland; it still took a beating, but was out of the range of the storm surge. It was a small building, but that was fine because we were barely there and were mostly in and out. That's where Glenn met Pratt as the team was sleeping together communally. But the small place, with so many in and out, was the problem. According to Pratt, Glenn caught her there alone and tried to . . . force himself on her." Distaste came through loud and clear in every syllable. "Pratt fought and got him off her. According to her, a well-placed knee let her get away. And as she was scrambling free, leaving him on the floor, he was roaring at her that he deserved to have sex, and her type didn't have the right to withhold it, that kind of thing. Called her all sorts of insulting names, including 'femoid.' "

Femoid—a misogynistic term for a subhuman, unintelligent female.

A flashing, red-alert signal.

Shock slammed into Meg. Glenn was a closet incel—an involuntary celibate, a group of men who turn their lack of success having sex with women into violence, hatred, and rage against them. That kind of rejection would entirely be grounds for murder for some incels.

"My God," Meg breathed. "I didn't see it at all."

"I hadn't either. He keeps it well hidden. Most do, from what I understand, until they lose it and go on the attack. Anyway, she lodged a complaint, and I handed Glenn off to another group doing SAR and, as far as I know, they didn't make contact again during that deployment. Then they both went back to their own states and, from what I understand, the whole thing fell apart into a 'he said/she said' kind of thing, with no physical evidence to back it up, or witnesses, and charges were dropped."

*So there was nothing for McCord to find, even if it had
been kept hidden.*

"Makes you wonder if this was the first time they'd
come into contact since then. Honestly, I didn't see anything between them to indicate they knew each other."

"He may have been playing it cool, and she may have
been trying not to give the situation any oxygen, hoping to
ignore him and have zero contact."

"She sure had contact with someone," Meg muttered.

"You're sure it was murder?"

"It's unlikely to be anything else. We found the kill site
about fifteen minutes from here on land. We found her
body about thirty minutes away by boat at the bottom of
the lake. A lake with only minimal currents."

"Accidental death certainly seems unlikely."

"Extremely. Pam, thanks so much for this. To say this is
a huge help is an understatement. I think you blew the
case wide open. Can you send me whatever notes you have
on it?"

"I can. Same FBI e-mail address?"

"Yes. And please cc: SAC Beaumont."

"I can do that. You'll see them by end of day today."

"Much appreciated. Thank you again." Meg ended the
call and sat for a moment, trying to organize her thoughts.

She got up and marched back to the fire.

Todd tracked her as she returned. "Anything useful?"

She stopped behind her own chair, but felt too restless
to sit. "I think we just learned everything we need to
know."

"Pam remembered them?" Craig asked.

"Oh yeah. You know how if you do enough deployments, they kind of become a blur unless something significant happens?"

"I take it from that, something significant happened?"

"Pam's group of five handlers and dogs was put up at a local, inland American Legion following Hurricane Michael. It was a small group, in and out a lot. At some point, when Pratt and Glenn were the only ones there, Glenn sexually assaulted Pratt. Or at least attempted to. It sounds like she nailed him with a knee to the groin."

"Nicely done," said McCord. "Did she press charges?"

"Yes, but the charges were dropped. No physical evidence, 'he said/she said,' no witnesses. It went nowhere. But there's more than just the assault. Afterward, it sounds like while he was rolling around on the ground, clutching the family jewels, he raged at her. Called her, among other names, a 'femoid.'"

Some of the faces around the circle were blank, but Craig and McCord snapped alert.

"Holy shit, he's an incel." McCord looked stunned. "I never picked that up in anything I found on him. But some of them camouflage themselves very well." He looked at Craig. "I bet if your eager-beaver agent could get a warrant for his electronics, you'd find he's a regular user of the Reddit incel forums."

"You can be assured I'm going to push him to do just that," said Craig. "I don't know if he's on-site still or if he left with Elan's body." He stopped, looking contemplative. "Elan . . . if we're assuming Glenn killed Pratt, then Elan was at risk as his alibi."

"With what we know about Elan and his addiction," Todd said, "maybe he thought Glenn was covering for *him*. If he was high, he may have thought Glenn alibiing him ensured his little problem was never discovered. He may never have known he was actually falsely alibiing Glenn. But that would have given Glenn a window of opportunity. If Elan was in a stupor, or unconscious, from the fentanyl on Friday night, he never would have noticed Glenn leaving. But if he was in that state, he certainly couldn't swear Glenn was there. His lack of an answer would have brought his drug abuse to light. So he lied."

"Maybe Glenn got nervous that Elan would let it slip he didn't actually know if Glenn was there that night," reasoned Brian. "Maybe he even confronted Glenn about it. If Elan admitted he couldn't alibi Glenn, you know Brogan would suddenly be looking to Glenn about why he'd lied. And if he looked hard enough at Glenn, he might have uncovered this connection to Pratt and the accusation of sexual assault. So, if Glenn thought his alibi was about to crack, he might have considered his only choice was to kill Elan." He looked up at Meg. "You saw him this morning. He looked genuinely distraught. But maybe it wasn't strictly over the death of his friend. Maybe it's because he felt he had no choice but to kill him to save his own skin."

"Prince of a guy," Meg said with disgust.

"And that note," said McCord. "The one Thatcher didn't write and they now need to compare to Glenn's handwriting. Maybe Fief wasn't the only one who overheard McGraw and Pratt arguing about cheating in the previous competition. If Glenn heard as well, then it would be natural he'd think after that first trial—where so many things went wrong—that Pratt was cheating again. Thatcher would have been the obvious partner, so he set up a meet with 'Thatcher,' knowing if it was true, she'd feel compelled to show up and that would be his confirmation. Then he lay in wait for her. Maybe to accuse her of cheating. Maybe to assault her again, or maybe to kill her dog and then her in retribution for the failed assault in Florida. Maybe all of it. Either way, we know the latter is how it turned out."

"We need to question Glenn." Craig stood. "I'll contact Brogan."

"Maybe we should wander over there and see where Glenn is," said Brian to Meg. "Go in to check up on him, since he was so upset when we talked to him this morning. Get your spare leash back. But we could keep an eye on him until Brogan arrives."

"That works for me." Meg bent and reached with her left hand for Hawk's leash, where it lay draped over the arm of her chair.

"Wait a second. What is *that*?" Brian sprang out of his chair and headed for Meg.

"What is . . ." Her voice trailed off. In everything that had happened, she'd forgotten what had come just before. "Oh."

Brian seized her hand and raised it to ogle her ring. "Oh my God, it's gorgeous. Congratulations!" He threw his arms around her and gave her a tight hug. Then set her back and stood with his hands on her shoulders to give her a light shake. "Why didn't you say anything? When did it happen? Last night?"

"Half an hour ago?"

"This morning? Babe, that's amazing." He caught her up in another hug. "I'm so happy for you," he whispered in her ear.

"Thanks, buddy," she murmured. "Now Todd and I can join you and Ryan in being an old, boring married couple."

That brought a laugh from him as he pulled back and gave her a smacking kiss on the lips. "You, boring? *Never.*" He let her go and held out his hand to Todd. "Congratulations. You caught the best of us."

Todd grinned. "No disagreement here."

Meg turned to McCord, finding him rising from his chair, leaving his laptop on the seat, a huge grin on his face. "Lemme see."

She held out her hand to him.

"Webb, we did good. It's perfect on her. Right size and

everything." He gave Meg a hug that lifted her off her feet with a squeak.

Todd looked over from where he was getting back slaps from his brothers. "Thanks again for your help."

"Anytime. You have to call Cara. And your parents," McCord told Meg as he put her down.

"I know. And I will as soon as I get a second." Her face went serious. "We have to deal with this first."

"We do. But take the joy where you can find it." McCord's eyes shadowed with memory. "Sometimes things can turn on a dime."

She rubbed his upper arm. "They can. And sometimes you have a team of friends who will find you no matter what."

"No matter what."

"Meg, congratulations." Craig held out his arms and she went into them.

Take the joy where you can find it.

She would. And then they'd nail Glenn to the wall for what he'd done.

CHAPTER 29

Oregon Tuck: A method of floating or vertically rolling over a waterfall in a kayak or dinghy. Named for the many large waterfalls in the northwestern United States.

Monday, October 21, 11:50 AM
Boundary Waters Canoe Area
Superior National Forest, Minnesota

Meg and Brian stood just out of sight of the campsite, flanked by their dogs.

"Ready?" Brian asked.

"Oh yeah." Meg glanced sideways at him. "Glenn's an incel and he killed Pratt because she rejected him. He let hatred of that fester over time. So it was a justifiable death in his eyes because she'd denied his 'rights.' It's really pissing me off." She stopped and took a breath, trying to keep the rage from rising. "I need to keep this tamped down. It's true, we haven't had the handwriting confirmed, but I think we know how that's going to go. And we don't know he had her meet him with the express purpose of killing her, but he clearly meant her harm. He could have apologized in public, out of hearing, but in sight of others. The only reason he pulled her into the backwoods was to do whatever he wanted to do unseen. And whether it was to assault her again, or to kill her for what happened in Florida, his motive was to harm, at the very least."

"At least. Though I'd say also to humiliate. She humiliated him the last time, and even if the charges were dropped and nothing could be proven, just the suggestion might have made him look bad to his superior officers, and he may have been fighting to get back from it ever since. I don't know much about incels other than what I've read in articles, but they seem to lay the blame for their failure to have sex firmly at the feet of women. Women are to blame for all their failures. Then combine that with the fact she bested him last time physically, and there could be significant rage simmering there, just waiting for the opportunity to boil over."

"It makes you wonder why she didn't back out of the competition. We all received the same e-mails. We all knew everyone who was coming."

"But think about when those lists came out—in the last two weeks. We signed up months ago. At that point, she would have had to make excuses to her senior officers. If they knew about the charges, they'd also know they were dropped, and innocent until proven guilty. Her continuing to raise the issue might not have gone over well with the old boys' club, if that's what her department is like. She may have felt she had no choice but to suck it up and come for the weekend. And don't forget the thirteen thousand dollars, which had already changed hands by that point. Back out, lose the money, and get nothing for it."

"Maybe her motive to win this competition makes more sense now with this new information. Maybe she felt she needed to win to improve her standing in the eyes of her superior officers, which had fallen because of the incident with Glenn. And then to find out he was coming? No way would she want to let him bring her down again by backing out." Meg glanced to where Pratt's tent still sat, physically separated from the others. "Once she got here, she tried to stay separate from the other handlers. But the competition fix was already in motion, and she was bound and determined to carry on with it. So she brazened her way through it."

" 'Brazened her way through . . .' That makes me wonder if some of her bravado was a show for Glenn."

"You mean the scene with Fief?"

"Yes. She was absolutely horrible for no reason. She'd already won. But was that actually a performance for Glenn? An I'm-such-a-bitch-don't-mess-with-me move?"

"Maybe. Or maybe she really was that horrible. We'll never know for sure. Now paste on a cheerful we're-coming-for-you smile, and let's hold Glenn in place until Brogan shows up."

"You want to see Brogan arrest him, don't you?"

"I can't lie, I really do. Then I'd like to walk away from him, knowing he knows he had it all wrong."

"Which will be amazing. Let's put that in motion. Come on, Lacey, let's go find the bad man."

They sauntered into the campsite, as if they didn't have a care in the world. Meg noted Glenn at the far fire and purposely strolled over to greet everyone seated around the fire closest to the road, including Fief and McGraw. They spent a few minutes there, chatting. At one point, Meg spotted Todd and McCord passing by, as if on their way to the washrooms or the main beach, casually glancing over to see how things were going.

Nosey parkers.

But in many ways, she couldn't blame them. They were both hip deep in the case, but didn't have any place in the final takedown. They'd timed their drive-by too soon. Nothing to see . . . yet.

Meg and Brian broke off and headed to the farthest fire.

The usual contingent was seated around it, including Glenn. Meg stopped to chat with Claire before circling around to Glenn and Dix.

She forced a concern she didn't feel to shine in her eyes. "Damon, how are you feeling?" She dropped a hand onto his shoulder in solidarity.

"Better. Sorry I walked off this morning. It's been . . . hard."

"I'm sure it has. You'd known Gerhard for how many years?"

"Five. And I know he had his struggles, but he was a good man."

"I'm sure he was." *Keep him talking.* "What's going to happen to Odin?"

"He belongs to the department, so I'll bring him back with me." He looked down at the shepherd lying dejectedly at his feet. "He has years of service left in him, so they'll assign him to a new handler. Poor guy. He loved Elan, and Elan loved him."

"They get so attached to us. If he realizes what's happened, he must be devastated. Though I think staying with you and Samson helps. You're both familiar."

"I'll stay with him as long as they'll let me." Glenn's gaze flicked to the road as Craig and Brogan appeared. Brogan's gaze was fixed on them around the campfire. He stepped into the grass and headed directly for them with no hesitation.

Meg watched him for a moment, alarm rising.

She wasn't the only one to spot him, as Dix also caught sight of them. "Look out, here comes trouble again. Brogan's headed directly for us. I bet he has more questions."

Glenn's gaze flicked to the oncoming agent, but his face remained placid. "Then I'm going to go get Samson and Odin a couple of bully sticks. Keep them occupied for the next twenty minutes until Brogan bugs off." Rising, he casually walked to his tent and disappeared inside.

She leaned into Brian. "What the hell is Brogan doing?" she whispered. "Are we sure this isn't his first case? He might as well be carrying a sign announcing his intentions."

"High on his own power and probably thinks there's nowhere to go."

"If Glenn has any suspicions they're after him, he could come out of his tent with a weapon. Do we know if he has a firearm with him?"

"No idea. But he could."

Brogan and Craig approached the fire, Craig looking vaguely irritated, both of them searching the surrounding faces for Glenn. Meg indicated the tent with an index finger, but before Brogan could change direction, the sound of a snapping branch came from the woods behind the tent. Whirling, Meg caught sight of a figure darting through the trees to disappear into the foliage.

Glenn was escaping.

Meg bent and quickly unleashed Hawk. "He's making a run for it. Hawk, come!"

She sprinted to the tent and past it, casting a quick glance at its rear panel. A long slash ran down the rear of the tent from top to bottom—he'd taken a knife to it rather than risk the sound of the zipper opening. And now he was trying to get lost in the forest.

If they'd ever had any doubts about his guilt, he'd just blown them all up. Most of the time, it was the guilty who ran before they were accused. Glenn must have been waiting for the boom to fall, had seen it coming, and was trying to avoid a crushing blow.

Running free, Hawk sprinted at her side, ducking under branches and through the underbrush with more grace than Meg. Behind them, she could hear Brian and Lacey pounding after them. She could only assume Craig and Brogan brought up the rear, but she knew Brian would stay with her; whereas she didn't know how fast or how long Brogan could run. Or Craig, who strictly coordinated when he was out in the field with his teams. She knew he exercised regularly, but he wasn't used to distance running the way she and Brian were from regular training. They'd stay with Glenn, even if no one else did.

Out of the woods, over the dirt road that led to the boat launch where she and Hawk had stood down by the lake on Friday night, and then back into the trees. Two minutes of hard running, and while she couldn't see Glenn in front of her, she thought she could still hear him. More than that, she could tell from Hawk's forward tilted ears that he did. She tried to judge where they were from the map in her head, and with a jolt, she realized where Glenn was heading.

The beach. Where the boats were moored.

Escape.

But it might also be a chance to catch him. He'd have to steal a boat in front of the pilots who manned them, who might object to someone running off with their equipment. And if they could close the distance on him, they might be able to intercept him first. The thought of taking Glenn down with a running tackle gave Meg a warm feeling that lit a fire under her feet.

Up ahead, the lake was now visible through the forest at about ten o'clock, but in front of her the light around the trees seemed brighter, and Meg estimated they were maybe thirty or forty feet away from the beach. Another twenty seconds and she heard shouts of fury rising from in front of them.

Glenn had made it through.

Meg bulleted through the tree line at top speed, Hawk about five feet to her left, toward the pandemonium on the beach. Glenn was in the water, pushing the nearest boat into the lake, spinning it parallel to the beach, and then hopping into it. On the beach, one of the divers was clutching his left jaw as he rolled to his feet from where he'd been laid out in the sand. Pilots and divers were running from the far end of the beach and from the line of tents in the forest above.

"Meg!"

She turned to see Todd and McCord sprinting down the hill toward her.

Away from the beach, Glenn had fired up the outboard motor and his boat was speeding into the lake.

Meg dropped down to a panting walk, scanning the incoming crowd for pilots.

But Todd had other ideas. "Come on!" he yelled as he ran past her, grabbed the nearest dinghy, and pushed it into the water. McCord joined him and then took over as Todd leapt into the boat. "Meg! Get in!"

Meg didn't hesitate. "Hawk, in the boat!"

Hawk raced for the dinghy, leaping in gracefully, Meg climbing in after him. She looked out across the beach, finding Charlie in the crowd. "Charlie!" When he locked gazes with her, she pointed to Brian and Lacey. "Follow us!"

Charlie nodded and waved Brian over to his boat.

"You know how to run this thing?" McCord called from thigh-high water.

Todd threw him a look that said *Duh* more clearly than any words. "Been fishing with my dad since I could walk. Been piloting for decades." He hit the start button and the engine purred to life. "Jump in if you're coming."

"Like I'd miss this." McCord pushed the boat backward into deeper water and then jumped onto the side and swung his dripping legs into the boat. "Next time, let's do this when it's a bit warmer."

"I'll make a note," Meg said. "Todd, he's getting away."

"Not for long." Todd backed them a little farther in a curve, and then shifted into forward and took off after Glenn. Once they'd cleared the other boats, he fully opened up the throttle and they skimmed over the waves after Glenn. He was a good sixty feet in front of them, spray flying from behind his boat.

"He's not going to stay in open water," Todd called. "He's been out on the lake a few times, so he knows how many small side channels there are. That's going to be his only chance to lose us, unless the battery in his motor isn't charged."

McCord dug a hand into his back pocket and pulled out his cell phone.

"What are you doing?" Meg asked. "You don't have a signal out here."

"No, but I downloaded maps of the area. I'll track where we're going manually based on our starting point. It could indicate where he might go. Or where we might get into trouble. It's not going to tell us anything about depth, but could indicate dead ends and so on. And where he could have gone if we lose him."

"Good idea." She turned around to scan the water behind them. "Two more boats are following. Brian and Lacey are in one with Charlie. There's another farther back. Looks like Craig and someone else. Probably Brogan. Because he hasn't screwed this up enough already. Not sure who's piloting that one."

"What did Brogan do?"

"Telegraphed his intent to Glenn, making him rabbit. Brogan has a lot to learn about technique. To say it's been lacking on this case is an understatement." She faced forward again, resting a hand on Hawk's shoulder to steady him as they bounced over the choppy water.

Glenn cut north and then west into the next large section of the lake, finally turning southwest toward the far side, where a series of three islands cut the lake into lateral sections.

Meg turned slightly so her words weren't lost in the wind. "I think we're gaining on him."

"He may not have the engine full open," Todd answered, his gaze fixed past Hawk's head and straight out over the bow. "Or it may only be a twenty horsepower. This one's twenty-five."

"Are we going top speed?" McCord asked.

"Oh yeah."

While breezy, it was brilliantly sunny, the light bouncing off the constantly moving water, glinting in blinding flashes off the waves. Bracing a hand on the gunwale beside her hip, Meg studied the far side of the lake. Part of the problem at this distance from the far side was that most of the smaller channels were hidden from view. Her best guess from their direction was Glenn aimed for one of the channels around the northern-most island.

Her theory bore out when Glenn suddenly swung north. For several seconds, it looked like he was piloting his boat directly for the shore, and then he disappeared.

"He's gone." McCord leaned forward, his eyes fixed on the spot where the boat had vanished.

"Got to be a channel opening there," Todd said, steering their craft in a direct line to follow, swinging out ever so slightly, and then arcing north.

And there it was. Only about twenty feet across, a narrow channel cut into the forest. From their previous angle, they weren't able to see it, but from straight on, it was clear as day.

"He'd have lost us if we were a minute or two behind him," called McCord, using two fingers to blow up the map on his phone for greater detail. "We'd have never seen him enter the channel, and would never have known it was there otherwise. You better slow down, some tight turns coming up here, according to this map."

"Got it." Todd slowed, but only slightly, not wanting to give Glenn any more lead than he already had. "Keep your eyes on the shore. He's out of sight for now. If he ditches and pulls the dinghy up and out of sight, and heads over-land on foot, we'll lose him completely." An experienced boater, he handled the S-curve with ease, keeping them neatly in the middle of the channel and away from the danger of the shallows.

Another thirty seconds had Glenn coming into sight again as the winding channel straightened out. And they'd gained on him. Todd opened up the throttle and they picked up a little more speed. Up ahead, Glenn kept glancing behind him, a mixture of fear and determination on his face.

"He's going to try to outrun us!" McCord shouted.

Behind them, Brian's boat came out of the curve and sped after them, then Craig's boat. They were still together; if one of them ran into trouble, the next boat could take up the chase.

As far as Meg could see ahead, it was all surrounding trees, making her wonder if Glenn truly knew where he was going.

His lead was now down to about forty feet. If he was trying to outrun them, it wasn't working.

Suddenly there was a horrible grinding sound of metal on rock, and Glenn's boat swung sideways, as if he was at-tempting to correct, or possibly head for shore, Meg couldn't be sure. The boat swayed forward again, just be-fore it pitched downward.

Meg watched in horror as the dinghy hung momentarily, bow down, the stern three or four feet in the air, the motor's propeller whirling uselessly . . . and then the boat went over.

Gone.

It had to be a waterfall, but how high?

Sitting up straighter, Meg craned her neck to see any trace of Glenn, even as Todd throttled down, cutting their speed. They got closer, thirty-five feet, thirty, and then Meg caught sight of Glenn's boat ahead, Glenn still at the tiller, in the water, down a level, though she had no idea how far.

She turned back to Todd. "I can see his boat. It can't be that far a drop."

"It can be far enough, but we'll have to chance it or we'll lose him," he called.

She nodded her agreement.

"We're not going over the way he did and risk the rocks below. We're going to jump it and aim to land in deeper water. Get in the bottom of the boat and hang on. And hold on to Hawk. We're not wearing life jackets. If we go over, we're each on our own." Todd revved the engine and the boat kicked forward.

Meg slid onto the bottom of the boat, her boots bumping against McCord's knees as he did the same. She slid her right arm under the rope that ran along the top of the gunwale, the rope digging deep into the lee of her elbow as she wrapped her arms around Hawk's middle, pulling him into the vee of her thighs. She glanced back over her shoulder to where Todd sat, jaw set, boots planted and body braced, one hand on the tiller and the other white-knuckled on the rope to keep himself in place. Past Todd, she could see Brian's boat, see the alarm in Brian's eyes as he realized what they were about to attempt.

Todd flipped the motor out of the water with about four feet still to go, letting inertia and the flow of the water maintain their speed.

Her heart in her throat, Meg had an impression of rocks and rushing water and furiously frothing foam.

Then they were airborne.

CHAPTER 30

Reasonable Deception: A legal doctrine that says police may lie to suspects during interrogations, so long as an innocent person would not be affected.

Monday, October 21, 12:37 PM
Boundary Waters Canoe Area
Superior National Forest, Minnesota

Meg curled over Hawk, her eyes clenched shut, the wind whistling past as they flew. They hit—*hard*—air whooshing out of her lungs in a gust as her body rocked, side to side, in concert with Hawk's. There was a huge splash and the boat swayed violently, but then steadied. The boat abruptly surged forward as Todd tipped the motor back into place and they were flying again, but this time over water.

"Everyone okay?" Todd yelled.

"Yes," Meg and McCord called in unison.

Meg let go of Hawk, who looked at her curiously, and pulled her right arm free, rubbing at the gouge where the rough cord had bitten into her flesh. Turning back, she finally got a look at the falls they'd gone over, a short drop-off, likely no more than five feet, but with a rough landing at the base. Todd's bet to jump them at high speed and land in deeper water had turned out to be the winner. Much better than teetering over the edge as Glenn had.

At that moment, Brian's boat came sailing over the edge, followed thirty seconds later by Craig's. They'd all made it safely.

Which was more than she could say for Glenn. Ahead of them, his boat appeared to be struggling and he kept turning around and looking behind him, his lead faltering badly.

Meg was certain he'd never have taken this route if he'd known the dangers of this channel. He'd likely seen it on one of his searches and thought it would be a good way to lose them. The problem was, he didn't have the lead that would have required. And it was very clear at this point he hadn't known about the waterfall.

"He damaged his propeller going over the falls," Todd called. "He stays in the water, we're going to catch him."

"He knows it too. Be prepared for him to ditch the boat and try to get away on land," McCord said. "Then the odds are even again."

"Actually, they aren't, and he knows it." He could try, but Meg knew they had something Glenn couldn't escape—the dogs. If they lost sight of him, and most likely they would in these thick woods, Hawk and Lacey would be able to track him. "He knows we have the dogs."

"He's not going to have any choice," Todd said. "Look, he's beaching the boat."

Glenn was steering directly for a small scrubby patch on the west side of the channel, clearly aiming to abandon the boat. Loud crunching and scraping echoed over the water as Glenn totaled the shaft and propeller of the outboard motor against submerged rocks at the shoreline. But as soon as the boat jammed against the side, Glenn was up, throwing himself at the bushes, then clawing his way into them, and disappearing.

"Get ready," Todd yelled. "McCord, let Meg and Hawk go, then jump out and pull the boat in. Meg." He met her eyes. "Be careful."

"Promise." Meg bent over Hawk. "Hawk, stand. Ready."

Hawk was poised at the bow, ready to leap. A quick look behind showed Brian and Lacey in the bow of their boat, readying to join the chase as soon as they made land.

Todd flipped the motor free again as the dinghy smoothly slid into a clear spot about ten feet short of Glenn's boat. "Go!"

"Hawk! Out." Hawk leapt onto land, Meg right behind him. "Find Glenn, Hawk. Find."

Hawk bolted into the bushes, Meg on his heels. She wasn't concerned Hawk didn't have a specific scent to follow; Glenn's being the freshest trail was all that was required. And Lacey would be with them in about thirty seconds.

They were in a dense area of the forest, away from any portage routes or hiking trails. It was hard going, a rocky area, full of old trees with winding, protruding roots. But for Meg and Hawk, it was just another day at the office, Hawk running about five feet ahead, both of them settling in to the run and pacing themselves. A steady rise sloped ahead of them, mostly populated with pine trees, but a sprinkling of deciduous trees made pops of brilliant color up the hill. As they climbed higher, the trees gave way to more and more granite, allowing them to climb faster.

Breathing hard, they made it up to the top of the rise. A quick glance over her shoulder showed Brian about thirty feet behind them and moving fast, so they waited, knowing it was worth the loss of time for coordination and strength in numbers.

"Hey," Brian puffed, "fancy meeting you here."

"Just out for a stroll. Seemed like a nice locale. Hawk, find."

"Lacey, find."

And they were off, the dogs shoulder to shoulder across the top of the rise. They ran near the edge of a sharp drop, where several tall pine trees leaned out on an angle, held in place by their massive network of roots tangled through the rocks. Far ahead, the wide blue waters of the next bay of the lake shone a deep, vibrant blue. Still, the dogs forged on, leading their handlers back down the slope, leaping from rock to rock until farther down, where granite gave way to dry leaves and soil.

Halfway down, the leaves were disturbed, swept downward toward the bottom, the dirt scrubbed clean.

"He fell here," Brian called. "Went quite a way down. Bet that wasn't without injury."

"You may be right. Let's make sure that's not us too."

They slowed their pace slightly, knowing they'd lose more time in a fall than they would taking a little more care. Reaching the bottom, they encouraged the dogs to pick up the pace again.

A loud snap came from ahead, the sound of breaking wood, followed by a strangled cry. Meg and Brian glanced at each other and sprinted as best they could after their dogs around trees and crashing through bushes.

It sounded like Glenn was getting into trouble. If so, he wasn't that far in front of them. Only a minute later, they leapt over the splintered remains of a half-rotted, fallen tree. From the width of the crumpled spot in the trunk and the depression on the far side, it looked like Glenn had stepped on the rotted wood, it had collapsed under him, and he'd gone down. Again.

And from how long it took for them to reach that location following the sound, they were gaining quickly.

That was when Meg caught the dark shadow moving ahead of them—Glenn in his black New York State Police jacket. They nearly had him.

Meg contemplated how to stop him. She'd taught Hawk how to attack on command, a skill that had come in handy only months before. However, she wasn't comfortable using her dog as an attack animal unless her life or someone else's was on the line. Luckily, the dogs, working in concert, had another skill they'd successfully used in Philadelphia.

"He's up ahead, I can see him." Meg's breath was coming hard at this point. "We're gaining on him. Send the dogs after him to corner and guard?"

"Let's get a little closer, and that should do the trick to get him to stop if we're right behind the dogs."

Another two minutes had them closing hard on Glenn, who, when Meg got a good view of him, was favoring his left leg. *Hurt during one of his falls, probably the first one, and exacerbated by the second.*

"Now?" she asked.

"Now," Brian agreed.

"Hawk, guard."

"Lacey, guard."

The two dogs shot ahead of their handlers—reminding Meg once again how much the humans on the team were actually a detriment to the dogs—Lacey running ahead of Glenn, Hawk staying behind, working in tandem to essentially surround him. Glenn stumbled to a stop while, on either side of him, the dogs lowered on their front legs, their heads low, teeth bared, both letting out ferocious growls.

Glenn stepped to his left and Lacey followed him, the increased volume of her growl letting him know in no uncertain terms she wasn't going to let him escape.

Meg and Brian dropped out of their run behind Hawk as Glenn spun toward them, only to come face-to-face with Hawk's bared teeth. In Glenn's fist was the knife he'd likely used to cut open his tent.

Alarm spurted through Meg at her dog being so close to

that blade, but she kept her voice level. "It's the end of the line, Damon. We know you killed Pratt and we know it goes back to you assaulting her in Mexico Beach, when she wouldn't put out for you. We also know you killed Elan to cover for your lack of a real alibi. He thought you were covering him, didn't he? But in reality, he was covering you. If that got out, you were caught in a lie that would make everyone look at you a lot more closely. So you silenced him."

"You women aren't smart enough to understand anything," Glenn spat. He looked at Brian, as if masculine support would come from there.

"I have to say, you were pretty smart in the way you managed a bad situation. Impressive thinking on your feet," Brian said.

Meg glanced sideways at her partner, and the expression of awe on his face. One she knew he absolutely didn't feel. But she had to hand it to him as a strategy to drag a few more details from Glenn, guy to guy, while he was off balance, details he'd never give up while seated in an interview room with his lawyer at his side.

"I mean, you probably didn't mean to hurt her, right? But she wasn't playing along. You sent her that note, the one signed by Thatcher. You probably just wanted to clear the air."

Glenn grabbed on to Brian's story like it was a lifeline. "Yeah. I mean, she wouldn't talk to me otherwise. She wouldn't even look at me. And I didn't want to attract attention. I figured it was the best way to meet with her in private."

"Did you know about the cheating?"

"McGraw told me he suspected something was going on. I bumped into him coming into the campground on Friday evening. He was *pissed*. He'd just had an argument with Pratt and he told me he suspected her of cheating.

Again. I know her kind." He flicked a glance at Meg. "Their only way to beat us is by cheating. So I wrote the note and signed Thatcher's name, figuring if she showed up, that was confirmation too."

"And she came?" Brian asked.

"She sure did. And I told her, I'd let bygones be bygones, and I'd keep her cheating in the trial on the down low, if she just did a little something for me."

"I mean, what would it cost her, right?"

Meg had to hand it to Brian, this was A1 acting. Since he was a decent human being, she knew playing along like this had to be turning his stomach.

"Right? But when I tried to get near her, she sicced her dog on me. I didn't have any choice but to kick it over the side."

Meg had to school her features into neutrality, when she wanted to leap at Glenn. The thought of anyone doing that to Hawk—

"She went batshit," Glenn continued, mirroring Meg's own thoughts. "Came flying at me. Bitch tried to push me over the edge after her mutt."

"Guess you showed her." Brian egged him on, since Glenn seemed to be slowing.

"Sure did. I had to fight my way back toward the trees. But then she started to scream, and you know how sound travels in open air like that. I covered her mouth with my hand, and she *bit me*!" The outrage pumped off Glenn in waves. "So I shoved her, and she fell backward into some bushes. Must have hit her head on a rock as she landed, because there was this crunching sound. Then she didn't get up again."

"Moving her body, that was so smart, and nearly had us. You needed to buy time to find that note. It had Thatcher's name on it, but the handwriting was yours. And your fingerprints, if you didn't wear gloves. You knew the clock was ticking. You also knew if a search was called the dogs would find her on land inside of about twenty minutes."

"Not that I could find the damned note." Glenn nearly snarled it in frustration. "I didn't have time to search her tent after I got back, but after the second training session, I snuck in from the trees and started searching. But then, the alarm was raised that something had gone wrong, Elan started looking for me, and I had to bail. I was going to go back, but then the tent got taped off as evidence and I never got the chance."

"How did you get her out there?" Still looking completely enthralled, Brian was trying to keep Glenn going before he realized through the fog of adulation that he was digging his own grave.

"A couple of the pilots brought canoes, as well as their outboards, and left them at the small boat launch to the west of the beach, so I snuck into camp and borrowed one. I'd walked that trail before, that's how I knew to have her meet me there. The trail goes downhill from that point to a low section, so I loaded her body in there and paddled out to an area that was supposed to be far north of any search site." The look he threw Meg was full of loathing. "What the fuck were you doing out there?"

"Following my dog." Meg matched his loathing with her own. "You may have thought you'd fool the humans in the area, but you'll never fool the dogs."

"You were never supposed to be out there for the dogs to smell her. Stupid, good-for-nothing bitch." He looked to Brian as if expecting support.

Brian finally let the act drop, his face morphing into its true lines, his expression full of disgust. "Don't look at me, man. I'm gay. I've never had sex with a woman either, but I'm sure if I'd tried, I'd have been successful."

"I'd do you right now." Meg couldn't help herself; she

simply couldn't resist twisting the knife in Glenn's belly one more turn.

Brian flashed her a grin. "Thanks, babe. It's the thought that counts." His smile fell away as he turned back to Glenn. "And you're wrong about Meg. She's clearly smarter than you. So much so, we're done here."

Crimson infused Glenn's face as he realized he'd been duped by Brian, and he swiped his knife toward Hawk. "Keep your goddamn dogs away from me."

"Hawk, back," Meg commanded. "Hey, Brian, look. He has a knife. What do we say to that?"

"I think we say this," Brian said casually, and they reached into their pants pockets in unison, both pulling out folding tactical knives, the blades springing free with twin *snicks.*

"We didn't bring our sidearms this weekend, but you know us SAR folk, we never go anywhere without our dogs or emergency knives." Meg's congenial smile melted away. "Put down the knife, Glenn. Between us and the dogs, you're not getting away. Unless you want to have additional charges levied. Brian, remember what happened in the last case when some moron tried to hurt one of our dogs?"

"You mean the felony charge of second-level assault against a police officer? Oh yeah, I remember."

"Unless you want that charge as well, I suggest you put the knife down. And you can try to get away, but you're not going far on that leg. Not to mention, the guys with the guns are right behind us, and they're going to be annoyed by your escape attempt when the dogs follow you to wherever you scamper to. You're outnumbered four to one. Do yourself a favor and be smart about this."

Indecision flashed across Glenn's face, but one last look at the two ferocious dogs convinced him he didn't have any choice. He lobbed the knife off to the side into the underbrush, away from the dogs.

"Smart move." Brian stepped a little closer and pointed at the dirt. "Now, flat on your stomach on the ground, hands on the back of your head." They waited until Glenn was in position, the dogs continuing to guard. Brian then turned to Meg as she folded her knife up and slipped it into the side pocket of her yoga pants. "You letting Craig know?"

"I'll text him our coordinates."

Ten minutes later, the area was swarming.

Craig stood by and let Brogan do the arrest, cuffing Glenn and reading him his Miranda rights. Then as Glenn sat on the ground, his back against a tree, his face a picture of rage and misery, Brogan called in reinforcements and transportation to camp and then to lockup.

Craig stepped away to make a phone call.

"Nicely done, guys," McCord said, moving forward from where he and Todd had followed Craig to the site and then stayed out of the way.

"As it so often happens, it was the dogs," Meg said. "He might have gotten away if it wasn't for them. We lost him visually in the trees, but the dogs never doubted where he'd been. He took a bad fall going down one hill and that slowed him down. I mean, we would have stayed on him until we caught him either way, but sooner works for me."

"Agreed," Brian chimed in. "We never got lunch. I'd like lunch."

"You know what? Me too. Anyway, the dogs surrounded and contained him until we could get closer and talk him into surrender."

Brian laughed at the memory.

Confused, Todd looked from Brian to Meg and back again. "That was funny?"

"Mostly sickening for me, because I played along with his women-are-dirt routine to goad him into spilling the beans of what happened." Brian couldn't hold back the smirk. "The funny part was when I dropped the act and told him I was gay. That I'd never slept with a woman either, but thought I could get one if I wanted. Then Meg offered to do me then and there. That *really* pissed him off."

Todd turned to Meg with arched eyebrows. "Did she now?"

Meg winked at him. "She did. It was glorious."

"It really was," Brian agreed. "He probably hates gays as much as women, so the thought that you'd stoop to having sex with me was a real kick in the pants." He held up a hand to Meg, who, grinning, high-fived him.

"He killed Pratt because he's an incel?" McCord asked.

"Yes. He told her he knew about the cheating, but he'd keep it quiet as long as she put out for him."

"Blackmail. *Nice.*" McCord drew out the last word, dripping with sarcasm.

"Oh yeah, he's a real hero," Meg said. "She objected, they fought, and he pushed her. When she went down, she hit her head. Brian and I can testify to his confession, if Brogan doesn't get it out of him a second time. Though, as you said, his electronics will likely also tell his story. But you know who I feel bad for?"

"Who?"

"The poor dogs who got the short end of the stick this weekend. Ava, who didn't survive. Samson and Odin, who will have to be reassigned. We'll have to make sure they get safely transported back to New York State."

"Craig will make sure of it," Brian said. "And speaking of Craig, here he comes."

They turned expectantly as Craig joined the group. "Good work, guys. Great job as always by all four of you."

"Thank you, sir."

"And Meg, I have a message for you."

"For me?"

"Yes." Craig slid his phone into his outside jacket pocket. "From EAD Peters. He says, 'Welcome back.'" Reaching into his inside breast pocket, he pulled out her black flip case and extended it to her.

For a moment, all she could do was stare at it. When she looked up to meet Todd's eyes, he was beaming. She took the case, the leather a familiar texture under her fingertips. "I'm back?"

"Peters was just waiting for the all clear from me. You're no longer a suspect in a murder investigation. You're back on the team."

Her smile was full of relief. "Thank you, sir."

Craig started to turn away, but then stopped. "Oh, and about the abuse accusation. Peters will be making a formal dismissal of the accusation, complete with the signed statements of eight of your current team members, FBI agent colleagues, and supervisors. It's going away, and will never appear on your record. More important, Hawk is safe in your care."

"Thank God," she breathed.

"Now I'm going to make sure this case is wrapped up, and then what do you say we get the hell out of this godforsaken wilderness?"

"Amen to that," Brian said with a fist pump. "Hopefully, never to return."

As Craig walked off, Todd pulled Meg in for a hug. "It's over. You can breathe now."

She wrapped her arms around him and just held on. "Feels like the first time in days. If we get you back to the boat, can you get us out of here?"

"You bet." He released her, but kept one arm around

her waist. "What do you say? Let's pack up and head for home today."

Suddenly there was no place she'd rather be. She could call her parents and tell them about the engagement, see her sister to show off her ring, and sleep in her own bed, secure in the knowledge she'd wake to find her dog still beside her. They'd be deployed together to help the injured and find the lost. A life together. Purpose.

"God, yes." She smiled up into his eyes. "Let's go home."

ACKNOWLEDGMENTS

Some books are harder to write than others, depending on what is going on in the world or in a writer's home life. In many ways, this book was written under higher pressure than many, so I am especially grateful to those who supported me and this manuscript during its creation:

Our amazing critique team, Jenny Lidstrom, Jessica Newton, Rick Newton, and Sharon Taylor—for always being game to step in whenever I need you, and, in this instance, managing a lightning-fast turnaround under deadline pressure with your usual thoughtful, sharp-eyed quality of editing. I am so thankful for all you do for each and every manuscript, and especially for this one.

Shane Vandevalk—for jumping into the title brainstorming game, and once again picking the winning title. Also, your advice on boating was great assistance to this non-camping girl.

Kane Thundertail—for providing backstory for his cadre of talented canine alter egos in this series, whether performing searches, providing therapy and comfort, or just being a human companion.

Nicole Resciniti, my agent—for your ready ear and constant willingness to assist in any way possible. And to the Seymour Agency team, including Marisa Cleveland and Lesley Sabga, for helping your authors reach a greater audience.

Kensington Publishing and its many arms, which make bringing a book to publication a real joy: Louis Malcangi, and his talented art department, for a wonderfully atmospheric cover that really captures the essence of the setting of the story; efficient editorial assistance by Norma Perez-Hernandez; and the outstanding efforts of communications and publicity teams, including Larissa Ackerman, Vida Engstrand, Lauren Jernigan, Kait Johnson, Alexandra Kenney, and Alexandra Nicolajsen. As always, it's wonderful working with you all and I'm so appreciative of all your work on *Still Waters*.

Esi Sogah, who once again was instrumental in steering the creation of this book, for always being flexible and the ultimate team player. It's always wonderful working with you, and this book was no exception.

Don't miss the other books in this pulse-pounding series

LONE WOLF
BEFORE IT'S TOO LATE
STORM RISING
NO MAN'S LAND
LEAVE NO TRACE
UNDER PRESSURE

Available now from
Sara Driscoll
And
Kensington Books
Wherever books are sold